For Melinda: Because Pink was your favourite, first.

Copyright © 2016, 2020 Malcolm F. Cross
All rights reserved.
ISBN: 979-8-6699-2029-6 (paperback edition)
Copy-editing: Jon Oliver
Typesetting: BookPolishers.com

This is a work of fiction. Names, characters, businesses, places, events, locales, and incidents are either the products of the author's imagination or used in a fictitious manner.

Content note: This book includes potentially upsetting material, including scenes of explicit violence; loss of life; ethnic, racial, and religious prejudice; and emotional distress.

http://www.sinisbeautiful.com

Contents

V: Blue	7
1. We Free	14
2. Pushing it	17
3. Home again	28
4. Medical Evacuation	36
5. New Blood	49
IV: Innocence	61
6. Winning Play	66
7. Losing Proposition	75
8. Money Men	93
9. Strategy Session	108
10. Heading Out	115
III: Lost	133
11. Born Killers	141
12. The Wall	148
13. Hostile Takeover	166
14. Home Cooking	175
15. Check, mate	182
16. Partial Stability	201
17. Mopping Up	205
18. Moving on	211
II: Honeymoon	219
19. Fixing Potholes	225
20. Battle Fatigue	234
21. Reasonable Cause	238
22. Packing Up	248
23. Lifting Corners	252

24. Game Theory   262

I: Leaving   273
25. Stone Sparrow   277
26. Wasted land   279
27. Real Blue   282

Acknowledgments   285
About the Author   286

V
Blue

::/ Dushanbe, Tajikistan.
::/ May, 2104.
::/ Edane Estian.

Fluid gurgled out of Edane's ear, dripping to the market's cobblestones. Part of the pool growing beneath his face.

Red.

He struggled to turn over. He couldn't hear properly. Voices were going too fast or too slow for him to understand, and automatic rifles kept roaring in coordinated bursts of electronically assisted over-the-horizon fire.

None of it made sense. Edane didn't understand. He couldn't roll over.

Pushing furiously at the cobblestones with his left hand, he fought to lever himself up, his fingers slipping in his blood, until the searing pain in his right side finally eased and he thumped over onto his back.

The gurgling noise in his right ear stopped. Had a clogged, underwater feeling instead, but his left ear was clear. He blinked, once. People were running by him, over him, shadowy in the corners of his vision. Something went *pop* in his ear and Edane felt the hot trickle start all over again.

The sky was blue.

Blue.

He blinked again. Didn't see the people, for awhile, or feel his armored collar digging into the back of his neck. Just saw the sky. The last wisps of smoke — from the mortars, it had to have been airburst mortars — were blowing away, leaving the sky a pure blue.

Edane had never seen anything so blue. Never. It was too bright for words. It made his eyes water. He didn't have words for anything like this, but he'd never had anything like this to try and tell anyone about. Never seen a sky so blue.

Blue.

He reached up toward it, but couldn't reach. Something was wrong with his right arm. Edane wanted to touch the blue, to hold it, to breathe it.

Someone stood between Edane and the sky. A little boy, with pale-pink skin, but not the pale-pink of a European, and he wore a skullcap over his dark, messy hair, so the little boy had to be Tajik.

The little boy stared at him, wide-eyed, and stepped around the pool of Edane's blood, frightened of it, skipped over something else, and made his way to another man's side. The man was already dead, and the little boy got his shoes dirty. The little boy pulled at the dead man's bloody shoulder, looked into his face, and lost interest, letting him go as he started looking elsewhere, calling "*Papa?*", his voice somewhere distant and to Edane's left, even though Edane was looking right at him.

Edane let his head sag. Saw something lying on the cobbles a little way away, between him and the dead man.

Oh. That was what was wrong with Edane's right arm. It was over there, on its own on the ground, and he was over here.

Edane looked down at himself, but he couldn't tell what was his ballistic armor and what was flesh and what used to be flesh. There was too much blood.

He stretched out his remaining hand, trying to reach, even pulled at the cobblestones, thinking he could drag himself, push with his legs, but he wasn't strong enough. His boots just slid over the slick flagstones. Edane felt like he might start crying — not because he was in pain, or because he was tired, or because he was going to die, but because he couldn't quite reach his right arm's wrist, couldn't even reach the limp fingers to drag it closer. He didn't want to lose it.

There was a foot next to him. Not his. Someone else's. A tall man. A local. He blocked out the sky, his silhouette made larger by the loose white clothes he wore. Everything about the man, except his dark beard and eyebrows, was clean and white. He bent over Edane, reaching for him, but hesitated, fingers twitching.

"Hey, hey! What are you doing?" Edane's brother said, the words repeated a moment later in Tajik by an automatic translator.

The man in white looked up. He stared in amazement and pointed to Edane's chest. "*He has a medical kit. People have been hurt, they need aid.*" The words came back, in English, from Edane's own translator. Just in his left ear. Not his right.

"There's a first aid station at the gates! Now get off him."

"They are busy with the worst cases, the gates are far, his medical kit is right here, and there is a person bleeding right in front of you!" The man in white pointed savagely at a woman behind him. "Now take his kit and give it to me, he is dying anyway, and I cannot touch him."

Edane, and his brother, both looked at the woman the man had pointed at. She wore a scarf over her head, face exposed — not the fully concealing clothes some of the locals wore — and blood was trickling down her face. Scalp cut. Those bled a lot.

"It's a minor injury," Edane's brother snarled.

"She is a person, he is a dog. Now give me his medical kit. I cannot touch dogs."

Edane's brother kept snarling, his teeth exposed, putting a wrinkle down the length of his snout. He touched the grip of his rifle. "Fuck off," he growled, ears back flat against his helmet, tail trembling in warning.

The man in white spat — leaving a bubble of white foam in Edane's blood on the market stones — and left.

Edane saw the sky again.

Blue.

Edane's brother knelt in the blood, pulling at Edane's uniform for a better look, and swore. "Edane's down!" he yelled. "I need the EM-STAB!"

"Coming up!" another of Edane's brothers answered.

"The fuck did that come from?" A fourth asked, watching the sky with nervous twists of the head.

Edane wasn't sure which of his brothers was over him. Or which one was fetching the EM-STAB kit. One of them had to be Sokolai. One of them had to be Esparza. Edane couldn't remember which of his clone brothers were scheduled to patrol Tajikistan's markets with him that day.

"It's going to be okay," Edane's brother said, hunching over him and blocking out the sky. Edane struggled, but he couldn't even move his head enough to see past his brother. Couldn't even do more than shiver, like he'd been running too hard and his muscles were spasming.

Edane's brother pulled open Edane's chest-pocket medical kit and sprayed a mockingly small amount of coagulant foam over the wound. Hands weren't enough to stop the blood flow, nor was the second tube of foam. The skinplast patch did fuck-all, and there wasn't enough left of Edane to secure a tourniquet to.

Sokolai — Edane saw the pocket name-patch, printed black-on-grey — tore off the front panel of Edane's armor, throwing the ballistic fabric and plating aside, then cut away his shirt with snub-nosed trauma shears. When he saw what he didn't have left to work with, Sokolai rolled Edane onto his side and lay on him, hip jammed into the crater where Edane's shoulder used to be, trying to staunch the blood under his body-weight.

"Where the fuck is that EM-STAB kit?" Sokolai screamed.

On his side, Edane couldn't see the sky anymore. His nose was wet in the mess of his own blood, and he wasn't strong enough to lift his head. Couldn't even reach out to try and get his arm back, either.

Edane hurt.

If the sky was pain, instead of blue, Edane hurt more than the sky was blue. And the sky was bluer than *anything*.

Something drooled off the pointed tip of his ear, it popped, and then he couldn't hear anything on the right side of his body anymore.

Edane went to sleep.

He missed the sky.

He woke up with Sokolai on his chest, and a new, almost pathetic spike of pain as Sokolai pushed a bonepunch needlegun up against his sternum and it spiked into him with a noise like a gunshot. "You still there, Edane? You still there?"

Edane tried to answer, but nothing worked. His head rolled to the left, muzzle hitting the wet stone, and he saw one of his brothers beating a man in western clothing to death, gore clinging to the red-brown fur of his brother's fists.

"Esparza! What the fuck are you doing?"

"He's the fucking artillery spotter!" *Thump*. "It's the fucking journalist! He's the one calling in the mortars!" *Thwuck*. "He was taking pictures of us. He was taking pictures of Edane — he stepped outside the gates *a fucking minute* before the strike! I saw him!" *Thuck*.

"Stop it Esparza, you're killing him!"

Esparza ignored their brother, and rammed his fist into what was left of the journalist's face. The journalist tried to fend him off. Esparza was six and a half feet tall, gengineered for strength out of a dog's DNA, and had been learning how to throw a punch since he was three years old. The journalist was maybe five-ten, skinny in that underfed refugee way, and badly hurt.

Esparza kept hitting him.

The journalist stopped moving.

Esparza kept hitting him.

Edane managed to look down at himself. Blood oozed around a tightly packed crust of coagulant foam running down his right side. Two needles were in his chest, both sticking out of his sternum, one connected by a trailing tube to a packet of synthetic blood plasma and platelets one of his brothers was massaging to push the fluid into Edane's body. Sokolai was fitting a syringe to the second needle. Orange-red fluid. BorGlobin, to help keep his tissue oxygenated.

Sokolai finished pushing in the first syringe, threw it aside, and broke open the top of another and pushed it against the port tipping the bonepunch needle.

Esparza kept hitting the journalist.

Edane let his head lull to the right, and the gurgling noise came back. He wasn't deaf. That was good, but there was a problem.

"What's that?" Sokolai dipped his head.

Edane tried again.

"I can't hear you."

"Hurts," Edane croaked.

"Oh fuck. *Fuck*. I forgot to give him painkillers." Sokolai kept pressure on the second syringe, pushing the BorGlobin into Edane's bones — and from there into his blood — as fast as the needle could take it.

Another of Edane's clone brothers came and helped, slipping a much smaller needle into Edane's arm.

The pain was still there.

Edane looked up at the slice of sky he could still see, and it was still so very blue, above the red-stained stone.

Esparza stopped hitting the journalist.

It started to hurt less.

The sky was very blue, but Edane couldn't keep his eyes open.

Edane's mothers danced together on the kitchen floor. They were very tall, so he must have been very young. Maybe seven years old, eight? It was soon after they adopted him, anyway. Soon after the Emancipation closed the barracks.

Beth and Cathy were barefoot, in their nighties, and looked very strange and very different and soft. They had explained to Edane who they were, and what their job was, and Edane hadn't believed them at first. It seemed absurd that anyone's mission profile would be to raise children, especially since Edane had been able to get food at the crèche and wash and dress himself ever since he could remember. And he *still* couldn't understand why they wanted to be called 'she' and 'her', didn't even know what those words — she, her, mother, woman — meant. None of it made sense.

They moved gracefully together, like they were rehearsing how to throw a punch or something, but there wasn't any violence to the motions and Edane had no idea what the point of the exercise was. They were smiling at each other, while funny noises played, like language — music, he knew. Edane hadn't liked music then, and he liked it a bit now if it was the right kind, the kind that his mothers were dancing to, but when they'd been that tall he hadn't known what music was.

Cathy's bare heel skimmed the kitchen tiles, which were covered in Edane's blood, but she didn't get any on her. Beth laughed, grasping Cathy's waist, spinning her around and around and around until they both stopped dead, staring down at Edane.

"Daney, are you alright?"

"I'm hurt, Cathy."

"Oh, oh baby. Call me Ma. It's okay. It's going to be okay. You've just hurt yourself, there's nothing scary about it." Cathy knelt down in the blood covering the tiles and picked Edane up. Held him, while Beth came in from the back, wrapping her arms around both of them.

Edane didn't understand why either of them held him, but his mothers did a lot of strange things. His mothers' kind of strange was okay.

"Daney. Oh Daney. Were you running? Are you alright?"

"I'm hurt real bad, Beth."

"Call me Mom. God, look at that, Cathy — has he broken it?"

"Don't be ridiculous, Beth, he's just skinned his knee."

"*That's* a skinned knee?"

"It's just been bleeding a long time. Why didn't you say anything, Daney?"

Edane bled into Cathy's nightie, slicking it to her skin with his blood. "They hurt me. They blew me up with a mortar bomb. They hurt me, Mommy." He felt tears prickle his eyes. He'd only cried twice in his life before. Only called his mothers 'Mommy' once.

"It's okay, Daney. It's okay. We'll put skinplast on it. Can we skinplast him without shaving his knee?" Cathy asked, looking at Beth.

"God, I don't know. Maybe?"

"The little boy didn't want to touch me. None of the Muslims like me. They hate me and they hurt me, Mommy."

His mothers clung to him, kissed his forehead and ears — he *really* didn't understand why they did that, but it felt good. "It's okay, Daney. It's okay. It's time to come home now."

"Time to come home, baby. Come home." Beth took her turn holding him, and his ruined shoulder drew slick trails across her torso.

"But I'm not ready to come home." Edane's head swam. "I'm not finished yet."

1. We Free

::/ San Iadras, Middle American Corporate Preserve.
::/ April, 2106.
::/ Ereli Estian.

"Ever think that the Emancipation was the worst thing to ever happen to us?"

Eversen leaned out over the railing, sticking his head into the hot, dry breeze. He shifted his jaw left, all the way, until it clicked. Then he shut his muzzle with a decisive snap. "No."

Ereli joined him at the railing and gazed out across the city. "I do."

"We're free," Eversen said, firm in his position now that he'd picked it. "We have rights."

"The right to what? Live *here* for the rest of our lives?" Ereli gestured out over the courtyard below, between West Wall Mansions and Heartland Heights — the two housing projects stuck out of Del Cora's poverty like concrete-sided warts.

Eversen didn't answer. They could both see San Iadras's other districts from here — the wealth surrounding the Uptown skyscrapers was like a slap in the face. Ereli, Eversen, and the brothers they lived with couldn't even afford *air conditioning*.

"It isn't all bad." Eversen folded his arms over the railing, staring out at the narrow slice of ocean not blocked by buildings, water stained scarlet by the sunset and framed by the black domes of the Defense and Decontamination Array on the far horizon. "The drill instructors can't terminate and replace us anymore if we get too badly injured in training to keep up."

"We don't get trained, either. Just told we should be like *that*." Ereli jerked his chin in the direction of the city. Of the money people, the office workers, the service economy. The world where earning a living and spending a fortune mattered more than anything.

"It's not such a bad way to live."

"Isn't it? We're chasing our tails over here, scraping together, what, thirty nudies a week? Each of us? In a *good* week?"

"Forty New Dollars, last week." Eversen kept his ears down.

"Meanwhile those fucking *Phillips* dogs get all the fucking employment they *want*. You know why?"

Eversen didn't answer.

"When they took *us* out of the vats, they made us into killers. When they took *them* out of the vats, they taught them actual goddamn life skills."

"They're all idiots," Eversen said, flicking his own pointed ear. "Floppy ears and dumb as shit. It makes them happy — you know that?" He grimaced, almost a snarl. "Working all day? Doing *nothing*? We're bigger, we're stronger, we're six inches taller than those mutts, easy, but they get work for three nudies an hour in warehouses and packing centers and they *enjoy* it."

"You don't?" Ereli put on a mockingly cool tone. "Sweating for eight hours with safety compliance officers breathing down your neck in case you try lifting fallen boxes yourself instead of waiting for some Phillips in an assistive frame?"

"*Fuck* them." Eversen banged his fists on the rail. "Everybody employs a Phillips, nobody employs an Estian — nobody employs *us*. It's not *fair!*"

"I told you," Ereli said. "The Emancipation was the worst thing that ever happened to us."

"At least we're not slaves." Eversen slumped back down. "At least we're free. Have rights."

"Okay. Not the Emancipation, then — when the corporations made us. *That* was the worst thing to ever happen to us."

"We didn't ask to be born," Eversen muttered. "So they decanted us instead."

"Exactly. And then they tell us we're free and leave us chronically unemployed."

"We had work in Tajikistan."

Ereli smiled, thinly. "We had *fun* in Tajikistan."

"Not all of it was fun." Eversen's tone was flat, dead. "Most of it wasn't. Shouldn't have been fun, anyway."

"That's what they say." Ereli jerked his chin at the city again. "Fighting's not supposed to be fun, killing's not supposed to be fun, risking death's not supposed to be fun. Sex and drugs and alcohol are supposed to be fun."

"They're not."

"They're not," Ereli agreed.

"Getting stuck in that house while the revolution rolled over us, spending days under siege? That wasn't fun."

Ereli slumped down over the railing next to his brother, adopting the same low pose. "It was kinda fun."

"Kinda. I felt alive, anyway. Like I had purpose."

"So I don't see what the problem is. Everyone deserves to have a purpose."

"I don't think it's moral for us to start a civil war just because we're *unemployed*."

"It's not because we're unemployed. It's because they don't have anyone to fight for them."

"Who? The Azerbaijanis? We haven't even finalized our pick." Eversen shook his head. "Everything still in quarantine zones with the Eurasian War's fallout, everyone in what's left of Bolivia, they all need protectors. If that was really why we were doing this, we could have started a war any time."

"We're *not* starting a war," Ereli said, carefully. "We're holding a crowdfunding campaign. It's different."

2. Pushing it

::/ San Iadras, Middle American Corporate Preserve.
::/ March, 2105.
::/ Edane Estian.

Edane stretched out his hands, and looked at them. His left hand was rock solid, while his right hand trembled uncontrollably. That was because, technically speaking, it wasn't *his* right hand.

He knew all the scars on his left hand. That dent in his middle finger, just beneath where the fingernail started? That was the suicide bomber back in Dushanbe. The clipped scar across his knuckles, a dark line of knitted flesh under ruddy red-brown fur, had been courtesy of glass in the streets when he caught himself on his fists, scrambling to his belly during a firefight. The dry scab across the back of his thumb, that was being a klutz when a cookery lesson from Janine hadn't gone as planned.

But his right hand? That was all a mystery to him. The ring finger and pinky were untouched, but there was an old burn that made the fur tangle across the back of his middle finger and forefinger, and it lined up perfectly if he made a fist. It could have been a fist to throw a punch, or a fist to grip something small and delicate safely. If he squeezed carefully at his right hand, he could make out the knots of old breaks that had been repeatedly broken, just under the knuckles on his right hand's long bones.

Edane had done that to himself, once. Punched too hard without a glove, broke his hand just under the ring finger's knuckle. That'd been with his right hand, too, but his right hand before he'd gone to Tajikistan. Before patrolling Dushanbe's streets. Before the mortar strike in the Tous marketplace. His right hand before shrapnel and blast force had torn pieces of him away. His right hand *before*.

He'd been lucky. A little more time spent bleeding into the marketplace's stones, and maybe one of Edane's brothers would have been sitting where he was sitting, puzzling over a left hand written over with mysteries. Scars without answers.

He waited for his can of meat to warm up in the sunshine, sitting in the shade under a tree away from the picnic tables and other players, most of his combat gear piled up beside him, wondering where the scars had come from and when the shaking would stop.

"You overdone it again, kid?" Marianna stopped beside him, on her way from the MilSim league organizer's table and back to the snack stand. "Something wrong with the arm?"

"No." He ducked his head away from her, and folded his arms — left over right, pinning the shuddering limb to his body.

Marianna grimaced, a narrow line of sharp teeth and gum on display, tail stiff. "Don't give me that shit, kid."

Marianna was like him. Gengineered dog. But smaller, and older, and that seemed to give her the idea that she had some kind of authority over him. As if she were his older sister — she might have been built from an earlier version of Edane's genes, but she didn't have command authority, she didn't own him, she just ran the MilSim team, his life was none of her—

KRAK!

Her helmet bounced off his skull and whirled away. She swung it around her fist by the chinstrap, and snarled. "Are you listening to me, kid?"

Edane winced away, rubbing his head. "Yes sir."

"Show me the arm."

Gingerly, Edane stretched out his right arm. She started prodding it, poking it, as if she knew what she was doing.

"You tear something again? I fucking *told* you to take it easy with the arm, Edane." She let him go, and he drew his arm back to himself, hunching over it.

"I don't think I tore anything," he muttered.

"You sure? You fucking tore something last month."

He glared up at her. "I said I didn't tear it." He looked back down at his shivering hand. "I think. I think I'm just tired or something. My arm's just tired." He shook out his right shoulder, looking away.

"You go easy on that thing." Marianna pointed at him accusingly. "Siegelbach didn't go and get himself killed so *you* could fuck up his arm. Nobody else is letting someone graft their dead arm onto your sorry ass, kid."

"The doctors said the nerves are only supposed to grow an inch a *month*," Edane snapped back at her. "It's only been eight months since I got it, and I can already use my hand. The graft's fine, I'm doing great, I do all my goddamn exercises and the physiotherapists say I'm getting function back faster than anyone they've ever seen, so lay off!"

"I'll lay off when you stop pushing yourself hard enough to tear those fucking nerves." Marianna growled, properly growled, a low sound of threat reverberating in her chest. She poked him. "Slow down. That's an order — and shoot *left-handed* for Christ's sake. Your aim out there's been *shit* for the last hour."

Edane didn't *want* to shoot left-handed. He didn't shoot left-handed before, he didn't want to shoot left-handed now, even if his MilSim rifle *was* ambidextrous. He looked away sullenly. "Yes sir."

"I'm keeping an eye on you, kid." She wagged her finger in warning and strode off back for the snack stand.

He watched her go, scratching at his right wrist nervously. He stopped, when he realized what he was doing, and when it didn't look like she was going to come back with her helmet. They still had twenty minutes before they re-deployed for the next round on the field. Plenty of time to rest, eat. By the time he got back out there with the rest of the team, his arm would probably have calmed down some. Probably. But he'd shoot left-handed anyway — that had been an order, in the context of the MilSim team, which she *did* have command authority for. But he was sick and tired of her butting in about his arm.

In defiance, he opened the can of sun-warmed meat right handed, twisting the little key in the notch to peel open the metal, and used the key's wire loop as a spoon to scoop out and eat the preservative jelly first. He had to take extra time, and duck his head close to the can, but he didn't spill like last time.

That was something, at least.

S<small>EMI-PROFESSIONAL</small> M<small>IL</small>S<small>IM</small> T<small>EAM</small> Eight-Eight-Zero, registered with the Middle American Military Simulation Sports Gaming League, Marianna Estian team leader, came in with a combined score of three hundred sixty-two points, ranking as fourth out of sixty semi-pro teams, and fifteenth in the combined semi-pro/pro table. Of the match's three factions, theirs — faction two — ended the match in a victory tie with faction three, with a points differential of thirty-five.

It was a very complicated way of saying Edane fucked up.

During the match Marianna had split the team into the usual two fireteams — her with Eberstetten, Erlnicht, and Svarstad; Edane with Ellis, Salzach, and Louie. She'd kept them roughly together, running parallel about a quarter-kilometer apart on a path hooking south-east and then bending up north across the playing field and into enemy territory, cutting through the forests towards the enemy hardline locations.

That part went okay — the hike was almost pleasant, without the distraction of a radio or HUD and waypoints, done electronics-off to keep from producing EM-signatures. Technically, of course, the MilSim's augmented reality goggles and tracking software and equipment were all still running to keep tracking the match, but as far as the experience of hiking went, it was a pleasurable three miles under thirty pounds of mock ballistic armor with all their equipment. Sure, it was hot, but there was plenty of water, and even Louie — the team's only human member, just seventeen — did okay. The under-armor circulation meshes they wore for cooling helped out a lot.

The trouble started late into their second round deployment, around about the time the team slowed down a little to let Louie catch up. That was expected, the kid didn't have the same stamina as the rest of the team, but that was when they wound up in a firefight behind the lines, and Edane's aim had gone to shit.

Oh, he'd shot left-handed. Curled his right arm around, gripping his left wrist with his right hand, barrel braced against the crook of his half-numb right elbow. It wasn't the most comfortable way to shoot, and it worked for him most of the time, but the jitters in his arm had gotten so bad that out of the twelve shots he'd taken, eight had gone off-target.

The planned, methodical search for the enemy hardlines had turned into an ambush and a scrambling run to find the on-field servers the hardlines were linked to. Radio links, especially long-range radio links, were too insecure and far too easy to jam, so hardlines in and out of combat zones were key combat infrastructure, almost as important as air and fire support. Successfully cutting the hardlines would net an immediate score of thirty points, but more importantly it would open up *all* off-field radio communications to EMWAR interference. Succeeding in EMWAR objectives like that — electronics, emissions, and electromagnetic warfare was key — had a knock-on effect worth a whole lot more than thirty points.

Four shots hit, which was to his credit, but eight of Edane's shots had missed. That had shaken him — he wasn't *supposed* to miss — and he'd fumbled a reload later, his shaking fingers refusing to guide the magazine into its well. That'd left him a few steps behind the rest of the team, unable to get out of cover fast enough, and he'd wound up eliminated as he'd concentrated on catching up rather than checking the environment around him.

One member down, it didn't take long for the team to lose another, and another… until only Marianna, Salzach and Erlnicht had walked back in off the field two hours later, victoriously carrying eight lengths of cut fiber-optic cable with them.

It shouldn't have taken two hours. It was supposed to be a victory, but Edane knew — the whole team knew — he'd let them down.

Not that it was obvious, by the way everyone was fussing over Louie.

Salzach reached over the van's middle seat, ruffling Louie's hair. "See?" he said, pointing at Louie's pad. "You're aiming better. Just had to develop some upper body strength."

Edane, in the front-left seat, beside the van's interface screen, shrank down, watching the road ahead, his ears flat. Salzach was probably just trying to encourage the kid, that was all. It wasn't a comment on Edane's performance — just on Louie's.

Louie had a lot of trouble keeping up, but they all liked having him around anyway. He was a kid, not a soldier. But Salzach had been friendly with Enzweiler, back in Tajikistan. And Louie's family had adopted Enzweiler after the Emancipation. So Louie was family, and if he wanted to hang around his foster-brother's clones, his foster-brother's clones were happy to let him.

"Yeah," Louie said, squirming under the contact. "Dad says I just need to eat more protein for dinner, then I'll build muscle…"

"Hey, just make them feed you something nutritious, like *meat*," Salzach said.

Louie stuck out his tongue, playfully disgusted. "Nah, we're gonna have chicken and 'fu."

"But that doesn't have *nutrients*." Salzach leaned forward over the middle seat's back, pressed against the van's roof. "Gimme a can of meat."

Obligingly, one of the brothers up front grabbed one from the little cardboard crate of chow they hauled along. Salzach had to turn the can around twice to find the part of the thickly printed label that had the nutritional information, amongst the ingredients and legalese. No smart-paper on the label to simplify the search.

"Now look, Louie, how are you gonna grow big and strong without your… Ethylened— Ethylene-*dia*—… shit, how do you pronounce this?"

The can got passed around, with various failing attempts to say it, until Marianna just looked it up on her phone. "You pronounce it *limescale remover*."

"*What!?*" Salzach burst into laughter.

Her grin had a sharp viciousness Edane couldn't help wanting to emulate. It was just the right mix of friendly and tear-your-throat out.

Marianna was kind of a role model for everybody. Even Edane. Natural, given that she'd been born ten years before any of his brothers. By the time of the Emancipation, Marianna's production run was almost grown up. Almost ready to put into use. Edane's run had been six or seven years old. Some of Marianna's sisters had transitioned straight from pre-Emancipation existence as owned people to private citizens in the same line of work — security and warfare. Marianna herself had been up to something she didn't like talking about in the depths of old Colombia, far enough south of the city that the borders of the Middle American Corporate Preserve gave way to old-style nation states. But now, now she taught self-defense and martial arts, and ran the MilSim team. And that grin, stretched across her muzzle, made Edane wish his face were just that little bit sharper, like hers.

"Meat's full of limescale remover, Salzach," she teased. "You're advocating we dump industrial cleaning supplies down the boy's throat."

Edane snatched the can back from the others to look it over, fighting off a smile — amused, not sharp. Cans of meat were familiar. Beautifully familiar. What he'd grown up on as a kid in the barracks. He'd lost track of the stuff for years, nobody seemed to believe that anything like meat could qualify as *food*, but some brother's family found someone still making it in bioreactor vats up north somewhere in Mexico, canning it just like the Mess sergeant used to dole it out. Edane put his phone to it, but the label didn't even have a smart patch to link to the web address, he had to scan it in so he could check their food safety certificates.

Meanwhile Louie was laughing so hard he was hiccoughing, and Salzach was slapping the kid's back. "I'm advocating we feed the boy some *real* food. None of this sauce and spice stuff. If it doesn't get pulled out of a vat in dripping strands of tissue and spun into a solid mass, it's just not *food*."

God, they were going to make Louie choke.

Maybe it was silly, enjoying this kind of thing. Laughing about it. But as a kid, Edane hadn't caught on to any of it. It had taken him years to understand what a joke was. Sometimes he still didn't think he understood.

Eberstetten, sitting in the front, was frowning down at his phone. He'd looked it up too. "It's a multi-use chemical. Ee-Dee-Tee-A. Ethyla-something-something." A short pause, his ears flicking back at the laughter behind him. "It's also for treating lead poisoning."

"See? So if you get riddled with bullets, just eat your meat, Louie." Marianna punched his shoulder, grinning still. "All that nutritious meat's gonna sop up the lead like a sponge, leave you just *fine*."

"Nah, nah, no way it's *not*!" Louie yelped, gasping for air between fits of laughter, face scarlet.

Eberstetten just turned and stared, ears flicking curiously. "I meant *real* lead poisoning," he clarified, cautiously.

Edane... Edane shook with silent almost-laughter, distracted from his problems, for a little while.

Eberstetten would get the joke eventually.

When they dropped Louie off, at his folks' place in the suburbs, Salzach walked him to the door. Stood there, tall and silent.

It was always awkward for the parents. Even Edane could see that much from the street. Edane knew the way those people looked, because his mothers had kind of looked like that when he'd been in the hospital. It'd been rough on them. Louie's folks, *Enzweiler's* folks, looked like nice people. A little reserved, holding back. Trying to hide the way they looked at Salzach, longingly, like maybe the bad news never came, and Salzach was really Enzweiler, and their son had never been killed on a cold mountain while trying to escape Tajikistan after the revolution kicked off, just a few days after Edane had been wounded.

Salzach, out in front of Enzweiler's mom, dad, and little brother, bore the weight of that longing silence longer than Edane thought possible. He smiled at them, gave Louie a friendly thwack on the back, and made the van rock when he got back in, slumping in front of the dashboard console.

He selected the bookmark for Ellis' place next, and the van drove itself out back towards the freeway.

With Louie gone, the real post-mortem could begin. Marianna unfolded her pad to its largest size, and took a sharp breath at the game map, showing their paths during the match as glowing lines.

"I fucked up," Edane said, breaking the silence. He folded his arms, left over shaking right, as Marianna flicked through the engagement's recording. "That's all I have to say about it."

"No, no," Erlnicht protested, shaking his head, ears flat back. "The mess started with that UAV. What the hell was up with that?"

Edane had forgotten about that. Their request for a UAV fly-by had been responded to with a loud, hydrogen-turbine drone that buzzed them at tree-top height. They'd expected something electric and near-silent. It hadn't given away their position, exactly, but it certainly hadn't helped them avoid fighting.

"Okay," he said, "that's where things *started*? But I fucked up. I took too long reloading, got left behind. That elimination was my own damn fault." Edane grit his teeth.

"Putting that aside," Marianna said, leaning over the map, "the thing with the UAV was bullshit. I talked with the coordination tent, apparently they were running low on resources, and their guy at the airstrip mistakenly sent out the wrong model, with the wrong AI mission parameters loaded. So, what we can take away from that is when shit goes wrong for somebody? It rains down on everybody else." She tapped the map's time control, skipping it forward. "Moving on."

The post-match post-mortem debriefing covered a lot of ground, but Edane didn't have the guts to say it, and apparently neither did anyone else. He was holding back the team. He'd fallen behind, because his coordination wasn't up to scratch, and he just wasn't good enough. It was right there in the stats — his accuracy had even fallen under *Louie's*. If Edane ignored his shooting immediately after starting, before his arm got tired, started shaking, he was miles behind Louie's accuracy performance, and best will in the world to the kid, but he was only human. Edane wasn't, Edane was supposed to be more than that.

Later, after they'd dropped off Ellis and Erlnicht, when it was Edane's stop, Marianna cornered him, exiting the van and slamming the door on Eberstetten.

"Stay in the van," she told him and Salzach and the others. "I'll help Edane with his things."

"But..."

"*Stay.*" And Marianna circled around the van, hauling Edane's armor bag out of the cargo compartment before he'd even finished getting his equipment bag over his shoulder.

Edane felt sure that this was it, this was when he got kicked off the team.

Marianna shouldered the armor bag and grit her teeth, and not in the way Edane wanted to emulate. "You listening to me, knucklehead?"

"Yes, sir."

"I told you to fucking go easy on that arm."

"I did, I'm shooting left-handed like you said, I'm even letting my right side take a rest." He held up his hands defensively, gripping his MilSim gun's bag in his left hand, not his right.

"No, you're not *listening* to me. I said go easy — it's not a goddamn secret that you got fucked up in Tajikistan last year, kid. If you were human I'd say it's a miracle you're even on your *feet*, let alone using your hand and growing your nerves back, but you are you, so I'd say you're doing *adequately*." She narrowed her eyes at him, teeth clicking as she slung her jaw left for a moment. "You hear me?"

"Yes sir."

"I am going to drag this team into the professional league bracket if it kills every last one of you little shits — except Louie, he's a rookie, he gets a year to live." Marianna took the gun bag from him and marched for the apartment lobby doors. "So you had better goddamn listen to me, Edane, when I tell you that you fucking take it easy with that arm. And to make this explicitly clear, that means you *slow the hell down*."

Edane followed her, warily.

"If you need more time to reload, plan for it, don't try and do something you can't. Okay? You're trying to act like you didn't get your ass blown up. That's bullshit. You aren't at everyone else's pace and you're not supposed to be — you hear me?" She set down the bags when they got inside, piling them in front of the elevators.

He didn't answer, this time. Couldn't answer.

"I don't care what the hell you think they made you for, what you're *supposed* to be capable of. Before you speed back up, you have to slow down. Heal, take your time, accept that you're not as fast as you used to be — accept that you got *injured*."

He looked away, and she grabbed the neck of his shirt, yanked him forward until he looked at her. "Man up, and stop pretending it never happened Edane. I've got no use for you otherwise. You hear me?"

"Yes, sir," he murmured.

Marianna shoved him back a step. Wagged her finger in front of his nose. "You fucking listen this time. No more 'I fucked up' out of you, Edane. Especially not in front of the rest of the team. You don't tell me you fucked up — I tell *you* that you fucked up. Got it?"

He nodded meekly.

She slapped him across the face for it. "Don't you nod at me, you little shit. You say 'yes sir' like all the other knuckleheads."

Edane grit his teeth, ears flat. "Yes sir," he ground out.

"Good boy." She half turned away, as if to leave, then spun on him — *thwack!* — beating him across the side of his skull with the heel of her hand. "Do *not* make me give you a fucking pep talk again," she hissed, pointing a finger under his jaw, at his throat, as if about to stab him. "This was fucking embarrassing."

Edane winced away, rubbing life back into his ear. "Sir yes sir."

"Goodnight, Edane."

"Goodnight, sir."

3. Home again

::/ San Iadras, Middle American Corporate Preserve.
::/ March, 2105.
::/ Edane Estian.

First thing after Edane got home, he stuck the stimulator pads the doctors gave him on his arm, their cables almost invisible in his fur. Leaving them on made his muscles twitch and fingers tingle in a way the doctors assured helped restore feeling and nerve function, but it didn't stop him from cleaning up the apartment. He put the sheer mesh nightgown back in the cupboard where it belonged, reclaimed the black lace underwear from under the couch and stuck it in the hamper, set the roses on the dining table straight, and generally put things in order. All with his left hand, of course.

He loaded up the dishwasher but kept the cheap mugs with the printed jokes on them aside to hand wash — Edane didn't understand any of the jokes, but Janine said they were jokes. The washer had a tendency to make them peel, and all of Janine's old joke coffee mugs had white specks where the joke parts had chipped out, and Edane didn't want that to happen to her new mugs. She liked coffee, and she liked drinking it out of mugs that said things like 'You don't have to be crazy to work here…', 'Today's a blue-movie Monday' and 'Work it', with a butt-slapping animation.

After that and getting her underwear in the wash cycle, he stripped down his MilSim rifle and took out the mud with an old, worn down toothbrush — the older the toothbrush, the softer the bristles. Oiling the recoil engine was strictly unnecessary, but checking the pneumatics and weights was part of his routine. It felt nice, reassuring. Like cleaning a real gun, and a lot of the parts — except for the recoil engine — were the same. When Janine's underwear was out of the washer, he threw in his uniform. His uniform and her underwear didn't mix. The uniform's fabric was rough-woven, actually hard enough to put wear and tear on Janine's lace. He didn't really understand why she had clothes that fragile, or why anyone would, but it was like her mugs — Janine liked things a certain way, so Edane respected that.

It was kind of nice, seeing how different she was, despite being so nearly the same as him.

When he'd finished cleaning up he took off the stimulator pads, went in the shower, and saw that she'd drawn 'E + J' on the shower door in soap, with a heart shape around it, so when the glass fogged up it was visible, and not before. He didn't get it right away, took him awhile to understand, but when he did, he smiled a little. Janine was *very* different to him.

He got out of the shower, set all their clothes out to dry, and afterward he sat on the couch with his MilSim goggles, and loaded up an augmented reality firing range simulation for sidearms to practice with, left and right handed, graphed his scores — better than last month's, at least — and spent a further fifteen minutes unable to think of anything else to do with himself until Janine came home.

She didn't have any set time to come home, but usually she got home before he was done with his firing drills. When Janine did come home tonight, late, it was with the winding, almost piercing scent of the Korean take-out from down the block that Janine always referred to as Chinese.

"Hi, baby." She blinked, surprised to see him at the door — but he knew the sound of her gait on the tiled floor outside her apartment.

"Hi." He couldn't help from wagging his tail, she just had that effect on him.

Janine let him take the bag of take-out, but stopped him from turning around to put it down with a hand over his shoulder. Her fur — a yellowy, sandy color — brushed over his as she snaked her hand up to the back of his skull, drawing him close.

He flicked his ears uncertainly, blinking at her as she pushed one lock of her very deliberately and artfully styled red hair to one side, and brushed her muzzle against his. This was one of those parts he didn't understand, but she didn't have to use any force to wrestle him into place, pulling his head down, down, until she could tilt her head and kiss him.

He'd seen his mothers kiss each other almost all his life — for longer than he was in the barracks, even — but actually kissing someone himself was... was strange. He didn't mind how it was warm, or how it was an excuse to stand near her, but when she did the curly thing with her tongue, groaning gently, he didn't know how to respond.

Instead of responding, Edane stood still, moving only a little, letting her push and pull him around until she seemed satisfied with his lip in her mouth, and released him with a smile. Then, with a sniff and a blink, she stared up at him quizzically.

"Did you use my shampoo?"

"Yeah. I ran out. That's okay, right?"

She pushed her black nose in under his throat, sniffed again, again, before leaning back and blinking at him.

He blinked back at her.

She was like him — kind of looked like a dog — but she'd been gengineered out of something else entirely. Something marsupial that just *looked* like a dog, but it actually had stripes? Janine had stripes, covering her back from her shoulder blades down to mid-thigh. She'd shown him — often. She was also smaller than him, a lot smaller. Warm to hug.

Edane liked hugging better than kissing. His mothers had hugged him a lot, a process he thought of the 'Cathy and Beth Maneuver', especially when they thought he might be sad, so he understood hugging a *lot* better than kissing. Kissing was okay, but he could hug Janine for hours.

She was good to hug. Tiny in his arms. Like just by hugging her, he could armor her against everything in the world that could ever hurt her, everything that could make her think she wasn't a nice person.

Janine took one last sniff, and squirmed, lifting her head to regard him with a quizzical glint. "You smell like rose petals," she announced.

"Yeah. That's what your shampoo smells like." He stilled the wagging of his tail. "Is that wrong?"

She looked at him without quite seeing him, thinking. "No," she said at last. "It's not wrong." She smiled up at him, stroked her hand down his jaw, over his neck, and patted his shoulder. "Weird, but kind of nice." She hesitated, before adding, "It's a little like I can smell myself all over you, which is… kind of *very* nice."

Edane let his tail wag uncertainly, relaxed his grip. "Okay."

She stood up on her tip-toes, kissed his nose, kicked off her high-heels and threw her bag on the couch, then set up a movie for them to watch while eating take-out.

Janine had gotten 'fu. Edane wasn't a huge fan of 'fu, under normal circumstances, but 'fu from the take-out place wasn't 'fu that looked like a piece of steak, trying to pretend it was meat. 'Fu from the take-out place was a kind of white block for dipping in all the weird sauces they had. At first Edane hadn't bothered with the sauce, just eaten, but Janine had found out and blinked at him and *made* him try all the different sauces until he liked one.

After the third try, he kind of liked the one soy sauce enough to choose it for his own, but Janine had persisted, and he almost couldn't remember a time when he *hadn't* liked the horse radish, even though it had only been a month or so since Janine invited him to move in with her.

It was nice, living with Janine. Much nicer than the hospital room he'd shared with some of his brothers, immediately after Tajikistan, and differently nice to the apartment he'd shared with some of his brothers after leaving hospital. Janine was a lot messier than his brothers had been, but she was different, and different was its own kind of nice.

After the movie they had sex, and Edane took another shower. Then Janine offered to join him in the shower, and Edane said no, that was okay, and she was waiting in bed after that with a kind of… hard to understand expression.

Edane thought she might have been mad, or disappointed, but apparently she wanted to experiment, showing him her stripes again, and other parts of her, and asking him to kiss her — so he looked at her, and he kissed her. She talked him into more sex, but this time things went a lot slower, and with more hugging — though hugging was *very different* when having sex, it was still hugging, still warm and something that made Edane feel good about how different Janine was. About how little she was, and how he could hold her, like he could protect her from everything.

Edane wanted a shower afterward again, though — he felt weird, a little sticky — but didn't think it'd be nice to Janine if he went and showered again, at least not that night, so he waited for morning.

"Edane?" Janine asked, taking her seat at the table.

"Yeah?"

She turned her head to one side, then the other, staring at her bacon and eggs. Smiling, lopsidedly. He'd drawn the heart shape with ketchup around the edge of her plate for her, and she was inspecting it very, very curiously. Hadn't even picked up her fork to eat, as if she didn't want to mess it up.

"Did you, uhm..." She leaned back from the table, palming at her eyes, hand folded over the bridge of her snout, frowning for a second as she thought about it. "Did... Did you do this for a reason?"

He perked his ears worriedly. "Yeah. Did I do it right?"

"You did it fine, Sweetie," she said from behind her hand. "But. Why did you do it?"

"You did the one in the shower."

She pushed her lips together, hard. "I see." She didn't sound too pleased.

"Was there a reason I was supposed to have done it?"

Janine shook her head, looking away.

He set down his pad, pausing the game replay from yesterday, and got up to join her at the table. "Tell me? I want to understand."

Her gaze wobbled over his face uncertainly. "Well. It's one of those romance things. I drew the shower one because we're..." she trailed off.

"In love," Edane said.

"Yes."

"And I love you, so." He gestured at her plate.

"Yeah," she looked away, awkwardly — her tail still over the back of her chair. "It's just that the little romantic gestures, they're... they're for togethery stuff, y'know? And you already ate breakfast." She gestured at his plate, waiting in the dishwasher's top rack for the next cycle.

He looked at his plate, then at hers. At Janine, directly. "Was that wrong? I got up earlier than you."

"I *really*, really appreciate you making me breakfast, Edane." She leaned forward, and kissed his cheek, before flopping back — a ruffled mess of thylacine (the thing she was gengineered from — sometimes called a Tasmanian tiger) and uncertainty. "Don't think I don't, but, it's just... didn't you maybe want to eat breakfast with me? Us together?"

Edane twisted his ears back, looking down at the empty patch of table in front of him, and the breakfast in front of her. "Oh." A pause. "I... I didn't think about it like that. I was thinking I needed to go over yesterday and tomorrow's maps, for the matches, and get in to the physiotherapist and... Sorry. Eating breakfast together didn't... didn't really cross my mind."

"It's okay." She sagged back, relieved. "Maybe we can try tomorrow?"

"Maybe." Tomorrow Edane was up early again, for training. Janine never managed to get up as early as he did, she only had to get to work by nine, but pointing that out felt like a bad idea.

"It's just a little confusing with you, Edane. Lots of, uh... mixed signals. And I don't always know what you're thinking when you do romantic stuff. You know?"

"I know." He got up, and leaned over the table to kiss her cheek, like she'd kissed his. "I'm still learning all that stuff."

"Yeah." She smiled, picked up her fork and swiped her bacon lightly across the corner of the heart. She sat there chewing slowly, watching him walk around her apartment. "We're both still learning," she said, brightly.

"Both still learning," he agreed, veering past her to kiss her cheek again — which made her smile all the more, so he knew he'd done *something* right.

He left her to breakfast and sat down to go over yesterday's maps again. He looked up again when she stood, taking her plate, with its still partly intact ketchup heart on it. Janine put it very, very carefully next to his in the dishwasher's top rack, her tail swiping side to side slowly as she smiled.

He smiled too, a little.

She crossed the open plan front room of her apartment — kitchen and living room both — and sat herself down on Edane's knee. "So, what are you busy with, Sweetie?"

"Yesterday's game." He showed her his pad. "Doing some thinking about ways to improve. Want to help? Always good to have someone to bounce things off."

He knew it was a mistake the moment he'd said it, but it just all spilled out anyway. He wanted to share things with Janine, things that mattered, like how his aim hadn't been too bad for the first hour or so of the game before his arm got tired, but...

But she smiled a little awkwardly, head pulling back from him in guilt, ears lifted in surprise. "I'd... I'd just distract you, Sweetie." She nosed in to kiss him briefly. "Maybe later, though." With that she hopped off his lap, and padded back to the bedroom, scrunching her hair into a tense, red tangle behind her.

The last time they'd tried talking about MilSim she'd gotten bored, hadn't really followed what was going on in the game. She'd needed things explained to her over and over — which Edane didn't mind, but she did. Janine had just sat there, struggling to keep up, getting more and more frustrated as Edane tried to rephrase things so she'd understand. It wasn't that she was dumb, or anything. Janine was smart — *so* smart. She just asked, without thinking, stuff like why can't the players just negotiate, and gotten *so* mad at herself for suggesting it even before Edane could reply, because she'd known it was stupid — she just didn't understand fighting. Not with guns, anyway.

Edane leaned over the couch's armrest, looking back at the bedroom door, and wondered if it made her feel kind of like Edane did, when he needed a shower to feel normal again, but he didn't dare go and ask her that. That might start a fight — the kind of fight Janine was good at, with words — and that was just about the only kind of fight that Edane never wanted to experience again.

4. Medical Evacuation

::/ San Iadras, Middle American Corporate Preserve.
::/ April, 2105.
::/ Edane Estian.

Getting into the second half of the spring season, things felt okay. The team's overall rankings were up, Edane's stretches of good performance at the beginning of each match and after rest breaks were getting longer, and he and Janine were very carefully not talking about things. Instead they sat quietly most nights, comfortable with each other, while Edane did his arm exercises and she relaxed after work. It was companionable. Nice, even though it was a lot quieter.

Gave him time to think.

He'd never realized how valuable that time was, but he'd never really had things to think about before — like Janine, and his arm, and his worries about the team. He wasn't really built for thinking. Not the way most people seemed to talk about it, anyway.

The kind of thinking Edane had done, still did — preferred, even — was the kind that happened between heartbeats when something bad happened. When there was something to react to.

Like the turret.

It was the third deployment of the day, last game before the mid-season rest week, so everyone was a little worn out by the last two months of play and extra driven to push hard, get their scores up before the break week and all of the teams had a chance to switch tactics.

The team was going after secure hardlines again. That meant slogging overland into enemy territory, the long way. Cutting through back zones, avoiding contact, running with their electronics off as much as possible, staying flat on their bellies while waiting for the mission coordinators to open up EMWAR assets and jam any local surveillance that might be around. This far back-field there weren't many enemy players. Leaving a team out in the middle of nowhere to cover nothing on the off chance someone was moving, that was inefficient. Instead, the enemy used fixed assets.

League rules for equipment budgets were meagre at this level of play. Standard play-theory for a fireteam of four said each member saved part of their individual budget, the team pooled the resources, and they got either a fixed automatic turret or a UAV. A full team of eight usually carried one of both, deploying the turret early for fixed defense or medium range fire support — getting the turret's heavy machine gun to fire in a ballistic arc over the horizon at something like a suspected mortar crew — and saving the UAV for light anti-vehicular roles. In this case, the turret had been left back-field.

Edane hadn't seen it. None of them had, it was lain under a chameleon cloth and set up on a ridgeline covered in scrub. The first thing they'd seen was the blazing muzzle flash turning the augmented reality special effects overlay in their goggles to explosions and tracers and nothing else.

Edane hit the dirt instantly. Waiting to topple forward was too slow, and diving forward kept the body in the air too long — the way to do it was to let your legs go slack and throw your shoulders down, as if starting a forward roll, except instead of rolling the ground came up and hit you like a hammer and if you had time, had foresight, you broke your fall with the stock of your rifle, but if you were unprepared — like Edane — you just let the ground do its best to break your ribs.

Going prone, that was the reflexive reaction. Then there was the thinking part. Figuring out the turret's line of fire, trying to work out if there were any others, calculating the possibility that the turret was linked into the enemy network or not, putting all those factors together in the blink of an eye. Edane thought his best bet was to crawl left, where there wasn't much more cover, but the contours of the ground would block the turret's line of fire.

An explosion of smoke bloomed nearby, flooding the world with grey. The smoke was almost dense enough to completely black out the sky, but Edane knew it was mostly AugR effects because the scent of it wasn't very thick in his nose, just a thin, water-based smoke effect, and what he saw was a hot, oil-black mess with metallic threads of chaff glinting and twisting everywhere. Thick enough he couldn't see the turret, not even with his rifle scope's tuned thermal imager, which meant the turret couldn't see him.

He got to his knees, hopped to his feet, and ran as low to the ground as he could, catching himself on his left hand every time he stumbled and throwing himself forward again in a mad three-limbed scramble.

"Who's hit?" one of his brothers' voices warbled through the murk.

Gunfire knifed through the smog, dark and invisible, but splittingly loud, the high velocity rounds screaming as they cut past Edane's head and towards the voice behind him. Edane yanked a grenade off his webbing, ripped out the safety bar with a spasm of his right hand, and lobbed it in the direction of the muzzle flash.

More gunfire, but this time the flash wasn't where it had been, the bullets were whining from a spot far to the right, tracking after the grenade... the turret had moved? The grenade exploded, shot apart at the arc of its throw.

Edane hit the ground, struggling to remember the lay of the land compared to where he'd last seen it all, and in desperation flicked his electronics back on. "It's not a turret, it's an Unmanned Ground Vehicle," he hissed over the newly established com-link.

A set of scarlet contact markers appeared in his booting HUD, as the weapon fired again.

"No shit," Marianna replied. "Oh, good. You're right on top of it."

As the local map finished loading up, he saw Marianna's marker a football field behind him, and Svarstad even further back — the rest were still electronics off, even though they'd obviously been spotted.

"Svarstad, distract that fucking thi—" Marianna didn't finish her order, Svarstad's LSW already spitting a line of glowing tracers through the smoke.

"Edane, *kill!*" she snarled.

No hesitation. He rose to his knees, sighted through the smoke at the muzzle flash of return fire ahead of him, and emptied his rifle in a single, two second, forty-four round burst that pounded his left shoulder to gravel.

His weapon clicked its last.

The turret — the UGV — fell silent.

"Think it's—" His ears rang. Not a real noise, a harsh tinnitus-pitched squeak playing in his earbuds, and the game's simulation of his electronics instantly cut out. For a moment he wondered if the match software had bugged out — that had happened once, a month or so back — but the AugR smoke around him was intact, still boiling clouds of oily black despite only the weak tang of chemical-tinged water vapor in his nose.

No, not a game bug — HERF, a high-energy radio frequency attack. Microwaves. He was being *microwaved*, his electronics burnt out with a concentrated HERF beam powerful enough to fuck with his ears. Those were deployed on satellites, sub-orbital aircraft and heavy high altitude UAVs. For one to hit you, they had to have a lock on you. He'd been close to the UGV when he'd killed it — it wouldn't cost the enemy team much to sweep the immediate area with HERF in the hopes of hitting a straggler, but he hadn't been *that* close. So they had to have some kind of lock on his location, had to have aimed it, and if they'd aimed it they knew where he was with precision, and if they knew that…

Before he'd even finished shaking his head, trying to clear of it the unfamiliar noise, he started running. Direction didn't matter, just running, because a heartbeat later there was an explosion where he'd been standing, the sound of a mortar shell airburst, and even if it didn't come with a blast-impact rattling through his body, a brief irrational fear took him, made him stumble down, lanced panic through him even worse when the second blast detonated to his left. He scrabbled back onto his feet, but his right arm shivered, sent him nose down into the dirt, and by the time he was up and running again, trying to evade a spiraling fire pattern he couldn't work out in the half-second available to him between panicked breaths, the noise was on him and loud and terrifying and the only reason he didn't collapse to the ground screaming was because he *hadn't actually been hit* — Edane had to remind himself of that very forcefully; he hadn't been hit with a mortar shell, it was just the game, just part of the game, he wasn't hurt at all. All that had happened was that his goggles were flashing casualty instructions at him, and barking, "*Casualty-Casualty-Casualty*," in his ears, and it wasn't real.

Just a game.

He gulped breaths of dirty tasting air, and lay down, like the casualty instructions told him, and looked down at his body fearfully. He was covered in blackberry jello, and so relieved he almost laughed. The wounds covering his torso, streaking his legs, were just AugR black gunk. At its worst, it looked like someone had dumped a bowl of half congealed pudding over him.

Edane lay back, able to shut his eyes and relax now, while explosions thudded both near and far, and twisted around to get his tail comfortable under his ass.

He opened his eyes, and looked up at the sky. It wasn't blue, just the roiling grey of the smoke sparkling with metallic chaff strips. Disappointing.

The casualty instructions flashed 'stay down and take no action' at him, and 'do not respond to questions or voice communications', so it was bad. Not immediately lethal, and it hadn't blinded out his goggles after he'd lain down, so he had to still be conscious by the game's wounding model. Kind of.

Edane grit his teeth. He wasn't a fan of 'kind of' conscious. Been there, done that, never wanted to do it again.

At last he heard Louie's sharp cry of, "Edane's here! I've got him!" Louie emerged from the smoke's depths, his expression frantic.

"Can he be moved?" Marianna called back.

Louie fell to his knees beside Edane, checking him over, asking him questions — none of which he could answer. "I don't know if he's conscious," Louie shouted back, ripping open Edane's medical kit. Louie squirted make believe AugR sealant foam all over Edane's belly, checked him again, and pushed a clinging pad down over his armor, representing a sheet of skinplast.

"Can he be *moved*?"

The kid didn't answer. As much in his own world as Edane had been. Hands shaking as he felt at Edane's neck and waited for the game's goggles to tell him about Edane's pulse. Tears building in his eyes as that pulse no doubt began to fade.

Marianna lunged out of the fog. "For the fucking tenth time, Louie, *we gotta move!*"

"I have to stabilize him first." Louie's hands were shaking as he pushed down harder on Edane's abdomen, a layer of AugR ink staining his fingers.

It wasn't up for discussion. Marianna grabbed Louie's wrist, and yanked his hand to one of the straps on Edane's armor. "Drag him," Marianna ordered, before sprinting off into the fog.

People always thought that a medevac had to be like in the movies, rescuer carrying the patient across a shoulder or in their arms or something, but that took a lot of strength. Edane could do it, sure, but over most terrain dragging was the better option. With a good strap to hold onto, just about anybody could drag someone else, and at a reasonably fast speed, too.

Edane did lift his head a little, to make things easier — that was *hardly* taking action — but otherwise Louie moved Edane by himself, back and out of the smoke into a curved gully between two patches of trees.

Louie looked a little shaky, and Edane wanted to congratulate the kid, help calm him down — he'd done *great*, after all, he was smaller than Marianna and he'd still gotten Edane moved — but the goggles kept telling Edane not to say a word.

Not while Louie started to lose Edane, forgetting that he needed to replace Edane's lost blood volume, and not when enemy players stepped over the gully-line and saw him panicking his way through first aid on Edane, instead of maintaining situational awareness.

"I SCREWED UP." Louie shook his head miserably. "I'm sorry, Edane."

They were sat in the back-bay of an equipment cart while it hummed along one of the side roads around the field, back to the rest area. Louie was slumped facing one way, feet up against the opposite wall, then Eberstetten facing the other way, with his boots against the wall next to Louie, and then Edane, his elbow on Eberstetten's toes.

Edane dipped his ears back. "It wasn't really your fault."

"Yeah. Worry about that later, work on what you can." Eberstetten rubbed at his face tiredly.

"That's what Marianna always says." Louie frowned at his hands in his lap, while the road rolled by.

Usually, the silence was comfortable. But Eberstetten yawning, tongue curled, just made the silence that much more obvious. Hardened it.

Edane leaned his head back against the bay's sidewall, splaying his ears out, flat against the rough fabric liner. Stained with ingrained dirt and scrapes and scuffs from years of muddy players piling into the vehicle. He listened to the engine's hum, the hiss of the tires on asphalt. Numb.

It hadn't been Louie's fault. Edane should have done better. Maybe... maybe if he hadn't stumbled on his right arm, getting up, he'd have gotten out of the blast zone. Maybe if he'd spotted sooner that the turret wasn't a turret at all, but a UGV, he could have had that extra moment to figure out what to do. A lot of maybes, but no answers.

"I'm sorry I messed up the first aid," Louie said again, scrubbing the back of his hand and wrist against his nose, all wet in the face.

"It's okay. Wasn't your fault." Saying that was getting to be a reflex. "First aid's just one of those things you have to practice."

Louie looked up at Edane uncertainly. "I got distracted, thinking. Thinking about how you got hurt."

He slanted his gaze down at Louie, just as uncertainly. "Wasn't like that, for me," he said. "It's just a game."

"Yeah, I know." Louie edged down, hunching his shoulders up. "But you got hurt with a mortar, and Eberstetten got shot by the UGV. Automatic fire." He palmed at his eye. "Like Enzweiler."

Eberstetten's ears perked in one stressed lift. "Aw, Louie, no…"

Eberstetten had been there. On one of the escape marches out of Dushanbe, post-revolution. After three days of madness that left Tajikistan a place where Edane's brothers were hunted, shot on sight as a particularly visible part of the fallen government's power. Eberstetten had been with Enzweiler, along with Salzach, a group of almost a dozen.

"I just. When I started to screw up with Edane I started thinking, thinking what if it was Enzweiler, and then—" The kid choked, a heavy sob, covering his eyes, skin red suddenly, his breaths wet and teary. "I was just, oh my God, oh my God, this is how Enzweiler died, and I can't save him and. And I wasn't looking and I screwed up and I got us knocked out and it's my fault and I'm sorry!"

Eberstetten blinked slowly, confused. Ears low, back. Edane didn't know what to do either.

"Louie… it's okay." Edane carefully set his hand on Louie's shoulder, pulled the kid closer.

"I'm sorry," he sniveled, pulling away, hesitating, then giving in and collapsing back against Edane, eyelids trembling.

Eberstetten pulled straight, sitting cross-legged, leaning forward, turning his head, this way, that. Half curious at how upset Louie was, half confused. Concerned. "Louie, it's okay. That's not even what happened to Enzweiler. You wouldn't have been able to do anything, nobody could have done anything, it wasn't anybody's fault."

"Really?" Louie looked up, choking on his own breath.

"Yeah. It was quick. There was nothing we could do. It was fast."

"Salzach told us. It was a machine gun. Like the UGV."

"Kinda, yeah. It was a Korel." Eberstetten held out his hand uncertainly. Let it thump onto the floor when Louie didn't reach out for it. Poor guy didn't know what to do with Louie's wide eyes on him.

"W-what's a Korel?"

Before Eberstetten even opened his mouth, Edane had tensed. He wasn't quite sure why, but the impulse to stay silent tugged at his spine.

"It's an anti-aircraft automatic support cannon. Big one, three rotary barrels on a motorized spindle."

Edane could almost taste the words on his lips. Staring at Louie under his arm, the impulse to try and do something, anything, to make the kid stop shaking was strong. And. And he'd asked a question, so maybe the answer would help him? Only it wouldn't.

"Oh my god," Louie breathed, suddenly like concrete under Edane's arm.

The answer wouldn't fucking help, and that was why Edane's jaw was clamped shut, keeping him from saying a single damn word, because as he'd learned in a dozen painful lessons — his mothers Cathy and Beth, Janine, Thorne, the folks at the market checkpoint — words could hurt people in a way Edane just didn't understand, and he knew that, and he knew enough to shut up and—

"It wasn't like he even got hurt, Louie. It was too fast. Enzweiler was standing up and then he was gone. Just pieces of him left."

"Pieces?"

"He got hit by a full burst, it wasn't anything like—"

"Shut up," Edane hissed.

"—like what happened on the field, he was just gone, and there was fog—"

"Eberstetten, shut the fuck up!"

"I'm explaining to the kid what happened!" Eberstetten snarled, teeth out. Not a grin. Just teeth on show, glowering at Edane.

Edane pulled Louie to his chest, even though the kid was shaking. Struggling. Sobbing, now. But Edane held him to his chest the way Cathy and Beth had held him whenever something bad happened, like by shielding the kid's head you could prevent trauma. "He doesn't want to fucking know!"

Eberstetten was waving his hands, now, hard sweeps, teeth grit. "It happened, okay? It fucking happened and I was there and I choked on him, I fucking sneezed, sneezed on his blood because it was all in the air and—"

"Shut up!"

"—upper half of his head was just lying—"

Edane jerked back his foot and stabbed the heel of his boot against Eberstetten's chin, had to do something to make Eberstetten shut up, but throwing Eberstetten's head back against the bus wall just made him madder, made him yell, "Why can't I fucking tell anybody this? Why can't I fucking say—"

Wham, and Eberstetten wasn't listening, but he'd caught Edane's foot, was wrenching at it, shoving it away, but somewhere in all that his reflexes fizzled out and his brain caught up enough for him to hear what Edane was yelling.

Heard, "Stop thinking! Listen to yourself! Get on schedule!"

Louie was insensible. Clawing at the front of Edane's uniform, sobbing.

Eberstetten went cold. Switched off. Ears going slack, pulling himself away, into a corner of the bay. Fingering his jaw.

Edane stared at him. Stared and stroked Louie's skull in hard half-remembered sweeps, just like Beth did when Grandpa Jeff died.

"I'm sorry," Eberstetten said, eventually, ears flat, taped tail curled against his leg. "I shouldn't talk about that. I… I got worked up."

A little while later Eberstetten made the shuttle stop for a minute, so he could vomit before they went on back to the rest area.

EDANE PUT HIMSELF in charge. Made Eberstetten go and eat something from the chow stand, and since the match clock was close to running out he went with Louie to get Louie's phone back from the judge stand, then forced Louie to sit and wait for his parents to get there. There was no way Edane was going to let Louie out of his sight and into an automated cab until he knew Louie was with the right people.

He wound up missing his redeployment round, kept Eberstetten there, and grabbed hold of Ellis when Ellis came back in after another firefight. Made them all wait, and when the rest of the team got back in, well… He had to hand command back to Marianna. Which meant an explanation. Which meant…

"He's a fucking kid, Eberstetten!" She had her helmet in one hand, seemed ready to bludgeon Eberstetten to death with it.

"I said I was sorry." Eberstetten stood with his head low, as if he could hide in the space between his shoulders.

"I don't get it," Svarstad murmured. "Louie knew Enzweiler'd died."

"Yeah." Eberstetten pointed briefly at Svarstad. "I thought maybe Louie thought Enzweiler'd been suffering like with a gutshot or—"

Violence was the tool of first resort. No friendly rough-housing, Marianna hit him so hard over the head with her helmet his ear started bleeding instantly, followed it up with very simple orders indeed. "*Get psychiatric aid! Do not discuss traumatic events with children!*" She drew up the helmet, glaring at him, teeth bared. "You hear me?"

"Yes sir," Eberstetten whimpered, eyes screwed shut. "Sir yes sir."

"Repeat those *fucking* orders."

"I'll get psychiatric aid. I will not discuss traumatic events with children."

Erlnicht dared raise his voice. "Louie's seventeen, Marianna."

She spun on him, finger raised like a stiletto blade. "He's not eighteen. That means he's a child, and he's my fucking responsibility while he's on this team, and this is not what his parents wanted for him."

Salzach dropped his jaw, let it swing side to side… at last shifted it left, left until his jaw clicked, and he shut his mouth, looking at Edane, then Eberstetten, then Edane again. "He was going to hear the details some time."

"Not when he was in tears because of screwing up the medical aid, not when I'd been fucking yelling at him all—" She halted her pacing back and forth under the rest area tree's branches, tail up, out, still as ice. "He didn't have to find out about it like that," she snapped.

Silence met her.

"Get that ear patched," she growled out, turning the finger of blame onto Eberstetten. "Anybody who needs to piss, go piss." She started pacing again.

Nobody moved, except for Eberstetten, marching over to the aid station, for the treatment of real wounds. Edane, Erlnicht, Svarstad, Salzach, Ellis. They all just stared, and after a moment of bearing the weight of the team's gaze, she whirled, stabbed out her finger at Edane, like it was Edane's fault, and yelled, "You're not at attention! You don't have to stand there like you are, so go finish off your canteens, fill them, drink until you need the Goddamn bathroom, and leave me alone."

Edane was the only one who kept standing there. Even Erlnicht loped off, casting a wary glance over his shoulder.

Marianna stood, palm over her eyes, long enough for them to get out of earshot before spitting out, "What?"

"It's okay. Wasn't your fault."

She cracked open her fingers, just looking up at him like he was crazy. "Louie's family, Edane. His people adopted one of us, he's family. We can't fucking do that shit to our family."

Edane dipped his gaze away, pushing his jaw left in one quick jerk, back, in brief, tired contemplation. "It's okay," he said again. "Wasn't your fault."

"I said go drink your water—"

"I don't take your orders like that. We play MilSim, but you're not my CO, Marianna."

She narrowed her eyes at him for a long moment. "You kids are so much easier to handle when you don't remember that."

Edane tried one last time, in case it'd work. "It's okay. It wasn't your fault." After all, it wasn't Louie's fault for screwing up, or Eberstetten's fault for opening his mouth, or Marianna's fault for yelling at Louie. At a masochistic stretch Edane couldn't help making, it was his own fault, for getting hit in the first place.

"Yes it was. I'm the one who put that kid in a team with the knuckleheads who stood and watched the foster-brother he worshipped get torn to kibble." She covered her eyes again, helmet dangling from her free hand, breath hissing between her teeth.

"It was an accident. Shit happens." Edane flattened his ears back.

Marianna just shook her head. So Edane checked both ways, to make sure that nobody was looking, not one of his brothers, not one of the players on another team, and stepped forward one step to apply the Cathy and Beth maneuver to Marianna.

After all. It'd helped Louie, a little, right?

She threw him off easily, jabbing the heel of her hand into his armpit hard enough to throw him over her foot, hooked behind his ankle. He thundered to the turf, legs sprawling, head bouncing off the grass, world dizzier than a carnival ride for just a little longer than it took him to realize he was on the ground.

Marianna stood over him, blinking at him, dumbfounded. "What the fuck was that?"

"A hug," Edane said, shuffling back on his ass, getting his hands under him.

"Oh." She stilled her breath. "Okay then." Her tone was calmer, but she didn't bother trying to help him up.

Not really a problem. Edane brushed loose grass off his backside and got up. "You looked like you needed one."

"Right."

"It's a thing to make bad feelings better, according to my foster-parents."

"Yeah, well, your fosters are full of shit." She settled her palm over her muzzle again. "Go drink your water."

"I said you're not—"

Marianna held up her helmet, eyes narrowed. "Don't make me beat the shit out of you. You ain't that big."

"Right." Edane averted his eyes.

"We've still got nearly forty minutes on the game clock, and we need to get redeployed and back onto the field. Now, are we done here? You going to go drink your water like a good puppy, and leave me alone so I can go talk to the off-field support controller?"

Edane lifted his hand to his temple weakly. "Sir yes sir," he murmured.

5. New Blood

::/ San Iadras, Middle American Corporate Preserve.
::/ April, 2105.
::/ Edane Estian.

Marianna could move fast, when she had to. "This is Eissen. Any of you know him?" She looked around at the gathered team, minus Louie.

Right in the back of the dojo Marianna worked at for her day job, between a pile of padding mats and a dusty rack of wooden sword things, Edane lifted his hand. "I do. I'm Edane."

Eissen grinned, a brief feral flash of teeth, pointing Edane's way. "Hey. I haven't seen *you* since the Tajikistan medevac. How you been?"

"Could be doing better." He waved his right hand, for effect, and Eissen jerked back, startled.

"The *hell* did you get that back…?"

Ellis grinned too — but in a much more human way. "He got a new arm stitched on last year. Nerves ain't all finished growing back, but Edane pulls his weight."

"If he doesn't drop it," Erlnicht chipped in, to more laughter.

"Alright, alright." Marianna snapped her hands in the squad-lead hand signal for silence. "Button up. See, Eissen? You already have a friend." She turned to the rest of them. "Until we know what the situation is with Louie, we're lucky enough to have Eissen in as a substitute."

Up front, Salzach cocked his head to the side. "You already play semi-pro?" he asked Eissen, ears splayed. Substitute players had to have a league ranking, which meant… "Aren't you already on another team?"

Occasionally teams doing really badly with no chance at a good ranking split up — that was the usual source for substitutions. But Edane didn't think one of his brothers would be caught dead on one of the drop-out teams.

Eissen shook his head. "I got asked to leave. I was on team Eight-Two-Seven."

"Why the *hell* would they drop one of us?" Salzach asked.

"You ain't heard?" Eissen asked, looking around. "Eight-Two-Seven's trying to go pro, and they're sponsored by Kennis-Purcelle Combat Games…" He searched for recognition in the others' faces.

The only person who looked like they knew anything was Marianna, and that was because she had her mouth clamped shut tight.

"The K-P are in talks with the league," Eissen went on, blinking. "They're lodging a doping complaint… Haven't you guys heard of this?"

"No." Edane shifted, glancing at Marianna. "I don't think we have."

"Our genes are too fucking good, man." That feral flash of a grin came back to Eissen. "They want to ban all furries — really, just *us* — from the pro level of the league. There's already an exemption for the genemodders, but apparently we've got some kind of unfair metabolic or genetic advantage they don't have. They want to get the league rules rewritten for the 2106 season."

Eissen kept looking around, that nervous grin appearing and disappearing, but nobody said a damn thing. Not a thing.

Not until Marianna clapped her hands sharply. "They ain't rewritten shit yet," she snapped. "And I have some *good* news for a change. We're about to be done with being team Eight-Eight-Zero." She zipped open a shoulder-pocket on her uniform and spread out a sheaf of shoulder-patches like a hand of poker cards. "We, provisionally and if you knuckleheads don't fuck this up for me, are gonna be the *Hallman Hairtrigger Hounds*."

She flung them at the team, one by one, and Edane caught his out of the air, blinking at it. They were pro? Semi-pro teams were referred to by their registration code, only pro teams got to pick *names*.

Edane opened his mouth to ask what was going on, but so did Ellis, and Erlnicht, and Svarstad, and—

"Shutcher yaps!" Marianna yelled. "We have a contract. You knuckleheads *are* going to sign it, and Hallman Electronics, a very nice custom fabrications company, are going to provide gear and pay us appearance fees at the maximum rate for semi-pro sponsorship. If we get into the top ten on the ladder by the end of the 2106 spring season, they will put up the registration money and we'll be a pro-league factory team — we have the remainder of this season, this year's fall season, and next year's spring season to do this. In exchange you will use their and only their gear, wear the logos, and let them use photos of us using their stuff in ads."

"But — *why?*"

"Because you knuckleheads made the mid-season highlight reels. *That's* why."

THEY MIGHT HAVE made the highlight reels, but Janine wasn't really all that interested. Not in the game, anyway.

"You move so *fast*. This isn't sped up, is it?"

Edane slouched down a little further on the couch, left arm loosely behind Janine, right arm wound up in nerve stimulators. "Nah. But it's got the effects on…" He started lifting his hand to gesture at the screen on her living room wall, but she did it first, tilting her head one way, then the other, as she switched between the feed's options with little shifts of her fingers in the air.

One way, Edane in the choking smoke and chaff beside the UGV he'd thought was a turret, while Svarstad distracted it. The other way, stripped of effects, Edane standing there in a few wisps of smoke — just enough for the AugR to work with — firing at the thing on full auto.

Then, after that, the team skirmished with the enemy faction's response team, coming to hunt them down in a series of rapid firefights. For the first time Edane saw where Ellis got taken out, intent on his target, forgetting that the enemy might have been coming up behind him — as they were.

"Which one is you?" Janine asked, staring at the screen.

"None of them. I was off the field, here."

"Oh." She sat back, leaning against his arm. "Can we fast forward to the next part with you in it?"

"I don't think there is one."

There was plenty more Edane wanted to look at, the commentary analysis on the way they dealt with the ambush, the exit path Marianna and the survivors took to sweep back around to the hardlines, deliberately hitting the enemy ambush team in the back before cutting the lines. But none of that, or the follow-up on the push across the middle field to grab a persons-of-interest objective, held Janine's interest whatsoever. In fact, she turned her back on the screen, scooting up to straddle Edane's lap, and pushed her nose into his face. "Wanna turn it off?" she purred, striped tail batting at his knees.

He pushed his muzzle against hers, back. Just mirroring what she'd done. Unsure, uncertain, still unfamiliar, even though this was one of the things she sometimes did. There were things that Edane didn't understand about 'relationship' maneuvers. Janine had explained it was like dancing, some things were for the lead dancer to do, some things for the follow dancer to do. Some things, like edging her hands up onto his collarbones, were more for the girl to do, and some, like putting his arms around her shoulders, were for the guy to do. Some stuff like that seemed entirely arbitrary, and the inexplicability of the rules behind it confused him.

She slowed, stopped, blinking green eyes at him from the other end of her long muzzle. He hadn't answered her. She knew he hadn't. Maybe even knew why, because Janine was smart like that.

She was so much *like* him. Just littler. Her muzzle longer, more slender. She could've been another canine, another dog, if not for being something very different. Thylacines were weird little extinct marsupial critters that just looked like a dog, but on the inside they weren't remotely the same.

Janine wasn't much like Edane at all. Not on the inside.

"We can turn it off if you want." He dipped his ears back, eyebrows up, worried about making her sad.

Softer, weaker, the electric life and joy in her ebbed out, she sank back on his lap, blinking at him slowly. Her ears dipped back, too. "You don't wanna turn it off? Maybe…" She leaned forward, pushed her muzzle alongside his. A quick touch of intimate warmth, and he did his best to respond, nuzzling into her cheek, cupping the back of her head before she drew back, her eyes gentle in front of him. Searching.

Whatever it was she was looking for, she didn't find it in him.

He lifted his hand and gestured the screen off, in case that'd help. It didn't.

"You like me, right?" Her voice was thin, strained.

"Yeah."

Something hard in her chest pushed out in her breathing, one puff, then another across his face. She hesitated. Asked, "Do you think I'm pretty?"

He lay his arms around her back, right looser than the left, to keep the nerve stimulators from smushing into her. He didn't know what she wanted, so he put his nose against hers. Pushed, gently, so their muzzles slid against each other. The way she had done it.

She shut her eyes, eyelids trembling for just an instant, before she lifted her chin, rolling the underside of her jaw across the bridge of his snout, settled in like that, with a more delicate, somehow more meaningful push of her nose against his. "Do you know what pretty means?"

She wanted an answer. He couldn't stay silent forever. He fought his impulse to keep his mouth shut, and whispered, "Not when you say it."

Janine's eyes opened uncertainly, and she blinked at him for a long time. "What do you mean?"

"I thought it meant nice." He looked away, slumping back against her couch. "I don't think you mean it like that."

"Well, I do mean it like that… but." She bit her lip for a moment. "Beautiful. What's beautiful?" She stared at him like she'd been shot. "Am I beautiful?"

He looked at her.

"Edane?"

He looked at her eyes. Her ears. Her muzzle.

"*Edane?*" She shook him, a tiny bit.

"I like looking at you," he said, softly. "That's what it means, right?"

"Yeah. Kind of." She did the Cathy and Beth thing all by herself. Lay her head on his chest, forehead pushed up under his jaw, staring into space. Her tension went away, a little, when he put his hand over her ear. Held her to him.

She didn't move, not one little bit. "What other things do you like looking at?"

He frowned. He didn't want to tell her. But he did. He wanted to tell her, because he'd never told anyone. Who else could he tell? None of them would ask. "The sky."

"The sky?"

"It was real blue."

"Oh." She shifted her head, a slight bit. Ear flicking against his thumb. "When was it blue?"

"In the Tous market. T-bone, we called it. I was on my back for a while. There was smoke trailing up, and that was black, but it cleared out and then the sky was real blue." He stroked her hair softly. Brushed it back and forth over her ear.

"When you got hurt?"

"Yeah."

"And that was beautiful." Her voice was so soft. Soft and strange.

"I don't know what beautiful is, Janine." He looked back up at the screen, blank and dead. "I don't think they made me for that."

"The sky can be beautiful," she whispered.

"Okay."

Her voice dropped again. So quiet he had to cup his ear to hear her. "Do you want me, Edane?"

"Is that a sex question?"

"Doesn't have to be."

"I like sitting with you." He thumbed her ear, gently. "It's calm and gentle."

She lifted her head a little, rolling her eyes to look up at him, blinking slowly. "They didn't make you to be calm and gentle, y'know." Janine sounded so hopeful. "You can be all kinds of things they didn't make you to be."

"Maybe," he whispered.

"Kiss the top of my head?"

He looked down at her. "Like how?"

"Like in the movies. Just curl down and—"

Edane had seen movies. He ground his nose in her hair, kissed her. Carefully pressed his mouth to her scalp, and she relaxed.

They sat like that for a while. Quiet, calm, and Edane didn't think about too much. Just felt kind of sleepy, but not like he needed a nap. Safe.

"Do you want to make love?" she asked him.

"We can if you want."

"That's not what I meant," she all but squeaked, voice tight, lifting up to look at him, blinking wetly.

"What did you mean?"

"Like if you... if you want... if you *want*... God." She shut her eyes on tears.

Edane pushed his muzzle against hers again. Kissed her. "Do you want to? We can if you want."

"It's not about me, I want to know what you want, Edane. I want to—"

He pressed the bridge of his snout against her mouth until she stopped talking. Until she held onto his fur with her teeth, while she blinked wet tears down her snout at him.

"I want you to feel happy," he told her.

"Make love to me," she whimpered.

"Okay."

Edane didn't really understand why it was so important. He did it with her anyway, to try and make her happy.

It didn't.

"Hit me."

"Okay."

Fire stabbed Edane in the gut. A wrenching tear in the fabric of his life, suddenly hot, suddenly real, a keyhole he could look through to spot a world where everything was right, everything was sane. A tiny fire-laced hole in reality that clenched up in burning rocky muscle.

His blood thundered in his veins, and for an instant, he wondered if this was what sex was like for Janine.

Only for an instant. He didn't have time for more.

Ellis's fist was jammed into his gut, knuckles twisted against Edane's shirt, and Edane caught the follow-up across the back of his forearm, throwing Ellis back through sheer physical weight of movement.

It had been a long time since Edane had broken a bone. He wanted to break a bone. Wanted to have a hurt he could understand again. None of this foggy 'how do I please the people I care about' bullshit, but something real and concrete, something he could hold onto, something he could feel a fucking *grudge* over, but he couldn't go back to Tajikistan and track down the bastards hopping over the border from their training camps in Uzbekistan and beat their heads in, couldn't rub their noses in the pools of blood and bodies left in the Tous marketplace, in the corpses of dead kids and the ruins of his arm. He couldn't do anything with that need except yell.

Yell, because sparring wasn't real fighting, and the rules didn't apply, he didn't have to be quiet, he could fucking *yell*.

"Eagh!"

Ellis's teeth flashed in his face. Anger, rage. Not at Edane. At the strength in his arms, shoving Ellis's fists aside, grappling for supremacy, digging in at the elbows, fighting, strength against strength.

The fight wasn't just against Ellis. It was against doing anything. Against doing dumb-ass things to hurt people — Louie, Janine. Against doing something dumb, making a mistake.

Edane twisted the tip of his thumb into Ellis's armpit, even as Ellis dug his fingers into Edane's shoulders, slowly twisting him to the side. But Edane wouldn't let that happen. He jerked back his fist, yelled again, and Ellis's shout was hot across his nose, breath wet with the stink of meat, wet with *pain* as Edane thumped his fist into Ellis's ribs.

It came down to a grapple, Ellis shoving in close, body against body. Wrestling for leverage. It wasn't unkindness that got Ellis pulling against Edane's right arm, dragging him into a lock. Wasn't even practical expediency. It was just that his right arm was the only place Edane gave way. Shoving at Ellis's throat, pushing his face away,

Edane could do that best with his left hand.

His right arm wasn't as strong.

He could pummel at Ellis's gut and shout and wrench against the pain of having his arm twisted, feel a tangled mix of joy that he *could* hurt so cleanly, so purely with his right arm after so long with it numb, then feel inadequate, utterly inadequate and lost and a failure because he couldn't slip out of Ellis's grip until at last there wasn't much point in moving. It wasn't going to change anything.

Ellis leaned in against his shoulder, his back, panting across Edane's ear, like Janine at night, but entirely unlike Janine, and Edane wondered what it'd be like with Janine.

Hurting her. Getting hurt by her.

He felt sick in the back of his throat. Was glad when Ellis eased off, loped back across the room to slump onto the garage bench. Edane wiped his tongue against the roof of his mouth, against the back of his hand, but it didn't take the sick taste away.

It was okay to hit Ellis. Okay to get hit. Bruising was okay. Bruising was healthy. But bruising was for Edane and his brothers, not for anyone else. He learned that quickly enough, when he'd gotten the surgery to let him have puberty. Puberty was different for him and his brothers. It didn't make them like the other kids, it made them aggressive. Aggression wasn't for anyone else. That wasn't allowed.

He wiped his tongue against his fur again and swallowed down a shivery breath.

Sometimes, he felt like if he hit Ellis hard enough, Ellis would understand. Ellis would understand everything Edane couldn't say. It was an insane, irrational idea, but probably no less irrational than Janine's idea that if they made love nicely enough, Edane would understand.

He took hold of the garage's wall and panted for breath, cooling off his tongue until his head felt less like a powder-keg. Outside, under the smooth high walls of Ellis's folks' housing block, on the asphalt between one building and the next, in the scuffed-away outline of Ellis's folks' parking spot in front of the garage door, Marianna paced, phone to her ear.

"Yes ma'am. I know. No, I don't want you to push Louie into talking to me if he doesn't want to." She dipped her gaze, taking a sharp breath. "No ma'am. No. Yes. Just like that. Let him know he's always welcome with us if he wants to play, or socialize. Anything." A pause. "Yes ma'am. It really is tragic. Eberstetten was with Enzweiler on the march, and... yes, ma'am. I'm sorry ma'am."

Edane watched her back. Thought about Cathy and Beth. About someone else having that kind of conversation with them. He shoved his nose against the crook of his arm as he leaned against the wall, and shut his eyes, listening.

"We all like Louie. It's... well, I think he was doing really well given his age, and the training time he could put in." Another pause. "No, no he's not really at anything like a pro level, ma'am, but we like him.

"We... we don't really think of it as him holding us back, ma'am. I think the consensus is more that we helped him go forward."

"Ever played football?" Ellis, behind him.

"Hnuh?"

Ellis wiped his nose off against his forearm, panted down a breath. "*Fútbol Norteamericano,*" he drawled, laughed. "That hypermasculine shit. They have a crapload of genemodded players. There's this one guy, a genemod tiger linebacker? I don't know what the hell he started off as — human or fur or what — but when they finished with him, *shit*. This guy can take the roof off a truck with his bare hands."

The idea of taking the roof off a truck bare-handed had weird appeal. "Could probably do it if I had a knife or something. Just an edge-tear in the sheet metal to get me started," Edane mused.

"That's not the point. The point is, they *like* overbuilt players. Safer to play if everybody's been toughened up past natural specifications. It's gotta all be in line with their medical safety board and registered and shit, but they don't treat genetic improvement as doping, right?" Ellis spread his hands.

Funny, how he wanted to be part of the team. Just to have a goal. An objective. Something comprehensible to chase down, like hardlines. No wonder the shit Eissen said had nagged at him, like it'd nagged at Ellis.

Like it must have nagged at Marianna.

He looked over his shoulder, out at her, done with her call to Louie's folks, standing at the far end of the worn away rectangle of paint in the asphalt. "Think we're gonna wind up playing football *Norteamericano* style?"

"We'd need to find some more players." Ellis bent over and poked at the door of the washing machine. The panel said 'wait', but it hadn't done anything for a while. The froth of soap and camo fabric was just sitting there. They had to wait. "Teams are bigger."

Edane slumped down onto the garage floor, staring despondently at the washer's glass window. They'd already loaded two more plastic tubs for the washer, but for some reason it was just *sitting* there instead of spin-drying, folding, and dumping the first batch of uniforms into another of the plastic tubs.

"Fucking thing," Ellis complained, flopping down beside Edane.

"Yeah."

Marianna's shadow fell across the concrete from outside. "Louie isn't coming back. We're keeping Eissen."

After a while, the washer spun up again. Stopped, foam dripping down the glass.

"I want Louie back," Edane rumbled.

Ellis was silent a little longer. Watching the rolling of water and fabric hopefully. Ears lifting in alarm when it spun, once. Stilled again. "Louie was fun to have around."

Marianna covered her face with her hands, struggling to keep the sigh in her. Not let it out. But she gave up, nodding. "I miss him too."

"Think if Salzach talked—"

"No," Marianna snapped. Shook her head more slowly. "No. No, the kid doesn't need Salzach around."

Edane looked up, wary. "How come?"

"He needs to mourn. He can't do that with carbon copies of his brother everywhere, with a violent death being re-enacted every time one of *you knuckleheads* gets shot down." Marianna flicked her middle-finger across the inside of Ellis's ear. "Hear me? head on a fucking swivel, Ellis. You are *not* getting tagged because you forgot to look over your shoulder again."

Ellis winced away. "Ma'am yes ma'am."

"That's *sir yes sir*," she hissed.

"Sir yes sir," he said. Didn't shout it, like at drill, just said it.

Saying it satisfied her. "Good. And you, Edane. You're ditching that pissy rifle. What were you, an eight?"

"I was White-Six." Back fifteen years ago. When he'd been a kid without a name, just part of the pack. When he'd known which squad and which platoon he'd been part of. When he wasn't a person, just a fireteam position. When ma'am and the female gender hadn't yet existed in his limited world.

"What is that? LAMW?"

"LAMW," he corrected. Not Ell-Ayy-Emm-Double-You, it was all one sound, *Lamm-whuh*.

Standard pack-pairing put evens with odds. Odd-numbered individuals were out front with heavy-barreled rifles good for anything. Even-numbered individuals hauled the specialist weapons. Light Support Weapons, which were rifle-caliber machine guns. Grenade launchers. Light Anti-Materiel Weapons — LAMWs — infantry-portable rifles in light cannon calibers for engaging light vehicles, infantry in assistive armor, UAVs, the works.

"Get a LAMW."

"But I—"

"I don't fucking care if it's got fin-guided-projectiles with a fucking gyro to aim it for you. If you need a crutch to shoot straight, get one. Hallman will fabricate whatever we want, and I'll make it work in the equipment budget. You're carrying a LAMW."

"Sir yes sir," he replied, doubtfully.

The washer turned over. Slung back and forth... and started to whirl, a blazing wheel of green and brown.

Marianna glared at it. "I've got seven of you knuckleheads now, so we'll do this the way we were designed to." She edged her ears back. Made the lines of her skull sharp. "If the league want to call us cheats, we'll give them something to really fucking cry about."

IV
Innocence

::/ Dushanbe, Tajikistan.
::/ May, 2104.
::/ Edane Estian.

Edane beat the stock of his rifle against the doorframe, the ancient wood flaking away under each deadblow impact. "Hey! *Hey!*"

In the dim corridor branching off the main street, the dark-haired Tajik locals stopped arguing with each other and bunched up tighter in the shadows to stare at him.

"We aren't accusing *anyone*," Edane said, waiting for the translator on his vest to catch up before going on. "We're looking for witnesses. Not making arrests." He lifted up his hands, showing his palms. Thorne would have approved, if he hadn't left the country, Edane hoped. "Did any of you see anything yesterday, before the man was killed outside?" He stepped back, gesturing at the street.

Silence. Dark eyes glaring out at him, all silent. Judging. Alien. He'd never been looked at like that, not in his whole life until he'd come to Tajikistan — the Muslims around here, they didn't like dogs, and they didn't like Edane.

"*Abhorred by God*," one of them muttered — fast and quick, voice low. The bud in his ear said it slowly, in three words, where the angry woman, her head covered by a shawl, had made it sound like a single curse.

Thorne would have been able to talk to these people. Thorne would have found an angle to take, a corner to lift. Edane didn't even know where to start, but he tried, anyway.

"Please. The man who was shot yesterday, he was like you, your brother, we're only trying to find the people who murdered him. He was a good Tajik man, he would have shouted if one of me tried to shake his hand. I don't want to shake his hand, I don't want to shake your hand, I just need to find out who shot him."

Confused grumbling from the man with the thick moustache shouldering in front of the lady. Not laughing — Thorne had been good at making people laugh, Edane couldn't yet — but they weren't trying to make him go away.

"Hsst." Sokolai, just to his side, hands lazily on his rifle, nodded his head out to the street itself. "That kid's moving again."

Edane glanced over his shoulder.

The little boy had been edging across the road, earlier. Walking back and forth, waiting for a gap in the traffic — dusty old cars, some manually driven, pushing goods and passengers through Dushanbe's streets. Edane had spotted him, wondered where the parents were. Now the kid had made it to the middle traffic island, was tottering along under his woolen coat as he crossed the rest of the way.

Elavarasa and Esparza were there, canvassing the opposite side of the street, knocking on doors, trying to find witnesses to the shooting. Elavarasa turned, blinking as the child pushed past some adults, reaching out to him, arms up.

Like he wanted a hug.

It happened sometimes at home. There were tourists who wanted photos of their children with furries — as if they were costumed performers in San Iadras's streets — so Elavarasa began to kneel.

The child exploded.

Dusty tan smoke billowed across the road, alarms blazed everywhere, the air punched Edane in the lungs and shoved him against the doorframe, something stung his finger, women screamed — the screaming always came first after a detonation. That high pitched wail after the bass *thud*. A quarter of the opposite side of the street vanished into the smoke, the sickly-sweet bleach smell of improvised explosives invading Edane's nose.

Falling glass bounced off the road, the cars screaming as they slewed to a halt. The few automatics on the road veered instantly to the curbside with hazard yellows flashing and warning alarms blazing.

Edane ran — stopped, dodging back as a manually driven car slashed past, its driver's eyes white-ringed with fear. Sokolai pushed past him, yelling, "Stay down! Everyone stay down, it's going to be alright!"

Heart hammering into his throat, his body sore from impact, left hand somehow bleeding, Edane pushed into the dirty smog, coughing even as it cleared.

A small pair of legs lay in the street, clothes stripped away. An arm. A howling Tajik man in western clothes stumbled away, the left side of his body all ragged red flesh and pockmarked skin, as if he'd been sandblasted, dust covering him. Elavarasa was sprawled in a mess of gore, his armor torn open, the lower half of his muzzle torn open, everything torn open, teeth visible through his throat.

The child had exploded. A suicide bomb? A *child*? Edane hadn't seen a trigger in the boy's hand. Remote detonated?

"EM-STAB, where's the fucking *EM-STAB?*" Esparza screamed.

Sokolai helped Esparza, tying off emergency tourniquets on Elavarasa's bleeding arms, his fingers gone.

The locals screamed, huddling in groups on the streets, running from their cars. If there was another bomb... Edane ran, breath howling through his lungs, tore the emergency stabilization kit off the back of their jeep, and tossed it down while Esparza called the Private Military Liaison Office, begging for medevac.

There was no one to shoot, no enemy, just wails of pain. Edane approached one of the wounded, the man who'd stumbled to the ground, blood pooling under him from his shredded skin.

"Let me help," Edane said, reaching for his first aid pack.

"*No, no, stay away from me!*" He swiped his hand viciously, eyes wild as he saw Edane's blood, lost his balance and fell back on the pavement, groaning.

Edane didn't understand. He knew the Muslims thought he was

dirty, that dogs were dirty, but he only wanted to help.

"*Please, let me.*" A younger woman, clad in the Muslim full black veil, just her eyes peeking out. She froze, hesitant, holding out her hands — which were bare.

Edane tore open the aid kit and set it carefully in her hands.

She didn't flinch away from touching him, though she carefully wiped his blood from the kit with her sleeve. The woman said, "*Thank you*," and bent to speak with the hurt man.

Edane wanted to thank her just for speaking to him, let alone *nicely*, but she'd already turned away. He scratched at his right wrist, trying to work out what he should do. The bleed on his finger didn't matter, wasn't even something that could be triaged. It'd go away on its own. He started getting the traffic moving again, waving cars on and past, making sure the people who'd fallen over weren't too badly hurt, getting the daytime crowd on their way home again safely.

That's what he was there for. To get all these people home safely.

FOUR DAYS LATER Edane was in the Tous marketplace, afraid of the locals. Not physically afraid. Afraid he'd have to talk to them. He was on patrol, rifle pointing at the ground, hanging off its sling, right hand on its grip, and his job was to watch them. The locals.

They were haggling over brightly colored things — be it clothes or candy or raw cuts of meat, cut out of *real* animals, it was all brightly colored — and passing back and forth little slips of paper that were supposed to be like money. Some of them had already spoken with him, asked him to stay away from their stalls, so he was standing away from the stalls, in a little clear patch in the crowds where people stayed away from him.

It was just his gun, he wanted to believe. But Sokolai and Esparza, a little way up at the gate, standing to either side of the big stone archway, had slung their rifles over their backs, and people were avoiding them, too. Which made Sokolai and Esparza's job harder. They had to look at people and compare them to pictures loaded in their goggles because the Tajik censorship of the internet limited the amount of bandwidth available for connecting to facial recognition services.

Maybe there was a reason the locals hated them so much. Maybe they were doing something wrong. Edane didn't understand it, didn't understand why one person would use religious insult-words and a woman dressed piously would calmly say thank you to him. He didn't understand why some of the little kids would pull faces and hide behind their parents, or why some of the little kids would explode.

He just didn't understand.

"That fucking journalist is back. What's his name? Gul? Bul?" Esparza grimaced, watching a man leaving the marketplace.

"Don't know," Sokolai replied, tone tired even through the limited bandwidth of their squad comms.

Esparza growled briefly, a low rumble, and Edane wondered why his brother hated the locals.

Then again, Edane thought, he knew why. It'd be easy to hate, to view them all as targets, part of the opfor, the tangos, the bad guys. Friendlies weren't supposed to spit on you, friendlies weren't supposed to call you names, friendlies were supposed to be *friendly*.

Maybe he hadn't done the right thing coming to Tajikistan. Edane had thought it'd be the right thing, it looked like the right thing from the inside of his mothers' apartment. It sounded so much better than trying to struggle through another year of college, where everyone knew the answers and Edane struggled to understand why anyone would care enough about high school to want to do it all over again as an adult with a different syllabus.

Mind wandering, his eyes flicked up. A hint of motion — he understood motion, understood reacting to it. The sky was blue above him, and in the time it took to swivel his eyes up the tiny fleck of motion blossomed out into a huge black cloud of smoke, thin trails lancing down at the marketplace.

Edane understood that too – that was a mortar shell airbursting at medium altitude to fire submunitions, and something pinged off the paving in front of him and he started turning away from the bouncing black submunition pod, twisting his right shoulder forward, and then everything hurt, and there was noise, and the mortar's submunition explosion kicked Edane away like a piece of trash.

6. Winning Play

::/ SAN IADRAS, MIDDLE AMERICAN CORPORATE PRESERVE.
::/ FEBRUARY, 2106.
::/ EDANE ESTIAN.

"SIX, MAKE IT go away." Marianna flicked her hand at the horizon, a blade chopping down on the distant target.

Edane pushed his shoulder down against the LAMW's padded back and levered the weapon around on its bipod. The bipod under the muzzle acted like a lever's fulcrum, turning each fractional shiver of his right hand and shoulder at the stock — less of a problem now, after Janine had taken the time to refine her massage routine over the break between the fall and spring seasons — into irrelevantly small shifts of the aim point. The strike indicator wobbled fractionally over the target, a UAV buzzing over the roof of the nature park's museum. Edane thumbed the lock control, the reticule blinked red, and the LAMW's pyrotechnic driven recoil engine rocketed backward into his shoulder.

The LAMW didn't actually fire anything, but so far as the MilSim's AugR was concerned a 23 millimeter fin-stabilized shell was in flight, an almost invisible blur streaking out at the UAV. The UAV was jinking — a standard random pattern — but the shell was semi-guided, thin and wire-like metallic fins contracting and curling under electric current to curve through the air, eating up the miles in one second, two seconds—

In AugR and through the LAMW's scope the impact was much more impressive, a tail of fire suddenly ripping through the UAV, shattered parts scattering, but in reality the drone's hull gently drifted down to a powered landing, even if it was wreathed in augmented reality flame effects.

"Strike," Edane murmured back. "Relocating."

Eissen was up first — unencumbered with anything more than his rifle, and forty spare rounds of the LAMW's oversize shells in eight brick-size magazines on his back — and beat through the brush beside the trail, opening a path.

Tearing the LAMW up off its bipod, Edane was up and after Eissen immediately, his arm shuddering familiarly under the weapon's weight as he twisted it under his arm, letting the body-straps carry most of the LAMW's weight. A dozen seconds later, the spot in the dirt torn up by the bipod's clawed feet exploded, a thudding barrage of mortar-fire locked on the precise location the LAMW's thunderclap muzzle blast had come from.

Edane didn't mind his arm shivering so much, anymore. It'd been bad during the first half of the fall season, last year — he'd needed full guided shells, complete with internal maneuvering gyros and explosive redirectional charges — but the numb spots in his palm had started disappearing around then. By the end of the fall season the only numb patches were streaks under his arm and over his bicep, and during the between-season break, over December and January, they'd been getting smaller and smaller under Janine's hands and the electrical stimulators. He almost had full use now, at the start of the new spring season, but the right side of his body still tired faster than the left. The LAMW weighed about two thirds of what Janine did, and that was still a little much for him to haul around for hours and hours without getting cramps and shivers. The body-sling helped, though.

Marianna looked up from her cover as they approached. She was further down the trail path and inside an irrigation trench, or streambed or whatever the map called it. Eissen got there first, skidding to a halt, and Edane bounded in over the trench's lip moments later, panting so hard his tongue flopped.

"Kacey?" she asked. "Any more targets?"

Kacey wasn't a member of the team — she played with the Merodeadores, a pro team with a sport ethic who insisted on wearing narrow neon strips on their gear, like cyclists or something. She was a little mixed-race woman, smaller than Janine, and also the only survivor of the Merodeadores' second fire team after they'd gotten ambushed. Handily, Kacey was the one with the high-grade EM detection kit.

She touched a control on her kit's board, making one of the box-mesh antennae further along the irrigation ditch wiggle. (It couldn't be just a ditch, Edane thought — why put goldfish and ornamental rocks in an irrigation ditch crossed back and forth with wooden bridges?) Kacey scrutinized the results, briefly checking a display strapped to the inside of her left wrist. "Nada, but there's a lot of Hedgemaze interference I can't filter out."

Hedgemaze was an EMWAR jamming system — artillery shells that dumped clusters of trailing wire antennae across the field and pumped random encrypted noise broadband over the air-waves, faking every kind of battlefield electronic transmission possible, making it that much harder to pick out legitimate electromagnetic radiance targets.

With only the vaguest flick of the chin as acknowledgement, Marianna edged up to the top lip of the trench, grabbing hold of the walking path's fence at the trailside, glancing left and right. "Four, why aren't you reporting target destruction?"

Svarstad and Erlnicht were set up about a mile away, in the map-segment marked 'Floral Gardens', flat on their bellies after having crawled around to the opposite side of the park with minimal electronics, doing it old fashioned, heads down and mud and camouflage.

"We've had no strike," Svarstad replied, voice low. "The automatic mortar installation is still operational."

"Fuck. I'll put in another support request," Marianna snarled.

This wasn't the first time. Off-field support was spotty, always had been, but some games... some games it felt like the team were being denied assistance *deliberately*.

It seemed like there were some players who just didn't like Edane and his siblings, especially now that they were playing under

Marianna's rules. Out were the standard man-portable UAVs and turrets every commentator on the game agreed were essential for a fireteam's equipment budget, and in was the paradigm they'd been made to fight by.

When Edane had been little, *really* little, he'd thought of it as pack-drill. Running, shooting, fighting, before there were really words to explain it with and everything was just barking — parroted phrases he hadn't understood were words. Sir-yes-sir, contact-down, relocate, hostile-sighted, all-clear, cease-fire, open-fire… People — the furless — the *officers* — hadn't spoken much to him, when he'd been that little. When he'd been White-Six.

He'd learned how to use and strip all kinds of guns — Matsushitas, Robhams, Kalashnikovs — before he'd been able to clearly read. He'd been part of White pack, one of thirty-two brothers from White-One to White-Thirty-Two, and even though they all crosstrained and took turns doing different things, ready to take up any role necessary, Edane had a special purpose.

To carry the Light Anti-Materiel Weapon.

The downsized training mock-up he'd carried as a child wasn't a real one, he'd known that — the real kind were taller than he was, that long ago. He passed it down the line every time the firing range instructor ordered them to trade weapons. Crosstraining was important, but at the start of each training session Edane carried one of the two LAMWs from the armory along with White-Fourteen, and even if one of his brothers had taken a turn cleaning it, he'd always been the one to put it back.

He'd been White-Six. He'd carried the LAMW. That was who and what he'd been, and who he was again.

It was like he'd been searching for who he was all his life, and then Marianna had handed it to him, wrapped up in grease paper and so freshly fabricated the grips still had printer's resin on them. Even if it was a MilSim toy, it was a LAMW. It was Edane's, and Edane knew who he was.

His brothers must have felt the same way — Svarstad and Eberstetten still carried LSWs, but now instead of a standard belt-fed light support weapon it was an eight-millimeter caliber heavy-barreled monster fed off two helical magazines, one stacked over the barrel and the other slotted in under the carry-rail. Ellis, who'd been an Eighteen, which was the same as a Two, hauled the specialist grenade launcher most games, although he switched with Marianna once in awhile. The rest all carried heavy rifles, same caliber as the LSWs, better at range than the usual five-five-six, six-five-nil and seven-six-two calibers most MilSim rifles represented.

They spaced themselves out wide, with or without electronics and comms, running in coordinated pairs more than a mile apart. They supported each other at extreme range, melted away from contact almost as soon as they were seen, moved smooth as a glassy razor over the terrain, slipping through the enemy deployment. The idea wasn't to use their brute force to resolve a conflict — their gear was heavy, though other than the LAMW and grenade launcher they had no anti-armor options — but to fight in short snaps of activity before disengaging, seeking to gather information, pinpoint the enemy, find targets for heavier guns and off-site support assets, and bring down UAVs and EMWAR assets while working with electronics off.

Their only real opposition during the fall season had been MA-Company, a pro level fireteam who wore dye in their fur while playing, made up of eight of Edane's brothers from a private military company, but MA-Company had specialized in dealing with Person Of Interest targets. That meant they bunched up while escorting the volunteers playing the role of generic non-combatants, hostages or VIPs depending on how you looked at the scenario, but MA-Company understood the dynamic, knew how to spread out thin and hunt Edane's team down.

It was exciting, familiar and unfamiliar all at once, exhilarating, the best game to play. Trouble was, not everybody wanted to play it. Nearly half of the dozen most popular commentators ignored Edane's team except to point out when they fouled up or highlight one of their plays as 'unfair', not within the spirit of the game.

After a couple of matches where the scenario organizers had randomly placed MA-Company and Edane's team together, those were the same commentators who'd complained of *collusion*. Of course they'd *colluded* with MA-Company, they'd been put in the same faction — Marianna had obviously spoken to MA's fireteam lead, Eisenach, and putting themselves into a double-stacked line three miles wide and a mile deep was *efficient*, not unfair. That they'd held an entire sector with only sixteen players was *amazing*.

After the second time it happened more of the commentators began to grumble, and by the end of the fall season it seemed like there was something fishy with the team assignments — MA-Company had been placed with Edane's team in six matches out of eight in a three week period, despite Marianna and Eisenach putting in an official request to the league to be placed on opposing factions instead.

MA-Company hadn't registered for the new spring season, though. They'd dropped out, and at one of Marianna's occasional barbecues they'd all shared meat and the occasional beer, talking about how shitty it was, but in the end MA-Company decided to bow out for a couple of seasons, try to find some private military work instead and open up the field, try and give the adverse commentators less material to use against Edane's group.

It wasn't *fair*. All the old stupid high-school slurs had come back out — commentators calling them the dogshit brigade, or skunkfuckers, which Edane *really* didn't understand.

And now the off-field guys in their tent out by the parking lot weren't responding to support requests.

They *needed* off-site firepower to function, and it wasn't like Marianna wasn't busting her ass cooperating with the ad-hoc plan the off-site coordinators had put together. But, of course, a team marking a target for off-site weaponry got points for that, and they'd barely edged their way up to a tie for tenth on the top-ten list at the end of fall season last year. It wouldn't take much to knock them back off it, with the spring season starting like this.

"Fuck it," Marianna muttered, after getting off the radio.

Edane shook his head to clear it and drew back from his spot at the top of the irrigation trench, ears dipping back. "Problems?"

"My handler went on rest break, and the new one's one of these fuckers who want us out of the league," she snarled, yanking open a pad. "I'm gonna talk to what's left of Seven-Forty-Six. They usually have a heavy UAV... We'll get this done with on-field assets. Kacey, Edane, Eissen, sort yourselves out. I want enemy anti-air assets *fucked up* in this corridor — do it." She swiped two fingers over the tactical map on the pad, tagged it, passed it to their uniforms' electronics, and then took off alone up the irrigation trench without even waiting for them to confirm.

The zone glowed, a mile-wide path moving up toward Svarstad and Erlnicht.

"You with us?" Eissen asked Kacey, casually pulling a brick-sized magazine from its pouch on his webbing. He double checked that it bore a black and red stripe — unguided general purpose explosive shells — and flicked it at Edane.

"Totally," Kacey said, head snapping up to follow the magazine's arc.

Edane caught it out of the air one-handed, left-handed, and stuffed it down in an empty pouch. He pulled out another magazine, consulting its display instead of being able to feel its weight to gauge how many rounds were left like with a real one, and threw the empty magazine back at Eissen. "Gimme the fin-guided solid core."

Eissen grinned down at her, switching the caught magazine and juggling another out to Edane with barely a glance. "Think you're gonna keep up?"

Had to catch the ammo two handed, this time — but Edane wasn't slowed down by his arm anymore, so long as he didn't push too hard, remembered he was a little clumsy at times and compensated.

Kacey looked up from grabbing one of her box-mesh antennas, glancing at Edane, gaze shooting up and down the LAMW hanging off his body-straps. A moment's consideration and she lifted an eyebrow at Eissen. "With him hauling that thing around, yes. Absolutely." She laughed. Eissen joined in.

Edane didn't laugh — he just strapped down his ammo pouches, bounced on his toes to make sure his gear was secure, and started running. Muscles burning, breath hot almost instantly, lungs stinging.

"Hey!" Kacey called after him, packing up the antenna. "Wait up!"

He thudded to a halt and grinned back at her and Eissen. "Way you were talking I thought you were going to give me a head start!"

She laughed — Edane felt good about that. Back in Tajikistan Thorne always used to tell him that making people laugh was the first step, and back then, Edane hadn't been much good at it. But he was learning how, bit by bit. Just had to find an unexpected corner to lift.

AFTER THREE MILES of cover-to-cover sprinting, hiking, dodging landmines, waiting for Kacey to jam wireless stationary sensors, hitting sentry-patrols and avoiding landscaping machinery — real, automated, and keeping the lawns and nature-park's gardens irrigated during the match — Edane was ready for a break. Nothing long, just five minutes to shake out his arm, sip some water, blow off a little heat.

Eissen was, too. Kacey, though...

Red-faced, she hunched over her pad, hardly able to speak between wheezing breaths. Her fingers were trembling on its screen. "Active electronic contact... at forty — *whfff* — forty-two degrees." Sweat dripped off her nose and blotted on the pad's surface.

Eissen snapped his head around, following his goggles' HUD to find forty-two degrees... he gestured at a park bench distantly ahead, made quick hand signals. *Observation position — landmark — halfway.* Halfway between them and the park bench, a walker's path forked around a patch of scrubby brush.

Quick as if he were barking, Edane signed back at him. *Firing position — landmark — quarter-left.* For landmark he pointed at the observation position. Eissen looked a little way left, spotted the piled stones around a flowerbed, nodded and started moving. The exchange had taken less than three seconds of snapped gestures, and they had the bare bones of an engagement plan in place.

Before setting off, Edane unhooked his water-bladder and drinking tube from his backpack and held it out to Kacey, with a slosh.

"Thanks," she said, only pausing to briefly clean the drinking tube's nozzle with her sleeve before sipping.

Some people, Edane reflected, treated him like he was people too, instead of something dirty, something disgusting. That was nice, even if in his heart he knew he wasn't people.

People couldn't hump it for three miles that quickly without getting entirely blown, people couldn't haul seventy-ish pounds of metal without complaint, people didn't learn tactical hand-signals from the cradle, people couldn't survive the kind of wounds he'd suffered in the marketplace in Tajikistan.

Maybe, he thought, glancing back at Kacey shaking with the exertion of keeping up with them, the folks complaining about Edane and his brothers playing had a point. Hell, even if Marianna needed to gobble pills by the handful to keep her metabolism stable — her earlier geneline hadn't benefitted from the ten extra years of development Edane's had — she could outrun, outshoot, and outfight just about anybody on the field, genemods included. (Edane included too, maybe — he could handle more weight than Marianna in total, but as a percentage of bodyweight she could haul fractionally more. And she had ten extra years of experience.)

He was better than humans, at MilSim. Much better. And the thought didn't sit well with him, because everywhere else in his life he saw humans doing better. They understood how to live life, they were more social, they could enjoy series shows without needing Janine to explain why it was fun… but at this, at MilSim, at fighting, Edane was *superior*. Built for it, engineered for it in a way they hadn't been.

It wasn't fair on regular players, in a way. He could see that. But it wasn't fair on him, either.

He pushed up, banking left from Eissen's line, and set the LAMW up in the spot he'd picked between the rocks, sighting in at forty-two degrees. He didn't see where the electronic contact Kacey'd detected was initially, but when fireteam Seven-Forty-Six's heavy UAV thudded its way overhead, Edane blew out the hidden defense turret on reflex the instant it unfolded to deploy its tracking radar antenna.

The UAV went on to deploy its single heavy anti-tank missile, ripping the enemy mortar installation to scrap metal. With the help of fireteam Seven-Forty-Six, the soon-to-be Hallman Hairtrigger Hounds took seventh place for the match, nudging them up into eleventh on the overall season's leaderboard.

7. Losing Proposition

::/ San Iadras, Middle American Corporate Preserve.
::/ February, 2106.
::/ Edane Estian.

Janine didn't want to sleep. Not sex stuff. When Edane got home after the match she was slumped in her underwear on the couch with a videogame gun that Hallman Electronics had given him, a pile of her lingerie abandoned on the floor and armchair. She had her toes spread on the coffee table, pushing forward a little to walk forward in the game, tilting her foot side to side to lean. The room was dark, lit up by an old pair of display spectacles perched on her muzzle. She looked in his direction when he got in, but didn't say anything.

She didn't say anything while he put his things away, or when he asked if she'd had dinner. Sat silently while he picked up her lingerie, the game gun clicking as she played whatever game the gun was for. Janine glanced down at the neatly folded stack of her clothes, then put down the toy gun on top, and stared across the room at the other wall through the spectacles, face lit by the lenses.

There were plates in the sink, so she'd eaten, and Edane didn't want to disturb her. So he tried going to bed, but she didn't want to sleep. She wanted to talk, appearing in the bathroom doorway after his shower.

"Edane?"

He looked at her. She looked at him. At his body, while he toweled himself off.

"Yeah?"

Janine leaned back against the doorframe. Watching his groin while she pulled off her bra. Her breath squeaked a little, through her nose, while she disrobed the rest of the way. Stood there, nude, one hand on her own belly. Watching him. Looking for a reaction.

He thought he knew what he was supposed to do. But instead he dipped his ears back awkwardly.

She bit her lip at him. "Edane?"

"I'm listening." It didn't seem polite, somehow, to put his towel on.

"You're listening." Now her ears swept back, now she released her lip.

"I'm sorry. I... I don't know what you want."

"Yeah, you do."

He flattened his ears against his skull. Wished he was smaller. Like he could hide. "I figured you were distracted with the game."

"I'd been trying on lingerie all day, and then I realized, it just doesn't work on you, does it? So I gave up." She gazed at his crotch. Up at him. Back at his groin. "Do you even get aroused, Edane?"

"Well yeah—"

"Not by touching, I mean. By thinking sexy things."

"I don't think sexy things."

"Maybe you could try?" She posed hopefully for a moment. Blinking those green eyes at him, hopeful. "My sister Jane spent a little time with one of you guys. Said it worked out eventually."

Edane didn't answer that. Just hesitated with his towel flopped over the side of the basin, uncertain.

"Christ, Sweetie. Don't you know if any of your brothers... y'know... have sexual relationships?"

Edane picked up his toothbrush. Toothpaste. Put the one on the other and stared at the brush. "Yeah. couple."

"Like?"

"Stolnik."

"And how'd that happen?" The hope in her smile got stronger. Got worse.

"He's been living with Stacy for three years." Edane didn't want to screw up that hopeful smile of hers. But it seemed inevitable. After all. Three years was longer than one. "And they were dating before that. Since seventeen."

Of course, a little thing like time wouldn't get to Janine. Not entirely. So she shifted. Presented her body, and even with her ears swept back uncertainly, kept up the hope. "So it took a while."

"Maybe, yeah."

"So, maybe, with, y'know… time and effort…" She pushed her foot forward on the tiles. Toes spread. Hopeful still.

"I should probably get to sleep early. There's another match tomorrow."

She frowned. Ears quivering back. "No sex before the big game?" she asked, trying to make it funny.

It wasn't the kind of joke Edane understood. But he could tell by how she said it, it was supposed to be funny. Kind of. He put his toothbrush in his mouth, switched it on, and buzzed his teeth clean.

"Look at me?" Janine ground her shoulders back into the doorframe. Posed like something out of one of her erotic magazines.

Edane looked, but it didn't seem to help. She squirmed a little. Maybe it was a dance of some kind. She flicked an ear. Just looked hurt, waiting for him to finish.

He spat foam. Rinsed his mouth. "We can make love if you want." Didn't look up at her, while washing his fur clean of toothpaste.

"Yeah," she murmured, voice strained, "but what do *you* want?"

"Do you want to have sex?" He looked at her, cautiously.

"Why are we back here night after night after fucking night?" she moaned, slumping back against the wall. Not a pose. Covering her face. Braced against that wall like it was better support for her than he was, and that hurt.

"It's just—"

"Just *what*, Edane?" She pulled her hands from her muzzle, leaned forward, almost like she was exploding in his direction. "You always fucking dodge it, and we make love, and you're like a cold fish. Our *anniversary* is next week, Edane! Moving in with me was supposed to be *special*."

"It *is* special! We'll, we'll do something nice — like a meal out at a restaurant? That's romantic, right?"

"Don't fucking dodge it!" She jabbed her fingers into his chest, hard enough he was scared she'd hurt herself. "Answer me, what do you *want?*"

"I want what you want. Okay?"

"That's not an answer, Edane."

"I don't want to make you *unhappy with me.*" He gripped the basin's edge, hard enough to hurt *him*. But the basin was just a thing. That was okay. Couldn't hurt porcelain. "Can't you understand that?"

"What *do you want?*" She gripped the side of the basin, next to his hands, leaning in, her snout right in his face. Demanding.

"I know what you want me to say, I know what you *don't* want me to say. Are you going to make me say it?"

"Say it."

"I don't want sex with you."

He'd never hit anyone that hard. Sent them spinning away, grabbing at the doorframe, gasping for breath. Never hit *anyone* that hard in his life, with words. Words weren't fists. His mothers taught him that. Sticks and stones, but words could never harm you.

Marianna had been right. Edane's fosters were full of shit.

"I'm sorry," he said, reaching for her.

She jerked away before he reached her. Out into the hall. "I already fucking knew that, Edane. I already knew that." She said it the way people pasted skinplast down over cuts.

"I'm sorry, okay? I'm not made like that. Maybe I'm asexual, I don't know."

"No?" Janine led him away, pulling her battered old bathrobe off the dresser in the bedroom. "Then why does this Stolnik live with Stacy? Why's Engelthal perfectly happy to hook up with Jane for casual sex? That's not asexuality, Edane!"

"I don't *know!*" He just wanted her to *understand*. Why didn't she understand? "I'm not Engelthal! I'm not Stolnik!"

"The point is they're your clones. It's *possible*. If you *tried*. If you put effort into this."

He stopped himself at the bedroom door, grabbing the doorframe. Kept himself from following her. "I do."

"No you don't. You put effort into everything *but* this." She swept up the belt bitterly, wrapping it around her waist while she sat down on the bed.

He bowed his head. Cathy and Beth had said, when he'd been a kid, that sticks and stones may break my bones, but words can never harm me. Bullshit, the words hurt. It was all bullshit. So he said so. "Bullshit."

"What?"

"You just want me to *know* already. You're the one who doesn't want to put in the effort, Janine, you just want me to know how all this stuff works and how to do it properly, and I *don't* know. I never knew, and you won't teach me. Every time I get it wrong or something doesn't feel right, I can't even ask you for help without making it worse!"

"It's a perfectly natural set of impulses, Edane," she hissed at him. "It's a basic fucking instinct." Janine just glared up at him, those eyes of hers glittery and cold.

He found bitterness inside him, to match. To play off her cold stare. "I didn't get *made* like you, Janine. Those aren't the instincts I got made with. Some of us weren't made to just *fuck* people like you were."

"Don't you say that!" Her voice turned to sandpaper and breaking glass. "Sex is important! It's beautiful, it's *making love!*"

"That's what I meant! Dammit, I got angry, I said the wrong word. I'm sorry, I wasn't made to make love." He forced his voice quiet. He didn't want to yell. Didn't want to shout. Didn't want to have that weird trembling feeling behind his eyes he didn't know what to do with. "I wasn't made like you."

"Don't you tell me how I was made! *Don't you tell me anything.* Get out, just, just fucking *get out*, Edane!"

She clutched the tip of her nose, other hand curled under her chin, glaring at him with cold wet eyes, body trembling, as if she could keep whatever was inside her from spilling out so long as she could just hold it all in with her hands. Edane didn't like seeing Janine like that. Didn't like hurting her. But he had. Because he wasn't any good at making love, or keeping her happy, or anything except following orders.

So shoved his gear into a rucksack for the game tomorrow, pulled on some reasonably clean clothes from the laundry hamper, tried not to wince at the sound of her slamming her bedroom door, palmed at the wet in his eyes when the trembling feeling got worse, followed her orders, and got out.

"AREN'T YOU EVEN going to try?" Beth sat with her elbows up on the kitchen table, her hair down, like it always was, first thing in the morning. Good and familiar, that.

Edane's ears hurt a little, he'd had them flattened out so much lately. "Please don't."

"Would it *kill* you to—"

"*Hssst!*" Cathy hissed like she hissed at the cats.

Beth wasn't a cat, wasn't even genemodded in that direction, but she reacted the same. Pulled up straight, blinking in surprise.

Cathy stroked Edane's forearm, his right forearm, in hard sweeps that made him push his spoon around his bowl of cornflakes. "Edane's having enough trouble with people wanting him to be something other than what he is."

"Well you're our son and I'm your mom," Beth said, pulling over her and Cathy's cereal, a finger in each bowl. She picked up a banana, peeled it, started industriously chopping slices into each bowl, alternating, one slice for her, one slice for Cathy, back and forth.

Edane preferred his cornflakes plain. Always had.

"I know," he said quietly. "I appreciate it. I just. I just think of you as Beth, the lady who made me part of her family. Not as what your role is in that family."

The right thing to say, for once. Beth rewarded him with a smile.

Edane had used his keys to get in. Been found out when Cathy woke up. He'd given them the bare details. For once his foster-parents weren't pressing for more.

The apartment felt nice. Familiar, and even if he wasn't any good at living life like a normal person, he still had a bedroom.

His old bedroom was still his old bedroom. It still had his bed, but it also had an arts and crafts table and it was where Cathy and

Beth kept their bikes, now, instead of in the living room. But he'd found his bed made, waiting for him. It had been comfortable, even if he didn't feel like he belonged there anymore.

Edane stirred the cornflakes into the milk with his spoon, trying to wet them, trying to stir it all into a steady uniform gruel. It took a while, like it always did. Gave him too much time to think.

"You know we're here if you need us."

He nodded. "Thank you Cathy," he said quietly.

"We're sorry if we pushed you into this, with Janine. We just thought you needed a little encouragement…"

He shrugged, slightly. "I needed it." He picked up his spoon, watching the gruel drip from it. "Like you said. I needed encouraging. And I was really happy with Janine. I really like her."

Cathy settled back, quiet. Picked up a piece of toast, staring at him. "Were you crying?"

He lifted his shoulders in a shrug. They felt too big. Even if these five rooms were his familiar childhood home, he'd been so short, so small, when he'd arrived. Cathy and Beth had been so much taller. Just his raw size made him feel out of place.

"Yeah." He palmed at his eyes tiredly. They were dry. But his fur was itchy. Tangled. "I guess I was."

The two of them shared a look. That perplexing parents-having-a-moment, what-is-our-adopted-child-doing, look.

"He cried when school broke up for summer. You remember that?" Cathy tapped the toast against her lips, blinking at Beth.

"Yeah. I thought he was developing emotionally." She smiled vaguely. Guiltily, almost, as she looked up at Edane. "That was the only time you cried, before Grandpa Jeff passed. Wasn't it?"

Edane ducked his head. He'd thought that he wasn't going to get to go back to school. That he'd never be allowed to have a schedule again, that it was all just *over,* and every day of his life from then on out would have to be a weekend. Weekends had been really hard until he'd learned how to give himself goals and objectives. He hadn't known it was possible to give himself orders, until Grandpa Jeff helped him work it out.

"I don't really understand crying." He scuffed at his nose with the back of his wrist. "I don't really understand much of anything."

"Powerlessness," Cathy said. "That's one of the big reasons people cry." She looked over at Edane, abandoned her toast and lay her hand back on his forearm. "But you're so smart, baby. So driven. You just don't see any problems in the world you can't overcome with a little effort, huh?"

He shrugged a little, thought about it. Thought about his arm, and picked up the spoon. Staring at the bowl as he held it. Steady. Just steady. And as he watched, the harder he tried to keep it steady, the more it started to tremble. Until the tremors were noticeable, and he had to jab the spoon back down into the milky gruel he'd turned his cornflakes into, to keep from having that itchy trembling feeling behind his eyes.

"Relationships aren't like that," Beth offered, voice soft. "People have their own things going on. It's not something you can solve for them, Daney."

"Yeah I could." He palmed his eyes, fighting the sensations behind his eyelids. "Like Cathy said, I just have to be someone else. I have to not be me. Then everyone would be happy."

"Baby…"

He was close to a foot taller than Cathy, now. She still called him baby. He might as well have been that small, physically, to match his stunted emotions. "I just have to be someone who gets what sex is. And someone who wasn't gengineered so they can call me a cheat. And someone who wasn't a dog, so nobody could say we were so dirty in the eyes of God that they could blow up little kids to get at us. And someone who knew how to fix all the problems in Tajikistan, so they didn't have to have a revolution, didn't have to throw mortar bombs at me."

They were so damn quiet, Cathy and Beth. And his palm over his face was so damn wet.

"And everywhere I turn there's one of me who did it better. Or had more luck." He sniveled at his palm, shaking his head. Eyes still wrenched closed, as if it'd all hold together. "I can try real hard, and I can make so many things happen. But I can't fix luck. I could have been standing out by the gate, like Esparza, and then I wouldn't have gotten hit by the mortar. Or I could have had less luck, and just died. But I can't *do* anything.

"I could lie to her. I could say I feel the things she wants me to feel." He snuffled at the wet in his nose. Like choking on half-inhaled water. Looked up at his foster-parents with watery eyes. Unable to see. "But that doesn't work, does it? So I can't fix this without being someone else. Janine wants me to be someone else and I'm not lucky enough to be someone else. So what do I do?"

Beth had to stand up to apply the Cathy and Beth maneuver, while Edane was sitting down. She couldn't do it if they both stood up. He was too big. But if he sat to eat breakfast, she could. She could wrap her arms around his head and hold him to her chest like she was protecting him, however impractical the position was. Cathy hugged Beth from behind, wrapped her arms over Edane's head too.

"You two know how these things work," he whimpered. "Tell me what to do."

"All you can do is cry, Daney. Right now, all you can do is cry."

Useful rule of thumb. If there wasn't anything else you could do about something, you could cry about it.

So he did.

AFTER THE MATCH he hadn't wanted to go back to his mothers, though he'd agreed to visit with them that weekend, and he'd left most of his game gear in the van with Marianna's blessing.

It had been a while since Edane had checked into a capsule hotel. Since before he'd left for Tajikistan. There had been one conveniently close to where he'd studied for his combatant licensing. Just the basic qualification, enough to register with the professional private military bodies, enough to meet employment requirements with the hiring agencies. Before Tajikistan, he and a few of his brothers — Sztebnik and Eichardt and all those guys — used to get drunk once in a while. He didn't like going home drunk, felt ashamed about it, occasionally slept it off in a capsule. He'd gone on a trip by himself up north once, one of Beth's odder suggestions. See if he could find himself.

He hadn't, but he'd stayed in a capsule hotel then, too, just because it was the cheapest place to stay, up on the southern fringes of the Mexican border.

The routine hadn't changed any. Edane paid. The telepresent receptionist on the front room's screen got the machine to offer Edane's phone the keycode, but since the encryption software these places used was dodgy as all hell and half malware anyway, Edane pulled one of the tags off his rucksack, cleared the smart-paper's memory, and loaded the key on that. Tag wasn't connected to his personal accounts, after all. He left, went down the hall.

Every single one of these places was a clone of the others, put together with more uniformity than Edane and his brothers had. Go through the first door on the left, follow the neatly painted lines on the floor and infographics on the walls. Take the hospitality packet provided, in extra large size. Empty pockets into it, including phone and the tag with the keycode. Go into a changing booth, get undressed, pull on the included dressing gown and slippers, stuff the previously worn clothes into the helpful draw-string laundry bag keyed to your capsule. Out of the changing booth, left again, open up both the doors on the booked capsule's locker. Stuff the laundry bag into the top section, so the hotel staff or bots or whatever could take it for laundry. Lock the rucksack in the bottom section. Take the rest of the hospitality pack to the showers. Use their shampoo, not enough for Edane's fur, really, but extra soap was provided. Dry off with the provided stack of towels. Use more towels than allocated, because the bastards only let the hair driers run for thirty seconds. What the hell, being damp didn't matter too bad. Out, again, left down the hall. Next set of changing rooms, just to get into one of the sets of papery pajamas they provided. Out again, right, down a blissfully white hallway, like a *friendly* version of the barracks, and to the capsule.

Edane's was right near the bottom. Just a tube, a little too short for him, but only by a little. Tall enough to sit up in, hunched. He shouldered his way into the capsule niche, barely broad enough for him, palmed the light control in the claustrophobic little capsule's screen, and twisted around, pulling the roller shutter on the end down.

Sealed away, in a calm uncolored environment. No sharp edges, everything smooth and rounded off.

He pulled the pillow up from the neatly folded stack of blankets in the corner, wedged it behind his head, and sat braced against the wall, legs stretched out, ears perked, just listening.

The capsule was quiet.

Still early in the evening. Not too many customers, yet. Residents, people staying a week or more, had a different section. The loudest thing he could hear was the faint pulse of blood in his ear, pressed against the capsule's plasticky roof.

The capsule's scratched screen went dark after a while, and his shoulders began to ache, especially the right one. He only really paid attention to it when settling down, dragging the pillow under his head, body turned slightly to the left, legs curled up to keep his feet from pressing into the shutter. The ache drifted out of his right shoulder. Edane thought about it, carefully twisting his right arm around in a slight curl. Prodding at his shoulder, everywhere from the line of scars down. There were numb spots. There would probably be numb spots for a long time. But the biggest of them felt smaller.

He could now clearly feel an ache when he was uncomfortable. That was good progress.

Edane held up his right hand, fingers spread. Staring at the burn across the backs of his fingers, still wondering where they'd come from, in the life his arm had led before being transplanted. When it'd been Siegelbach's arm. He braced his left elbow against the capsule wall, wrist twisted so he could keep one eye on his wristwatch, the seconds passing by, and waited with his hand in the air.

Counted past five, and six, and seven. Thirty whole seconds for his hand to start shivering, after aching under the thumping pressure of the LAMW's recoil all day. Thirty seconds to tremble, when once, after surgery, when he'd just started to get movement back, his fingertips had trembled all the time.

He held his hand to his chest, hugging it close, tight, to keep it still. The way Janine did, sometimes, holding it steady against her stomach.

He fumbled the hospitality pack back up from the corner he'd dumped it in and put his things up on the tiny recessed shelf. Keys, phone, wallet.

Waited. Just in case.

He stared at the black gap between the shelf and the capsule's wall, cracked open under strain. Maybe somebody had yanked on it, trying to sit up.

He kept waiting, but his phone didn't bleep at him. No call. No message. He picked it up and unfolded the phone so the screen was at its largest, checked the day's play highlights for all of twelve seconds before shutting it all off, rolling properly onto his side, and he opened the messenger program to stare at Janine's, *Good luck with your game today*, which he'd missed that morning because he'd already handed his phone in at the judge's stand by the time she'd sent it.

He had to wipe his eyes dry after a minute.

He thumbed in, *Okay to call you? I want to talk*. Getting that sent off made his thumb tremble, but that didn't have anything to do with his transplant problems.

The phone went back up onto the little shelf, and he lifted his shirt. Felt along his ribs on his right side. Checking for numb spots, even though there hadn't been any for months where the skin grafts from Siegelbach had gone in, where there had once been more scars than flesh. Started massaging his arm the way one of the hospital nurses had taught him, and how he'd taught Janine, which wasn't as good as the nerve stimulators, but was good for his arm all the same.

When the phone rang, Edane felt a pang of resentment. He wasn't ready to talk. He'd wanted to throw text messages back and forth, prepare himself. Think through what he was going to say. Instead he was scrabbling at his phone with crampy fingers, looking at it long enough to check the caller icon and answer it on speaker.

"Hi, Sweetie." Janine's voice was thick, rough-edged.

"Hi," he whispered, curling up, tail swept to his leg. Almost fetal, phone lain on the mattress, just beside his face.

Silence. Quiet, comfortable silence, tainted by all the discomforts between them.

"So, what's up?"

The light in the capsule, bright and white, felt invasive rather than comforting. Like the surgery table and hospital wards, rather than bright sunlight, or the fluorescent burn of the lights in the barracks when he'd been a child. He shut his eyes against it, curled up all the tighter. "Thought we should talk."

"Yeah," she said, voice soft and delicate. "We probably should."

"What do you want me to do?"

She hesitated. "I want to know more about what you want, Edane."

He thought about it, but not for very long. "I want to apologize. For what I said."

"It's okay."

Those two little words hit him like shrapnel, and he couldn't help but curl up, knees against the capsule box's wall. "I don't think it is."

"Oh, well." He could hear the smile in her voice. Tight. "It's probably true, anyway. Everybody only knows what you got made for because it's so obvious, Sweetie. Nobody put a label on you, nobody put a label on me. I probably got made for that, even if I don't like thinking about it."

"Probably not," he said, carefully. Soothingly. "You're so smart, you know? You know how everything works. People and culture and stuff."

"No I don't!" She wheezed laughter at him. "I don't understand how *you* work."

"Yeah, but that's because I don't work very well."

"Nah." Her voice went all soft again. "You're just *different*."

"Different's bad, normally."

"Yeah, well. You still think you're supposed to conform to standards, y'know? Run so many miles in so many minutes, carry so much weight. But that's not how life works, Sweetie."

Edane cracked open his eyes, slowly uncurling his right hand, gazing into his palm. "It's supposed to be," he whispered.

"That's how you feel about it, yeah. But we're all different. Even in our production runs. I mean. Like you said, you're not Stolnik."

"I yelled it at you, Janine." He offered it up – a fresh wound, ready for the salt.

But Janine didn't want to rub salt in his wounds. "Being different's hard for you, Sweetie. You don't want to be different, I think. Yeah?"

"Yeah," he murmured, waiting for his hand to start trembling, as he held it steady.

"The thing with your arm, that must have been *so awful* for you. I mean, getting hurt and all, yeah, but. Suddenly you weren't like everyone else, you know?"

"Yeah." He closed his left hand over his right, and pushed them both down between his knees, so he didn't have to stare at them. Didn't have to wait for the tremor; that would come around by itself. "I know."

"And the only thing that really makes you happy about it is, well… It's not about you making progress, is it? It's about you getting back what you lost. Becoming more like what you were."

"Probably," he murmured. "It's getting better. I wanted to tell you. Here and there, where I hold my breath, if I don't have to strain my arm too much, it's like it was. I don't tremble at all, for a little. Whole half minute at a time."

"That's great, Sweetie." Her voice almost held a smile. Almost.

"It's almost like it used to be." He stopped a second, thinking. "Like I didn't get hurt. Yeah, you're right. Like I'm not different. Like I'm how I should be."

She thought about that, then asked, "How should you be?"

He didn't immediately have an answer. But there was one question that drove him. "How do you want me to be?"

Janine was silent for a long while. That was okay, he didn't mind listening, carefully, for the slight sound of her breath. "I have a question, first."

"Okay."

"What is it you like about me? Why, why do you stay around me, why does what *I* want matter so much to you?"

He struggled to find a reason. To pick one out of the possible things she wanted to hear. But in the ache in his chest, there was something he knew sounded stupid. He said it anyway, eyes wrenched shut. "I like doing your laundry for you."

She made a squeaking sound. A crying sort of sound. "Laundry?"

"Yeah," he whispered.

"You moved in with me so you could do my *laundry*?"

"Kinda."

"It's okay, Sweetie," she said, voice shaking. "I can do my own laundry."

"I know," he whispered. Wishing she'd just… just understand. "But you do mine too. And you smile at me, and, I smile at you." He gnawed at his lip, rolling over in the capsule's confines, batting his shoulder against the wall. "It's *important* to me. I don't know how. We have a routine. We're more efficient together."

"More efficient." She laughed, not quite bitterly, through her tears.

"Yeah."

"Is that what you like about us? More efficient?"

"Yeah. I like it a lot."

"God. I'm the least efficient woman in the world, Sweetie."

"No, you're not. And you're always so happy when everything works out. You do something and I help you, and that makes *me* happy, 'cuz I got everything right for once and you smile at me and I knew it and I didn't need anyone to yell it at me or write me a report card, I just *knew* 'cuz you smiled all the time."

He ground his knuckle against his eye-socket.

Crying was bullshit. It made his fur all snarled up and made his eyes sting, gave him a headache.

Her voice was tiny. "It sounds important to you."

"It is," he groaned. "It really fucking is."

"Like I'm important," she added.

"You are."

"Like being *together* is important?"

"I don't understand why, but it really *is*, Janine. That's why making love with you's okay, it makes you smile so much. That's why I do it with you. 'Cuz you want it and 'cuz I want you to have it, 'cuz it's so important to you."

It was like he'd pulled the pin on her. She just blew up, in a tiny wet sound, as she sobbed, harder, harder, until it cut out entirely. He jerked up, staring at the phone… greeted by a 'call muted icon'.

Irrational panic took him and squeezed Edane in its fist. Was she alright? Was there a problem with the call? Was it anything other than what he'd learned, that Janine didn't like it when people heard her cry?

She came back. "Christ. God." Another sob. "Jesus *fuck*. Sweetie, that's not why you have sex with people," she spluttered.

"I… I don't see any other reason to do it."

"Sweetie. Oh my God." She sobbed explosively down the phone. "The only reason you have sex with somebody is because it makes *you* smile."

"But it *does*."

"Not for the reasons it should. Not for the reasons *I* want you to smile when we make love, Edane."

He twisted his face against the pillow, wiping his eyes, shaking his head. Both at once.

"I want you to be happy," she squeaked, "and I want you to be the person *you* want to be. Not the kind of person I think you should be, or those soldier guys tried to make you, but the person *you* want to be. And I want you to be my lover, I want you to look at me and tell me I'm beautiful, so I feel beautiful. I… I want to put my mouth on you and just make you *glow* with how beautiful the pair of us are… and… and…"

His eyes hurt the way hers must have been hurting, just then. "It's not like it doesn't sound nice. It sounds wonderful. I wish I could feel it like that. But…"

"But you can't. And I don't know how to teach you to, because…" The sound of her blowing her nose broke his heart. "I just want someone to hold me and tell me I'm beautiful, Edane. I'm not strong enough to stand and look at myself in a mirror and try and figure out what the hell I am and whether or not I'm pretty. I need someone to tell me that. And I'm not strong enough, I'm…" She halted, struggling for her thoughts. "I'm not even brave enough to even think about what fixing our relationship really means, I just keep kinda hoping it'll fix itself. I can't wait for you to learn how to make me feel how I need to feel, let alone teach you. I don't know how to teach you that."

"You're pretty," he whispered against the capsule wall.

It made her cry all the worse, but she didn't hang up. Didn't mute the call. Just spluttered for breath until she could wheeze out curse-words. "Fuck", and "shit", and "Christ". She eventually calmed herself back down to a whimpered, "Thank you."

"Just not in a way I can see by looking at you," he said. "I have to know you, I guess. I think that's what pretty means, anyway."

"I think you understand what pretty means a little better now," she told him through her tears.

"I think you're brave," he replied, quietly. "Plenty brave."

"Y-yeah?"

"Yeah. I mean, you didn't run away from those things, even if they hurt. Like the Drill Sergeant used to say, pain is your friend. You can't be a brave person, and think pain is the worst thing, or even a bad thing. You have to endure that. So maybe there isn't a solution, but you didn't run away from trying to find one. That counts as brave, too."

"God. I wish there was a solution. I think I understand you better too, now, Edane. And I think you want to be my friend? Like. Really close friend, like. Life partner, almost. Like… like lovers without sex."

He kept his eyes very, very tightly shut. "Yeah. Can't we be that? Whatever that is?"

"God, Sweetie. God." She sniffled over the phone. "You're more than that to me, Sweetie. You're… fuck. I need you more than that."

"But I don't have what you need me to give you."

"You give me so much, Edane. *So much*. Don't feel bad. Please. I'm sorry."

"It's okay, Janine."

"We want different things and it's close enough it could almost work, but you'd have to be someone else and I'm not who you need me to be and I need more, want more than you can give me, and…"

He whispered that it was okay at her, over and over, soothing her until she spluttered a last sorry, and hung up on him. He dragged his knuckles over his eyes and lay back in the tiny cell of space the capsule gave him.

He'd lied. It wasn't okay.

8. Money Men

::/ San Iadras, Middle American Corporate Preserve.
::/ April, 2106.
::/ Ereli Estian.

Ereli banged on the door until Eversen opened up Stolnik and Stacy's apartment and stuck his nose out.

"You got the stuff?"

Wordlessly, Ereli lifted up eight bags of Chinese takeout, four dangling from each hand, stinking of sauce and the wet, starchy heat of rice.

"Food's on!" Eversen yelled, stepping back and letting Ereli bring the food to the kitchen counter in an awkward waddle — with that much shit to carry, there wasn't anything he could do *but* waddle.

Eversen followed, then helped line up the bags and peel down the plastic, lifting out and restacking the steaming plastic shells of rice and beef like MREs on a shelf.

Stolnik — wearing a pair of custom dog-tags with little pink hearts stamped in the back — broke away from the pack of brothers sitting around the coffee table first, picked up a pair of paper-wrapped chopsticks and broke them open with ease. The two lengths of wood sat easily between his fingers, as naturally as Ereli might hold a sidearm.

Stolnik opened one of the shells, and with a snap of the chopsticks was holding a scrap of beef and rice, chewing on it a moment later.

It was weird, *really* weird, watching himself demonstrate a skill Ereli knew he didn't have.

Ereli gave Stolnik his bank card back, and Stolnik juggled the food expertly while pocketing it, before taking a second shell and veering off to sit with the lone human in the apartment — presumably Stacy.

Picking up the sticks, Eversen fumbled them into his hand, repositioning the one on top against his middle finger, kinda like Stolnik had held them, but every time he tried to nab a slice of beef out of his shell the tips skewed apart, beef slipping back onto its bed of rice.

Ereli didn't even try, picking up a shell and a plastic spork, instead. "How's the crowdfund going?"

"Five nudies or something." Eversen frowned grimly and tried the chopsticks again. "Hasn't really started, we're just setting up the accounts, but somebody already found us."

The room wasn't quiet, exactly, but Ereli's brothers were more interested in the arrival of food than the crowdfunding total, even when the big numbers on the wallscreen opposite the couch bumped up by two and a half New Dollars.

"So. Where's Scheuen? What's the money plan?" Ereli asked, stuffing his face.

"Here, look at this." Eversen turned and pushed through the group around the coffee table, snagged a loose pad, and walked back, dumping it on the kitchen counter in front of Ereli, open to a social networking site.

The text was unfamiliar — almost like the English alphabet, though with more accent marks and weird curly stuff on the Cs. Almost readable, but a language that looked like made up nonsense to Ereli. That was his lack of understanding talking, though — what one man ignorantly took as nonsense was another man's culture. What he *did* understand were the videos playing in tabbed out links.

"That's Szydlow getting killed," Ereli murmured. "Back in Tajikistan."

"It's part of our advertising campaign, now," Eversen replied. "What happened to Szydlow isn't shown."

The footage was grainy, mostly taken from governmental closed circuit surveillance, probably stolen pre-revolution before the Private Military Operations Centre was overrun.

A city street, dust rolling across the tarmac. Paint-cans slopped out of a window above a tank column, splattering over the visors and camera lenses, blinding one of them almost instantaneously. A heartbeat later a flaming car rolled out of a side street, pouring black smoke across the column's middle — two brothers, turned blocky by the low frame rate and the speed of their motion, came in against the blinded tank, one with a four foot long crowbar, the other with a can of gasoline.

The crowbar went into the gap between the tank treads and its wheels in one stab, and a quick levering motion detracked the vehicle as it started rolling backward. A tank further back shot through the smoke, machine gun rounds splattering grey flecks all over the blinded tank's hull, but Ereli's brothers had already run back to cover — the gasoline burning in a roaring pool over the tank's engine air intakes, a fiery mess under its hull.

That hadn't been the run Szydlow had been killed on — that happened later, from what little Ereli remembered of the panicked communications traffic that day. Tanks had crossed over the Tajik border from Uzbekistan, supporting an insurgent push. Ereli's brothers only had riot gear to fight with, expecting a protest. They'd had to improvise.

A few moments later the footage cut to another view, flames and smoke boiling around the detracked tank while it spun in a helpless circle, slamming back into the burning car and forward into a building, all its traction on one side lost, unable to escape the inferno. The instant that one of the tank's hatches opened up, one of his brothers marched up, muzzle wrapped in wet rags, tearing the fleeing crewman out of the hatch and bodily throwing him off the vehicle before reaching in and pulling out fistfuls of electronics. Meanwhile the tank driver was beaten to the ground by another brother with the stock of a shotgun, then a bottle with a burning wick was passed out of cover and smashed over the open hatch, spilling flame everywhere…

About a dozen of Ereli's brothers, and some locals brave enough to put down the grievances they were protesting over long enough to protect their little northern town, had disabled and destroyed four of the six tanks that had attacked in hopes of taking control. The other two vehicles had retreated.

The lesson seemed obvious to Ereli — don't take tanks into crowded urban centers without specialist infantry assistance, especially not main battle tanks built to snipe at each other from kilometers away. Built up areas were ruled by unmanned ground vehicles, deployed automatic turrets, and infantry, not heavy armor. But the mistake the Uzbek-supported factions made seemed to be teaching the people of Azerbaijan a different lesson.

Five New Dollars popped up on the wallscreen, added to the total — thirty-five in total, now. The comment that scrolled under the transaction was simple and to the point: *'Nesimi's police killed my son. I have no hope.'*

Ten nudies and a few cents more brought the words, *'Is this real? Can the capitalists really fight like that?'*

Ereli thumbed around on the pad for a translation, and the whole crowdfunding information page flashed into English for him.

'Your government is built to protect one man's interests. Ilhaim Nesimi has been lining his pockets with your nation's money since he led the post-Eurasian War coup d'état and took power in 2074, and he thinks he is safe from justice. He and his family spent more on foreign investments in 2105 than was being spent on food, education, and healthcare over 2105, 2104, and 2103 combined. With your help, he and the government he put in place will fall within the month.'

Ereli looked up at Eversen, ears flat back. "This is really happening? Azerbaijan?"

"Yup."

"Who the hell figured we could do it in a month?"

Eversen pointed across at some of the brothers on a couch in the corner. "Scheuen and one of the guys from the Kennel. Based on our battle-plan."

"Our plan is a *guess*. It's a spec-ops raid to murder a dictator for a hundred thousand nudies. Any dictator, we weren't specific."

"That's where we start. It has to begin with a low-key covert insertion — like starting a guerrilla war by invading a city."

Ereli set down his shell of rice, closing the lid, and picked up the pad. "That's been done once or twice. But we'll need to support our teams on the ground — that kind of operation could last *weeks*. They'll need ammunition, food. Can't rely on the locals to provide it, either."

"Not without a consensus, but once Nesimi's gone…"

"Revolution should pick up speed by itself. You think revolutionaries would feed us?" Ereli frowned down at the pad uncomfortably.

"Just because one set of revolutionaries hated us doesn't mean others won't like us."

Ereli didn't answer that.

The revolutionaries, back in Tajikistan? They'd spent a lot of time trying to kill Ereli and Eversen. Even though Azerbaijan's would be a completely different set of people, people who'd hopefully be friendly, calling them revolutionaries still sounded bad.

More brothers arrived with each passing hour. The total on the wallscreen rose up to six hundred, edged its way to two thousand. By the time it hit two thousand five hundred, the lawyers and executives showed up.

Three men and one woman, all human — probably all mildly genetweaked to fit into their roles in life. Thin suits for all of them, the men cleanshaven even though it was a little past midnight, each of them alert with glinting eyes that flashed to their wristwatches and phones as often as other people's faces. Their bodyguards came too — one of them was an old-model dog, one of the female production run that'd been decanted ten years before Ereli. She didn't speak much, though she did exchange a brief handshake with a brother named Elwood.

They were all from Andercom West. Here to advise by the request of the private military companies they helped found.

The executives – a guy and the gal – were shortly discussing the legalities of what they were doing, which was in effect asking people to pay for a glorified assassination/kidnapping contract. That conversation swallowed up Eversen, while Ereli joined in with a group talking about regime change with one of the lawyers specializing in international treaties — what it would take for other global governments to recognize whoever stepped up to replace Nesimi's regime as the legitimate government of Azerbaijan.

Apparently it wasn't an issue that came up very often, because, "Generally speaking, when a regime's overthrown it's because another national power's installed a new one. The backing national power ensures international recognition."

"But we don't have a backer on this," Elwood said. "The only money in this is out of Azerbaijan, right? On the other side of the room they were saying we need to limit donations to Azeri citizens only or we'd have *no* fucking chance of having this called legal."

"I don't think this situation's come up before," the lawyer sipped from a paper cup of delivered coffee one of the bodyguards had brought up. "Occasionally — especially in some of the Northern Persian autonomous territories — an ethnic diaspora backs action and calls in foreign fighters, either calling for aid on shared religious grounds or purely in an attempt to reclaim a homeland. But no one like that's asked you to come in, you're... offering services, as it were."

Ereli leaned in, dipping his ears back uncertainly. "Can't whoever steps up just do what the MACP did? Sit down, bang out some treaties?"

The lawyer paused at that. Smiled, thinly, his dark red-brown skin tightening around the eyes. "When the Middle American Corporate Preserve formed up in the fifties and entered into treaty negotiations, it did so backed with about six and a half trillion New Dollars in business assets."

"Azerbaijan's got oil money," Ereli pointed out. "We shoot the guys who own it, nationalize the industry. Then they can bring something to the negotiating table, right? Oil money's why nobody gives a fuck about removing this guy, isn't it?"

The lawyer's smile broadened. "I like you. Who are you?"

"Ereli." He shoved his hand out.

The lawyer shook it. "Jay Narang. The Azeri oilfields have been giving their last gasp for a long time now — they were thought to be dry until the recent fracking run — but it's possible. That's how the old post-soviet dictators did it, oil and caviar. And the price of fossil petrochemicals is rising considerably now that the Sub-Saharan and Western African Treaty Organization has legislated a ten percent land area limit on its biofuel agriculture…"

Apparently, negotiating shared more than a little with fighting. Except the ammunition — law and money and all that bullshit — was about as much fun as a bottle rocket. Give Ereli a SHED-WAP tipped missile any day.

A cry went up around the coffee table, the group at the screen hollering over each other in excitement. "Twenty thousand! *Finally* fucking hit twenty thousand!" "We hit the twenty-kay mark." "Twenty thousand — we need to incorporate *now*, or the bank's going to freeze the fundraising."

The incorporation paperwork was complicated, even for Andercom's lawyers to hash out, and they'd come prepared with a private chipcase server full of case law to run search algorithms across. Loopholes were closed, references made to some fishing rights dispute and how ownership was resolved for a tiny island off South-East Asia that was mediated by the UN, documents got drawn up, and by the time Ereli was into his second shell of rice the fund was at forty-five thousand New Dollars and the call went up.

"We need a minimum of six signatories to incorporate the fund, as a signatory you're going to be legally responsible — and culpable — for the receipt of and use of any money generated through crowdfunding. Any volunteers—"

Hands shot up around the room. The lawyer laughed. "Okay, we have volunteers, but there has to be at least one witness per signatory — how many of you are here?"

There were far more volunteers to sign than witnesses. Witness? *Fuck* that. This was a chance to do something, to be responsible for something — to have a duty, and goals. And it sure as hell didn't mean starving in an apartment, waiting for his dignity and self-respect to erode away. Ereli pushed through the clumping crowd, with the only abstainer not trying to get a piece of the action sitting in a quiet corner of the room with the human woman who owned the place — so that must have been Stolnik.

"Okay, okay, uh. Where's Ereli?" Jay the Lawyer asked.

Ereli thrust himself forward, grinning. "I'm Ereli!" His brothers pushed him through the press, wrestling him forward until he was up against the kitchen counter, listening to Jay explain the incorporation document to him, waiting until they loaded the page he could sign on.

Bit by bit, the funding total on the wallscreen jumped up. A thousand nudies here, then quiet for ten minutes, then a trickle of donations in fives and tens and hundreds, pushing up the total. Twenty-five thousand, thirty thousand…

TRYING TO PLAN out the invasion of a sovereign nation from Stolnik and Stacy's living room grew less and less viable as the night wore on. For one thing, there wasn't enough space to move — the living room was a crush of Ereli's brothers. For another, it was impossible to get the privacy needed to make a simple phone call.

"We are being overheard," the voice on the other end of the connection said, grim and serious.

Ereli twitched an ear and looked back inside. He'd been forced to retreat to the apartment's balcony, outside into the relative cool of three AM. "I understand that, Mr. Karimov, but there really wasn't any other way to get in touch."

Ereli waited over the brief pause as the phone software finished translating him, listened to the brief shadow of Panah Karimov's own words in Azeri before the English translation began. "It is not as though I have any confirmation that you are who you say you are."

Ereli turned his back on the others indoors, and retreated to the balcony's furthest corner, leaning out into the night air. "Likewise. For all I know your granddaughter—" a pleasant girl studying in the political safety of neutral Georgia "—transferred my call to her politics professor, not her grandfather the opposition militia leader."

"Hypothetically speaking, if you are who you say you are, what do you want in exchange for this *miracle* of deposing Nesimi?"

"Nothing. We've already been paid."

"By this *crowdfunding*?" The translator warbled, injecting an emotive hiss.

"That's right. We've received over five hundred thousand New Dollars. By the incorporation charter of the Private Azerbaijan Civil

Protection Effort, holding those funds, we are beholden to make an effort to depose Nesimi's government."

A pause. "Why are you doing this?"

"We've been paid to."

"No, *why?* Why Azerbaijan? Why do you even care about a country so far from your own?"

Ereli swung his jaw left, all the way until it clicked. He cleared his throat. "Ever thrown a dart at a map, Mr. Karimov?"

"No?"

"It doesn't matter where the dart lands, it's going to land somewhere people are living, somewhere people care about." Ereli pinched his fingers over the tip of his nose, the end of his muzzle. "You have a dictator problem, and a disaffected population willing to pay upward of five hundred thousand nudies to get rid of it. We need work. That simple."

"And you want us to fight a war because *you* started one?"

"No, sir. We didn't start the war. Azerbaijan's legal citizens did by hiring us via crowdfund. And I don't want you to fight it, either — I want to know what support you can offer a covert team inserted into Baku. I have a lot of materiel I need to move into the country, and if I can buy some of it from you that's going to make my life a lot easier."

"You want guns, ammunition?"

"Food and ammunition. We'll be bringing our own guns, but I need to know what caliber rounds you can provide so we can get the right hardware printed up—"

A wave of human noise rose up behind Karimov's voice. Voices crying out in shock.

"Something has happened," Karimov snapped. "Please leave the connection live, I will be back."

The call blanked to hold, and Ereli was left staring at the phone's connection icon.

"All you had to do was confirm whether or not you guys use seven-six-two like everybody else over there…"

Shutting down his phone's interface, so it'd buzz at him when Karimov was ready to talk again, Ereli tiredly stretched out his shoulders and opened the balcony's sliding glass door to get back inside.

The room was quiet, at least. Which you'd expect of someone's living room at just past three. But not when it was this crowded.

"The fuck is going on?" he asked, edging in beside Eversen.

The number on the wallscreen, linked directly to the crowdfund, had bugged out or something. It kept failing to refresh, the number cutting off mid-update and flicking its way up.

Eversen shook his head silently, clicking his muzzle's jaw side to side.

It'd been five hundred and ten thousand or so when Ereli had stepped outside to call Panah Karimov. It was flickering its way up to eight hundred thousand, now.

"Eversen?"

"Shh. Elwood's on the phone."

Elwood was one of the brothers up front, head bowed, nodding silently to whoever was on the other end of the line. He paused, gestured at the screen to flip channels, and stepped back.

The jarring orchestral sting of a newsfeed's headlines sang into life, talking heads appearing immediately after the logo.

"In this hour on Eastern Interests — Northern Persian warlords deny seeking biowarfare agents, Tibetan farming co-op displaced by storm, and Azerbaijan's growing dissident crackdown."

"Fast forward the feed, man," one of his brothers demanded. "I can't, it's *live*," another snapped. "Is it the same footage? Has anyone found the pirate feed they're talking about?" "I found an old recording of one, but it's not whatever's happened…"

Bullshit about the various autonomous territories in Northern Persia flashed by — wild eyed guys like darker Tajiks talking in subtitles crawling across the screen. Tibetans and refugees from India hiding in nomadic tents as contaminated rain lashed down, while the news anchor talked about biowarfare fallout from the Eurasian War. Then there was the inside of what looked like a large restaurant that'd been rented out, people dancing like out of a retro dinner party, half in western clothes and half not — darker haired than most white people, their skin not much darker, more Mediterranean, but different facial features to Italians and Greeks. It was some kind of wedding.

The bride was in a green dress with a veil, completely out of place — kinda Muslim looking. The groom wore a formal Western suit with one of the lacy, hand-embroidered skullcaps kids used to sell on the streets of Dushanbe. But this wasn't footage of Dushanbe, it was Baku — Azerbaijan.

Then a guy in a suit that screamed secret police thug walked up and broke the groom's nose, another tore off the bride's veil to reveal streaked mascara and misery.

It was about then that Stolnik took Stacy — Ereli had been properly introduced — to another room, and Eichardt had the pirate feed open on his PDA lain out on the coffee table, with its screen stretched out as big as it'd go. Some watched it over brothers' shoulders from behind the couch, others leaned in next to Eichardt — Ereli had to lay across his brother's knees to get a glimpse.

None of them were watching the wallscreen's newsfeed anymore. They were watching the pirate feed's raw footage, that'd been chopped up into news-sanitary segments.

The wedding in Azerbaijan, the party having gotten started in the middle of the afternoon — a couple of hours ago. Apparently the internet was censored inside the country, and while the banking system was run by external Swiss interests and allowed for money to be moved with minimal government oversight — making the crowdfunding possible — the actual news about the crowdfunding campaign hadn't spread very quickly.

The way the crowdfunding page had been set up was so that a version of it could be spread phone to phone, with direct file transfer and on pages loaded into chips. And the biggest points of transfer turned out to be social gatherings — apparently the Azeris liked big dinner parties and weddings and things.

So did the Ministry of State Security: Azerbaijan's equivalent to the Tajik Ministry of Internal Security. A nice name for spies and thugs and black-ops types, all aimed at their own population. Secret police.

What the newsfeed had called 'plainclothes policemen', and what Ereli thought of as fuckers who attacked non-combatants, lined the wedding's guests up outside the dinner party hall. Later in the afternoon, by the angle of the light.

That's when Ereli thought a firing squad would show up, but no. Mobile cranes, the block and tackle looped back on itself, were used to haul the partygoers up by the neck. First singly — the groom and bride left struggling, kicking out to reach the ground a bare six inches under their feet — and then in twos and threes and fours, guests forced back to back, then lynched around the necks together and dragged up, their own combined weight digging the metal cable in under their chins until their skin broke.

It took these people a long, long time to die. Most of it was filmed from a nearby building, by young women continually ducking down out of sight and gibbering in fear in their own language, one Ereli didn't understand, but he didn't have to. The tone in how a person said something meant a lot more than the words — that was something he'd learned as a child, when the same bark of sound produced two different ways meant very different things.

Pirate internet wireless in Azerbaijan was pretty efficient, especially when they didn't mind losing a few nodes by letting them broadcast long enough for the government to find them.

The government was killing its own people to try and keep word from spreading that maybe, maybe there was a way out from under their oppression.

Apparently the government's efforts weren't working, because the crowdfunding total hit a million New Dollars and kept climbing like there wasn't any tomorrow.

For a lot of people, there wouldn't be.

CRISP, ARISTOCRATIC TONES spoke on the newsfeed behind them. "Well, Chris, it's clearly terrible, and the United Kingdom is at the forefront of demands to impose sanctions on Azerbaijan *now*."

"But don't we need more than just sanctions? Don't we need *action*?"

The official, some cut-glass accented government PR drone, was just as much a copy-and-paste nobody built to fit his role as the Andercom lawyers had been, or as Ereli was. There were five hundred and eighty-two clones who could fit Ereli's role *exactly*, and he didn't doubt the same was true of the talking head on the screen.

The guy smiled. "Well, Chris," he said, "the situation very much does need action, and the international community is already sending a very firm message to Nesimi's government that this crackdown will not be tolerated through the use of economic sanctions and boycotting."

It didn't matter how often the interviewer butted heads with the guy — the official was a pro, knew that his role was to spit out the same meaningless nonsense over and over and over.

Kind of like Stolnik, except Stolnik's role was to get them back on track, over and over and over.

"All we need are drone strikes here, here, and here. We can take them down in no time at all—"

"This *isn't* tactical planning," Stolnik yapped again, like a broken record. "We need a plan, we need a concrete strategic plan to organize ourselves, how we handle the tactical situation is *easy* for us."

One of their brothers started talking about rifles — Stolnik cut him off. "This is officer level shit. Not holding the guns, *planning*."

"I understand you. I wasn't trained for that," the brother who'd spoken up — Eichardt — replied.

"None of us were," Stolnik muttered. "Look, it's simpler if you slow down. Stop thinking about how you make the kill — think about what you need for it, where that's going to come from. How you're going to wind up holding a gun in the place you need to be, how you're going to get fed on the way there and back…"

"Food's on the Ammule, everyone knows that," Elwood cut in, a sarcastic edge on his voice.

Stolnik smiled, but didn't laugh. "I guess if we can get enough Ammules to follow us around, then we don't *need* a plan, do we?"

Ereli *did* laugh. Most of the time, with an Ammule following you around — a four or six legged cargo bot loaded up with supplies — you didn't have to think about where ammo or food was coming from, just fight.

"Look," Eversen said, voice serious, "the regime is attacking its own people. That's nothing new, but they're doing it because of the crowdfunding campaign — what's the total at?"

Ereli glanced away from the map for an instant. "Eight million."

"The regime *knows* we're coming. You understand that? We just launched a crowdfunding campaign with the stated goal of putting the regime's decision makers in chains or in the ground. We just declared *war*. They're probably putting up automatic turrets in Baku, and we don't even have a toe in the country."

Ereli clicked his jaw side to side. "He's going to run. Someplace he feels safe."

"Maybe he's got bunkers somewhere, but he's also got like a gazillion mansions in Baku, owns half the hotels himself. Chances are at least some of them are fortified. Safe and comfortable," Eversen replied.

Elwood flattened his hands on the map, pulling its focus around to Baku. "It's like they tried building San Iadras, but without a decent plan. Look at this mess."

"That's about what they did," Stolnik murmured. "Lots of oil money, so build all the pretty skyscrapers. But they didn't think about what the buildings were *for*, they just threw that shit up because it looked good and fed their egos. Then the Eurasian war fucked them up and they did it all over again."

"They can boobytrap this place to hell and back," Ereli muttered. "Nesimi and his guard unit can just sit there as long as they want, get prepared specifically to kill us. I don't know that inserting covert teams will be enough. We need proper information on where the hell Nesimi *is*. We need high level access to their internal tactical network."

"We're not all coming back from this," Eichardt murmured.

"None of us have to die if we do our job right," Stolnik replied sharply.

"Unless the other side does *their* job right."

Stolnik bowed his head, growled at the edge of hearing — a deep, bassy rumble. "Every time in your lives you've felt fucked up and wrong because you were different, because office work doesn't feel right, because society is too hard to understand?" He slapped the counter, hard. "That's them, the regime, right now. They're the ones who're confused and ignorant. We're the ones who were made for this — *us*. None of us have to die.

"We're going to do this right. And we have to do it now, because the people we've been hired to protect are being attacked, and we're on the wrong side of the world. We can put teams on the ground *now*, not to neutralize Nesimi, but buy the rest of us time to move on him in force. So, let's figure this shit out without whining about how difficult it is, and get organized to go show Nesimi that his people are voting him out of office to the tune of eight million nudies."

"Nine and a half, now," Ereli said.

"To the tune of nine and a half million nudies," Stolnik corrected himself. He straightened up, glancing at the screen. "Fuck. How much are these people going to spend?"

"Oh man. If we hit the stretch goals, the regime is in *such* deep shit."

9. Strategy Session

::/ San Iadras, Middle American Corporate Preserve.
::/ April, 2106.
::/ Ereli Estian.

It wasn't that luck was a key ingredient in war, but beneficial circumstances helped. Ereli had been in the right place at the right time, spoken to Jay Narang the lawyer, made a good impression, had been made signatory to the incorporation for what was the 'Private Azerbaijan Civil Protection Effort' on paper, and was now 'The Liberation Fund' on the news feeds that were giving coverage. A good start, so far as Ereli was concerned.

He wasn't a leader — they didn't have time for leaders — but he *was* one of the first users of the tactical bulletin board, mapper, and operations organizer one of Elwood's guys set up, as if they were playing MilSim. Turned out to be the same planning software package, just the actual military edition. After getting set up and discussing it with the others, he got three approvals from the other signatories — a group of fourteen brothers — and added his own for the four signatory agreements required to start signing off funds to pay Andercom a thousand five hundred nudies an hour, letting Ereli rent time on Andercom's hardened Low Earth Orbit observation and communication satellites.

The Azeri army was in motion. It took an hour and a half's work for Andercom's image interpretation staff, included with the hourly rental, to find and identify all of the known Azeri tanks — forty of them rusting in a yard a hundred miles west of Baku, and the rest split between an operation heading West, to their Armenian border, and East, into Baku itself. The tanks were vanishing between the skyscrapers, hidden from view until a satellite's orbit brought it into alignment with the messy street grids.

Infantry was on the march, Azeri riot police holding back crowds of protestors, grounded passenger aircraft blazing white in the sun at the airport.

"Look at that, they're corralling the protesters." Elwood let his jaw hang slack, before biting back down on one of the catering sandwiches they'd brought into their newly-rented offices, the middle floor of a Midtown skyscraper given over to short term furnished leases. The wallscreen had been left displaying stock market graphs by the previous tenants, the prices rising and falling in real time, but they'd switched it to the news.

The news wasn't good.

Not everybody was protesting for the same reasons. According to some independent journalist named Stone Sparrow on the news feed, even though they were all Muslims, that didn't make them the same. There were different kinds, like Protestants and Catholics and Reformists and more. Most people, just like in San Iadras which was technically Catholic, either ignored religion or called themselves Muslim because that's what their country was. Some protestors campaigned for the rights of the church — the mosque, whatever — some complained because women wore the veil, others complained because they didn't.

The Muslims being rounded up and pushed in ragged lines after being pulled through burning protest barriers, these were the religious ones — the ones who wanted the state to recognize a religious marriage, the ones who had ideas about stopping five times a day for prayer, the ones who said the government-backed Imams and preachers and holymen were scaremongering liars who exploited people's fears about other sects and the West. They didn't want to be attacked because they chose to wear a beard, or chose not to. They wanted a woman to decide if she wore a veil, not the mosques and not the government, not the unwritten law that said women dressed in religious clothes were oppressed fanatics and said the ones dressed like westerners were 'whores'.

The religious people were stacked up next to the other religious people who said some historical figure married another one, so someone inherited something else — Ereli didn't understand the differences between the Sunni and the Shi'a, but he knew it was one worth killing for. Some of the religious people thought women shouldn't be educated, and some of them believed education was for everyone — men and women both — wasn't just a right, but a holy duty passed down from the Prophet himself.

They were all different, the only thing they had in common was that they called themselves Muslim, and in the face of government oppression they begged for whatever they thought was sanity under the name of their God. That let the government brand them extremist no matter what they really believed, and that's why Stone Sparrow was able to hide and watch as the protesting Muslims were pulled from the protest barricades and pushed into vans even if they hated each other, pushed in elbow to elbow, man and woman, equal under the law.

Except there wasn't enough space for all of them, and the three or four Muslims left behind were pushed down and left to wait in the gutters for the next van.

Then there were those who weren't playing the religion card at all, the young and the alienated, screaming for justice. The families whose loved ones had been killed or disappeared or branded hooligans or arrested on made up drug charges, only to disappear into prisons for years on end — or forever. Journalists and human rights activists, all branded traitors or spies. Refugees who'd fled the contaminants of the Eurasian war, all accused of being there only to leech off the state's meagre hospitality.

And when the activists and refugees didn't fit in the trucks, when the zip-tie handcuffs ran out, they were pushed into the ground and held at gunpoint with the Muslims.

Then the neo-fascists came, the angry rebels, those who wanted to fight and were emboldened by the protesting crowds who'd come out to try and shout their government's violence down, throwing bricks and paving stones, Molotov cocktails, bringing out weapons to shoot at the police.

That's when instead of guarding the Muslims and activists waiting for a van to take them away, so the secret police could vanish them into some inner-city prison, the riot police shot their prisoners. Blood ran in the gutters, and they stacked up more bodies of captured protestors and rioters — neo-fascists, activists, and Muslims alike — slaughtering them in the crowd's crush like battery farmed hens.

Blood oozed along the gutters, both on Stone Sparrow's feed, and on the satellite imagery of the riot.

And the money?

The money kept flowing in. Twelve million, now fifteen million, twenty, thirty… The same Swiss bankers who'd helped the oligarchy hide its money, the ones who'd taken over when the local banks failed for being too corrupt, were now helping Azerbaijan's citizens anonymously send their money to these foreign dogs who promised so much, but had so far done nothing.

The more money that came in, the more blood the government was willing to spill, putting on public news conferences that listed the names of those brought in for questioning with dark hints that the names mentioned wouldn't be coming home again. The more terrible the oppression, the more desperate the people became, the more money that fell into the Liberation Fund's lap.

Ereli needed to stop it. He had a duty to stop it, one signed into the incorporation documents with his name. And he had a plan to stop it.

But he was only one dog. He needed the other five hundred and eighty-two.

"You're distracted," Eversen said, squinting out into the noonday sun.

Ereli clasped the jeep's wheel, even though he wasn't driving on manual. Just needed something in his hands to squeeze. "No shit."

Eversen leaned forward, squinting out of the windshield. "That dirt path there. Second left."

Ereli waited, then tilted the wheel fractionally — the route planner pinged its assent, and he sat back, waiting for the jeep to take the left turn. They were out in the open country, San Iadras a silver blot behind them. Green everywhere, and so many *trees*. Ereli hadn't even known this was out here, barely twenty minutes away on the freeway.

"You okay?" Eversen asked, glancing across the cabin.

"Every minute I dick around, wasting time, somebody's dying." He released the wheel, and picked up his pad, scrolling through the discussions on the planning board. "It's not a good feeling."

"You're not dicking around, you're gathering manpower."

"If that bitch would've just let me plead the case over the damn phone…"

"Don't call them bitch." Eversen ducked his head and pointed out to a red-furred shape waiting by a van ahead, beside a rocky field. "They don't think it's *remotely* funny."

Marianna, the team leader, was waiting for them. Standing annoyed, ears erect, teeth bared — when the jeep stopped, she was at the window in an instant, knocking at it.

Ereli clicked open the door, but before he could get outside, she was snarling at him. "Our team is *this* close to going pro, you understand? We're not your recruitment resource because you knuckleheads kicked a hornet's nest!"

"I need to talk to them — Eissen told me he was interested yesterday."

"I am not handing you my fireteam on a silver platter," Marianna said, ears flat back against her skull. "We do not ship out because you said so, you get me?"

He was taller than her. Six inches taller, easy, but even forcing her to look up at him once he'd stood, she didn't back down. Didn't stop jabbing her finger into his chest, either.

"This is war." Ereli clenched his fists — he *sure* as hell wasn't going to back down to her, even if he wanted to. "I'm not going to drag anyone, but I would've *thought* this is what you wanted."

"What we *want* is pro level sponsorship and a spot on the league tables. This is a sport we're playing, it's the goddamn final quarter of the season. We're not just fucking cooling our heels daydreaming about some asshole coming along to push a real gun into our hands." Marianna jabbed her forefinger and middle finger, braced together, into Ereli's ribs. Hard — like fucking *stabbing* him. "You don't dial me up and tell me to bring my players to your office. Understand? You're lucky I'm letting you talk to them, they're supposed to be training."

With that she stalked off, leaving him to follow her. He glanced back at Eversen — Eversen just shrugged, leaning against the Jeep's roof — and set off after her.

Her team was what he needed. Exactly what he needed. Seven of his brothers, sat around a red-hot cooker pad, waiting for the labels to burn off a stacked pile of food cans. They had a fluidity to their motions, a kind of grace — comfortable with their own physicality.

Ereli envied them, he hadn't had an excuse to get back into that kind of shape since Tajikistan.

"Listen to him. Don't agree to shit — if you don't take at *least* an hour to think about what you'd be throwing away I will tear you bastards to pieces, so help me God."

"Yes ma'am," one of his brothers replied.

She wound up, as if to backhand him — "Ellis you little…" —but he ducked away, laughing.

"Just pulling your chain, Marianna. Jeez."

"I'll kick your ass," she muttered, turning around to face Ereli. She shrugged, gesturing at the group. "You can talk to them now."

Ereli glanced back, making sure Eversen was still with him — trailing behind by about twenty feet, letting Ereli take all the fire — and looked around the group. "Eissen?"

A hand went up, on the right.

"Okay. For the rest of you, I'm Ereli — I'm part of that Azerbaijan thing you've probably heard about."

"Hey Ereli. I'm Eberstetten."

"No shit? This is Eversen." Ereli bobbed his head at his brother. "We haven't seen you in *years*."

"Not since Tajikistan."

"Not since then," Ereli agreed.

"This Azerbaijan thing, it's crazy," a brother replied — Ellis. "It's not actually going to fucking work, is it? I mean you guys had a couple of million this morning, but…"

Ereli lifted his wristwatch and thumbed it, checking his tickers. "We're at thirty-eight million, now. We've got an operation planned, equipment and armor's already available, but we need manpower."

"Dogpower."

Despite himself, he choked back laughter. "Which one of you was that?"

"Edane." The one next to Eissen, the bulk of a LAMW against his shoulder, lifted his hand.

"Right, well, we need dogpower..."

BY THE END of the song and dance, half of them were interested, half of them weren't. Eberstetten was wavering either way, Ellis kept bringing up how their team was clinging to ninth on some kind of ranking table.

As if a ranking table mattered.

Ereli thought about it, staring out of the window as the jeep took him and Eversen to the next address on their list.

"What do you think?"

"Hm?" Eversen looked up from his pad.

"What do you think our chances are with the MilSim teams?"

"Lousy." Eversen ran through the list of other active MilSim players, more of which they were going to try and meet in ones and twos and threes — there weren't any teams with as many brothers on it as Marianna's, and all of these teams were out running exercises in the boonies. "They're happy with what they're doing here, no reason to pull up stakes for us."

"Maybe we should turn around and beg," Ereli muttered. "I figured the money would sway it for us. We need teams ready to move out by *tonight*."

"Money isn't what matters to them. Doing something that makes them happy does — you happy?"

"No. But I've got a duty."

Eversen smiled slowly. "I don't know about you, but duty makes *me* happy."

"In a way, it makes me happy too," Ereli mused. "I just wish people weren't dying because of it."

10. Heading Out

::/ San Iadras, Middle American Corporate Preserve.
::/ April, 2106.
::/ Edane Estian.

They had ninth spot. *Ninth*, and if the team held onto it for four more weeks, then Hallman would take them pro. They'd been working for this since Edane had first met with the team and asked Marianna if he could join, to keep him in shape, for his arm. It'd been a year and a half since then, nearly two since he'd been hurt. Edane couldn't stand it, just couldn't fucking stand it.

They got themselves ninth spot on the season's leaderboard, and now this. He hadn't set out to go professional, but the semi-pro contract gave him enough that he hadn't been leeching off Janine, originally. Paid for his nightly stay in the capsule hotel, now, keeping him in a neat, no-nonsense pattern and routine of playing and eating and training and *not thinking*.

He hadn't been made for thinking, for feeling. Been made for fighting, he knew that now, better than ever.

Eberstetten didn't want to go, not when Ellis pointed out that him and Salzach had *barely* gotten into the most valuable players consideration list last Saturday, and semi-pro registered players got into the MVP lists once or twice a season. Erlnicht had a night job playing club doorman somewhere, friends. Didn't want to lose either. Svarstad wasn't sure whether he wanted to leave on almost no notice, but he thought he might take a week to think about it, if this mess lasted that long.

Eissen… Eissen had this haunted expression all through the rest of their exercises, plinking at pretend targets in AugR — kept looking at Edane, and Edane kept looking at him. As if Edane knew what Eissen was thinking, as if Eissen struggled with the same thought of *what if I hadn't gotten hit*, the same nagging feeling that he hadn't really *been* in Tajikistan because he'd gotten medevaced out of the country just before the revolution hit.

Except Eissen hadn't been wounded — he'd been captured along with the human contractors he'd been working with, got taken down to a police basement cell and tortured until him and his friends broke out on the revolution's first day, running over the border before the real shooting started.

Edane slumped back in the team's van, palms over his face, as Marianna talked to the rest of the team about the upcoming Wednesday match, shooting the shit about all the possible scenarios that might come up, which way she'd bid for targets and ask for support, what she'd do if antagonistic off-field controllers denied them artillery.

One by one the team members got dropped off, first Ellis, then Salzach — Erlnicht changing into his night clothes, bathing himself in stinking cologne to fit in before hopping out of the van and walking down to play bouncer at his club before sunset.

Almost without noticing the time pass, Edane was alone in the van with Marianna, with nothing to distract them except the purr of the van's tires on the way back to the freeway.

"You know you have to make up your mind before the end of the night, right?" she asked. "That knucklehead's suicide mission needs you ready and at the airport by one fucking AM."

"It's not a suicide mission," Edane mumbled. "It's forward infiltration. Get on the ground, get in, secure infrastructure and delay the Azeri army's operations until reinforcements arrive."

"And if it doesn't? If the money for reinforcements doesn't get kindly donated by an appreciative population, and you wind up all fucking alone out there? You know what it's like playing without support — do you *really* want to wind up stuck in hostile territory without even Louie to back you up?"

He laughed, weakly. "I miss Louie."

"I do too."

"An actual warzone's no place for him, though."

"It isn't. But is it a place for you?" she asked, head cocked.

He pulled himself forward, edging around the van's seats until he flopped down onto the bench across from hers.

Marianna stared at him silently.

"You're not talking me out of this, exactly, are you?"

She smiled. Not a pleasant smile, not a friendly smile. Shark's teeth and broken glass. "Oh, kid. I'd beat sense into you if I could, but that'd be pushing you just a *little* far. What was it you said to me? I'm not your commanding officer?"

He scratched at an ear tiredly, looking away. "Well. You're not."

"If I could beat you into thinking I was, I'd tell you shut up and get in line like a good puppy." She let her jaw hang slack, swinging it left and right until it clicked. Shook her head slowly. "But let's face it, kid. You might be one of my knuckleheads, but your heart isn't in this, is it?"

Edane didn't answer her. Flicked his ears tiredly, head bowing lower and lower. "I appreciate what you've done for me," he said, at last.

"Don't force me into beating the shit out of you with that touchy feely shit, kid. Just don't. Look at me like an equal, okay?"

He lifted his muzzle, warily met her eye.

No shark-tooth grin from Marianna this time. Just a tired expression, almost the same as his own.

"I did my time," she said. "After the Emancipation, I signed on with Andercom and ran my little ass around the Ecuadorian jungle in a suit of assistive armor you would have *died* for, kid, and I shot people, and I hunted down and killed those idiot warlords who thought they were better than the corporations. I saw two of my sisters die, and hauled one out before our shitty metabolism could kill her after she got kidnapped without her pills. The friends I worked with died around me, and I killed people 'cuz a little voice in my ear sitting in an office somewhere in Downtown told me to.

"I did my time, kid. I might not have gotten fucked up like you did, but by the time you were getting out of high school I'd done it all, and I'd had enough. I am older than you, definitely have more life experience than you, am probably smarter than you, and I have *been* there. Okay?"

Marianna blinked expectantly at him.

He blinked back. "Okay."

"There will *always* be someone else stupid enough to go get themselves killed in a war somewhere, Edane. You don't *need* to go. Trust me, even if the powers that be decided we have the need to do it printed into our fucking *genes*, that war will get fought without you."

"I know that."

"Good. Now, MilSim's a game. It's a good game — it hits all the buttons for making me feel like I'm living how I got built to, meeting challenges without hurting anybody, positive usage of aggression, teamwork, all that bullshit. I'm happy that it's my life's work right now." She shrugged her shoulder, breaking eye contact. "Much as I love it, it's only a game."

He watched her looking away, looking out the window, looking everywhere but at his face. "What are you saying?"

"I'm saying that I don't blame you if a game isn't *enough*."

"It's not that the game isn't enough," Edane muttered. "It's been good to me — it's kept me going, my arm's almost normal these days. I want to get that pro spot, I do, it's just…"

He frowned, palming at his face. As he pushed at his eyes, a stark sky-blue popped up in the colors behind his eyelids, unbidden.

"Unfinished business." Marianna clicked her jaw again. "You went to Tajikistan, expecting I don't know what, but you got your ass blown up. I thought that was what was bugging you, that you'd been fucked up, that you couldn't hold a rifle straight—"

"I can do that now," he interrupted. "I can use solid core unguided, switch off the scope and make a kill at a mile if I have to."

"I know." She lifted her hand for him to stop, nodding. "I know. But that's not what's been eating you up, is it?"

"Janine… We talk sometimes, and—"

"We'll get to that. But you didn't leave just your arm in Tajikistan, did you?" She stared at him. "Why'd you go in the first place, kid?"

Edane hunched in on himself, head bowed, shoulders forward. He'd spent so long arguing with his mothers, they'd tried to talk him out of it, get him back into school. He'd been twenty-one, twenty when he'd made the decision. He covered his face again. "Fuck," he breathed.

"They took you out on your back, but you went in there on your feet. You get me?" she slapped him, hard enough to hurt, hard enough to *make* him look at her. "You were supposed to walk out of that country on your feet. That's what you expected going in, wasn't it?"

He nodded, lamely.

Marianna shook her head. "I don't think you're going to shake this until you've come back on your own terms, kid. When you choose to come back to civilization — not when you get dragged back."

"Maybe."

"You listen to me on this. I've been there."

"What about the team?"

She exploded in laughter. "Kid, kid. Jesus fuck, *kid*. Have you not seen what the league is doing to us?"

"Yeah, but…"

"They're running us out as fast as they fucking can. Oh, we're going to hold onto that nine-spot. Maybe if you and Eissen stuck around we could claw ourselves up to seventh, and we'll probably hold our ground if we bring in a couple of substitutes… but there ain't gonna *be* a team by the time you get back." She snorted. "Hallman's nice to us, but they ain't stupid. No professional league for us to parade their gear in, no sponsorship."

Edane nodded, staring down at the van's floor, ruined by booted feet and mud and simple brutal use. He scratched at his right wrist, fingertips questing through his fur, even if it wasn't *his* wrist, really.

"I've been called a lot of things in my life," Marianna went on. "Bitch is the best of them. But doping? Cheater? Never, and you've seen how I pop the pills." She shook her head slightly. It was true — Marianna took somewhere between eight and twelve of them every four hours, like clockwork. No timer, no alarm, but she always had them within a couple minutes of the hour. That's what screwed up genes did for you — taught you how to take metabolic drugs on time so you could keep living. "Anyway. If this fight in Azerbaijan lasts past the end of the season, and they put their little get-out-of-dog-free clause into the league's rulebook? You'll probably see the rest of us out there. So, don't worry about leaving us behind, kid."

He hesitated. "Marianna?"

"Yes, kid?"

"How much more life experience than me do you have?"

"Aww shit." She slumped back, propping her head up on her fist. "Your girl."

He dipped his face in a brief, slight nod.

"How long have you been broken up with her?"

"Two and—"

"No!" She stopped him, one finger up, and dragged out her phone. A moment, two, as she clicked through to his playing stats. "It happened just before match two in February. Right?"

"Sounds right," he sighed.

"For what it's worth, as your team leader, I think you need to straighten that shit out. Either get over it or get back together — your reaction times have been middling. Distracted..." Marianna grimaced, waggling her head noncommittally. "You've always been a little distracted, but it's been worse lately."

"I don't know what to do about her," he murmured. "If I go to Azerbaijan..."

Marianna watched him awhile, her voice somewhat soft. "If you go to Azerbaijan, then what?"

"I don't know." Edane shook his head. "It was all going so great with her, for a year."

"What happened?"

"Sex problems."

Marianna recoiled away, disgust pulling at her features. "Oh, don't give me *that* shit, kid."

"She wants it, and I don't." He waved his hands helplessly. "I don't know what the hell I'm supposed to do."

"You're supposed to *stick it in her*, champ." Marianna bit back a laugh with a coughing snort. "Jesus, kid. Relationship advice, okay, maybe I can help you out, but sex advice? All I have to do is like a guy enough to put up with laying on my back for fifteen minutes at a time without decking him." She squinted at him. "The hell does she want sex out of you for, anyway? There's better fun."

"She thinks it *is* fun." Edane kept his gaze slanted out the window, unfamiliar embarrassment heating his face. "She has all these crazy ideas about it — wants me to call her pretty, like I understand what that means."

"Ha! She wants *you* calling her pretty? Unless she's got a face like a Kellinger-Dewy twenty-three cal, that girl's fucked… Well, she *ain't*, but you know what I mean."

"I like her," he murmured. "I like her and I don't know what to do, Marianna. I've never liked *anyone*."

"You like those parents of yours — the mothers."

"Not like this. Not this much. Putting up with the sex is worth it, but. But she needs me to want it too, and we can't talk about it without hurting her 'cuz she wants me to want it so *badly*." Edane ground his fingers against one another. "I liked living with her. It was like we fit together," he concluded, fingertips stacked into each other.

Marianna grimaced. "I've had that. Guys taking it personal that I don't enjoy having them tire themselves out on me. Then they get all pissy and want to fuck someone else, like I care." She exposed her teeth. A thin, sharp white line. "Now when a guy — or a gal, I guess — tells you he just wants to be *friends*, if he can live up to that? That's a fucking test of character."

Edane flicked his ears back and forth, staring at his laced fingers.

Marianna watched him evenly, cheek against her palm. "You want encouraging advice or advice that helps you walk away?"

"You're the one with life experience."

"You're the one with your artificial balls on the chopping block."

Her gaze was cold, when he lifted his eyes to meet it. "I don't think I'm going to be able to, but I want to try and fix it with her," Edane said.

She clicked her jaw side to side, gazed out of the window at the streets outside. "I had a good thing, like your thing with your girl, once." She lifted up her finger, counting off the single instance. Her hand drifted to cover the tip of her muzzle, as if she'd said too much. "Just once, you understand," she added. "It made stupid sentimental shit *fun*. The sex was... enhh, but the look on his face afterward made me happy."

She tapped the end of her nose, thoughtfully. "A lot about it made me happy," she concluded. "Not a better kind of happy than killing, or a worse kind, just. Different... A way I ain't had again, so far."

"What happened?" he asked.

Marianna glared at him. "It got to let's just be friends, and I didn't call him as much as I should've. I went away to my little *la guerra*, then came back from the jungle to find out he had a new friend, a *girl*-friend, and I couldn't be the kind of friend I'd been with him without ruining that for him." She lifted her shoulder in an awkward shrug and resumed watching the streets outside. "Now we're not so close. It's six years later, and I still miss him."

Edane looked away. Something in her expression was too private for his eyes.

"It's not so bad, kid. Life sucks sometimes, and it was fun to have while it lasted." She shrank down in her seat and folded her arms. "But for what it's worth, here's what life experience says — you do what I didn't, and you call her before you pack for your suicide run. Just in case you can fix it. You will blame the *fuck* out of yourself if you don't. You hear me?"

"Sir, yes sir," Edane said. "I hear you."

"IT'S NOT A good time, Sweetie..."

"Please, Janine. It hasn't been a good time since I walked out. I want to talk to you."

In the privacy of what used to be his bedroom, pacing the familiar floor, he felt slightly more able to talk. Maybe it was being in friendly territory, visiting his mothers, maybe it was more than that.

Janine snuffled at the phone. A wet sound, displeased — not in tears, but miserable. "You're just gonna leave, Edane. That's what you're telling me, that you're leaving for this Azerbaijan place."

"I don't want to leave without talking to you first."

She made a petulant noise. "Why couldn't you have called me to talk last week, huh? Or the week before?"

"It's the middle of the MilSim season, and I was afraid to talk to you and I figured it could *wait*. Please? I don't have much time."

"Fine. Where do you want to meet? My place?"

"I'm visiting with my mothers before I go, but I'll meet you wherever you want."

The connection was quiet a moment, two. Muted again, but she hadn't been crying, her voice was too level, restrained — more likely she'd been swearing. "I'll come meet you there. But you come down to the street to meet me, okay? Alone. I'm not doing this in front of your moms."

He smiled, just slightly. Janine could call them that, he couldn't. "Okay. Thanks Janine."

"I'll... I'll see you in a bit," she muttered, and closed the line.

Edane turned his phone over, watching her messenger icon blink from 'on call' to 'busy'. He folded the phone up and stepped out of his room, careful not to bang his knee into his mothers' bicycles, and padded down the short hall to their bedroom.

Cathy was laying in the dim light, back propped up with the bed's pillows, Beth laying back against her belly, a pad in each hand. Photos on each.

"Oh, look at this one," Beth murmured, passing one of the pads up to Cathy.

Cathy idly scratched Beth's scalp with one hand, took the pad with the other. "*Ohhh*," she breathed. "He was so little, then."

Edane leaned back, then stepped forward again. Louder, so they could hear. They always said he moved too quietly.

Cathy looked up with a blink, smiling, holding out her arms. "Come here, Daney."

"Why'd you have to grow so *big*, baby?" Beth shuffled to one side, making space for him, hugging him tight as he sat down between them. "You were *so* little, and then you were just the right size, and in a heartbeat you were all grown up."

He accepted the pad from Cathy, looked down at a picture of himself. Hard to judge age, but he remembered the shirt. He'd have been thirteen, maybe fourteen. Not very long before he had new testicles implanted, giving him the right hormones to develop — he'd been castrated at decanting.

"Sorry," he said. "I didn't mean to grow big. I'll do better next time."

Beth laughed, so did Cathy, until even Edane smiled a little.

"And you were always *so* polite. Always 'I'll do better next time.' Where'd you pick that up? You didn't do that right after the Emancipation, it wasn't the barracks, was it?"

He shook his head. "Grandpa Jeff. I asked him what I was supposed to do if I was unable to perform well for you, one time you were both at work and he was minding me. I figured he was going to tell me to... I don't know. Go do push-ups or something, but he said I should apologize and try to do better, so..."

Cathy sat up. Couldn't reach his head, to pull him down and comfort him, but she held him too. Her arms didn't wrap around him as tightly, she couldn't reach far enough around him to hold her own elbows anymore. "Dad was *so* fond of you, Edane. And proud of you too. I'm so glad you got to spend time with him."

Edane thumbed at the pad until he found one of the birthday pictures. The old man — he'd had Cathy when he'd been in his fifties, youngest daughter with his second wife — holding up a glass of one of the expensive kinds of alcohol he'd liked, smiling at the camera. Edane, a little younger, staring quizzically up from under his arm.

Edane put the pad down, gently. "I liked Grandpa Jeff."

"We know, Daney."

"I don't think Grandpa Jeff would've been happy that I went to Tajikistan, though," he said, voice stretched. "Or that I'm going to Azerbaijan, or that I killed anybody."

Cathy frowned, a complicated expression. "Probably not," she agreed. "But he'd be happy that you were trying to help people, both times."

Beth got up, bending down to kiss his cheek. "I'll go make tea." She smiled, and walked down the hall. It was funny, how much noise she made doing it, even though she was much smaller than Edane.

Thinking about Grandpa Jeff was hard. But Edane made himself do it anyway. "He probably would've liked MilSim, though. He liked sports."

Cathy laughed. "Probably would have, if you could get him to stop watching tennis."

Edane nodded quietly and picked the pad back up.

It was filled with his life before Tajikistan. He searched back and forth, eventually found one solitary picture from after he came back — before the graft, but after he'd healed enough to be able to sit up on his own. He was up on a hospital bed, right side turned away from the camera, talking to Beth. He almost looked whole — the only reason he could tell his shoulder was missing was because of how the hospital gown sagged on his chest.

"I'm sorry I went away," he said, softly. "I'm sorry we fought — I should have listened."

Cathy just smiled at him, softly. "We should have listened, Daney."

They joined Beth in the kitchen, and Edane just drank hot water instead of tea. When Janine arrived, calling him, his mothers were gently turning in each other's arms, bare feet skimming over the tiles, softly humming the music together as they danced.

JANINE SMELLED FUNNY. Not humorous, but strange. He didn't understand why she smelled like that. Not right away — why would anyone smell like other people? But then he remembered, sex. And she looked miserable, hair tied back loosely instead of brushed, her fur standing up all over her face like she'd just washed it, not shampooed it.

At least, Edane thought, he hadn't been stupid enough to ask her why she smelled like that.

"I'm such an idiot," she muttered.

He stepped along beside her, wandering along the square, right-angled pathways that gradually cut down underground to the little row of nighttime cafés from his mothers' apartment. "You're not stupid."

"Yeah, I am. Goddammit, Sweetie." She shook her head. "We

should have talked before — I saw that thing on the news. God, it's so horrible."

Edane nodded gently. "They want me to go and, uhm. Fight."

"Yeah."

"Tonight," he clarified. "So I can be deployed before local sunset there, tomorrow."

"*Fuck*," she breathed, shuddering next to him.

"I wanted to talk to you, first."

She stopped in her tracks, abruptly enough he had to turn back to face her. Janine held up her hands. "Edane. Before this conversation goes any further, I have to tell *you* something."

"Okay?"

"I've been sleeping with other men. In fact, I just got out of a hook-up to come and see you, okay?" She looked at him as if this meant something. "You understand?"

"I think so."

"I fucked other men, Edane."

"Okay."

"Doesn't that matter to you?" she asked, voice high-pitched, almost squeaky.

Edane carefully tilted his ears forward, to be attentive, to let her know he was listening. "Uh."

"Oh God. I was hoping you'd forgive me," she went on. "I'm sorry, Sweetie. It was just easier for me than being alone, y'know? It's just, it's just casual stuff, it doesn't *mean* anything…"

He did the Cathy and Beth thing. Held her, his arms gentle on her back. Waited until she paused for breath, "Can you explain this to me?"

"What?" She looked up, eyes damp.

"I'm not mad or anything but, I just don't understand. Is you having sex with other people something that's supposed to make me unhappy?"

"Well, yeah. Unless you don't want to get back together."

He frowned, ears splayed. "Oh." Cleared his throat. "Well I want to get back together with you, but I don't understand why I'd be sad if you had sex with other people."

"Edane, sex is special, it's important to people, it's—"

She blinked wetly up at him, and he shrugged, a little helplessly.

"I can try and be unhappy about it if you want, Janine, but I'm not hurt or anything. I still love you like before."

She kept staring at him, and shook her head ever so slightly. "You are so different to me, Edane."

"Am I?"

"Yeah. I figured telling you about this would make me feel like a slut or something, and I do, I guess but..."

She hugged him, and he held her close, nose buried in her hair — even if it smelled funny.

Janine sighed against him. "You don't make me feel *dirty*," she whispered. "Everyone else makes me feel dirty, when shit like this happens."

"Could take a shower," he offered, stroking her hair.

She smiled, just a little. "You know I don't mean it like that."

"Just trying to make you laugh."

She snorted, which was *almost* a laugh. "Am I forgiven?"

"Yeah, if you need to be."

"Okay." She nodded gently against his chest.

"You're important to me," he said. "Real, real important to me."

"You're important to me, too."

"Is it okay if I kiss your hair?"

"Yeah." She held still.

He did, and they went down to find somewhere to eat. Eventually settled in at an automat diner, her drinking a coffee, him the same, just to fit in with her.

They talked about what happened. The sex thing. The not living together thing. About the ways it hurt her, and, with Janine being patient as he figured it out for the first time by saying it all aloud, how it hurt him. He wasn't used to being hurt like that. In ways people couldn't treat with coagulants.

He told her about how the rest of the season had been going — that Marianna had said some of his stats and scores were a little down, which made Janine smile. It took him a while to understand why she'd be happy about his performance taking a hit, instead of being sad he wasn't doing well. She told him a bit about the other guys she'd been with. No real details, but Janine mainly told him about how the one made her feel how she wanted to feel — pretty — right up until she went home, alone, and then she felt very not pretty. And the other one didn't make her feel pretty, but did get her off — Edane asked her if there was a trick to doing that, because he was never sure if he was doing *that* part of sex right even after doing it on and off for a year, and she spluttered tiny giggles into her coffee.

"No, Edane," she said, dabbing up the spilled coffee with a napkin. "There's no real trick but, God. I don't know. There's stuff you could do, we could talk about that, but… not in *public*."

"Okay." Edane shrugged. "It's one of those things I kept wanting to ask about, but. It didn't feel good to ask."

She looked at him over her coffee. "I can see that, Sweetie. I put a lot of demands on you and never really gave you time to catch up."

He nodded, a little.

Janine took a sip, shoulders shrinking together. "I read the scoring rules for MilSim," she said. "Watched one of your matches — I *kind* of understood what the commentators were talking about."

"Which one?"

"A month ago? A Saturday, you had a…" She put the cup down and drew rectangles with her hands. "Big thing. *Big* gun."

"The LAMW?" He said it slowly for her — *Lamm-whuh*.

"No, you always have that one. It was, uhm. A gazebo? A *shed*, it was definitely a shed!"

"An AT-missile launcher, with a SHED-WAP. It's a kind of warhead for missiles. A dual warhead, with armor piercing and a soft explosive." He nodded. "I remember that game — I picked it up off one of the friendly teams."

"Yeah, that." She nodded, looking away, embarrassed. "Sorry, I don't like looking ignorant — anyway, you did *so* great. It was impressive, I had you on while I was cleaning the apartment. Saw you blow up the thing on replay. You did good."

He smiled a little. "Thanks."

"You're welcome."

"I don't think you're ignorant because you don't understand this stuff, Janine. I think you're *smart*. You understand *everything* I don't."

She smiled back, just a little. "I know." She shrugged a shoulder. "I like that feeling. It's just that I've never had anything in my life I couldn't pick up and understand like *that*," she said, clicking her fingers. "I didn't like struggling in front of you. I still don't."

"It actually made me feel a little better," Edane said. "Like I wasn't the only one struggling, for a change."

"You're stronger than me." She picked up her coffee, looking at him fondly over it.

"Only physically." He leaned against the table, staring down at his own cup. "I didn't realize the feeling pretty thing was hurting you so much. And for a year?"

"Not all of the year," she said. "Just some of it — some of the nights, really. I liked all the days."

"The days were pretty good," he said, nodding.

She hesitated. "Remember what you said, about bravery and pain?"

"Yeah? Pain is my friend?"

"And you can't be brave and think pain's the worst thing there is? Well. Wouldn't we be better off not being in pain? Better off being together, if that's what we both want?"

"Maybe." He bowed his head. "Probably. If I move back in, does the anniversary counter start over, or do we have the first one after I'm with you for a week?"

She laughed, and they talked about that for a bit. Calendars and anniversaries and things he didn't understand, but she did. About moving in together — she didn't want him to, not yet, but said it might be okay after they'd talked a little more, figured some things out. Given her time to decide what she wanted to do about the other men she was sleeping with. But, of course, he couldn't move in with her. Not then.

"If I'm going to Azerbaijan, I have to leave for the airport by midnight."

Janine lifted her watch, then stared into her coffee, looking for answers there. "You'll have to leave soon, then."

"Yeah. And I need to go back up and say bye to my mothers."

She stirred what was left of the coffee with her spoon, dumping in a packet of sugar. "Would you stay if I asked you to?"

"Yes."

The clinking of metal in ceramic stopped cold. When he looked up, she was staring at him like she'd never seen him before.

"What?" Edane asked.

She let the spoon rest. "I thought you were just. Just going, and this was making things were okay before you left."

"Kind of is."

"I didn't expect you to say you'd *stay* if I asked you to. When you called, I thought you were leaving to get away from me, Sweetie."

Edane shook his head. "No. It's not that."

"Then what?"

"The sky was blue."

She stared at him for a moment, searchingly. Then Janine somehow clicked, straightening up. "When you got hurt? In the marketplace? Tous?"

"Yeah. I didn't think you'd remember me telling you."

"It was important to you, of course I remember. You told me… last year?"

"Yeah."

"Going over there, to fight. It's important to you, isn't it?" She kept staring at Edane, until he looked away.

"It is," Edane said.

Janine stirred the sugar into her coffee, staring at the spiraling liquid. "Tell me."

He told her. About the sky being blue, and the black smoke. About choking dust in his mouth, and pieces of little boys on the ground — Elavarasa nearly dying on the street; Thorne giving Edane advice and telling jokes. He told her about what it was like holding a LAMW, both as a child in the barracks and now. He told her about the Muslims who hated him because he was a dog, and how much he'd appreciated the few who didn't. They ordered another coffee for her, and he stumbled over what it meant to kill someone. The difference between watching someone die, and coming to the conclusion that someone had to be killed because otherwise they'd hurt other people. The feeling he had when it happened — like he'd won, like he was important, a fulcrum that the world turned on because he'd stopped the person who'd been trying to kill him — or the civilians — from achieving their goal, and killed them instead. The sick war in his own head about what that meant, if it was moral to kill.

He told her what Marianna said.

"I walked into Tajikistan whole. I chose to go there, Janine. But I didn't choose to come back."

Tears glinted in her green eyes, her coffee held to her mouth. Staring at him.

Janine sipped from the cup, and set it down. Gently put her hand on his, in a way that was warm, but he didn't understand. "You need to go, Edane. And if you choose to come back — I'll be here for you."

He set his hand on hers, and he didn't understand the warmth behind his chest. "I'll come back," he said. "If only to visit, I'll always come back."

III
Lost

::/ Dushanbe, Tajikistan.
::/ March, 2104.
::/ Edane Estian.

The warning lights on the perimeter fence flashed a dull pink, rain coming down in big drops that thudded into Tajikistan's dry earth and were swallowed up immediately.

Contaminated.

The rainwater dripping off the rim of Edane's wet weather cover — an oval dish of plastic, like one of the Chinese refugee traditional hats, strapped over his helmet — was theoretically awash with chemical and biological contaminants left over from the Eurasian war. Maybe one raindrop in a thousand was laced with one of those tiny killer spores, or had caught up a dust particle laced with the crop-killing caustics that got swept off the dustbowl and built up in cracks in the ground and stagnant pools over decades until it reduced fish in untended garden ponds to a thin layer of oozing scum on the surface.

Edane eyed the rivulets of water pouring off his cover, too fast to count. One drop in a thousand was enough.

Edane didn't like the rain, here. Apparently the rain had been like this all over the world for a few years, just after the Eurasian War, when the out of control biowarfare agents got into the water cycle and all the wars everywhere petered out as people turned their time and attention to surviving, instead of killing each other. Here, in Tajikistan, with the dead flats of Mongolia somewhere over the mountains to the east, there were contamination warnings every few weeks.

It'd be nice when the clouds went away again. Left the skies clear.

Even if Thorne and the rest of his teammates working for HPC international were fully vaccinated, they didn't take chances with the rain. They trudged back in from patrol, coming in through the north end of the highway checkpoint that marked the border between the mountains and the city of Dushanbe, crossing the line in the sand between quarantine and vaccination, between trusted local civilians and the unknown rural population.

The HPC international team left their armored personnel carriers parked five hundred meters up the highway, in the fenced-off inspection area where the vehicles would be washed clean with bleach after the rain stopped. Thorne and the other European private military contractors bounced along the highway in their rain-slicks, wearing their ricepicker tops — what they called the conical version of what Edane was wearing — with the brims bent down on the sides, sluicing water past their shoulders. They moved heads down and hunched forward.

Edane had their personal IFFs up, the system in his goggles pinging them as he glanced over each. He handed his brother Sokolai the volatiles sniffer — theoretically to be used on pedestrians walking in and out of Dushanbe, but there would be none today — and jogged out to meet the old man.

Edane's tail was bound up in waterproof tape, but even waterproofed it got cold when he leaned forward and the water ran off it, though the cold wasn't as bad this month. It was mad, the safety regs here, with rain. Especially when Edane watched the civilians in it, letting it get on their bare skin — the rurals drinking it, as he'd seen out in the hinterland on patrol, thinking fresh rainwater to be safer than the standing barrels they watered cattle with.

Thorne lifted his hand as Edane got closer. "You should see what we found," he croaked from beneath the brim of his ricepicker, face wrapped in a filter mask, goggles up on his forehead. The corners of his eyes crinkled, partly from age, partly because he might have been smiling. "Shaw, pass up our prize trophy."

Shaw, a much younger soldier, gestured for his squadmate Ellings to turn around. He plucked an object from the strapping of her backpack, and brought it up, clasped in thick weatherproof gloves.

A pinched, dirty silver cylinder. About the length of Edane's arm. Heavy. A mortar bomb, unfired, propellant charge locked in under its tailfins, ablative shielding untouched by anti-ordnance lasers and covering the warts of its submunitions like a silver skin. Edane didn't know the exact make, but he recognized the arming pin, still in, and the electrical firing socket, still covered with its port protector.

"Just like the dissidents have been throwing into the city every other night," Thorne said, proudly. "Pulled it out of a cache we found and blew the rest — this one's our souvenir. Already cooked it," by which he meant passed it under radio waves intense enough to burn out every scrap of circuitry in the device, "but I think we'll ask the armorer to drill out the explosives and leave it inert before we take it home, just to be on the safe side."

Edane took the bomb, turning it over in his hands while he walked in with them. He'd never seen one before — only heard the rattle of fragments and submunitions bouncing off buildings, the distant boom of them airbursting at night. "This isn't an autoloader bomb," he said, checking again for clamping points. "This is for hand-loading. The dissidents aren't using automatic mortars?"

"No, son, no." Thorne shook his head emphatically. "It's tubes in the hillsides. Not even real mortars — just some half-buried piping angled at the city, and a phone cabled into the bomb. Bloody impossible to find once it's in, and they just telephone up with some coordinates, and the fin guidance does the rest."

Edane didn't know whether or not he liked the mortar bomb. Automatic installations were one thing, with a gimballed turret and autoloader — an actual weapon. Weapons could be misused, but they were supposed to be for fighting with. Buried mortars in the mountains, aimed so you could only hit Dushanbe, all you could do with that was try and blow up civilians. This was something different to a weapon of war. Something that felt wrong, just holding it.

He gave back the bomb, but helped when Shaw struggled to put it back on Ellings's backpack, and walked Thorne and the rest through the wire cage of the checkpoints.

"You going to put it in your house?" Edane asked. "For your grandchildren to look at?"

Thorne shook his head a little. "No. Down at the Cockerel and Hound, I think. It'd look fine on the wall, wouldn't it Shaw?"

Shaw nodded, smiling. Not dutifully — glad to be going back home.

"What's the Cockerel and Hound?" Edane asked.

"Our regular pub at home. Just down from the Kent office."

Kent was a district of London, Edane thought. Kind of like the Esplanade back home, but greener. "You're really leaving?"

"We have to, son. When the government ramps up their internet censorship at the end of the week, we don't have enough exempt bandwidth to send our telemetry home. It wouldn't be legal to work here, I've told you this before."

"You could get re-registered. Military Contractors registered in the MACP don't need the monitoring telemetry, just combatant licensing. K-Level licensing is a five-day intensive workshop — you could be back by the end of the month."

"And what happens when I shoot someone without a live-linked feed to verify it was all nice and legal, hmm? Then Her Majesty's government put me under a mercenary's investigation the moment I step back home — no thank you."

"Andercom's lawyers…"

Thorne laughed. "You know what the tabloids at home say about Andercom West?"

"No?"

"Call them the bloody SS thugs of the corporate Nazi Reich."

Edane flattened his ears back against his helmet. "The who?"

"Nazi?" Thorne glanced back, eyebrow raised. "Don't they teach you anything in South America? The Second World War, son — Britain's finest hour!"

Edane shrugged. "Middle American Corporate Preserve," he said, lamely. "We didn't get a lot of wars in history class."

"Got Coke and McDonalds and Disney, I bet."

"Disney," Edane agreed. "We had that in media class. I don't know McDonalds."

"Bless him. A dog who doesn't know about McDonalds." Thorne's teammates laughed. "Then again, perhaps that's for the best!" They laughed harder.

"Was that lifting a corner?" Edane asked, glancing back. "Derailing the conversation by making people laugh?"

"In a way. But for it to work I'd need to make you laugh." Thorne stopped at the inner checkpoint, looking at Edane, but the corners of his eyes were crinkled in a different way, this time. "I'm not sure what makes you laugh."

"Me either," Edane said. "Please stay, Thorne. I can't talk to the locals like you can — you've seen how they look at me and my brothers. With you gone it's almost only going to be us left."

"I can't." The old man patted Edane's shoulder, the thump of it warm, even if it was deadened by layers of protective uniform fabric. "But it's a hell of a thing, this. Never had a dog tell me to stay, before. Always the other way around."

Edane bobbed his head, the once, looking down at Thorne's hand. "I get that joke," he said, smiling just to show willing.

"Good. But it's no joke when I tell you *not* to stay, Edane." Thorne let his hand drop to the butt of his rifle, hanging off his shoulder sling. "Censorship's the last resort of tyrants before everything falls to hell. This country's going nowhere good."

"I know," Edane replied. "But where else can I be a soldier, Thorne? It's either here or Ecuador, and the weather's never this nice in Ecuador."

Thorne laughed, turning to look at Dushanbe, misty and blurred in the falling, poisonous rain. "Well, there is that."

"Did I do it right?"

"Hm?"

"Lifting a corner. Derailing the conversation with something funny. I do it right?"

Thorne looked back up at him, and the corners of his eyes crinkled the right way, like he was happy. "That you did, son. That you did."

EDANE DIDN'T MANAGE to do it again. The locals just stared at him, even when he tried to tell the jokes in Tajik instead of English, so he gave up and let the translator do the talking for him. His Tajik wasn't all that good, anyway.

The Private Military Contractor Liaison gave out different jobs in the weeks and months that followed Thorne's departure. Instead of just handling checkpoints like before, and going on patrol with Thorne and the other Europeans, now Edane and his brothers had to do the city patrols by themselves. It was harder, after the police strike in Kuktosh wound down with the government giving in.

In response almost all the police started striking, or starting go-slows, doing the bare minimum of work in protest. Sitting back and letting local militants scream and riot, leaving Edane and his brothers to hold them back from the parts of the city that the government wanted kept safe — which were almost always the only parts the rioters wanted to wreck. It got bad, really bad, when some of the rioters started trying to take over, declare themselves the de facto authorities. The dissidents, the ones being backed by Uzbekistan, they even tried rolling into a disputed town with tanks during one of the riots. Three of Edane's brothers had died there, but the government was still barely in control.

Barely in control wasn't the same as in control.

There had been nobody to stop it when rioters and protestors swarmed into the eastern camps, where the Chinese refugees lived after the Eurasian War. It didn't matter that they helped farm and run the city, like everybody else, it didn't matter that they were citizens too, nobody stopped it when the dissidents crying out for revolution lynched a dozen refugees over street lamps. Nobody ordered Edane to intervene, nobody did anything except wait for it to happen again.

The only time Edane got ordered to do anything was when a relative of a government official got shot, and then he had to go door-to-door in downtown Dushanbe to try and find witnesses, as if *he* was a police officer, because the police weren't doing anything.

At least it was dry, again. Dust boiled up into the road as the street's potholes took another car's tire, rocking the vehicle like it'd been hit by a mine.

Edane and Sokolai were taking one side of the street, Esparza and Elavarasa the other. Edane had been talking all day, and getting angrily stared at, so he didn't want to be the one to talk to the people behind the next doorway, but Sokolai had talked to the last ones, so it was Edane's turn. He hesitated as long as he reasonably could, sipping water from his pouch, getting his mouth wet before moving on.

The local people dodged around him, left a clear space around him and Sokolai as they went about their business. Things were busy, today, but a little kid up on the sidewalk caught Edane's eye. Walking back and forth in a big thick woolen coat that was wrong for the weather, stepping out into the road on his own before ducking back onto the sidewalk when a car or truck or something roared by.

"He's going to get himself run over," Sokolai muttered.

"Wonder where the parents are." Edane glanced around, hoping to spot some worried looking women, or maybe men — men could be parents too, he reminded himself. Nobody. "Sometimes kids are out alone," he said.

"Yeah, in the rural villages." Sokolai shook his head. "Ain't seen it in town so far."

The little boy wandered up the road, checking on the traffic, looking for a place to cross. Edane watched him a little longer, then pushed the drinking tube back into the pouch pocket. "Okay. Let's do the next door."

"Right."

Edane tried to put the little kid out of his mind, and Esparza and Elavarasa across the road too, and brought up his rifle's stock to bang on the next door. It was a little alleyway, a dim little corridor. A man had opened the door, women were looking out. "We're looking for witnesses to the murder in the street yesterday," he said.

By the time the translator finished saying it all over again in Tajik, the people were arguing with each other, yelling. Edane sighed and lifted his rifle to bang against the doorframe for their attention.

Somewhere behind him, the little boy searched for a way across the road.

11. Born Killers

::/ Saatly Farmlands, Azerbaijan.
::/ April, 2106.
::/ Edane Estian.

The sky wasn't blue, but red, scarred by the sunrise.

Edane, Eissen, Sieden and Siegen. On the march. A hundred and ten kilometers as the crow flew, thirty of those down in six hours, with forty-five actually covered on the ground thanks to the terrain's realities. The air was blessedly cool, astonishingly crisp and clean. Edane's feet hurt.

They'd been shipped on a charter flight to Turkey. A big fat bribe had bought them the run of a military airfield — that was the way to fight a war, with bribery, but the crowdfunding couldn't rustle up enough to simply pay off the old government and get them to fuck off.

Eissen and Edane had met Sieden and Siegen on the flight, between cat-napping and coordinating with the others. Self-organizing into fireteams. Sieden and Siegen were a sequential pair — Cyan Twenty-Five and Twenty-Six — who managed to be adopted together after the Emancipation. Neither spoke very much, but they didn't need to. Nods and agreement got them further.

Most of their gear was stock — leftovers from Tajikistan and work in Bolivia, bought off Andercom and the subsidiary PMCs that'd closed down. The uniforms all fit, the camouflage still cycled, but it felt strange to be wearing someone else's uniform. So Edane had blacked over the name strip with a marker and written his own name and production serial number into the uniform's lining.

From Turkey they'd been dropped by a swing-jet VTOL plane, ten kilometers short of Azerbaijan's southern border with North Persia. Other teams had been put down north, in Dagestan — still others were working their way up the southern coast.

Edane's group — code-tagged as Hunt-Three — had drawn the short straw. They had the smallest distance to cover, the most direct route, no significant border fortifications... instead of one of the wire-framed collapsible cars some of the other teams had gotten, Edane got spiked with a needle in either thigh.

There had been only so much space on the charter plane, and the wide-gauge needles were a whole lot smaller and lighter than collapsible cars. They contained strings of slow-release corticosteroids, some kind of glucose mix that was supposed to keep his muscles fueled for six or seven hours, an enzymatic release implant specifically banned for use in athletics, and a woven chemical mat unfurling under his skin that was seeping new drugs into his system depending on the metabolic markers it detected.

Edane's feet hurt. They weren't supposed to, and his boots were strapped right, but there was fuck-all he could do about it. Just keep moving under the weight of the LAMW over his back, following Sieden and Siegen. The two were bouncing over the terrain at a pace that varied between a jog and a sprint, never slowing for longer than it took to flick their goggles on and off to check the sky before running on.

Now, as dawn broke, even Sieden and Siegen stopped in place and pulled their goggles up onto their helmets, blinking out at the sky and farmland before them.

The crop was young, a lake of rippling green stalks stretching up to their knees. The crop tenders were silhouetted against the changing sky. Black staves sixty feet tall, their mirrory heads turned to face first light like mechanical sunflowers. The tenders moved slowly. They were tall and slender robots, braced on long arms that almost seemed rooted to the ground, swaying in the breeze, stretching and bending, pumping fluid through their limbs with the pressure of the wind.

Black spikes against the horizon, as far as Edane could see. An endless thinly scattered forest. Their mirror-heads twitched, flexing to collect the sunlight and reflect it down at the ground, bobbing points of focused light skimming between the narrow rows of the crops. Each one focused on a weed or tracked after a bug — sometimes sweeping over the scuffs left in Hunt-Three's wake.

The crop tenders were basically mindless automata. Built to do one thing and one thing alone — kill. They did it slowly, or quickly, in an ecologically friendly way. Using sunlight to burn out individual crop pests, slowly scorching the leaves of weeds until they died, like a swarm of kids going after individual ants with magnifying glasses.

On his way past one, curious, Edane slowed down and shoved at its trunk with the stock of his LAMW. The tender swayed, the EMWAR gear Sieden was carrying registering not even a gnat's-fart of a transmission from the telephone-pole beasts. Edane ducked under one of its thin side-limbs and glanced back at it as it mindlessly used the dawn's light to focus on a lost seedling, determined to kill it no matter how long it took.

Edane wondered what corporation built the robots, and whether or not he and it had shared any designers. If some reference in the crop tender's engineering specifications pointed to the same references in Edane's project documentation.

His feet hurt. He ran anyway. They hurt no more, and no less, kilometers later when the team encountered their first real piece of resistance. A black-topped road.

Siegen knelt beside it, while Sieden checked the feed from the plastic-cased panel antenna on his back.

"Solar charged smart-road," Sieden announced. "Part of Baku's road network. Pressure-sensitive. No idea if it's networked into military intelligence."

The light was clear, but Edane couldn't see a fucking thing on the horizon yet. No skyscrapers, no sign of life, just dry hills and irrigated green patches broken up with more and more rolls of dusty earth the further he looked in their direction of travel.

Eissen remained silent, sipping his water. Bricks of ammunition strapped to every part of his body, the magazines black under the camouflaged strapping holding it all together.

Eissen was carrying slightly more weight than Edane, but better distributed over his body. The LAMW Edane had been given was an unfamiliar mass pulling at either his right or left shoulder, depending on how he shifted it on the body-strapping. He'd had enough time on the plane to get familiar with it, some German design he'd never met, and the basic mechanical principles behind the loading and firing mechanism were comprehensible enough. Even so, it threw off his stride and he hadn't tried firing it yet. An unfamiliar weapon, even though he'd locked his MilSim LAMW's scope to it and burned in new hardstate software chips with the fabricator on the plane.

The LAMW wouldn't be much good against the road surface, though.

Siegen pulled down the cloth of his facemask, panting into the air — his mouth visible this close as a blot of erroneous heat marked up in Edane's goggles with an outlined overlay. He didn't speak, just gestured.

Query — move around obstacle.

His brother Sieden covered his goggles with a hand, blanking out the world so he could check the map in virtual space without distraction. "Bridge five-and-a-half kay east. Might be able to get under the road there."

Eissen looked left, right — up at the real threat, the sky above. "If we ping the road, what's going to make us look different to civvie foot traffic?"

Nearest contact — settlement — four kilometers — follow linear landmark, Sieden responded in four snaps of his hands, pointing alongside the road.

The Azeri government would have to have some fairly intensive search algorithms running on their road network to pick up and tag their footsteps as questionable, but the risk wasn't worth it — Andercom's EMWAR people would have set up custom AIs to look for exactly that kind of anomalous foot traffic within two hours, and the Azeris had a head start of nearly two days.

Hunt-Three had no commanding officer, no set leader, but Edane and his brothers set off in perfect coordination after discussing the problem for a couple of minutes.

The road was an anomaly in the landscape. Beautifully made, eating light to power itself and store energy for the contactless vehicle chargers along its length, probably lain at a cost of millions of nudies a mile. And the first crossroads leading onto this beautiful road was a dirt track cut out of the earth with spades, leading through a farm fence and alongside a neglected field laying fallow.

The second crossroads was almost worse — cracked asphalt that'd gone without maintenance so long it was really just lumps of flat stone, rather than a single contiguous surface. It was a side-road leading into the settlement Sieden had mentioned; a village, its main street patched over with tar and concrete, but still obviously neglected when they checked it over through the bulky matte lenses on their rifles.

The village's name on Sieden's map didn't match the one on the beat-up sign, and Edane wasn't sure how to pronounce either of them. Perhaps the name had changed and the map hadn't updated, or maybe there had never been the money to replace the sign — it didn't look like there'd been the money for anything. The only reason the road looked like that was because it was part of the network leading to Baku. The place had been left to rot by the government, right next to a road that'd cost more in public works funds than had been spent on the town in its entire history, Edane guessed. Hell, even the automatic turrets laying siege to the village were cheaper than the road.

There were four turrets that they'd seen and tagged — a pair on each of the two roads leading out of town. No dead people in the streets, but the occasional flash of heat in windows revealed an uncovered face, and the buildings were warm enough that at least some of them were currently being heated. Trails of smoke rose from their chimneys, as though Edane had stepped back into an exclusively fossil-fuel burning society.

Four turrets, holding twenty times that many people hostage, keeping them bottled up instead of protesting, or running for the border. Not a nice thing to do, but efficient, even Edane had to admit.

"We can't just leave them," Eissen muttered.

"I can nail all four turrets from here if I have to," Edane replied, head ducked to the glass part of his LAMW's scope, not just watching its feed in his goggles. "We can clear it, take one of the local's cars to make up lost time."

"Like the plan," Sieden murmured. "Me too," Siegen added.

None of them did a thing except think about it. Muse on it. Oh, they all wanted to be heroes. Edane could feel the need churning in his gut — but none of the people besieged in their own homes were in imminent danger. There wasn't any efficient way to deal with the problem they could come up with between the four of them, even if there were dozens of emotionally satisfying options.

If they took action, the turrets would lose their connections to whatever network they were on. Sieden's EMWAR kit could theoretically link up with home for someone to remotely set up a man in the middle attack — replacing the downed turrets' signals with a falsified one, telling the Azeri regime's network that everything was just fine while Edane and the others destroyed the turrets, but that would both eat time and open themselves up to signal interception by the enemy. And if it went wrong — there was a good chance it would — the Azeris would be able to send a few overflight drones to search for them. Detection was the major threat. They were even communicating vocally — voices didn't carry nearly as far as radio waves and couldn't be picked up with EMWAR gear. As for the car to make up for the time they lost… that'd have monitors built in, and show up on aerial imaging much too clearly.

Something flashed red in the town, and a loud warning played — toned like an industrial hazard message, barking a few short words Edane didn't understand over and over. Someone down in the town, who'd dared take a step out of their own front door. A disposable monitor stood in the middle of the street, its warning lights whirling around and round.

The civilian, a grey-haired old man, backed up and shut his front door.

This wasn't the mission. The mission was to run another sixty kilometers and get into position to move on Baku by nightfall. Infiltrate the city, tie up the Azeri army in time-wasting guerrilla harassment.

Edane uploaded the contact coordinates to their electronic person-to-person networked map — murmured commentary to it. Eissen had already flagged the town with a brief overview of the situation, Edane added his opinion that the place needed urgent relief and bumped it to high priority.

"Can you guys mark it too?" he asked, packing up the LAMW. "If we all mark it, it'll receive higher priority on the system if it's just one of us. That way the system will flag it for attention sooner, once we update with the rest of the task force."

Sieden and Siegen did it together — they'd never used a MilSim style coordination map before. "Like that?" One of them asked.

Edane checked, nodded, and folded in the LAMW's bipod, slinging it back over his shoulder.

They cut around the village and found the short bridge keeping the road level over a fold in the land, kind of like an oversized culvert. They had to belly-crawl underneath, but got through, and set off running directly cross-country toward Baku instead of following the road's curve towards the coast highway.

One of the follow-up teams would get rid of the turrets. Maybe a UAV, if any could be brought up. The village would be helped, in time.

Edane glanced back, once, to spot the white glare of one of the village's buildings, then powered down his uniform's electronics other than those required to keep his camouflage updated and turned his back on them.

It wasn't a good feeling, abandoning those people. Worse than the ache in his feet by far, but Edane ignored the guilt as easily as he ignored the pain.

Baku by nightfall. That was his objective. He ignored everything else, and ran.

12. The Wall

::/ Baku, Azerbaijan.
::/ April, 2106.
::/ Edane Estian.

Edane limped after Siegen and Sieden, something wet gathering in his boot. He didn't want to think about it, didn't want to show weakness, wanted to fight and fight and fight, but that wasn't the responsible thing to do. Not right now.

Room clear, Eissen gestured through the flat-topped, two story building's upper window as they neared.

Sieden stalked forward, his long assault rifle's stock tucked partially over his shoulder, grip held tight, body turned to pull the weapon in close to himself and shorten its length relative to his body. Making their way inside with silent footsteps, sweeping slowly, looking for trouble. There wasn't any — just a cat lying silent on a pile of rags, green eyes blazing up at Edane as he passed by. The lower floor seemed to be an office of some kind — desks and chairs, anyway — lots of storage. The upstairs was open, a long hall with working areas and weird horse-shoe shaped machines he'd never seen before, with needles. The map profile for the building, once they set up the weakest connection they dared to, was for some kind of clothing manufactory, but there weren't any cutters or fabricators. Just the U-shaped needle machines.

Eissen thought it might be manual clothing manufacturing, but Edane, Siegen and Sieden didn't think so — hand-made bespoke clothes were expensive, a big money business, and this place was a shithole.

Nightfall was coming. They had to prepare. Get updates, upload what they'd found, find out what had changed, set up cameras, prepare, eat, drink.

The attacks on the north border through Dagestan had gone well. Azeri army units had been pulled into skirmishes across the northern sectors of the country — grids labelled A, B, and C on the coordinated map with no regard for local provinces or borders. No deaths among Edane's brothers so far, four hundred and five kills based on automated analysis of rifle and scope camera trigger-pull footage.

Hunt-Two had been pinged by UAVs while they were driving — two stabilized casualties, the rest of Hunt-Two were still pulling their wounded brothers in random patterns to nowhere in specific, attempting to get away from the area before the next set of UAVs came up to replace the ones shot down. Hunt-One had yet to make any kind of report at all, silent since they'd crossed the border sixty kilometers from where Edane's Hunt-Three had.

The ultrasonic probe from the medical kit, and the doctor back home, said that Siegen had hairline fractures in both shinbones.

"*How* far have you run?"

Siegen checked his goggles. "One hundred eighty one kilometers, three hundred and eighty two meters, over fourteen hours, fifty-two minutes. Is that medically relevant?"

The human doctor stared at him through the screen. "No. If I tell you to take plenty of bed-rest, you won't listen, will you?"

"Sir, no sir."

She blinked at Siegen, confused. But Siegen had probably spent more time with his brother Sieden than humans, never really getting acclimatized to ideas like male *and* female.

They splinted Siegen — according to the doctor, Edane had something called an avulsion fracture. One of the tendons connected to the side of his ankle had partially ripped off a shard of bone, leaving it barely connected to the main bone mass. Had to be bandages, tight bandages, because surgery wasn't an option. He pushed splint-bars into his boot's straps, locking his ankle, too. Laced it real tight after cleaning the patch of skin and fur that'd been rubbed down to bloody meat by the fit of his boot — lacing it tighter didn't make walking any less painful, but the support kept him from needing to limp. Eissen had the same thing on his knee.

None of them pretended not to be in pain, not to the doctor. They listed their problems as rapidly and efficiently as they could — she directed them to apply bandages and coagulants. Not a combat first aid specialist, but she did, at least, have a little experience with Edane and his brothers. She didn't bother suggesting pain killers, and they didn't ask. These weren't those kinds of wounds, and they had work to do.

Bracing themselves with strapping under their armor, clean socks, tightened or loosened boots as required, splints and bandages, pulling out their athletic under-skin implants and jabbing in fresh ones to ease the nagging ache in their muscles to an almost pleasant burn — that would be enough. It had to be enough. They had to be ready for the night's work.

The doctor checked their blood chemistry remotely, warned them that they were all wrecks in dire need of sleep, food, and water, and signed off to give remote treatment and advice to the next batch of brothers.

They tested the tap water, found it to be clean of contaminants, and drank until they couldn't. Ate their rations, rearranged their backpacks, took five minutes to check their social networks — Edane's mothers had sent a quick video from the kitchen, just a short 'good luck and be safe', Janine had sent something a little longer and heartfelt in text. He responded to both as quickly as he could — the MilSim team and Marianna's message, *'Don't make us look bad'*, didn't need a reply beyond a click on the thumbs-up beside it.

The sky was red again, after being blue for so very long. Soon it'd be black.

Nightfall was coming. Killing was coming.

Edane's feet hurt, and his back hurt, and the patch over his thigh covering the second implant site was bleeding a little more than the first one had. There was satellite imagery of Azeri kill teams moving north, no doubt there would be more in the city proper — soldiers whose whole goal was simply to kill Edane.

It was, he thought, almost exactly like the car ride to Grandpa Jeff's. Being cooped up, and helpless, and knowing that there was a huge yard waiting for him and vat-grown globs of meat for the grill in the trunk, and that Grandpa Jeff was gonna come over and ruffle Edane's ears the *second* the car doors opened again. Except Edane liked being a little bit hurt, and this time when the car doors opened, he was going to kill someone. It was a good feeling. He hated that it was a good feeling, but couldn't help from smiling anyway.

Grandpa Jeff wouldn't like it.

DETECTION WAS NO longer the threat it was. With hundreds of buildings to use as cover, and hundreds of random heat sources to blend in with, they even walked across the roads without much fear.

There were sixteen of them in the city proper. The faster they got to work, the sooner more of them could get in.

Edane's first position with Eissen was a rundown office block, blowing the building's connectivity node and beating down an Azeri night watchman with more patriotism than sense, leaving him disarmed but still walking with a clear message, albeit ran through their translators. *Vacate the area. There is a public emergency services building three blocks northwest, attend it for medical aid.*

Fifteen minutes later Edane was cracking a hole in the upper floor's walls with an entrenching tool, ripping out bricks to open up a shooting position, while Eissen set up grenades in the other rooms to mousehole the walls.

The streets were relatively clear in this part of Baku. The protests were happening further out where the poor lived, this was the money part of town, the part the protestors were being kept out of. The part where the army and riot police were organizing themselves and handling logistics between anti-protest actions.

Three shots. One through a police car's engine, the LAMW leaping into Edane's shoulder for the first time, rocking back perfectly into position on its bipod, though the hydraulic shock-absorption cylinders were squeaking — too new and unused, the seals yet to soften. A second shot through an equipment locker in the back of one of the riot police armored vehicles, throwing shreds of body-armor and broken riot shields in a conical plume across the vehicle's interior, possibly wounding one of the drivers, but not — Edane hoped — killing him. The police weren't for killing; they wore, until the rules of engagement were updated, the wrong kind of uniform.

The right kind of uniform had cut-glass creases and a speckling of color over one shoulder, an oversized visored cap — the semi-formal wear of a desk jockey, but a desk jockey in the army and wearing a sidearm. Sadly one life was currently not worth the seventy-five nudies each armor piercing solid core shell cost, so Edane waited a few seconds until the man ran for cover behind another police car, and then shot him through it.

The desk-officer's body fell out from behind the car in a limp two-part fall, flopping with a snap like he had a brand new hinge installed somewhere he'd never bent before.

Something about the scarlet under the street lights made Edane's gut tighten. Made him *happy*, sang in his nerves — the guy was barely a combatant, barely fighting, but Edane knew it was the men behind the desks who did far more damage than he ever could. He reminded himself of that, his thoughts gloomy, his heart and gut *singing*.

The suppressor locked over the LAMW's muzzle dripped steaming foam, its baffles slowly spinning down and slinging droplets across the ceiling and floors alike. It didn't make the noise appreciably softer, but it did transform the telltale thundercrack of a LAMW's blast into a muffled uneven roar, different every time thanks to its dynamic baffles, which could be enough to confuse triangulation software's interpretation by altering the signature sound of a given weapon.

"Anything else worth shooting?" Eissen asked mildly.

Edane handsignalled *negative* and pulled up the LAMW. Eissen blew the grenades, and the room filled with smoke and dust, hot even through Edane's facemask. A hole grenade-blasted into the stairwell got them downstairs without entering the hallway. They marched over broken desks and computers to get at the mousehole the next grenade had torn through the exterior wall. Eissen kicked brickwork and boards out at the edges before slithering through — Edane unclipped the LAMW and passed it outside before following, the first buzz of UAVs in the air *already*.

Edane heard the uneven stutter of a rifle somewhere to his left — could only make out Siegen by the IFF querymark that popped up when Edane focused in his direction. Siegen adjusted his point of aim, fired again, the buzzing of UAV engines turned into the grinding of dying lift fans, and then the other half of Hunt-Three was moving. Edane stopped in an alley to haul the cooling net in his facemask back up, cooling each inhalation and exhalation through a grid of capillaried fibers that sweated water chilled by a chemical pack, both to help hide the heat of his breath and to cool him down as he ran with his brothers, leaving the shoot site behind them.

Edane struggled with the feeling of having killed someone for the fourth time in his life, because this was the first time he'd killed someone who hadn't shot at him first. But that was the LAMW's role. *His* role. That's what he'd done on the MilSim field thousands of times.

The fifth time was barely half an hour later, backed up in someone's bedroom.

The locals had been aware something was happening when their building's internal network went down, and their commercial electronics lost their signal thanks to Sieden's portable EMWAR unit and a remote connection to an EMWAR server back home, providing falsified signals to feed into Baku's city network. Even so, they hadn't expected having the dogs start beating down their doors. They hadn't wanted to leave — who the hell wanted to leave their home? Many of them didn't understand, the children especially.

"*We paid for you to save us, we paid for you to save us,*" a particularly young one cried at him, caught up in his or her mother's arms. They were too young for Edane to figure out their gender, and he didn't understand if the clothes and their colors meant girl or boy over here.

"This city is a war zone," Edane told them through his vest translator. "The fighting is here now, you need to leave safely. The government will fire on this building now, you need to evacuate."

Not all of them did, and not all of them supported what was being done. At least one of them, Edane figured, would call up the local police when they got out from under Sieden's EMWAR jamming.

He did his best to find a room as far away as possible from anywhere occupied, far from where the people who couldn't bear to leave, who didn't want to leave, were barricading themselves up in their bathrooms. It turned out to be someone's bedroom, a big double bed with pictures beside it of two Azeri people, a man and a woman. There was an 'I love you' cat meme picture on the wallscreen's powered-off desktop. A hardcopy book, maybe the Koran, was open on the dresser — but the man was cleanshaven, and in none of the pictures on their walls did the woman wear a headscarf.

None of the people they'd asked to leave the building had spat on him because he was a dog. Some of them had called him that, dog, look at the dog, the dog says we must leave, but never in a way that made it sound like an insult.

Edane had thought all Muslims hated dogs. That's what it'd been like in Tajikistan. Why not here? Was it the Western clothes? They dressed like people dressed back home, their apartment wasn't all that different, though every bathroom Edane had seen had a kind of bidet on a hose, or something similar for washing, not just toilet paper.

A perfectly normal family had lived in the apartment that was now his shooting position. Their skin was a pinkish color that was a little different than what Edane was used to in white people at home, and their hair was pretty dark, and some of their things were different, but they were a normal family and Edane and his brothers had thrown them out, and in case they had to come back here to fight later, Siegen and Sieden were hacking mouseholes in their home's walls for better room-to-room access, but without setting up any boobytraps — they'd agreed that would be wrong with so many civilians still around. One of them might try to get home.

Blackish-yellow plumes of smoke were coiling into the sky on the horizon, the protest barricades lighting up the smoke from beneath. Armored fighting vehicles — army, this time, not police — were rolling jerkily across a square about half a kilometer away, their dismounted infantry peering into storefronts with flashlights, not goggles. Edane wasn't sure whether it was because they didn't have adaptive night vision that would let a user peer into the shadows without the city's illumination washing out the rest of their vision, or if the flashlights on the ends of their rifles were supposed to be scary to the civilians, but all the flashlights did was turn them into targets.

Edane spotted the soldier wearing an EMWAR kit only because the panel antenna wasn't strapped to his armor, the way it should have been, like Sieden's, but riding high on top of his backpack instead. Edane destroyed it and killed him — hitting him so hard between the shoulders that his head broke off when he hit the ground. The LAMW shell cut through someone behind the EMWAR soldier too, but non-fatally, tearing through the leg before blowing a crater into the street surface further back still. Eissen let rip with his heavy rifle, killing five more in one stutter of gunfire, leaving a trail of bodies over the street.

Now the family that lived here's window was broken, and an automatic turret on one of the passing armored fighting vehicles was spitting chains of lead over their building's facade, breaking through windows and chewing into brick, uncertain exactly where the shots had been fired from but knowing which half of the building it had been.

Edane hoped the people who had stayed behind had gotten sufficiently low to the floor. That the people who had gone down to the ground floor had piled enough furniture against the walls, were sitting under their tables and in their doorframes, like waiting for an earthquake, in case the building got hit with something heavier than a machine gun.

Again, they left.

Hunt-Three struck again and again, at a tempo of around one engagement every forty minutes because of the time it took to clear out civilians and cut holes for exfiltration. But it worked.

The human soldiers were either asleep on their feet or buzzing on stay-awake drugs, chasing Edane and his brothers, forced to send out more and more patrols, wasting their resources on trying to hold the city instead of hitting the protest barricades. UAVs buzzed over the city all night, getting plinked down one after the other by Siegen and Sieden, shooting so much they had to top up their suppressors twice with the water-polymer gunk that helped distort the noise and prevent automated triangulation.

His foot hurt, and all his joints were swollen. There was something wrong with his left hand, for a change, making it click funny when he bent it all the way back — so he didn't.

Edane didn't sleep, either. When daylight came the job didn't stop, the objectives changed.

EDANE ATE A leisurely breakfast at ten-forty five AM, gathered with Eissen and Siegen and Sieden in a partly looted supermarket, while everything else changed, too. The news on the local pirate wireless, and even on the official channels, was going crazy.

Edane and the rest of his brothers in the city had been branded terrorists, a screaming man was bawling at the UN to sanction not Azerbaijan, but the government-backed terrorists now on their soil, blaming everybody — the *Norteamericanos*, the Western Europeans, the MACP, *everybody*.

Edane washed out his water pouch and left one of his used up chemical coolant packs to cook in a microwave with the first sachet of the three chemical additives needed to reset it. Ate a sandwich he made from stolen food — cold canned fish gunk and rice cakes, choice limited by what had been left by the looters. Watched the clipped down news reports from the uncensored internet that had been highlighted as 'worth five minutes' and loaded on the operation's chat forum.

It was hilarious, watching this Nesimi guy talk. Like he lived in some kind of bizarre alternate universe where his regime hadn't just been executing protestors in the streets, hadn't been grabbing people out of their homes. The UN promised a full investigation into the matter, which meant they'd get to it in a few months when everything was over, the uninvolved governments promised full cooperation, and the MACP sent one of the Tri-Corporate Special Interest Group PR people to explain to Azerbaijan's government, patiently, that the Tri-Corp's charters did not allow it to interrupt legitimate commercial activities, and that all persons recorded as leaving the MACP with firearms were duly accredited and certified, and that their identities and further details could be applied for in a freedom of information request which would be processed after ninety days due to one of the trade secrets protection acts.

In short, go fuck yourself and apply for the information like the rest of the public and ethics watchdogs had, sending in the correct forms and everything. Edane wasn't nervous — he had combatant licensing, he'd signed his liability of litigation waivers. The only sticky part was whether or not his employers — the brothers running the crowdfunding — had any authority to employ him, but that was their legal responsibility, not his. Unless he deviated from their rules of engagement, of course, or if he followed rules of engagement that weren't legal, like shooting non-combatants.

The part that wasn't funny was what the Azeri regime were doing inside the country.

They were taking civilians hostage. The secret police were rolling up in armored fighting vehicles with explosive reactive countermeasure pods on the sides and hauling away one or two members from every family.

"We will deal with this disrespect for authority," they said, seizing private electronics, searching for evidence that money had been sent to the crowdfunding addresses. When it had, they dealt with the disrespect for authority by taking whoever owned the phone to jail and bringing them back hours later, dead, in a zip-up bodybag for the family.

That wasn't supposed to be what happened. What was supposed to happen was Edane saved the local people and killed the bad guys — the government — and then everything would be good, and his mothers could be proud of him.

This was worse than making the family move out of their apartment so Edane could use their bedroom to shoot from. This made Edane angry. He hadn't been angry for a long, long time. Not angry like this, anyway. He was angry enough to count the shells he and Eissen had left, and sit with a calculator working out how many he could waste killing people with before the next chance to resupply. He wasn't angry enough to fudge the numbers based on last night's engagement, wasn't angry enough to say fuck it — he set just two shells aside for killing people, explosive unguided ones, and told himself he'd use them to kill the soldiers — the presidential guardsmen — doing the kidnapping.

Edane was angry, but he wasn't angry enough to waste ammunition.

IN THE HOURS of daylight, heat was less of a problem. At least, the kind of heat that Edane shed — easier to camouflage it when there was sun-heated asphalt around. More brothers had arrived — Hunt-Four and Six had made it in after breaking down the northern border posts, dodging around the response to get into Baku's northern reaches, and were in with the protest groups, talking them into abandoning the barricades one by one, getting the idiot right-wingers to put their guns down and leave instead of fighting an army with decades-old cast off weaponry.

With the civilians out, Edane's brothers turned the protest barricades into shooting galleries, scattering terrified police who were left alone so long as they didn't shoot back. As news of that little fact spread, the police started throwing down their arms and running the moment there was gunfire, whether it was Edane and his brothers or even just the noise of the army shooting someone.

That was good. Strategically speaking, turning an enemy combatant into an enemy non-combatant was up there with wounding one of them badly enough that they needed three or four other people to hold them together and handle medical stabilization — reducing effective manpower far more than just blowing someone's head off would.

Better able to move in the daylight, Edane and Eissen made use of every opportunity to avoid detection. Walking over hot roads, their camouflage set to concentrate on an aerial perspective and blacking out to match what was under them instead of behind them. Moving at the same time of day civilians were, as they struggled to get out of the city or gather what they needed to survive — medicine, food, water.

Some civilians were stranded in parts of the city as the police and army clamped down, turning crossroads into sandbagged bunkers. Other civilians were outright assaulting each other — sometimes these were people who seemed exactly alike to Edane, and he couldn't work out what their problem was. Sometimes it was obvious — foreign refugees, darker skinned ones from India and Pakistan, lighter skinned ones from China and the eastern reaches of Russia. Humans had a *thing* about skin colors, and in some places the refugees had been mistreated for years, and they thought it was their turn to mistreat others. More often the Azeris formed groups to march them out of the neighborhood, as if the refugees were to blame for the government — Nesimi had originally been from North Persia, not Azerbaijan. In some places where the political apparatus had fooled the locals they threw out and occasionally killed the refugees, claiming the refugees were funding the terror campaign on their city.

Edane had only shot soldiers in uniform and destroyed materiel belonging to the armed forces or police. He wasn't a terrorist — the police and civilians were.

Eissen and Edane split with Siegen and Sieden, who decided to concentrate on local UAV and electronic resources, while Edane wanted to disrupt the civilian kidnappings. Eissen was willing, but didn't think they could do anything. He was right.

The armed forces ran house-to-house searches, trying to hunt down protestors caught outside their strongholds, campaign funders, or even the locals trying to hold together their uncensored pirate wireless network. Edane put in an intel request for assistance in finding one of the broadcasting nodes, and within five minutes he got a quick verbal report from a young man with an accent he couldn't recognize — some kind of intelligence and information support group that had been hired to help out the Liberation Fund.

It gave him a location. He and Eissen yanked the tiles out of the roofs of two neighboring buildings, making holes in the attics for firing positions, lay an old ladder between the roofs for building to building access, and set up watching one of the longest running pirate nodes.

When the army showed up in their armored fighting vehicles — the kind with explosive reactive countermeasure pods, so it was the presidential guard — Edane didn't shoot them immediately. He waited for them to get out of their vehicles, start moving house-to-house.

He'd read a thing in school, which must have made the teacher who assigned it feel like a comedian, about Pavlovian conditioning and dog training. Edane had understood it immediately.

If you did something bad, you got punished. That way you associated doing bad things with being punished, so you stopped doing bad things. Do that to the soldiers and maybe they'd learn the way the police had learned, and start surrendering.

Two soldiers with electroshock batons dragged a woman out of a building, jabbing her with the ends until she fell down in the street. That was when Eissen shot them, two muddy roars of his rifle from the other building, and they fell over — the woman remained on the street, clasping at her head in terror, curling up into a tiny ball.

When another soldier picked up a baton from his vehicle, going to get her while they detonated smoke grenades, Edane shot him, with one of the explosive shells.

In front of his squadmates.

Pieces of him flew back out of the growing cloud of smoke, spattering across the vehicle's armor, his bare arm laying loose on the vehicle's roof like a pale length of bloodied rope.

Edane's goggles took a feed from Eissen's viewpoint, projecting an AugR image of his view across the smoke, bent and warped, to try and fit Edane's perspective instead, uneven 3d shapes popping up where the person-to-person network's image processing thought they should be.

Edane didn't shoot the guys trying to go and find what was left of their buddy, and he didn't shoot the one in the vehicle who was probably calling for UAVs.

He didn't even shoot the ones returning fire, shooting at *all* the buildings nearby, shattering the tiles above Edane's head. Nobody went to try and take the woman again, they left her alone to go back inside, screaming, so he didn't shoot any of the others. That was their reward. So they'd be conditioned not to go after the civilians anymore.

Edane and Eissen left before the VTOL arrived, a gunship big enough to hold pilots, shooting explosive shells bigger than the LAMW's 23 millimeter ones into the positions Edane and Eissen had used until the roofs caved in.

Eissen stared at him, when Edane explained why he'd only taken the one shot, later. Shook his head, almost disbelievingly, but he helped Edane do it again — though this time Edane shot the shell into the passenger compartment of an armored vehicle with the same serial number as one he'd seen used by soldiers who'd killed protestors on the news.

It might not have been the same soldiers inside, but it was the same unit — the presidential guard — and they had *just* opened the back doors after a drone overflight had buzzed by, turning camera lenses over Edane and Eissen's spot on top of a building — but the sunlight had heated the building's roof, and Edane and Eissen's camouflage gear gave them the same colors, and they'd picked a low spot, pushed in against sidewalls to minimize their shadows. Nobody knew Edane was there. The presidential guard thought they were safe, just like how the local people probably had felt safe before the guard had started kicking in doors, and then Edane had shown them that they weren't.

None of the soldiers in the other vehicles went into the buildings to go house-to-house, looking for people to take back to the prisons, hostages to hold to try and make people stop sending Edane's brothers money.

There was a lot of money. Which meant reinforcements, soon. On the discussion forum there were rumors about UAVs being available that night, but definite information was being filtered out in case the enemy had access to their tactical network's lowest levels. Edane didn't think the enemy did — the discussion forums and most of the software was the same as in MilSim, and people tried to cheat in MilSim all the time, but nobody had broken the encryption on a realtime basis yet. They'd only ever broken the encryption after the fact, long after matches were over.

Later in the day Edane and Eissen were asked to help deal with UAVs, so they found a position and Eissen fed Edane guided shells, which he fired off in bursts of five — going through a whole magazine in a single session, fin-guided munitions smashing heavy and midsized drones out of the air.

He tried hitting one of the bigger VTOLs, which apparently *was* piloted, but after he'd blasted a hole in the armored section that was supposed to hold the cockpit, behind blast shields that could lift to expose windows in an emergency if the cameras didn't work, it didn't fall out of the air — only turned and limped away.

Maybe if he'd used an explosive armor piercing round, but he was running out of those, and those were the only kind he had left that would get into a heavy drone's armor block.

They went through most of their ammunition, killing UAVs giving the rest of their brothers trouble — there were almost forty brothers in the city, now, all of the Hunt groups except for Hunt-Two, who were still hiding in the hinterlands, waiting for pickup. The local reports, the official ones, claimed there were a division of two hundred clone dogs and offered a five hundred thousand Azeri Manat reward for information, which was about twenty thousand New Dollars.

A good day's work. The night came again, and Edane had a chance to stop long enough to check his foot. The flesh was bleeding again, fur matted into his sock, his foot swollen into his boot so badly and painfully he didn't even try to take it off to replace the sock, just cut out the wet part and stuffed in as much bandaging and gauze as he could before lacing it back up tightly. His collarbone and shoulders were bruised from the LAMW's kick, worse than when playing MilSim because his MilSim gun had better hydraulic shock absorption.

For the first time, Edane felt tired.

He didn't know how he'd explain to his mothers what he'd done over the course of the day. Hunting soldiers, not just trying to stop them, but trying to *scare* them.

He decided not to — instead he told them, and Janine, that he wasn't hurt, and that things were okay. Technically speaking this was something called a white lie, which Edane had learned to be important sometimes, but it was true, really. He wasn't hurt in a way that would threaten his health, only in ways that made him uncomfortable and in pain.

He hadn't slept in almost two days. He didn't have proper reinforcements yet, but they were coming.

He had a fight with Eissen. Not a big one, no snarling, but some shouting.

"We didn't fucking achieve *anything,* Edane!" Eissen showed him his pad. The satellite imagery. A view from above of the woven wire fences lain out in a grid of cages, each grid square full of people — full of civilians. "They still took hostages — they still *executed* fifty people today. We could have been hitting their EMWAR antennas, taking down more of their UAVS—"

"We shot down *thirty* UAVs," Edane snapped back.

"And we spent four hours on *scaring* the presidential guard. Twice. It didn't stop them rounding up sons and daughters out of every fucking neighborhood outside of the protest barriers!"

Edane kept his teeth grit. So did Eissen. Glaring at each other in the basement they'd stopped in to patch themselves up.

"Someone has to make them stop," Edane murmured.

"We don't have the manpower to hit the Ministry of State Security buildings. So *maybe* we should fucking accept we can't do shit about that, and help break their networks, hit their short-range UAV refueling stations."

Edane didn't want to admit he'd been wrong. Didn't want to admit he'd been angry, had let that guide his choice of objectives, didn't want to admit he'd wasted time, didn't want to admit he'd killed soldiers who hadn't even *known* to fight back.

He didn't want to, but saying it was the responsible thing. So he did. "I got it wrong."

"*Affirmative,*" Eissen snapped — but he didn't rub it in any more than that.

They sat in silence, eating ration bars, because they hadn't found any food.

Eissen flicked through the pad's screens. "I want to move to capture/kill work," he said, at last. "Deal with Persons of Interest."

"The LAMW's no good for that," Edane said, stating the obvious. "I don't have the munitions to waste on individual personnel."

Eissen glared up at him, and Edane looked away. He should've saved those two explosive shells for equipment, for setting off stored munitions or fuel instead of killing people. But he hadn't been short of munitions for achieving support requests by other Hunt teams in the area, so far.

"I know," Eissen said, and started unpacking the webbing holding the spare magazines to his body. He didn't have to check them — could feel their weight, unlike in MilSim. Set the full ones down on the floor carefully, dropped the empties where he stood.

"You abandoning me?" Edane asked, blinking at the piles of ammunition.

"I'm taking a different objective. If you can find someone to trade the LAMW with for a rifle, I'd prefer to stick with you, but..."

Edane hugged the weapon's bulk to himself, disturbed by the very idea. "No, no," he murmured. "I'm keeping the LAMW."

Unloading the half-full magazines one by one, Eissen set the shells down carefully in neat rows, keeping the color-coded tips together. Explosive, guided, unguided. "You don't really *need* a spotter. All I'm really doing is hauling your ammunition for you, and we've gotten through most of it."

"Yeah," Edane replied, laying a hand on his belly. It felt weird, even through his armor. Cold or twisty or something.

"What are you going to do?" Eissen asked, picking up another magazine.

Edane slipped on his goggles, gestured through to the requested objectives screen. He cleared his selection — red checks indicating completed objectives vanishing along with the grey circles showing uncompleted ones. Picked through the priority list. "Anti-UAV cover, I guess," he said tiredly. "Shooting down enemy eyes is still a popular request."

"You'll be okay alone?" Eissen asked.

Edane nodded. "For tonight, anyway."

Eissen picked up his pad, thumbed around… and in Edane's goggles his IFF marked Eissen as a member of Hunt-Adhoc-2, along with four other brothers. "Maybe check with Sieden and Siegen," Eissen suggested. "They'll probably want help."

"Probably."

After finishing their meals, and getting the magazines topped up with the shells that were left, Eissen went upstairs and out into the darkness of the night. Edane sat by himself for a little, hugging his LAMW.

He'd done the right thing, he thought. Not because he'd actually done the right thing, but because when he'd been a child the trainers said that if he ever felt *compunctions*, whatever those were, he should remind himself that he was doing the right thing until the feeling went away.

It didn't take very long for his worries to vanish, and Edane was *certain* that Grandpa Jeff would have yelled at him about that.

13. Hostile Takeover

::/ San Iadras, Middle American Corporate Preserve.
::/ April, 2106.
::/ Ereli Estian.

By the time Ereli got back into the office, the first commercial plane taking brothers into Azerbaijan — the Hunt groups — was still a half hour away from Turkey, where bribed Turkish military airlift assets were waiting to deploy them at the borders.

Ereli had never realized money could buy so *much*. It was like with money, and the right contacts, a battlefield became easier to fight on by an order of magnitude tied to how much money there was to spend.

There was a *lot* of money. So much of it that they had set aside a section of their temporary Midtown office just for accountants and bookkeepers to handle invoices and check funds and make the money *move*, which was basically easy — money shot off faster than bullets — but keeping track of it was the hard part, couldn't just weigh the magazine in hand and know how much had been spent, like with bullets.

Another part of the office was full of lawyers, now, most of them constantly on their phones talking with case history researchers and people overseas — *none* of the lawyers looked happy, but their end of the operation was more of a long term risk management thing, except when it came to negotiating for support from neighboring countries — nobody wanted to accept the next planeload of Ereli's brothers.

Ereli didn't see why they couldn't just send more money to the Turkish military, bribing them again, but that idea made the lawyers *very* unhappy.

After talking to the lawyers for a while, Ereli checked the project management system in the office and just to reward himself for helping the lawyers settle into the office, he assigned himself a fun job. Sourcing gear for the next plane out of the country.

They'd already raided Andercom West's inventories for every piece of gear that'd been custom-fit to his brothers for the PMCs during the Tajikistan boom in business, and there wasn't much left, so now Ereli had to arrange the fabrication of what they needed. He had to go to custom fabrications firms one by one, getting that guy with a circuit printer to start on EMWAR kits, this guy with the right kind of looms to start printing camouflage uniforms with chameleon circuitry specifications so they could recolor properly — that stuff was the easy part.

For every item not specifically for killing people with, there was somebody in San Iadras with an automated fabrication setup and the right kind of printers or automatic cutters and shapers to spool out the gear on demand, for a price. And since Ereli and his brothers were all the same size — give or take a few fractions of an inch, since different exercise regimes and nutrition over the intervening decades had plenty to say about bone structure no matter what their standardized genes said about it — he could order the gear mass fabricated without waiting for specific fitting measurements.

The hard part was guns. Bombs. Automatic mortars. He'd bought a license to produce forty automated mortar tubes from Hacker-Meyer-DeVilliers, but none of the fabrication shops he could find were either set up for that kind of heavy metalwork, or licensed to independently work on lethal technologies.

Some of the lawyers were working on that, but in the meanwhile, every small scale fabrications specialist he spoke to said there was *one* guy in the city who had the *perfect* rig for doing UAVs. So Ereli drove out to meet the guy.

"Saigon Salcedo," the guy said, shaking Ereli's hand. He looked like a rat. A *literal* rat, regular human sized, thin, with black fur and white hair. A clone run Ereli hadn't met any of before, with a bunch of gold rings through both ears. "And that there is Glacier Fabrications,"

Saigon said, with no small amount of pride, gesturing at his outdoor garage. "Oh, and this is my wife, Anne Treyer."

Anne was about the same height as Saigon was, a skeptical looking human woman, close-cut hair... same set of gold rings through both ears. "I can't *believe* you're willing to do this," she said.

Ereli blinked at her, at first thinking she was speaking to him, but no, she was talking to her husband.

Saigon flicked his tail agitatedly. "It's all above-board, I checked, and you *said* we should do something to help those protestors."

"Donate to International Human Rights or something, not make bombs." She kept her glare fixed on Ereli.

"I'm not going to *make* bombs, and besides, it's going to pay off the rest of the mortgage..."

The couple argued, and Ereli peeked into the garage.

White-shelled robotics were packed into every available space in the building, manipulator arms and tool heads, rolls of sheet metal stacked on spools, a block of what Ereli recognized as polymer printers. It was like something out of a dedicated multi-purpose fabrications plant — but Ereli hadn't been able to get any of those to work for him, they were all booked up producing consumer goods.

After the married couple had finished their argument, short and snappy statements that ended with a kiss, Anne marched up the fire escape of the nearby four story house and into the upstairs apartment. Saigon's energy ebbed down to nothing, watching her vanish upstairs, then the black-furred guy joined Ereli at his garage door.

"Mostly I, uhm... I do custom robotics for enthusiasts. That's my specialty — scientific probes, recreational remote flyers, that kind of thing..." He wrung his hands together, awkwardly.

"I ain't ever met any of you before," Ereli said, blinking into the interior of the garage, before looking back at Saigon. "Rats?"

"*Mice*." Saigon corrected.

"Mice," Ereli repeated. "Well. I think you know what I'm looking for."

"I can't do guns," Saigon said, spreading his hands. "Not licensed for that, but I can fabricate observation drones — I've got a construction cage I can set up, for assembling things that are bigger than the garage…"

"Can you show me this thing in operation? Get it to turn something out? Demonstration piece, just to show me the fabricator's running smoothly."

"Oh! Sure." Saigon leaned in, pulling a pad from a niche in the garage's inside wall, and flicked through it. Pulled down the garage door, before things swung into motion. "Gotta run it with the doors shut, local noise pollution issue," he explained, and hit the button.

"How much did you want to charge?" Ereli asked, leaning in to peer through the door's observation window.

"Depends on the pieces. Materials plus three hundred and fifty an hour? This *is* rush work, and I have loans to pay…" He swayed side to side, smiling nervously. Ears up, flared out.

The interior of the garage turned into an insectile birthing chamber rendered in sterile white. Pneumatic rams struck at the steel — the noise reduced to a muffled thud by the door and walls. Whirling arms tore and stripped, a blower fan shot the cutting swarf and metal splinters away with blasts of air from the back of the garage.

"We don't mind paying a rush rate. How much is the loan for?"

Saigon hesitated. "I don't know that I should discuss finances…"

"We need armed UAVs," Ereli said, bending down to pull open the garage door as the arms fell silent inside. He pointed at one of the metalwork arms, the one with the pneumatic rams. "That thing can handle hardened alloys?"

"Uhm, yes," Saigon murmured, "but like I said, I'm not licensed for lethal technologies…"

"We'll buy you," Ereli said. He reached in and picked up the demonstration workpiece. It was an interlocking set of metallic slats, with numbers etched into it. Six inches long, maybe. The middle slat came out when he tugged on it. Looked kind of like a schoolyard ruler.

Saigon stared at him. "Buy me?"

"Yeah. Hey, what *is* this thing?" Ereli asked, sliding the middle slat back in, turning the thing over.

"It's a slide rule. Kind of an antique mechanical calculator. Now what do you mean *buy* me?"

"Yeah." Ereli squinted at the numbers, trying to figure out how to make the slide rule work — he couldn't. Must have been some trick to it — he put it back down. "Our lawyers set up a procedure for it. We buy out your loan, buy your business, then we run you under our license for lethal technologies. There's a buyback clause, and we'll sell your loan to whatever bank you want afterward, but in the meanwhile we're happy to employ you on a contract basis. Three hundred fifty an hour is *fine*."

Saigon stuttered something, blinking. Cleared his throat. "That, uh. That sounds kind of complicated…"

"Yeah, our lawyers made me memorize all that." Ereli got out his phone, and wallet, and offered out the contract. "Here's the contract they drew up, and here's fifty nudies to hire yourself an hour or so of legal aid to make sure it's legitimate. All good?"

Saigon the *mouse* looked down at his pad, loading the contract up, and got out his wallet to accept the payment. "Uhm. Yeah, I'll… I'll call your people?"

"You do that." Ereli slapped his shoulder, though not too hard. "I have another dozen fabrication guys to talk to by lunch — war on, and all that. Oh, and if it helps any, you can tell the wife that you're working for those protest groups. They're the ones paying for this."

"Uh. I'll, uhm. I'll try that on her. Thanks."

"What am I supposed to tell them?"

Ereli pushed past a hanging rack of body armor, the suits heavy on their frame, and struggled between the too-close together desks with a grimace. "I don't know, Juan. Maybe tell them to get *on schedule*."

Juan didn't have as much trouble following, clutching his pad as he dodged the swinging armor before stepping between the desks with ease. Being small made the difference in a crowded office, Ereli supposed. "There *isn't* a schedule," he complained.

"It's an expression." Ereli sighed. "Have you got the intelligence contractors on the mission network?"

"Yes, but they want to know who to talk to. Who's in *command*."

Fucking humans. No initiative. Ereli grimaced, and turned to loom over him. "Congratulations, Juan — *you* are in command. Order them to find and respond to requests for intel assistance on the mission network as efficiently as possible. Okay?"

"Me?" Juan squeaked, backing up a step, two. "I'm just an admin temp."

"You have a management qualification, right?"

"Yes…"

"So *manage*. Each field request for intel assistance needs to be responded to, make sure everybody gets some help. Teams in active conflict get more help, and teams resting or taking down-time can be delayed, okay?" Ereli chopped his hand out at the bank of desktops and screens across the office. "Go do it. If you have trouble, ask for help — don't rush it and fuck it up, do it as slow as you have to, so you get it done right."

"Okay." Juan squeaked out a breath. "Slow and right. Slow and right," he repeated to himself, veering away between the desks.

Most desks were still unoccupied, but there were clumps of life. The lawyers, the bookkeepers — and now the liaisons, like Juan, managing contact with the hired contractors.

They'd opened accounts with Andercom's intelligence services, UAV programmers and operators, and the brother-owned Private Military Companies that weren't already involved. One of the other incorporation signatories like Ereli was already negotiating with some of the European PMC conglomerates, who had a lot more experience with peacekeeping.

The office felt like a madhouse to Ereli, but that was only because their employees still had no idea how to tell the difference between he and his brothers. If they had a problem, they grabbed whichever brother was closest.

He found Eversen in the office's meeting room, where a group of their brothers were crowded around the wallscreen for a briefing — nobody cared about the pretty boardroom table, the map on the screen was all that mattered.

"After monitoring social media failed to produce meaningful results — too many Azeris are losing connectivity to their social media — we managed to set up a polling system through the comments attached to crowdfunding donations themselves," a brother with unfamiliar dog tags — possibly Stelborn — explained. "The Azeri regime are more afraid of the banks seizing their personal assets out of the country than they are of us right now, so, the banking systems are still wide open. By using analysis on the pledging notes with each crowdfunding transaction we've identified support for these specific goals…"

An automatically generated bar chart popped up, notation tacked to it. Ereli could see that ending President Nesimi's rule was high in demand, but so were things like protecting the protesters and halting the regime's kidnappings — they'd started taking hostages to try and halt the flow of donation money. Rescuing specific loved ones, securing specific areas, those were popular too — but everyone had a different loved one, and everyone lived in a different neighborhood.

"As you can see, there's a very large divide between the amount of money pledged, and the number of people pledging," Stelborn said, switching between graphing it on a dollars donated basis, then showed it by a count of each person making a donation. A ton of money was tied into requests for locking down the parts of Baku the rich people lived in, but far, far more individual people had pledged with requests for protection in the poorer areas, swept off to the sides of the highways and infrastructures.

"How we're going to prioritize this, I don't know — thankfully we don't have any contractual requirements to alter the operational budget or our deployment specifically based on pledging requests, but I think we need to integrate these objectives onto the network."

"Can we link it in like squad support requests?" "If you do that the regime might send us a million pledges just to flood the support objectives system." "Maybe we can get a software guy to write filters…" Brothers began to babble, searching for good solutions.

Meanwhile, Eversen collared Ereli, drawing him out to the edge of the briefing. "You get us our assignment?"

"Not yet, but I have a line on some support work in the backyard…" Getting shipped into Azerbaijan was on a mission specific basis, and right now brothers, or teams of brothers, had to put in bids on missions towards specific objectives. As a signatory Ereli had access to money, a *lot* of money, but it wasn't money he could spend on getting him and Eversen onto a plane. "The popular stuff is getting a lot of interest, a ton *of* bids from the PMC teams. Very well organized, we want them in there more than us. Best bet for getting us in-country is to take work going in to talk to the locals, get equipment where it's supposed to be… same as the office shit around here, but on the ground out there."

"That ain't *shooting*," Eversen complained, though with more amusement than bitterness.

Ereli got out his pad — well, one of the office's pads he'd assigned himself, and showed Eversen. "All needs doing," Ereli said. "And it gets us on the ground with guns. Once we've completed the mission profile, we can find different objectives to take."

"Just so long as we ain't stuck in this office for the duration of conflict, I'm happy."

The image on the wallscreen changed — a different brother pushed his way forward, apparently some consensus having been reached on the pledging problem. "Okay, so, next topic. Tactically and strategically we're getting somewhere, but we need to start talking about the actual long term goal here. Getting the cops collared and the civilians safe are secondary objectives, even if they're important — our actual stated objective, and the one that matters, is seizing political power and dismantling then replacing the current regime.

"The lawyers want us to talk to opposition parties, find one of them to use as a replacement, but we're already getting some hefty bribe offers from factions I've never even heard of, and I don't feel right handing power over to these guys even if it's clear that we're going to have to accept corruption for now and beef up our slush funds. Now, since it's not like we give a shit about international law anyway, I want to put forward the possibility that after we seize power we set up a transitional authority based on polling via crowdfunding pledges until a better solution comes into play. It's already a system we've seen that works in a military context — we just got hired to achieve a military goal — so we just need to set up a new crowdfund for policing, a hospital fund, a street lighting fund, all those civil services, then let the people figure out what they want for themselves until things shake out…"

"That couldn't work, could it?" Ereli asked Eversen, squinting, ears flat. "Voluntary taxation?"

Eversen shrugged, ears perked. "Be nice if it did…"

14. Home Cooking

::/ Baku, Azerbaijan.
::/ April, 2106.
::/ Edane Estian.

The picture in Edane's sights was fuzzy. All of his electronics were off, everything stone dead. He couldn't afford to be detected. Carefully, fingers trembling, he adjusted the tiny focus knob in the scope's open manual panel. The view through the sight sharpened.

A pane of broken glass, a thousand hairline cracks.

Behind the spiderwebbed glass window, in a building's interior three quarters of a kilometer away, Azeri soldiers. The dinner-plate sized crucifixes of short range reconnaissance UAVs were lined up on a table.

Edane leaned left, right. Pivoting on the LAMW's bipod. His crosshairs passed over the corner of a workstation — he could see the screen's glow turning one of the soldier's faces an acidic blue-white.

Left a bit, left a bit more. Crosshairs on the brick wall, just in front of where the control station must have been behind it.

He pulled the trigger.

The wall shattered, brick fragments blown out to all sides in an expanding ring of grey dust, the broken glass in the windows fell away — plastic shards exploded out of the control station inside the room, the operator was screaming, waving a hand missing fingers, the UAV one of them was working with picked itself up and started circling the room's interior like a bee without a brain.

Foam sloshed out of the end of the LAMW's suppressor, boiling steam as it bubbled up.

Edane's ears rang.

His foot hurt even worse, now.

He'd spent what felt like days alone, hunting equipment, network gear. Killing EMWAR operators while destroying their kit, steadily working toward completing his assigned objectives as coldly and cleanly as possible, without giving in to the urge to cause mayhem, simply to kill, as had been acceptable in the first few nights.

The first night's objective — to force the Azeri army into overdeploying, stretching thin, running itself ragged to deal with a threat perceived to be much, much larger than the hunt groups — had been achieved.

Now Edane's brothers controlled three airstrips inside the country, and reinforcements were flooding in every time they could black out the country's air defense network. Which was becoming increasingly common, now that there were UAVs of their own in the air.

Even so, Edane didn't risk sticking around.

He jerked the LAMW up, grimacing at the wet, hot, tight feeling in his shoulder, and lay it against his chest while he got up and left the building.

There weren't many civilians left in this part of Baku. The streets were lifeless as he made his way out through a mousehole leading into a back alley. Even the trash seemed dead, lifeless as errant gusts blew it around.

He heard a pop, and his body tensed. Then it came, the stuttering bangs of submunitions going off, rattling the streets, shattering glass — a mortar bomb. Clouds of smoke billowed past the alley mouth and the building behind him creaked.

Fucking mortars. Edane shot them when he could — stubby pintle-mounted automatic things, installed in courtyards and on top of buildings, wired into the Azeri force network, relatively fragile if hit right — but there was always one more of them to drop ordnance on positions of suspected enemy fire.

Silence. Only one bomb had come in.

Just the one felt like an insult, but there was a *lot* of suspected enemy fire in Baku. The rippling roar of LSWs went off regularly, then the controlled double or triple-stutter of rifles, just like how Edane had been taught to shoot as a child. Sometimes he heard the occasional boom of another LAMW, echoing in weird ringing patterns thanks to their suppressors. The whip-crack of their shells cutting through the air were supposed to be a far cleaner, more obvious sound, though Edane hadn't heard it yet. Didn't hear it behind the gun, after all.

Edane limped through the alleyways, disturbing a nest of terrified cats who scattered out in all directions, so he turned back — he didn't want to warn anyone he was coming, and a dozen disturbed cats would be more than warning enough.

He was tired. He hadn't slept in days and days. Hadn't seen the point in it, somehow — not since splitting up from Eissen. Edane's whole world had closed down to mindlessly hunting and killing, and he didn't like how proud he felt because he was able to function like that. Because he was *efficient*.

When the noise was quieter, and he'd found a quiet spot between buildings the mortars would have trouble hitting him, he switched on his electronics long enough to find a supply dump and oriented himself toward it.

UAVs tore past overheard a little while later. Not enemies hunting down his signal, he thought, he hoped, but all the same he circled around and around before finally looking for a door into one of the waterfront office buildings. The first one he found was mined — he could tell because the door was closed, but the lock had been shot open. Nobody bothered shutting a door without a reason, without something to protect behind it.

Edane switched his electronics back on, no wireless except for his IFF, and moved the focal point of his helmet's cameras across the door. The IFF pinged — there was a mine, and it was friendly, so he waited for the mine to authenticate him, and then he went through the door, shutting it carefully behind him.

Two floors down in the underground parking lot, amidst silent cars, a space heater was burning. Cans of meat hung from loops of wire just barely above the electrical filaments, their labels scorched.

One of his brothers lifted a hand to him, standing up from a chair beside a bank of automatic monitors, flicking through images of the building's surroundings.

The brother blinked, looking Edane over. "Shit. You've been out here since the start?"

Edane nodded. "Affirmative."

"Well. Come on in and take a load off — welcome to Forward Base Gamma. Food's there, there's a tank of water down the ramp there," his brother said, pointing at the vehicle ascent and descent ramps, "and we've got a field-hospital one floor under that. I'm Sipnitz."

"Edane," Edane said, unclipping the LAMW from his body-harness. "Armory?"

Sipnitz spread his hands in a shrug. "Hasn't been unpacked yet. We haven't been here long enough to need to re-arm. It's over there if you want it."

He pointed at a row of plastic crates, next to a rural cargo vehicle, open-backed with Azeri plates. Edane blinked at it, tiredly. "You get that vehicle on the way in?"

"Yeah."

"Village surrounded by turrets?"

"Yeah. We cleared that out and told the civilians to evac. No idea if they did, but they let us buy a couple of their cars."

Edane set the LAMW down, and more than just the weapon's weight left his shoulders.

HE DIDN'T WIND up unpacking the armory, but Edane did visit the field hospital. It was a full telepresence rig, the doctor back home who treated him tutting as he cleaned out the athletic implants in Edane's thighs, washing them out before gluing the points shut. "No more of those," the guy said, manipulating Edane's limbs with the surgery arms, running multiple ultrasounds of his feet. "Your muscles are getting beaten to putty — you're so swollen up and tight because the tissue's torn itself to shreds. Needs time to heal."

"Right," Edane murmured.

"See that bone?" The doctor asked. The screen filled with his face shifted to a rotating view of Edane's innards. "Dislocated. And that Avulsion fracture's much worse than it was in the last file on record for you, it's caused some bleeding and swelling."

"Need surgery?"

"Not immediately. For now I'm going to print out a custom brace for you. It should fit under your boots, but if it doesn't just get it printed into a new boot." The rig spat a square of smart-paper out at him. "Take this to the pharmaceuticals supply locker and dose yourself as directed. That'll help your feet and your shoulder. As for the rest of the damage you've done to yourself, rest and corticosteroids are your best option. *Please* put everything back where you found it when you're done."

"Okay. Thanks." Edane liked this doctor. Not so squeamish. He went and got the drugs, carefully following the directions on the smart-paper to open the right coded drawers, and made his way up the parking ramps, getting water on the way to drink it all down with.

When he got back to the heater, he discovered it wasn't just Sipnitz in the base, along with the two brothers he hadn't met on guard duty in the building above the parking lot. Now another patrol had arrived back.

The patrol had newly arrived in-country, and were tired. One's ear was almost torn off, the blood staunched with coagulant foam. His helmet, hanging off the back of his armored vest, had a white-streaked furrow down the side and over the ear-gap, a bullet wedged at the end of the furrow. A hell of a close thing.

Edane lifted one of the cans of meat on its wire from over the heater, dunked it into water to cool off, then carefully hooked another can by its key to replace the one he'd taken, and sat down to eat on the bench seats that they'd torn out of cars left in storage down here. His uniform — old and beaten up by days of activity — was immediately commented on.

"Here's a guy who's been in country for a while."

"Uh huh." Edane snapped the key off his can of meat, jabbed it into the little notch, and began turning it to get the thing open. "Hiked in, even."

"Nice. Would've liked to do that myself. We got in this morning — been clearing the riot police out of the protest areas. They're shoot to kill now, you heard that?" His brother smiled. "They put out an announcement — anyone doing violence to civilians is shoot on sight, and that's the riot cops. They've got fuck-all for firepower, but the army show up *real* fast when they start screaming."

Edane nodded vaguely. "That's good," he murmured. "Violence against the civs needs to stop."

"Yeah. I'm Enzow," the talkative one said, leaning back to show off the grey text on the front of his camouflage. "That there's Scartho," he went on, pointing at a brother hunched up over his meal, ears flat down, almost cringing, lost in his own world, "and that's Sokolai next to you."

"*Sokolai?!*" Edane twisted to the side, blinking. "I'm Edane!"

Sokolai looked up, amazed. "Jesus."

"You two know each other?" Enzow asked, grin fading a little.

"Fuck yes. We were in Dushanbe together—"

"—This guy held me together after I got hit. I didn't know you were still working—"

"—Where the hell did you get a new arm?" Sokolai laughed, breathlessly.

"Got it on loan. It's good to see you, Sokolai."

Sokolai did it first — put his can of meat down and reached out. Edane reciprocated, hugging him, tight. A bear-hug of a clasp, squeezing so hard and fast it was like hitting him, before releasing, just staring at each other.

"I am so fucking glad to see you in one piece. I thought you might have died." Sokolai squeezed Edane's shoulder. His right shoulder.

"Still here," Edane said. "After all, I'm just as tough as you are."

Sokolai gave up on his current assignment by the time they'd finished their meat. Enzow had laughed, shrugged it off easily. It wasn't anything like when Eissen left — no, there was a reason for Sokolai's departure, and a good one.

They formed a new unit then and there, registering it as Pair-Thirty-One, and caught up with each others' lives. Apparently Sokolai hadn't been doing too well — bad experience in Tajikistan, during the revolution. Edane felt bad for not being there, for having been medevaced, but Sokolai didn't blame him. From what little Sokolai said, he blamed himself.

Just like how Edane blamed himself, for most things. But Sokolai was interested in the MilSim — said he'd have to check that out, maybe subscribe to it. Was pleasantly surprised to hear that Edane was seeing someone, apparently Sokolai wasn't in a relationship himself, but lived with some people, could kind of understand the impulse. No sex for Sokolai either, though.

After the armory was unpacked, and Edane put in an order for it to manufacture new shells for him overnight, he picked up his new brace — which barely fit into his boot — and went off with Sokolai to find a place to sleep.

In the end they lay together, back to back, warm and safe in a niche between a concrete pillar and a wall, two more levels underground, tails wagging against each other until sleep came, guns in their arms.

It felt good having his brother here with him. Knowing that after they slept they could get up and fight, side by side. Edane snugged down, warm, and pushed his nose against his armpit, eyes shut.

Tomorrow would be better. So much better.

15. Check, mate

::/ Erzurum, Turkey.
::/ April, 2106.
::/ Ereli Estian.

After the plane's dark interior, the light outside was blinding. The sunlight was a whole different color here — when Ereli had left San Iadras it had been raw and yellow. Here, hours later in the back-end of Turkey, it was cold and white.

Their rented hypersonic commercial airliner still had its Haversham logos on the tail, though the dynamically colored parts of its hull had been greyed out, removing its arty paintjob and helping it fit in with the other planes lined up on the military airstrip.

Most of the planes were commercial, since those were the air cargo shipping options that could be hired on a same-day basis. But commercial was good. They were fish-gut style transports, planes whose flight frame — nose, wings, engines, ribs — lifted off its cargo fuselage, leaving the cargo in place while the rest of the plane's frame picked itself up to fly back with hardshell canvas covering the gaps in its frame. Typically they were used by tycoons, delivering their manually driven sports cars somewhere for the weekend, but they were just as good at hauling shipping containers on short notice.

The airstrip had an antique style tower, and an emergency relief aircraft was sitting in its shadow, belly-open, insectile fabrication gear churning out last minute gear and custom weight-bearing webbing for brothers stepping out of the planes. Two cargo containers were propped up on stilts, forming a lean-to over their contents — a row of metal fabrication shops, caged up with plasma arcs blazing, spitting out and crating missile engines for building payloads for the delta-wing UAVs parked on a taxiway, the crated engines immediately picked up and loaded back into the other end of the fabrication shops by the engineers, already starting to fit them to warheads.

"Where're our guns?" Eversen asked, turning around and around, while engines roared from every side.

Ereli checked his pad. There was a logistics map of the airstrip's layout, even though they were due to clear out by that evening — ship it all into Azerbaijan, assuming Ereli and Eversen could install man portable air defense turrets around the captured airstrips, ensure a safe place to land their gear. He navigated himself and Eversen through the tangle and to a machine shop where brothers were already lined up, checking the printed tags on racked guns fresh from the printer.

"Eversen and Ereli!" Eversen yelled, fighting forward. "Our orders up yet?"

A group of eight brothers at the front of the queue looked up, faces sprayed with colored dye, and checked the tags rapidly. White passed Eversen his rifle, Pink gave Ereli his.

The weight in his hands was a relief. The boxy device was exactly what he'd asked for on the plane — telescoping stock, double-lensed above and below the barrel for easy binocular rangefinding, socketed and railed in case he needed to stick more gear on it. Eversen's was solid-stocked, longer barreled, fed off helix magazines instead of boxes, almost a Light Support Weapon.

Ereli pulled one of the empty magazines off the print-sprue taped to his new gun's foregrip, gave the spring a push, and slid it home in the gun's magazine well. He looked up to find Eversen had racked one of his helical magazines, too, and was already dry firing the weapon at the ground between his feet.

Eversen grinned. Ereli grinned back.

"Let's find *bullets*," Eversen yapped excitedly. "And then armor! And let's find that air-defense shit we're installing and *get in-country*."

"You get the bullets, I'll get the armor. We'll meet at the shipping stand and find the crates we need to baby into the country. Okay?"

"Affirmative." Eversen turned and started hunting down the

small arms armory.

Behind the chain link border fence, the Turkish air force guards stared disbelievingly at Ereli and his brothers over their moustaches.

What. Had they never seen kids given free run of a candy store? Giddy, Ereli ran for the armor racks.

::/ Baku, Azerbaijan.
::/ Eissen Estian.

The clock was ticking. Eissen bowed his head again, gaze-flicking through his goggles' menus to reconfigure his camouflage for the sixteenth time. It fluoresced everywhere shadow fell on him, gave him the same even blend of color as the wall behind him, but he had to keep manually adjusting the expected enemy viewpoint instead of letting it use one of the automated profiles defined by the direction he was looking in.

Somewhere, someone screamed. Not unusual for this part of the city over the past few days — the war had mostly dodged these moneyed districts, but pent up aggression and dissatisfaction with the gap between rich and poor, combined with the complete disappearance of the police, had made for more than a few horror stories as people marched into the rich part of town and took what they thought belonged to them.

Eissen didn't have time to deal with every instance of looting and pillage. There was only one horror story he was interested in now. Scharschow, across the roadway, flashed a thumbs up, and ducked around the street corner, backing up to one of the stone sections of the skyscraper behind him, melting into the grey. Their gear wasn't good enough to provide camouflage against the reflective windows that were the fashion everywhere in this part of the city — the area put together like a cheaper, run down mimicry of San Iadras's Downtown and Uptown skyscrapers with the city streets dead and flat.

Eissen waited patiently.

The convoy purred silently out of the skyscraper's shadows, swerving around a dead cat's body on the asphalt — as though one of the feral animals infesting the streets could be dangerous — and continued on around the corner.

The road was wide here — six lanes. Impossible for pedestrians to cross, but the roads weren't for pedestrian benefit — anybody who was anybody in this town had a personal car.

Ismayil Nesimi, president Nesimi's only son and presumptive heir, had three limousines and a presidential guard armored fighting vehicle running escort, just to sweeten the deal.

The limousines were gaudy, snub-nosed things, long and thin and low to the ground, armored windows black, wheels all turning independently to grip the road as the silent electric things navigated the streets.

Eissen focused on the front car, heart thundering in his chest — he was practically out in the open, at one end of an open cross-walk between skyscraper lobbies. A hostile UAV hissed above the scene, a black speck in the narrow slice of sky between the towers.

Eissen waited, waited. The rough, almost familiar voice of one of Marianna's sisters — Malinka — purred through his earbuds. "Stud-Five and Stud-Seven, incoming. We go on the strike."

He huffed once. Twice. Harder, pushing air through his mouth, boiling the heat on his tongue away through his filtered camo facemask. Tensed, relaxed, tensed, relaxed —

The drone above them vanished in a scattering of grey mist and components, blast reaching Eissen's ears a moment later, the cars slewing to a halt. The armored vehicle's turret popped up, started tracking the sky. A delta-wing UAV jack-knifed around a corner, hovering on its own thrust for an instant before it fell like a bird coming down off its perch, missiles streaking from its upturned belly.

The walkway trembled under Eissen, blown out at the opposite end by a missile, the rubble falling across the roadway, crushing the front of a limousine trying to escape. The second, third, and fourth missiles all hit the armored vehicle in its side-door, one after the other until the black wound torn into the car exploded outward in a pressurized blast, the AFV's hydrogen cells pierced through the internal cabin and boiling out of the vehicle in a screaming tongue of fire.

The second delta-wing UAV, Stud-seven, scythed through at thirty feet over street level, direct-fire cannon under its belly swiveling in quick jerks, like a chameleon's eye, blasting out the limousine's wheels one after the other with stuttered bursts. Anti-aircraft missiles buzzed after it, bobbing and twisting above the lip of the street's canyon, searching for an opportunity to safely dive beneath the skyscraper tops without damaging the buildings. Stud-seven had no such concerns, blowing out an office's windows and diving through, sending glass crashing down precisely where Eissen had been waiting.

He wasn't there anymore.

He was running down the rubbled remnants of the walkway, pointing his rifle at the gap in the armored vehicle despite all occupants blatantly having been neutralized within the hydrogen-fueled kiln of its interior, because that was his job. "Armor clear," he yelled.

Erkner shot one of the bodyguards getting out of the lead vehicle, side-stepping in a wide rolling circle, his camouflage struggling to keep up.

Eissen took another bodyguard in the back of the head as the man straightened up above the height of his limousine's roof, throwing him forward onto the mulched remnants of his face with a tap of two rounds.

As Eissen got closer to the car he dropped his rifle, the angle of his body-strapping carrying it under his arm and out of the way, and drew his pistol. Held it low against the limousine's side window, angled forward towards the windshield, and held down the trigger for the quarter-second it took the gun to blow through all fourteen rounds. He ducked aside as the broken glass sagged, reloading — Scharschow stepped in, ramming his rifle stock through the armored glass, gouging a hole in the splintered mass big enough to get a fist through, and Eissen aimed the pistol through instead.

"Open the door!" he screamed, bobbing side to side to keep on target through the miserably small gap.

He screamed it again when the limousine started moving, helplessly scraping across the asphalt on its two left wheels, wobbling in the wheel wells. The limo's AI had no idea how to protect its cargo now.

Gunfire further up the line as brothers got into one of the limousines — throwing dead and wounded suited guards aside...

The door creaked open an inch — Eissen grabbed it, tore it open, and levelled his pistol at the interior.

One bodyguard in front with a cut-down shotgun — dead, no matter that he was holding it over his head. Second guard in the back — dead with a rapid jerk of Eissen's trigger-finger. Target in the middle seat...

"Got the target!" Eissen grabbed Ismayil Nesimi, a short (six-two — almost all humans were short to Eissen) pale-skinned man with distinctive dark eyebrows, fingers digging into the man's shirt-collar, and pulled him out of the vehicle one handed, throwing him to the asphalt.

Ismayil cowered, hands lifted. "You can't do this!" he screeched, in English. "This is an illegal kidnapping! You can't do this. I demand a lawyer!"

"A *lawyer*?" Eissen dropped onto the man, knee over his midsection, pinning him down, arm crooked to hold the pistol high, beside Eissen's face and out of Ismayil's reach, angled down towards the man's throat. "You want a *lawyer*? You're the head of the fucking secret police!"

An echo of engines thundered through the streets. The distinctive thudding of a helicopter's blades — the invading force had no helicopters, piloted or UAV. Azeris. Incoming, and fast.

Behind him his brothers and Malinka swarmed the limousine, plugging EMWAR gear into it — Scharschow dropped down and tore through Ismayil's pockets, stole his phone and watch, throwing them over.

Ismayil dropped his hands long enough to screech, "All you have is accusations! You can prove nothing!"

"You think we have to *prove* something? You think this is going to *trial*?" Eissen laughed. "Shit, buddy. We're going to *kill* you."

"What? What about my rights? A right to a trial, western democracy — that is what you claim to be bringing!" His eyes boggled out in fear.

"But we're not in charge yet," Eissen hissed. "You are. This country's operating under *your* law."

He scrabbled at Eissen's chest, yanking at his uniform, squirming as if he could get out from under him. "No, no, please no, I'll pay, my father—"

"We have his network access. We don't need him anymore," Malinka purred over the comms.

Eissen shot him in the face. Once, twice, a third time — a fourth through his scrabbling hands as Ismayil clutched at the bloody mess he was screaming through, a fifth, a sixth — Eissen aimed higher, for the brain instead of just maiming the man's jaw, and emptied out the rest of the weapon.

Thirty seconds later they'd stripped every byte of data out of the man's electronics and passed every high level access account within them over to their off-site hackers. By the time the Azeri rapid assault team found somewhere to land, Eissen and the others were gone.

::/ BAKU, AZERBAIJAN.
::/ ERELI ESTIAN.

"WHERE'S THE PRESIDENT?" Eversen yelled.

Ereli pointed over the front of the boat. Ahead of the captured pleasure-craft's nose rusting oil derricks were still thumping at the bed of the Caspian Sea, hunting drops of oil. Beyond the metallic forest of derricks sprouting from the waves, artificial islands jutted from the coast. A glistening network of glass and green fronds, interlocking walkways, beautiful under the blue sky.

The Khazar Islands. Someone's attempt to put heaven on Earth just a short drive down the coast from downtown Baku. "Army's blocking the roads, checkpoints fucking everywhere," he explained. "But they ain't gonna last long!"

"Why?"

"Check the mission map!"

Eversen ducked his head, gaze-flicking through his goggles' menus…

He froze solid when he saw it.

Ereli had signed off with the rest of the signatories. All other objectives, except for suppressing Azeri air defense, had been put on hold. For every dog in the city, every friendly UAV and allied contractor, there was only one target.

Ilhaim Nesimi, president of Azerbaijan.

Or, at least, his personal phone.

The Azeri military information technology wing had been all but severed over the past few days of fighting — embedded EMWAR specialists killed, forcing them to overstretch themselves to support their men in the field. Most of their gear and software was off the shelf, developed overseas. There hadn't been any challenge in cutting into their network and isolating the commercial electronics linked to it, once Ereli's brothers had captured administration level access from the Ministry of State Security and handed it over to Andercom West's contracted hackers.

The president, or his phone, was pacing in a room on the seventy-fifth floor of the Aliyev Hotel. Going round and round and round.

The boat angled itself in towards the islands, the shimmering water between them locked in a crisscrossing pattern of canals. The luxurious Khazar Islands weren't all they were cracked up to be — the receding Caspian Sea had left some of the smaller sky-scraper topped islands on dry land, the main canals and pools and locks had all been deepened and dredged out to keep the water in place.

Ereli sat back and grabbed the railing as the brother at the boat's console put it on manual control and called out, "Brace for beaching!"

The brother swung his finger over the control pad, and the boat banked. Spiraling in towards the shallowly angled coast beside the main canal, at the edge of the Khazar Islands. On one of the footbridges linking the islands, crossing over the canal, two soldiers stared and pointed — Ereli flattened his ears against the bassy double-boom of Eversen shooting at them. The target slumped against the railing — the other man, running, was picked off by a brother closer to the front of the boat, and abruptly the keel hit the coastline. The pleasure-craft skidded out over exposed seabed and towards the old marina, now six feet above sea level.

Ereli and Eversen bailed out — seconds later the boat was clear, and brothers were running for the marina. Something popped overhead — Ereli's helmet cameras caught it, pinged him to look up. He did — madly spinning parachutes, bright in the sky.

"*Apeygesms!*" A brother screamed an instant later, the acronym spilling out of him in a rush.

APGSMs. Anti-personnel self-guided missiles hanging in the air on their parachutes. Scanning for targets, pinging IFF and waiting for responses. And when they didn't get an IFF response...

A parachute fluttered loose, tumbling end over end as the missile it held dropped. An instant later the rocket motor streaked toward the ground, painting a thick black line of smoke — one of Ereli's brothers vanished in a black-grey cloud tinged with scarlet mist. The name in the goggles was Enzow.

An instant later something small and hot and astonishingly hard hit Ereli in the muzzle — an explosive fragment. Hard enough to rip through his ballistic cloth mask, hard enough to tear through his cheek, hard enough to lodge between his gum and lip and pour blood into his mouth.

Ereli stumbled, spat, and pulled himself in behind the concrete pillars holding up the marina, making it there three steps behind Eversen, an instant after a second line stabbed down from the heavens and dug a chunk out of the marina sidewall one of his brothers had been scrambling up over.

Heartbeats later there was a black flash — a second flash, smoke blossoming over them. A drone buzzed by, low altitude, popping glowing flares into the sudden smokescreen over their heads, thick wads of silvery ribbon churning and twisting down before the UAV detonated another smoke pod, screening out the sky in a churning black layer.

Cover.

Ereli pulled his mask down, grit his teeth, and yanked the metal shard from his mouth. Stood for an instant, spitting blood in front of Eversen, and stared at the wicked, curved little bit of metal, crosshatched in a diamond pattern — the missile's metal casing, engraved to break into tiny parts. It was bloody in his hand, small and lethal and twisted.

Ereli stuffed the thing into his dump pouch, and before he'd even finished, Eversen was squirting coagulant foam over his face. A hard slap. "You set?"

Ereli nodded, pulling his mask back up. A wary glance overhead — a missile slammed down through the black layer coating the heavens, hit the exposed seabed fifty meters from any of them. "Cover!" He yelled and crouched down next to the concrete pilings.

The rest of the missiles rained down, striking blindly but in an orderly pattern, explosions rocking from one end of the marina and over the seabed until finally blowing up the boat — trying to kill the rest of them through the smoke.

No luck for the missiles — when Ereli and Eversen got up onto the marina and into the artificial island's streets, the worst hit of their brothers who hadn't been killed in the first attack was pulling himself up and over the marina's edge, beach-sand and coagulant spray gritting his belly.

Nesimi would need more than fancy hardware to kill Ereli.

::/ BAKU, AZERBAIJAN.
::/ EDANE ESTIAN.

EDANE LIMBERED THE LAMW at waist-level, replaced the magazine, and nodded to Sokolai. *Ready*, he signaled.

Sokolai nodded once — rifle held up with his right hand alone, armed hand grenade in his left. He released the grenade's cocking lever, starting the fuse, and counted off with bobs of his left hand, the both of them nodding in time.

Three. Two. One —

Edane blasted out the doorway's top hinge with the LAMW, aiming with the barrel-camera's picture in his goggles. The shell punctured the armored doorframe, tearing it, and the upper hinge, out of the wall with a colossal scream of steel, peeling the hardened security door apart like an orange. Edane was already taking cover by the time Sokolai had flung the grenade in through the ripped-open corner, ducking down to the doorframe's side the moment the grenade blew in a cut-off roar.

Sokolai shouldered down the rest of the door and stepped into the smoking security room, rifle pointed left, right, up, down — no combatants were still standing. The walls smoked. *Clear*, Sokolai signed, and began to stalk on through.

Edane followed, keeping the LAMW low to his body, clutched tight against his hip, half the view in his goggles interlaced with the gun's point of aim.

They were in the Khazar Islands — getting in had been a pain. Everyone was dodging around the Azeri army, avoiding contact instead of engaging, except for the UAV operators laying down cover fire. A little more coordination would have been nice — a blocking force to hold attention, while the rest of them moved around — but it was all good. The Azeri army were spreading themselves paper thin, and once they were inside the protected zone of the Khazar Islands, that made things beautifully easy.

The security room they'd just hit was on the bottom floor of the Heydar Aliyev Memorial something or other, a fancy office named for the cult of personality around one of the nation's former dictators, and was where the building's systems were controlled by the guards. As it was, the guards — probably army, except for one corpse in the corner — were dead now, instead of monitoring the building's systems.

Sokolai checked the corners, kicked the corpses — one was alive enough Sokolai lifted his rifle, as if about to shoot it through the head. He hesitated.

Edane said, helpfully, "Coup de grace is technically illegal, if he doesn't go for a sidearm."

"True." Sokolai lowered the rifle and used his foot to pin the man to the floor by his helmet. "You surrender?" Sokolai asked, chinning at his translator to say it over in Azeri.

The man just groaned, so Sokolai waggled the guy's head for him with a shift of the toe — making him nod — then kicked his sidearm out of its holster, and started pawing over the man to see if there was a first aid kit on his uniform.

Meanwhile, Edane got the elevators running and the emergency stairwells unlocked. For good measure, before unplugging his pad and its EMWAR software suite, he uploaded a rootkit for the off-site hackers, and helped Sokolai provide the legally mandated minimal first aid they were supposed to give prisoners and wounded combatants, then flagged him on the mission map for emergency services or someone who wasn't busy fighting a civil war to come and deal with.

"Upstairs?"

"Upstairs," Edane replied. Upstairs would give them *perfect* sight-lines.

But before they got through the lobby, something bad happened.

It started with the lights flickering out. The elevator door jammed, just as it was opening in front of Sokolai.

Then Edane's ear clicked. Once. Like there was a grasshopper inside it. His goggles blanked — all his feeds going dead at once. The click happened again, stronger — even worse. A hard rattling inside his head from nowhere, his tongue felt like it was being doused in vinegar and metal foil, then his vision pulsed white-blue twice, just as the clicking was joined by pain that got worse and worse and—

"The *fuck* was that?" Sokolai moaned, pulling off his goggles. His camouflage was frozen, the dynamic countershading gone. He rubbed furiously at his ear.

Edane checked his electronics. They were dead. Everything was dead — the building silent around them, even the air conditioning off.

"We just got HERFed," Edane breathed.

"What?"

"They just burned out all our electronics with a fucking microwave beam — *they know we're in here!*" He yanked at Sokolai's shoulder and started running. The lobby's constantly revolving door had jammed shut, none of the side doors opened — Sokolai blasted out one of the full length windows with a blaze of gunfire, and the pair of them crunched out across the broken glass and into the sunlight outside.

An enemy UAV bounced off the paving in front of them, stone dead. A second followed it — one of the cruciform camera drones. In the distance, a pair of brothers were looking around, bewildered — and past them, Azeri soldiers were standing up, waving back at a group of them around a stalled out armored vehicle...

It wasn't just Edane and Sokolai that'd been hit by the HERF. The whole fucking Khazar Islands had been burned clean.

Sokolai pulled the dead electronic scope off his rifle and flung the scrapped thing aside. Then he lifted his rifle to his shoulder, sighted down the iron sights, and shot twice.

One of the bewildered Azeri soldiers fell.

Behind the soldier, behind the stalled armored vehicle, a pair of tanks rolled from the mainland highway and onto the bridgeway into the islands. They shouldered the stalled out armored vehicle off the road, making way for the perfectly functional ones behind them.

"Shit," Edane murmured, stunned.

Sokolai grabbed him on the run — half dragged, half led him off the street and towards cover.

The grinding sound of the approaching tanks grew louder. Behind an ornamental fountain, Sokolai and Edane ducked down, met the other two brothers they'd seen. One had a pink splotch of dye covering the exposed part of his face, the other a yellow-amber.

"Hi!" Amber introduced himself. "I'm Elwood and this is Eschowitz."

"From *Mark Antony*?" Edane gaped.

"Yeah?"

"I'm Edane, from—"

"Triple-H! On the MilSim fields? And you?" Elwood looked to Sokolai.

He shook his head. "Sokolai. I'm not a MilSim player."

"Huh. Well, good to meet you. Either of you got anything to hit those tanks with? All we have is eight pounds of AGX."

"Seven," Pink — Eschowitz — corrected. "We used one of the charges already to get through that wall."

"Oh, yeah. Seven." Elwood shrugged.

"I've got four bricks of AGX," Sokolai replied. "And he's got a LAMW."

"It ain't enough to stop an armored column," Edane pointed out.

"No, but it is enough to slow it down while we blow the bridge." Elwood pulled down his mask, teeth exposed in a feral grin.

"With eleven pounds of AGX?"

"Hell, just *one* pound is more than enough to light off the munitions in those tanks…"

::/ BAKU, AZERBAIJAN.
::/ ERELI ESTIAN.

ERELI GOT PUT in a microwave. The dial turned over to eleven. It didn't burn, not directly — the radiowaves hit and shook molecules. Atoms. Pushed energy into the circuits he carried. Fired off nerve impulses, made phantom noises buzz through his ears, lights flash in his eyes, made pain scythe him off his feet and onto his knees and—

It was over. Light UAVs dropped out of the air, crunching into the ground, smashing into the hotel ahead.

All around him brethren swore, getting back up. Camouflage — those who had active camouflage of some kind — frozen. "HERF!" Some yelled, when others didn't get it, shuddered where they stood.

But the exterior of the Nesimi Hotel wasn't a good place to freeze up, even if the Azeri soldiers had been hit just as hard.

The dogs recovered faster than the humans. Their gunfire ripped across the rear garden and pool area — the Azeri return fire, when it came, beat through the pool chairs and tilted umbrellas, spewing plastic shards in all directions, wrenching back and forth over the concrete paving and tearing out the brickwork.

It looked impressive. It *was* impressive. But the dogs' hiccoughing double and triple-taps weren't aimed to suppress, force people into cover, or throw off the enemy's fire — weren't there to intimidate, but to *kill*.

Somebody got taken in the throat to Ereli's left — staggered on his feet, and while steadily bleeding all over his camos calmly limped into cover behind the poolside bar while returning fire. The brother hit the floor like a sack of bricks the moment he was out of the line of fire, another sprinting up and skidding to a halt while ripping an EMSTAB kit off his pack before vanishing in a boil of smoke cover and chaff ribbons.

An Azeri officer yelled orders to his men — he fell over, two holes drilled in under his exposed chin, helmet ballooning out behind him.

The door was too much trouble. So to get inside, one of them blew open the spa complex's walls and doors with an anti-tank weapon. They pushed into the hotel through burning hair salons, even as Azeri reinforcements began to arrive — Ereli spotted the whining hull of an active UAV, shot at it — missed, shot again, again… led the target, shot, and the thing came apart mid-air, its rotors tearing itself apart.

The popping noise of APSGMs overhead was accompanied by a scream of warning, and Eversen and the others lagging behind charged through smashed windows and into the hotel barely in time to avoid getting killed, the missiles scything down both on the few brothers left out in the open, and the Azeri forces.

There were more of the Azeris than of the dogs. A lot more of the Azeris, all with their IFF burnt out.

Ereli glanced over his shoulder, wondering who'd had the bright idea to send the APSGMs down on that mess, spotted Eversen behind him, and joined the flow of attack pushing through the luxury center's corridors and into the ornate lobby.

Just as they began rising up the cavernous marble-floored and gilt lobby's stairways, the building shook, smoke pillowing out of a brand new crater torn through the upper floors. The mezzanined catwalks high above the main lobby came tumbling down.

"Armor!" A brother screamed, running from his place at the reception desk seconds before a burst of machine gun fire lanced through the glass facade and into the wall behind the desk, showering chips of stone across the floor.

Someone stopped in the middle of the lobby floor, on the glossy stone between the walkway's crumpled rubble, and lifted a rocket launcher. He stared over the sights, aiming it near-blind with the thing's electronics dead — but the purely mechanical firing mechanism worked just fine, hitting the rocket motor in the back and sending it spinning through the air, wobbling without its internal guidance.

The explosion tore through the active-camouflaged tank's forward tread, burning the asphalt-black covering its armor to a crisp ash white. Ereli ran for higher ground — so did the rest of them. At the best of times a stand-up firefight was the last thing any of them would want, preferring to shoot and retreat then shoot again, but against a tank, pulling back took even more urgent priority.

Outside the hotel, more armor was rolling up the mainland road towards the biggest of the bridges onto the islands. Two tanks, three, four, six — Ereli barely registered counting them as he got a glimpse running past shattered windows, and before he had time to finish the count two of them exploded simultaneously on the bridge itself, throwing smoke in tight plumes through each and every porthole, then tongues of fire jetting through the gaps as the internal fuel reserves began to burn…

He spotted two camouflaged figures dropping off the side of the bridge into the water, and a heartbeat later the tanks' munitions stores went — the tanks' full stock of APSGMs, explosive shells and reactive armor going off in a single rippling sympathetic detonation.

The bridge lurched under the tanks' weight, folded, and an instant later the Azeri reinforcements on the mainland were cut off. The bridge crumpled entirely, throwing up white plumes as the rubble hit the water below.

An infantry carrier stopping to disgorge its passengers exploded the instant it opened up — the next to open its doors did too, exploding shells blasting into their interiors with the muffled, drawn-out thud of a LAMW firing.

Okay. Someone else was handling the armor. Ereli nodded to Eversen, and they returned to their objective, running for the stairwells — the building's elevators were down.

Seventy-five fucking floors of stairs later, and thirteen bodyguards, two Azeri soldiers, and two pistol rounds lodged in Ereli's armored chestpiece, they burst in on an empty luxury suite. One of the chairs was overturned. Bottles of wine and vodka, a jar of caviar, all left open and abandoned on the tables.

"Some party," Eversen murmured.

"The fuck did the president go?" Ereli snapped. He stepped out, looked both ways — a stairwell down? But no, brothers were pouring up out of all of them, panting for breath, aim steady as they checked left, right.

Ereli yanked his mask down and sniffed the air. Tried to follow the traces of vodka and food out into the corridor — lost it. Found it again. His nose wasn't that good, ability to scent close to human — in the genetic tweaking that'd made him he'd lost olfactory acuity in favor of the visual, but that was okay.

Couldn't smell a goddamn sign on the wall with exit directions no matter how good your nose was.

"There's a helipad — five floors up!" Ereli yelled. "Do *not* let that bastard get away!"

The word was passed up and down the ranks, and Ereli charged back up the nearest emergency stairwell, hot on Eversen's heels. They burst out into the hallways, stalked down them at a jog, guns leading the way.

Someone was saying something in Azeri behind a heavy set of double-doors — Ereli gestured at it. *Prepare to breach.*

Brothers he didn't recognize stacked up on both sides of it — he kicked through and they swarmed in around him, behind him.

A glass waiting room, leading out to a helipad anchored to the side of the hotel. Men in suits — bodyguards. Pull trigger, pull trigger — no, not at that guy, his uniform too ornate, no sidearm — him? No, he's already been shot…

Ereli froze, the only sound the after-echo of gunfire.

The guards and soldiers were dead, in slowly growing pools of blood. Three old men stood just outside the helipad door, the wind blowing past them and inside.

"Don't move!" A brother behind him yelled. "Don't fucking move!"

Ilhaim Nesimi, the man who clawed control of Azerbaijan from its previous, marginally less corrupt ruler for life, stood red-faced and desperate, his gray hair blowing around his skull in tight whips as a helicopter approached.

The helicopter's hull leaned backward as it slowed to land.

Nesimi tensed, as if readying to run. The military officer beside him in the big hat, just as old and too highly ranked to be armed, stepped out in front of him, shielding him. The other official, another old man, cringed away, clapping his hands over his head.

The helicopter edged up to the pad, Nesimi stepped toward it — someone barked a warning, but Nesimi went on, hand outstretched.

Two holes punched straight through the helicopter's cockpit, trailing broken glass and shredded metal behind the shells as they exited with a glossy red wake of the pilot's gore. A third shell slammed into the midsection, tearing into its engine — no exit wound, but the helicopter screamed, tilting as it lost power, finally clipping the end of the helipad with a squeal of metal before falling away into open air.

Three distant roars of a LAMW washed past them a few heartbeats later, the shells having reached their target long before the sound of the gunshots arrived.

Finger on the trigger of his rifle, back of his left wrist supporting the barrel with a set of zip-tie cuffs clutched in his hand, Ereli stepped closer. "Lay on the ground!" No helpful repeat, following a moment later. The translator on his vest was dead, too. "Fucking dammit. Can someone translate that for me?"

Apparently the three old men understood English. In the face of the rifles pointed at him, the military official got to his knees, then down on the floor.

President Nesimi turned his head, looking longingly beyond the lip of the helipad, at the open space so very, very near at hand. "How is this possible?" he asked, voice rough. "How is it possible you have done this to me?"

"Eighty-seven million New Dollars of donations make a lot of things possible. Lay down on the ground — you're being taken under custody by the Private Azerbaijan Civil Protection Effort as an unarmed belligerent pursuant to section five of the AD-MACP private military operations guidelines."

Nesimi bowed his head, holding his wrists out behind his back. "Everything I did, I did for my country. I am a patriot."

"Yeah?" Ereli grunted, cuffing him. "I'm sure the oil money didn't mean *shit* to you."

16. Partial Stability

::/ Baku, Azerbaijan.
::/ April, 2106.
::/ Ereli Estian.

Smoke pillared up into the sky above Baku. Fires, raging helplessly out of control. They'd been burning all day, but as night neared, it was finally possible to do something about them.

Dark-skinned North American contractors from Detroit were patrolling with the emergency services — two planeloads of them had been waiting in Germany for the signal to fly across, and with the commercial airport taken over, more manpower was arriving every hour to help out. The streets were mostly empty, but the flashing lights and sirens of fire engines were blazing through anyway, chased by captured armored vehicles with their sides splashed in white and neon yellow paint.

"You don't think that's going to be an issue?" Eversen asked, watching the fourth team of contractor-peacekeepers pull out, rolling across the now secure highway towards the coast and the Khazar Islands.

"Hm?"

"The dark skin. Most of the locals here, even the refugees, are light skinned." Eversen shrugged uncomfortably. "Humans can be funny about that."

Ereli flattened his ears, and grimaced — the hole in the side of his muzzle aching where the skinbonds pulled at the raw flesh. "I figured they'd like it better than us. Muslims don't like dogs."

Eversen took a step forward into the shattered glass of the street.

Empty, now. The only echoes of gunfire coming from the far east of the city at the moment — although there was an enemy push in the makings on the main commercial airport out west, it hadn't started yet.

"I haven't gotten much of that, out here," Eversen said. "None of the people terrified of touching me thing. Maybe the dog thing was about Tajikistan, not about Muslims."

"Maybe. But you haven't seen all that many civilians, either."

"No. That's true. Been busy."

Ereli patted Eversen's shoulder, and moved past him, heading down the street towards the nearest checkpoint. He'd been able to rechip most of his gear, though the displays in his goggles were still fried after the HERF. Had to lodge a transit request with a pad, instead. And a low priority request, since they weren't in combat.

They waved as they approached the checkpoint and the fire team of North American mercenaries waved back — not like Ereli and his brothers really *needed* to be IFF checked. The checkpoint itself was made up of some overturned cars, sandbags filled with rubble, and an automatic turret sitting on the pedestrian crossing island at the road junction.

"How's it going? You good?" the contractors' front-man asked.

"We're good." Eversen smiled, just as naturally as the human had.

"Yeah. Just waiting on a pick-up," Ereli added.

The front-man flashed a nervous thumbs-up. Ereli returned it. A couple of the group — North Americans were a lot more socially forward than Ereli was expecting — came up, making small talk, clearly very interested in the brothers, in trying to get their heads around working without a commanding officer. Well, the contractors had a commanding officer — part of their internal chain of command, all of them employed by Huxton Security — but that Ereli and his brothers didn't even have officers blew their minds, even when Ereli showed them how the tactical software worked.

"Taking over a city's a relatively simple task," Ereli said. "What we did was be selective about where we struck. Keeping an eye on the enemy is more to keep out of their way than to find targets. Engage, attack, melt away."

"And it's been what, four days?" Specialist Verge — an Anglo-African American, he'd been very quick to correct Ereli, *not* a Mestizo or Mulatto — seemed amazed.

"Six," Ereli said. "About five since our spearhead entered the city — six since this whole thing started."

"Wonders of that MACP neo-capitalist service economy," one of the others joked. "Just click express delivery, pay up, and you can have whatever you want, even regime change, *right now*."

They all laughed at that one.

With the regime beheaded the next step was cracking the ministries — work already underway, now that the Azeri governmental networks were infiltrated. The more civil-works oriented ministries — law and justice and street cleaning types — only needed a team of Ereli's brothers to show up. Stuff like the Ministry of State Security, that still needed brothers to break in, throwing out the army forces holding the buildings, free the civilian hostages the regime had taken. Most of the army were starting to surrender, though if that was because their president had been captured or because their battle networks were fucked, Ereli couldn't tell.

The situation outside of Baku was worse, militarily speaking — infantry and armor bedding down in the hinterlands so they'd be impossible to dislodge, UAV airstrips found to be empty when strikes were called down — but Baku was the major population center, where most of the money was coming from, and thankfully there were relatively few reports of the military taking its aggression out on the local population outside of the city's center.

"You going to stick around, mop up the ministries?" Ereli asked Eversen, when their transportation arrived — a patrol of their brothers in a pair of pre-fab buggies, happy to give them a lift back to Forward Base Gamma. "Or you wanna come help me arm the interim police force?"

That'd been Ereli's idea — shipping in non-lethal weapons to arm the locals with, put together a temporary force so the people could police themselves. It was popular on the crowdfunding polls, and one of the political opposition militias — that Panah Karimov guy they'd failed to buy ammo from — had volunteered to help recruit for it.

Eversen glanced back, over his shoulder at one of the plumes of smoke eating into the early sunset. "Yeah, I think I'm done with fighting for now," he said. "Let's go make peace instead."

17. Mopping Up

::/ Baku, Azerbaijan.
::/ April, 2106.
::/ Edane Estian.

Edane and Sokolai were getting good at their entry routine. Edane took down the door with a shell — there were plenty of shells, now that all the armories were running. Sokolai took down the rest of the door, kicking or shouldering it down. Edane followed him in, occasionally needing to fire off a second shot from the LAMW to help clear the room.

It felt good. Real. Cleared out his nose and let him get the scent of explosives and death and rubble deep into himself.

They were running with about two thirds of their electronics functional — they'd had time to rechip and replace what they could — he'd had to throw away his old scope and get a new one — but the printers in-country were swamped with orders, they didn't have everything they needed. A flight was due in tomorrow morning with basic replacements, but for now there wasn't anything to do but soldier on.

"Armor, north-east, second intersection," Sokolai hissed from behind Edane.

Edane picked up the LAMW, and turned, edging across the housing block's flat roof, between drying lines for clothes. He lifted the weapon awkwardly and rolled to his back, bench pressing the LAMW up until its scope got a peek over the sidewall.

The LAMW's barrel was hot to the touch. The suppressor was long dry, its outer casing heat-cracked. They'd been fighting a long time.

Edane lowered the LAMW and looked into the scope's viewfinder, playing the scope footage back. He found the tank, marked it in the playback — the viewfinder showed him a tag where the vehicle was. About a half-kilometer away.

The housing block was part of a row of connected buildings, roughly in the middle of a wide, open square. Good sightlines, and plenty of structure to eat up the tank shells.

Edane stripped one of his three remaining Shaped High Explosive Double-Warhead Armor Piercing shells from its magazine on his hip, drew the LAMW's bolt lever back — thumbing the chambered solid core shell back down into its magazine before the extractor pulled it free — and manually loaded the SHED-WAP directly into the chamber.

Sokolai crabwalked in beside him, ducked down. He held out his phone, the tank's make and model — UTR-77 — displayed along with the schematics. Two pin-lined paths marked possible points of vulnerability, one through the roof and down at an angle into the tank's frontal optics wiring junction, and a second through the turret and into the autoloader.

Edane tapped the phone, dragging the pin-lines down, shifting their angle to better match what he had off the roof. He shook his head. "Can't do it from here. Need to get over to the other building, or wait 'til it gets closer."

A shake of the head in turn, Sokolai's teeth grit. Sokolai switched the phone's display back to the linked stick-eye disposable cameras he'd set. One had been burned out by the tank's targeting laser. In the feed from the other two they could make out the huddled forms of infantry. "I better get downstairs before they start trying to come up," Sokolai said. "Help when you can?"

Edane nodded. "Yell if you need me."

Sokolai nodded back, and pulled up his facemask — the camo inactive, reset to a murky brown-grey-black pattern. He hitched up his rifle and crawled into the narrow roof access door, back downstairs.

Edane edged back to the roof's edge, ear perked into the grilled gap in his helmet, listening. Tanks were loud, while they were charging their batteries or running at speed, burning fuel in turbines. On electrics, though, they could creep along, silent but for the crush of their weight.

He tapped the button under the rim of his helmet for his comms, gazing into the wristwatch he'd strapped around the LAMW's forestock. He touched the wristwatch's little display with his forefinger, navigated it through the communications web, sent a request through to UAV operations in his city-sector. It only chimed twice before the connection was accepted. "We have tanks coming up towards the airport at Pair-Thirty-One's position," he said.

"Still no strike capacity available Pair-Thirty-One. Stud-Four will be on station in forty minutes."

Not good enough. Edane grit his teeth. "Do you have any alternative capacity?"

"Alternative capacity, Thirty-One?"

"Yeah. Like a distraction. Or observation."

A pause from the other end of the connection. "Can-do. Overwatch and a *distraction* in T-minus three. Hope you like countermeasure flares, Thirty-One."

"Appreciate it, operations."

"You're welcome. You are now on hold, but please stay on the line."

His earpiece chirped. Edane touched back to Sokolai's channel. "Operations is getting us some overflight support in under three minutes."

Sokolai kept his voice low. "Firepower?"

"No strike, she said, but overwatch and a distraction."

"Distraction? What's that supposed to... whatever. They're stacking up to come inside downstairs. That tank's angling to support them. Going to need you here soon."

"I'll try not to keep you waiting..."

Edane crept up to the roof's sidewall. Listening. He tensed his ears, turning his head... he couldn't be quite sure where the tank was. All he could make out was the clatter of tank treads as the tank moved, an inconsistent sound — only audible when the vehicle's suspension flexed, otherwise the rubberized rollers deadened the sound, and tank treads moving slowly could be whisper-soft on hard surfaces. Hard to pinpoint it from sound alone, but he had a rough idea.

His earpiece chimed at him. "Feeding you oversight now, Thirty-one."

Edane wished his goggles still worked. He had to use the wristwatch strapped to his LAMW, and the tiny screen was almost useless.

The infantry were entering the building, and the tank's chassis was turned to present a corner of its front tread toward the building, cannon levelled in their direction. There were other white splotches of heat in the area, but the signals interpretation software and operator had tagged them as non-combatants.

"Distraction?" Edane asked.

"Coming up in minus thirty…"

Edane scrabbled back round onto his back, laying the LAMW down the length of his body. He planted the bipod between his feet, shoulders braced against the washing-line post immediately behind him.

"Minus twenty…"

He unlatched the magazine, stripped off the shell on top — a solid core armor-piercing round — slapped the magazine back in, and rearranged his shells like he had before, this time pushing the solid core into the chamber. First the solid core, then the SHED-WAP. He thumbed the fire selector to two-round burst.

"Minus ten…"

Edane touched in under his helmet, switching back to Sokolai's channel. "Distraction incoming." He set his feet against the bipod's legs.

"Got it."

"Three, two, one—"

A black streak cut between the buildings across the plaza and exploded in light, a roaring sound of flames accompanying pouring red curtains of fire across the buildings — the UAV dropping a trail of dozens of blindingly hot flares, like a long bouncing string of stars, before it hopped over the rooftops and vanished back over the horizon.

Edane sighted in on the tank, aimpoint in his scope guided by the oversight feed, and pulled back on the trigger. The LAMW shuddered on the bipod legs, fighting against his boots, sending painful jolts up his ankle and along both knees, cracking into his shoulder what seemed like once — the two rounds fired so close together that the hole punched by the solid core round tearing through the roof's side-wall had barely started shedding dust before the SHED-WAP blew through in the solid core's wake — striking the tank directly in the divot the solid core had torn out of its armor, the paired warheads working in just the same fashion as they did in larger anti-tank weaponry.

The first shaped charge was highly directional, a solid blast of force on impact, funneling hot gas, molten metal, and shockwave pressure into a tightly focused point — a point hit an instant later by the secondary charge, plummeting through the gap and smearing on impact, like a ball of clay hammered into every tiny crack the first charge had torn and melted through the armor plate. A bare instant after impact the deformed charge exploded — tearing open the gaps and shredding the armor plate, and what was behind it, to pieces.

In this case, what was behind the armor plate happened to be the tank's loading mechanism. Something burned out in the barrel with a thump — the chambered shell going off — and the un-armed tank shell crashed through the building's walls and tumbled out the other end of the housing block, smoke billowing up from the cannon's end. More black smoke began to boil from the loader — the emergency hatch blew out a few heartbeats later, the pair of crewmen stumbling out and sprinting away before anything else detonated.

Tank knocked out, the infantry below were yelling at each other — a man screamed in response to a muffled thump downstairs, a grenade. Edane hauled himself up over the roof's edge, LAMW held rifle-fashion, and he snapped off a solid core shell at the men below. It crashed through a man's shoulder and down his left side, gouged a crater out of his leg as the shell skimmed out. The yells turned to screams, gunfire roared inside the building, a long burst that tore out of a downstairs window, spraying fragments of brick and dust. One of the soldiers threw their gun away… then another did the same, falling to the ground and covering his head.

"Four down, three surrendered — I need you down here," Sokolai hissed.

Edane peeked over the roof's edge again, shoulders sore. "Get down and drop your weapons!" He yelled, translator on his vest repeating it almost as he said it.

Two soldiers looked up, from beside their maimed, bleeding comrade. Made eye contact — Edane tensed, ready to shoot… but the man on the left threw his gun aside, and the other simply looked back down to his wounded comrade, hands bloody as he tried to hold his friend together.

Fifteen minutes later, after getting downstairs with Sokolai, and disarming the enemy in groups, cuffing the men inside first with zipties, then the ones from outside in groups of two, they'd somehow captured all of the enemy. And the Azeris were laughing. Laughing, even though two of them were dead, and some of the others were waiting on a medevac.

"Twenty four of us. Two of them!" the officer laughed, tears in his eyes.

One man looked ready to fight, after he'd been disarmed and cuffed, but when the officers started talking like that, he slumped on his knees, relieved.

"We surrendered the platoon to two of them," the second replied, hunching over to wipe his eyes on his shoulders. *"My God, we'd have been killed if we hadn't lost this war!"*

The laughter was infectious. Even Edane and Sokolai were laughing, by the time the contactors arrived with emergency medical kits for the soldiers, bringing the news that the airport was still secure, that the last of the Ministry of State Security's facilities in the city had been successfully raided and prisoners, from the protests of days before, freed.

"War's over," Sokolai murmured, tears in his eyes — not just from the laughter. "We don't have to shoot anyone else."

Edane perked his ears, tense. "You crying?" he asked.

Sokolai thumbed at his eyes, startled, looked down at the wet on his ruddy fur. "Yeah. Maybe." He blinked, hard. "I'm just glad this is over."

18. Moving on

::/ Baku, Azerbaijan.
::/ April, 2106.
::/ Ereli Estian.

The plan was to head north, to meet with one of the opposition leaders. Panah Karimov, formerly of the pre-Eurasian war's state sponsored media. An old man now, he'd spent the decades since Nesimi's coup dodging the regime's arrest warrants while holding together what amounted to the country's only political opposition — which, given Nesimi's crackdowns, had become an armed militia out of necessity.

Ereli tapped through the dossier on the man, still bearing Andercom West's branding on each document. He tilted the pad around to get a better full view of one of the photographs. Karimov and the Aliyevs — family members of the previous regime — in Baku, summer of 2045. City was nicer then, a little flatter. In the picture he was a dark-haired young adult, beaming on the arm of a cosmetic-surgery and genetweak beautiful woman — if they even had genetweaking back then. The Caspian Sea was deeper, and there weren't quite so many oil derricks out on the water — certainly not the forests of steel they'd dodged on the way in to the Khazar Islands. He held the pad out to Eversen across the interior of the armored vehicle — the interior was scarred, and it reeked of wet paint, even on the move. "Here's the last publicly available photo of the guy we're meeting."

Eversen took it, showed it to the brother beside him — Srednoi — and passed the pad down the line. "It's a little out of date."

"Sixty *years* out of date." One of the brothers laughed.

Waiting for the pad to make it back around to him, Ereli sat back. "Man's our link to getting ahold of local manpower, though. An intermediary said he could get us upwards of ten thousand potential recruits for the intermediary police."

"Trained, or untrained?"

Ereli shrugged. "If it is trained, it's going to be of the three months in boot camp variety."

Eversen shook his head. "We were barely getting started, with five years of training."

"Funny. Most humans I talk to don't remember as much out of their childhoods as we do. Certainly not so much that sticks."

A shrug in turn, while Eversen considered that, swinging his jaw side to side. "Not like forgetting something's going to make them harder to sell. Human kids don't get trained like we do, they're people, not products."

"True. Not most of them, anyway."

"You know a human trained from childhood as a product?"

Ereli gestured vaguely back the way they'd come. "Some of the young political activists I met around the city seem like they've been raised for this, almost. Waiting for this day... lots of ideas about how they want to run things."

"I kinda like the crowdfunding and voting thing. Needs some work, though," Eversen said. "Everybody wants to pay for hospitals, nobody wants to pay for roads."

"Yeah, well, when people need a hospital they notice it's not there, when they need roads they forget—"

The world tilted ninety degrees, then ninety degrees again. Ereli's ears rang. Shockwave concussion beat his chest to mush. He hung from the webbing of his seat — his rifle fell away from his lap and clattered to the roof above with a dozen others. There was a bulge in the sidewall, something screeching, a sensation of motion as the vehicle skidded on its roof — the enclosed space suddenly felt very hot, very tight, all the blood was in his head, his legs dangling uselessly in space as he hung upside down.

He saw a brother deeper in the suddenly dark passenger compartment banging at the seat webbing's buckle with the palm of his hand. Tore it open only to plummet down. Something smelled like burning, Ereli couldn't hear clearly — he couldn't lift the catch on the buckle. Too small for his fingers, somehow. Ereli yanked his knife from his belt and jammed it into the catch — twisted. The knifeblade's point snapped off — did it again. The catch gave and he slipped down, clinging to the webbing, falling onto his feet. Grabbed Eversen — cut open the shoulder-strap, the hip-strap, helped him to his feet.

Picked up a rifle off the floor, any rifle, even if it wasn't his. Shouldered his way out after the brother who got the passenger hatch open. Couldn't breathe properly — air was too thick, too hot. Fires lit the road, smoke everywhere.

The armored vehicle was on its roof, the other four of the convoy were ahead and behind — the one furthest back was nothing but scrap, the car up front burning but on its wheels, hatches open.

"Where?" Someone yelled. "Who—"

Tracers cut through the early-evening dark, bullets ripped a brother off his feet and onto the asphalt. Ereli shot back, quick double-taps at the origin of the tracers, at the flash between the buildings on the hillside out left.

"Under attack, this location, immediate support required, multiple wounded." "Contact north-east." "Contact west." "Contact north — Contact down, relocating."

Who the hell was shooting at them? The army? The army wasn't *out here*. It didn't make any sense, this area was supposedly under control of Karimov and his supporters.

There wasn't any cover except the armored vehicles. He ran up against the burning hulk's side, right where some kind of ordnance had smashed in the sidewall — that made sense. He was afraid for a second, that he'd be in the line of fire, but it made sense. The armored vehicle was on its roof, it was upside down — the impact site was facing away from the direction of attack.

He lifted the rifle — not his rifle. The rifle's electronics were confused about his location, but he sighted in north, then north-east.

West was behind him — west was the open field behind him. He turned, found a target, shot — shot — started moving after the second recoil against his shoulder, not bothering to check his hits, looking for more cover, looking for something to shield him from both the north-east and the west, from both forward-left and the right, but there wasn't anything so he ran for the gutter where the road's paving ended and the dirt next to it began but the tracers lanced straight *through* him, pain complete and utter as his own guts fogged the air and he crumpled onto the ground, all the muscles in his belly giving up at once. He hit the road, clawing at it, dragging himself an inch at a time for the gutter.

It was right *there* and his body hitched again, spasming, and Ereli just had to get into the six inches of cover it'd give him, had to find cover then shoot then move to the next bit of cover and he'd be okay, that was how firefights worked, you shot and you took cover and you shot, he just needed to get to cover, just had to get over whatever it was he was leaving on the ground and everything was slick with blood now and *fuck* them, he'd get to the gutter he could reach it just a little bit further, just a little bit further, just—

::/ BAKU, AZERBAIJAN.
::/ SREDNOI ESTIAN.

"THERE! FUCKING *THERE!*" Srednoi pointed again, just as the machine gun somewhere out to the right opened up again, scattering chips of asphalt and blasting through the poor bastard stuck on the asphalt.

His brother Skarlin didn't respond, hiking up the grenade launcher to his shoulder. *Pam, Pam, Pam,* the thing made muffled thuds of noise launching one grenade after another — they flashed as directional charges blew mid-air, flinging them further up the hillside, between the buildings the enemy were using for cover. Explosions thundered out as each grenade found a target, the gunfire stopped. But the enemy were also behind them, there were targets out west and—

::/ Baku, Azerbaijan.
::/ Skarlin Estian.

"Srednoi? Srednoi! Man down!" Skarlin dropped the grenade launcher and grabbed Srednoi's armor carry-loop, dragged him in behind the blown out vehicle as fast as he could. Brothers were spreading out to all sides, gunfire lancing out in every direction. "Hold on, Srednoi, hold on…"

He crawled in behind the armored vehicle's wheel, pulled Srednoi's limp weight just a few feet more, then stopped to assess the wound.

Had to do triage, had to follow the procedure. Fuck. *Fuck*. He hadn't done this since he was seven years old. Bleeding. Had to check on the bleeding first. Srednoi was bleeding from the throat. Big, messy wound. Skarlin pushed down on it, tried to apply pressure, stop the flow — there wasn't a flow. "Shit, shit…"

He turned Srednoi's head to the side. There was an entry-wound, almost lost in the mass of his fur, just over his ear. The throat-wound was an exit wound. The bullet had gone clean through Srednoi's skull and jaw.

What the fuck was Skarlin going to say to Srednoi's dad? Coming out here for this was just *work*, just getting back to their roots, it wasn't even supposed to be dangerous — brothers with experience were doing all the point fighting, Skarlin and Srednoi were just there to operate heavy weapons, police the locals, they weren't supposed to be getting fucking *ambushed*, weren't supposed to be dying.

The armored vehicle exploded. Threw Skarlin away like a doll a kid was done playing with, left him ragged on the asphalt, a mess of pain. Pain was his friend. Pain told him he was alive and kicking. Pain was good. He tried to stand up — couldn't. Tried again — still couldn't. He looked down and there wasn't anything left of him anymore, just ragged meat at the ends of his arms and blood pouring off his face onto the road surface underneath him, every part of him not wrapped up in body-armor gone — no ears, no tail, no fingers, one of his feet gone.

He tried to get up again.

And again.
And again.

::/ Baku, Azerbaijan.
::/ Eversen Estian.

Ereli was dead. Eversen lay belly down in the dirt gutter beside the road, bleeding into the dust and staring at Ereli, not more than ten feet away.

Dead.

They'd been talking and then the car got hit and he didn't know who killed Ereli or how or when, but there was a lot of time to think between the *CRUMP* of detonations around him. Anti-armor rockets, he thought.

He gripped his rifle tighter, eyes fixed on the darkness around them, out left and right of the line and travel. Towards Ereli's corpse and back away from it.

The last attack had finished off one of the armored vehicles up ahead. The brother who'd been huddled behind it tried getting up one last time, mess of missing limbs waving helplessly, and then all the fight left him.

Eversen grit his teeth, ducking his head.

It'd been worse than this. He'd seen worse than this. Support was coming. There hadn't been any support in Tajikistan, in Tajikistan it'd been worse than this, the Tajik special forces had come and it'd been worse than this.

This was a cakewalk.

Ereli was dead.

This was still a cakewalk. Look at them, look at that contact there — Eversen lifted his rifle to fire — *tap tap,* and started pushing himself backwards along the gutter, breathing hard and fast, pain of the gunshot in his thigh close to overwhelming. That man, coming to inspect the wrecks? He hadn't been wearing a uniform, he'd been wearing civilian clothes, carrying a rifle — not even any helmet, which was why Eversen had shot him in the head. Not even a real soldier.

Another rocket hit the asphalt nearby, the shockwave rolling through Eversen's body like a punch — bits of rock stung his tail and side, skittered past his nose. Eversen pointed his rifle left, where the rocket had come from — thumbed the rifle's controls the way he had as a kid, hoping whoever owned the gun had kept to the old system. They had — the scope lit up in a confused thermal blur, but there was a trail of heat left painted on the ground where the rocket's exhaust had washed over cold grass and asphalt and along the wall of a building, and *there* was the point of origin, and Eversen twisted his body in the dirt and fired once, twice, three times. Ducked his head in fright at the crack of a bullet passing overhead. Pushed backward again, grinding himself into the dirt. Away from Ereli. Away from where his brothers were dying.

"Support on-station, hold tight," a voice in his ear told him.

He huffed at the ground, trying to hide the heat of his breath with his body, for all the good that would do. Eversen held tight.

They were going to meet Panah Karimov. They were being attacked by irregulars — by un-uniformed combatants, not the Azeri army. Un-uniformed combatants like Panah commanded. Panah would've been able to guess the route, he'd done this, or one of his people had sold them out.

Why? *Why?*

Eversen and his brothers had just fucking *liberated* the country, dismantled a regime that'd oppressed them for decades, a regime that had been killing the people brave enough to protest, even throwing their journalists in jail. Eversen and his brothers had just killed the bad guys. *Why* were the civs doing this?

A face in the dark. Human, so Eversen shot it. He didn't care who it was, nobody was going to kill him, *nobody*. Fierce heat bubbled up in his gut. Pride. Eversen was going to live and the people who had attacked him were going to die.

Support arrived — drones whining overhead, cannons blasting at the ground, pulping the earth into sprays of dust across the enemy positions, tearing men open and cutting them down as they ran.

Eversen twisted and shot as their attackers fled, grit his teeth and aimed, and fired, and ran on his shot leg toward cover even if it was only a hump of dirt, and fell into formation with his brothers, sweeping west, then north, then east again, clearing the area while the drones scythed past overhead.

They found sixteen dead human bodies, and body-bagged seven of their own after sending another eight back into Baku hooked up to Emergency Stabilization kits.

Why had they been attacked? Who the hell had they been fighting for, if not the oppressed people of Azerbaijan, like Panah Karimov? Why couldn't there be peace?

Someone told Eversen, later, that Ereli had listed him as next of kin.

Over and over again, Eversen asked himself why.

II
Honeymoon

::/ Dushanbe, Tajikistan.
::/ January, 2104.
::/ Edane Estian.

There was blood in the dirt yard, out behind the civilian housing row next to the security base, and Edane didn't understand why the Muslims had done it. Why they'd killed that sheep with knives, pinning the struggling animal down, its throat slit, bleeding it out into plastic buckets.

When he'd asked one of the Private Military Contactor Liaisons about it, he'd been told it was Eid-i-Kurbon, a religious festival, something about eating food with family and getting together in friendship — but that still didn't explain why they mutilated the sheep.

It was cold, too. No matter how Edane lifted the collar of the coat he'd bought — too small for his shoulders — he couldn't keep his nose out of the cold. So cold that in the mornings there was ice on the rare patches of grass, from the dew frozen solid. On really cold nights it even covered the dirt, a thin blanket of white, but it wasn't snow. Edane had never seen snow. Edane had never been cold before, either, not with his whole body. He'd only touched cold things like drinks, been a little chill standing under an air conditioning vent, but never *cold*. Not like this.

He was far away from home and almost all of the people here had the same skin color, and even when there were differences — mostly among the refugees — they all went around in blocks of pale pink and dark pink and dusky brown, not mixing. Like there were rules here nobody talked about. None of them had genemods, none of them had even changed their skin to a new color.

The water wasn't safe, either. All the faucets had signs warning about contaminants. Some of the signs were live and showed particulate counts, but most were just paint on aluminum with scanner codes to point phones at live warnings. All the signs warned to run the water without touching it for five minutes before using any, even in some good hotels.

Tajikistan wasn't the same as home, but Edane understood it better.

There was always someone who said what to do, a list of objectives on the barracks board in the morning. Some of Edane's brothers were already there, working with him — more were arriving at the PMOC base outside town every day. There were bad guys who tried to kill Edane sometimes, when he was patrolling in Dushanbe's streets with the other mercenaries, and Edane shot back at them. Easy. But even if he understood it here, he didn't feel like he belonged.

Edane lifted his rifle, shouldering it to shoot back, and lightning-strike quick Thorne slapped down the rifle's barrel toward the ground.

"Hold fire!" he barked, just like one of the drill instructors, so Edane did, patiently watching the target pry up another stone from a gouge in the road where the old asphalt had been worn away.

The target wound back, threw it — Edane's brother Sokolai a little further along the cordon line turned his shoulder into the strike, catching it on the dense ballistic padding of his body-armor, and started to lift his rifle. Lowered it, glancing warily along the line towards Thorne.

Edane wagged his tail the once. He liked being told what to do by Thorne. It meant he didn't have to work it out for himself.

The target shouted something in Tajik Edane didn't entirely understand, but amongst other words he heard the word for dog — *Sag!* — and the target's tone of voice was hateful and angry. The translator on Edane's vest didn't say it again in English, so he couldn't be sure, but he felt like whatever the target said had been meant hurtfully.

The civilians were protesting, and the PMC Liaisons had sent Edane and his brothers to help reinforce the cordon around the square. Ordinarily the police would do it, but the police were on strike and rioting in Kuktosh — a remote district of Dushanbe to the south-east.

Thorne leaned forward, his lined face marked out by a dusting of grey stubble under his jaw. "Hold fire! Safe weapons and *leave* them—"

Edane was already dry-firing his rifle at the dirt between his feet, magazine removed after throwing back the bolt to drop the chambered round, by the time the clacking of weaponry up and down the cordon line had caught Thorne's attention.

The old man stared at Edane beside him, thumping the magazine back into place — weapon safe and uncocked, unless he chose to yank on the cocking handle. Edane blinked back, neutrally.

"So, they didn't just make you lot to shoot down protestors at the drop of a hat, eh?"

Edane hesitated. "Sir, no sir." He held his rifle in front of his chest, fingertip curled over the trigger guard, well away from the trigger itself. "That man made himself a belligerent — he was armed."

"The boy's younger than you are, and it's a *stone*." Thorne gazed at the crowd ahead of them, its ragged near edge made up of people chanting in Tajik, waving signs. Some carried tools — shovels, the handles for pick-axes — but Thorne had explained that this didn't qualify them as armed belligerents until they actually tried to start hitting Edane and the others with them. "Not a reasonable threat."

Edane had been trained to kill with stones. Not by throwing them, and with larger stones than that, but improvised weapon training had taught him that stones were reasonable weapons. He didn't correct Thorne, though — the old Brit didn't like it when he did that.

"*They send filthy animals to oppress us! Foreigners, instead of our own countrymen! Why? The government does not have the support of the people, because our own countrymen would never bar our way — they would join us and march!*"

The speaker was impassioned, raw. Edane hadn't seen anything like it outside of social studies class in high school, even if the translator's flat tones deadened the impact of what the guy was saying. He was a wild-haired man, the black curls falling into an arrowhead around his face. No little religious skullcap on his head, like a lot of the other men, and he was cleanshaven. Young.

Thorne wagged his finger across Edane's face, commanding attention, more for the benefit of Edane and his brothers than his own men — the other European mercenaries in the cordon line already knew what Thorne wanted. "Stay in place. If they start throwing things, step out of line to dodge them. You do not shoot at anyone unless they're pointing a gun at you."

"Sir, yes…" Edane tensed. None of the other mercenaries were responding. Just staring silently ahead — one or two separating out Edane's brothers. Keeping them calm, as Thorne had explained, earlier. Making sure that Edane and the others had an example to follow in the soldiers at their sides. "… sir," Edane finished lamely.

Thorne shouldered his way out of the cordon, and slung his rifle back, holding up his hand. *"Excuse me!"* He waved sharply at the wild-haired man — Thorne didn't bother to use the translator as he approached, speaking in Tajik.

"You see? They send the foreigners and their dogs to hold us back from liberating ourselves, rob us of our livelihoods—"

Thorne pushed his fingers into his mouth and whistled — a harsh, attention-getting screech.

Silence fell for a moment. Even the wild-haired man was staring at Thorne now.

"Excuse me!" he repeated. *"You would prefer to be policed by your own countrymen? The citizens policed by themselves — that will give you safe streets?"*

"Of course!" the man hurled back at Thorne, waving a fist.

The ragged front of the protest crowd stared on, falling into the slow gibbering whisper of many people speaking to each other in low tones.

Thorne stepped back, gesturing past the cordon line at the jeeps the mercenaries were using as transport. *"Well, would you like me to drive you to Kuktosh? It's only an hour away, and your countrymen, the police, are making the streets very safe for the citizenry there."* He paused. There was laughter — nervous, not from the ragged front edge of the crowd, those waving their weapons, but from those further back — the ones simply bearing signs. Thorne went on. *"They're breaking into shops and people's homes — not marching against the government like you. Are you so very sure you would prefer your countrymen to police you?"*

The wild-haired man turned back to his supporters, calling for their attention. *"Don't listen to him, our brothers in Kuktosh are fighting oppression, it is only government propaganda—"*

"I can drive you to Kuktosh right now. Maybe we better do that if you're so eager to join in. Edane, restrain him," Thorne called back.

Edane slung his rifle, marching forward, tearing one of the zip-tie handcuffs from his belt pouch, marching on the protestor — the man backed away in fear, fell to his knees. *"No! Leave me, I do not want to go to Kuktosh, leave me be!"*

Thorne waited long enough for Edane to get close before whistling again, sharp. "Edane! Halt." The old man turned to the crowd, spreading his hands. He smiled, with teeth. *"Oh, so he doesn't want to go to Kuktosh?"*

Some of the angry protestors stayed angry, some were frightened… some laughed at the wild-haired man as he got to his feet, stepping away from Edane, swearing at him — calling him a tool of Satan and a dozen other things, friends of his coming through the crowd and pulling him back through it.

The laughter got a little louder. While Thorne rejoined the cordon line, the protestors in the thick of the crowd started trying to get a chant going again, waving their signs in an unfamiliar alphabet Edane couldn't read, a mixture of Cyrillic letters and Arabic swirls. Nobody was listening to the wild-haired man anymore. The boys throwing stones were skulking at the back of the crowd, not so bold, now.

Edane rejoined the line beside Thorne, rubbing at his wrist. Picking through his fur uncomfortably. He didn't like being called a tool of Satan, even if people had laughed at it.

"Something on your mind, son?" Thorne asked.

"I don't understand what just happened."

"Lifting a corner, that's all. Easier to flip something over on its head if you find a corner to lift."

Edane looked down at Thorne worriedly, and brought his rifle back around to his stomach. "Corner to lift?"

"Make people laugh and they stop thinking. Halts their train of thought. Make a man look ridiculous, and even if what he was saying had been taken seriously moments before, he's a laughing stock now — nobody will listen no matter how legitimate his argument." Thorne hissed between his teeth, shaking his head. "Poor sod's right. Mercenaries should *not* bloody well be policing this crowd, that's for sure."

Edane twitched an ear.

"You don't quite follow me, do you, son?" Thorne smiled strangely up at Edane.

"Sir, no sir." Edane looked down at his feet for a moment, then up at the quieter crowd, the signs moving in unison as they chanted their complaints — almost musical.

Edane liked music, a bit. His mothers played it all the time.

"I'd like to learn, though," he added. "How to lift a corner." It seemed like a way to deal with belligerents that Grandpa Jeff would've liked.

Thorne's smile changed. Crinkled the corners of his eyes, now. "Well. Perhaps it's not too late to teach an old dog a new trick, eh, son?"

"Sir?"

"That was a joke, son. You're what, twenty? That's ancient for a dog."

"Twenty-one." Edane paused. "I don't understand that joke, sir."

"Call me Thorne, son." The old man gazed levelly at the crowd.

"Thorne, yes Thorne. Would learning to speak Tajik help?"

Thorne's expression got crinklier. "It wouldn't hurt."

19. Fixing Potholes

::/ Baku, Azerbaijan.
::/ May, 2106.
::/ Eversen Estian.

DEAD BODIES DIDN'T smell right, and Eversen couldn't work out why.

They couldn't find a morgue that could take all the dead — the city's morgues were already overflowing with the dead, civilian and combatant alike. Instead, they'd cleared out a tiled restaurant kitchen, a big block of a room, fittings torn out with refrigerant equipment piled against the walls, door covered with tacked up plastic sheeting.

Sixteen sheet-covered corpses on the floor to the left, seven on the right.

Was it because they were old dead? No, Eversen had smelled that before, the start of decay and rot, worse. But these corpses were being held at low temperatures, their decomposition held back. The sewage-and-blood scent of bodies, always mingling with the perversely food-like scent of raw, torn flesh. Yes, there was that, but… was it the sweat, maybe?

None of the corpses were sweating. The sweat on their skin was old, drying, none of the natural processes of life refreshing it — as though something had been frozen and cut off mid-way, the very smell of them like a photograph torn in half. It was obvious there had been life, but now…

Eversen leaned harder on his cane, a simple length of metal tubing one of the fabricators had done no more than stick a bend into and cap off with a plastic heel.

"Who were they?" he murmured, pushing his weight back onto

his good leg despite the surge of pain through his thigh, entry and exit wounds burning under layers of coagulant foam.

Stelborn consulted the pad. "Don't know yet. We're decrypting the national databases, but running face recognition comparisons between these and the social networks has to wait until Andercom's day office opens. Time-zone fuck-up."

Grimacing, Eversen let the cane slip in his grasp. Twisting it to drop the handle to the floor, gripping its heel to poke the hook in under the nearest sheet and pry it back enough to gaze at the grey, strangely white but not ethnically white face beneath.

The corpse was Caucasian as they came — Azerbaijan was part of the damn southern Caucasus — but the corpse wasn't *white*. White meant Anglo or Euro, white meant democratic, white meant *capitalist*. It meant the same as African-American or Afro-Costeño or Libres or Black, meant the same as Anglo-African-American or Mulatto or Mestizo, meant the same as any other word for any other ethnicity. It had fuck all to do with skin color, it meant *friendly*, having an ethnicity meant *human*, and the corpse was one of the enemy combatants who'd killed Ereli and by virtue of that had been ejected from the fucking species, the same way Eversen had been legally added to it by the Emancipation.

The corpse was something else. It wasn't even Azeri. It was alien, different, *wrong*.

Its sweat didn't smell right.

He twitched his cane aside and let the sheet fall. "Find out who they were."

"Eversen? What about them?" Stelborn wordlessly gestured the pad to the right. Towards the other seven bodies.

The much bigger bodies, sheets over the heads lifted by muzzles where the heads lay intact.

Eversen flattened his ears back, staring at them. "They're all still dog-tagged?"

"Yeah. There are cases where we've had trouble matching remains to bodies, but it's just scraps of flesh — all the loose limbs are matched to bodies."

He should have gone to find Ereli. Said goodbye. Taken a last look at his dead brother's face. But Eversen was Ereli, now. He'd inherited Ereli's signatory status.

Fuck it. They were designed to be interchangeable anyway.

"Process them as per whatever documentation they filed." Eversen dug his cane into the kitchen-slash-morgue's tiles and limped to the door. "Remember to make sure medical's cleaned them out for organ transplants, first."

"Juan, slow down." Eversen palmed at his forehead, wincing. "What'd they say?"

"The streets are *ruined*." Juan, back in San Iadras and on the other end of the connection, was still talking fast, but pausing more between sentences. "The protest barricades are still burning and they're too big for the local neighborhoods to pull apart. There are holes in the streets."

"Holes in the streets." Eversen shuddered, again, and crushed the phone against his forehead for a moment. "Juan," he murmured, phone back at his ear for an instant, "can you write this up? E-mail me? Now is not a good time."

"Sure, Ereli — I mean. Eversen, sorry. Shit. Yes, sorry, Eversen. I'll get on that."

Eversen ground his head back into the pillow, snapping off the phone.

"You sure you don't want more by way of pain management?" the nurse asked, watching the robot rig nervously.

Eversen shook his head, and sagged back. His thigh was locked into a steadying frame, while the mostly pre-programmed robot went through its routine. It had gone in through a keyhole cut into a shaved section of his thigh above the gunshot wound, the robot's head worming its way around in there, tearing out dying and infected tissue then gulping it up, gobbets flying through the attached vacuum hose.

It hurt, but *fuck* hurt. Eversen needed to be on schedule. He'd only stopped working because the scan had shown the wound in his thigh wasn't healing right — no internal bleeding, but the wound channel, where the bullet had torn into him, wasn't doing well. The bullet's impact had stretched his tissues out around it, like dropping a bowling ball into a pond. Like a pond the body was mostly water, but instead of splashing out, the flesh stretched and tore, cells and capillaries ruptured.

He would've been healing alright if he'd just kept flat on his back, but he had Ereli's job now. He had to check in with the rest of the brothers who'd signed the incorporation documents for the fund, had to sign off on every new chunk of budget before it could be released to one of the subsidiary corporations formed to tackle problems on the ground. Eversen had to make sure the citizens were fed, that the power stayed on, that the remnants of the Azeri air force were kept out of the airspace — they had some kind of high altitude plane with a HERF dish that they'd used twice so far, but it had circled off over Uzbekistan, disappeared under cloud cover and now nobody was entirely sure where it was, or even if it was in the hands of Azeri loyalists or the Uzbek government.

Had the Uzbeks done it? Had they backed the ambush team that'd hit the convoy, that'd killed Ereli, the way they'd sent tanks into Tajikistan years ago? Was it the Neo-Aliyevs — the faction made up of rich civilians members of the old regime's family, many of whom lived in Dubai after being run out by Nesimi? Was it the religious radicals, angry about dogs? (Maybe not. Eversen hadn't met even *one* religious person in Baku who'd out and out hated him for being a dog, although he had been invited to stay outside the mosque rather than going inside while they fetched one of the community leaders.) It probably wasn't the protestors, the youth opposition leagues who'd been howling for free elections and free press — they had that now. The right-wingers, the militias?

Maybe it'd been Nesimi's loyalists? There were a couple of Eurasian warlords who were nominally Azerbaijani, people who'd lived here as children, some like Nesimi who had tenuous ties to the region. The exile factions, the opposition militias, the right-wingers? That seemed unlikely — Panah Karimov had disavowed all knowledge of the action, had turned over access to his people's equipment and weapons even if they refused to leave their mountain strongholds.

According to the facial recognition report, none of the bodies Eversen had inspected were members of Karimov's faction. None of them were even family members of any of Karimov's men and women, and, according to the Andercom intelligence officer Eversen had spoken to, that seemed to clear them. Family was important here; if you joined a militia, so did your siblings.

Even so, it was a long march between hearing that and *trusting* Karimov. Like hell Eversen would let them get ahold of weapons, even non-lethals, and start playing volunteer police.

Fuck. It was supposed to be simple, supposed to be easy — come here and shoot the *one* guy — but now that they'd turned the rock over and shot the bastard they'd found a dozen factions crawling around underneath, clicking their claws and making hissing noises, all impossible to tell apart. It'd be easier if they'd actually shot Ilhaim Nesimi — they had him locked up under the old court-house, awaiting a suitable legal system to be built to try him, instead.

The suction stopped, and the surgery robot started pumping something into his leg. It felt cool, and numb, and when Eversen dared open his eyes to peek, the glop being shoved in was blue-green.

"Am I going to be able to walk on this?" he asked the nurse.

The man — woman? Eversen wasn't sure and it didn't matter — the *nurse* nodded. "Oh, sure." They smiled. Then frowned, theatrically. "In about a week."

"I need to be on my feet today."

The nurse shook their head. "No can do. We can put you in a wheelchair if you like."

"Can't you splint it? Brace it? I have a cane."

"It needs rest. A wheelchair's my final offer. For at *least* five days. You already tried walking on it, don't try it again."

Eversen slumped back, staring at the ceiling. He wanted to go and take revenge, shoot whoever the hell was responsible. But he'd already shipped Ereli's body home, and still had no clear idea as to what the hell had happened at the ambush.

Eversen grimaced, pulling up his phone, and logging into the tactical network. "Well, thank you," he muttered at the nurse. "I'm sure there's some kind of job that needs doing from a wheelchair…"

EVERSEN'S FIRST THOUGHT was that he had no idea who these people were, or why they were sucking their tea through sugar cubes clenched between their teeth and encouraging him to do the same. As if the correct consumption of tea and sympathetic tuttings about his wheelchair were at least half the reason he'd been summoned to speak with them.

The objective listing on the tactical network was low priority — meet with local politicians, almost all of whom had put in requests to meet with the commander, the organizer, the top dog, the head of this coup from nowhere.

Bud in his ear, translating jokes he didn't understand, Eversen hauled himself out of the wheelchair, waving off the business-suited attendant and their beverage, limping the two steps to the desk, and thumping his palms down on it, hunching over the seated man.

Malik Najafov. Third or fourth from the top of the Citizen's Democracy Party. The CDP, or 'VDP' in Azeri, was a political organization which had shed all of its links with Nesimi's government hours into the assault on the Khazar Islands, and was now swallowing down a mixture of politically conservative and somewhat communist supporters in its first attempts at openly campaigning for votes.

The man's office had physical paintings on the walls, not screens, and gold and brass knick-knacks in glass-topped and scarlet cushioned display tables, along with silver carafes and jugs that served no purpose Eversen could comprehend. Malik sat square in the middle of it all, at a desk the size of a bed with recessed panels for the desktop workstation inside. His attendants leaned in at the sides, almost indistinguishable — cousins hanging out at the office, all smiling and saying nothing.

"I'm not here to pay a social visit," Eversen growled out. "You requested a meeting — I'm here. What do you want?"

"*Don't be so rushed,*" Malik purred, the oily tone filtered out in Eversen's earbud. "*We have plenty of time. Please, sit down.*"

Eversen exposed teeth. He knew how to smile at humans, showing teeth politely, but that wasn't what he did. Not now. "I'm so pleased you have plenty of time. If you don't get to the point I'm leaving."

Malik and his cousins shared a brief, serious look. "You are… highly placed in the Liberation Fund's forces?" Malik asked, in English. Asking it gently, prying. Uncertain as to how much respect Eversen was due. "We have been told that there is no commander."

"I hold signatory-of-incorporation status." Thanks to Ereli. He gestured at the chair, waited for it to roll in under him, and lowered himself into it. "That's as close as you're going to get."

"*Signatory…?*" Malik looked helplessly to the man on his right. The man shook his head, helplessly.

Malik smiled, falsely. All white teeth and good humor and something dumb and blank in front of his eyes shielding whatever thoughts were razoring around the man's head. "Then, please, let me not waste your time. We have many concerns. The establishment of a democratically elected government to follow your Transitionary Authority, is there a timetable?"

"The in-house lawyers are setting up a central court system to handle arbitrations. Randomly selected juries from the citizenry are aiding and authenticating the selection of judges from the Azeri population with the oversight of the European Union High Commission." Eversen ground his knuckles over his face tiredly, and got out his phone, tabbing through for the speaking notes someone in the offices back home had prepared for him. "Once the central court system is in place, delegates will be selected by democratic vote to form a parliament within the Transitionary Authority which can begin to ratify and amend the draft constitution that the TA has suggested, and the process as a whole is expected to be complete by the end of the month. Draft constitution allows for one to six weeks of political campaigning and discussion to take place before the elections, so, call it two months before the new independent government's established."

"I see."

Folding the phone flat, Eversen pushed it back into the front pocket of his uniform coverall.

Eversen almost wished he hadn't checked in with the local street patrols for backup — if there was an attempt to assassinate whoever had been sent to the meeting, maybe he was better off dead than sitting through this shit.

"This information is readily available from the Transitionary Authority's front-house office," Eversen said. "Is this all you wanted a meeting for?"

The reason Malik Najafov was third or fourth from the head of his party was because, as Eversen understood it, they were hoping to push him as their presidential candidate. The man at the top had actual business to perform, but down here, a couple of inches under the line of fire, Malik had time to push his own agenda.

"There are questions I had about the proposed citizen police force, how you are selecting officers and commandants..."

"It's off," Eversen snapped. "Plan wasn't fit for purpose. We're subcontracting to peacekeeping service providers vetted by the United Nations."

"Ah." Malik blinked away surprise, and a little disappointment, before stroking his chin.

Eversen stared, levelly.

The politician gestured away two of his cousins from the desk, directing them to clear away the tea service, and leaned in conspiratorially. "And the actual money in the Liberation Fund? What happens to this when the new government is in place?"

Eversen pricked up his ears. "The remainder of the fund, after dispersing hazard, disability and bereavement payments to combatants and settling all other debts, is being released through the Transitionary Authority to the governmental body formed by its elections."

"And these... disability and bereavement payments." Malik's lips quirked, a knowing look in his eye. "They are likely to be... extensive?"

"They're capped at sixty percent of contractor payments or six months equivalent non-combat duty pay, whichever's lower. It helps defray insurance costs. That's standard practice as per AD-MACP private military operations guidelines." Eversen leaned forward, in turn. "Materiel, ordnance, and support equipment not being rented or otherwise contractually redistributed on disincorporation is also to be handed over. At present the hand-over fund's net usable total is at thirty-six million New Dollars and growing, which translates to something near to a billion of your Manat. A lot of that will be spent between now and then fixing streets, but you can ask accounts for access to the quarterly audit when that's done. No, Mister Najafov, we are not running off with your citizens' money, if that is what you are asking."

"Please. Malik *Bey*, not Mister Najafov. That is how we address each other in Azerbaijan, Eversen *Bey*."

"I don't concern myself with your nation's culture, language, or social niceties, Mister Najafov. That's not what your country hired us for. Me and my brothers come cheap, *not stupid*."

"I am concerned for my people." Malik lifted one of the tea-glasses, a stubby little shotglass, in salute. Sipped, no sugar between the teeth. "I must be sure we have not traded one dictator for another. You understand?"

Eversen smiled thinly, all teeth, no joy. "I can understand that you wouldn't want another dictator around, Mister Najafov."

20. Battle Fatigue

::/ Baku, Azerbaijan.
::/ May, 2106.
::/ Edane Estian.

Edane knew that holding onto the LAMW on patrol was irrational — what he *needed* was a cut-down folding stock rifle, but it was hard, emotionally, to let go of the cannon. Hard to let go of the war and settle into the required routine.

The routine where he stood alone on the coast side plaza where the Azerbaijan National Flagpole stood hundreds of meters up into the sky, so high up the wind could be nasty enough to shred the flag to tatters while there was hardly any breeze at all on the ground. He was supposed to keep an eye on the crowds and provide a rapid response capability in the event of violence anywhere across the bay of Baku, but instead two men in touristy clothes came up and tried to stab Edane to death.

The knives were relatively small, easily hidden as they approached. One of them tried to distract Edane, asking if the city was really safe now, where ex-president Nesimi was, while the other went around to Edane's right side. Edane caught the knife by reflex in his right hand — a bad reflex, but he'd never been afraid of getting cut. The little blade shredded his palm ragged, even through his combat gloves.

The knifeblade snapped as Edane twisted it away, his left fist shot into the first attacker's face, then he drove the back of his elbow into the second man's face before he could finish sinking his knife into the mesh weave of Edane's armor. The knifeblade tangled up on the fiber — he should've let the first one stab him, too, but there was always the possibility they'd aim for his throat — so he kicked the second's feet out from under him and rolled him over with another kick. The attacker was bloody on his back — nose and upper lip pouring blood as he sprawled out.

Edane had expected more of an attack than that, so he drew back from the scattering pedestrians, calling for backup, but… there wasn't any follow up attack.

The two men? They hadn't really come to *kill* Edane. Sure they'd tried, though it was a lousy attempt, but they weren't part of a larger effort.

They were angry men, attacking Edane because of what he represented to them, not because he was a dog and Muslims hated dogs — Edane hadn't been treated like that yet in Azerbaijan. No, it was because he was the closest they could get to the political authority now towering over them.

Edane and his brothers had stolen their revolution. Ignored their passion and their hatred and their need to be free, their years of struggle, and pulled their government apart in a way they could never hope to. Now Edane and his brothers were putting in place systems of power and authority that wouldn't enfranchise them the way they hoped to be — no young activists in the limelight, just a new crop of the same old politicians as before, discussing the laws they'd put into play when the new government was formed.

They weren't trying to kill *Edane*. They were angry, because what he represented was between them and the political power they wanted — *they'd* wanted to bring down Nesimi's regime, become Azerbaijan's heroes.

There were no heroes, just a bunch of dogs on the streets.

"I guess I understand where they're coming from," Edane said, checking the skinbonding across his palm for tears or leaks. He wiped it down again with disinfectant, sitting in the new barracks — a dirty old hotel, still full of grenade-blasted mouseholes in the walls and rubble in the corridors, being rented at cut rate after the battles. "They care about who runs this country. I don't. I never did."

Janine, the world away, sat, hands under her chin, gazing seriously at him out of his new phone, propped on a cracked ply-plastic dresser. "No," she agreed. "It's like you with me. Isn't it? Being part of something. You're not a part of them."

Edane sat, regarding the wounds on his palm, which would now be just another set of scars on his body, mapping out his life. "Yeah. I'm not part of this," he said. "I don't care who runs this country next, so long as they don't kill people."

She watched him, levelly, quite still.

He dipped his ears, looking back at the phone. "It's different. Fighting. That's for when there isn't another option. You're not supposed to kill people unless there isn't any other way to keep everybody safe."

"I know, Sweetie."

Edane gazed at her. Wondered if he could dare try and explain to her how blowing soldiers to pieces to terrify their friends was keeping people safe. Or describe that moment when Sokolai was about to coup-de-grace someone they'd wounded.

Or explain any of it.

"Like the guys who tried stabbing me," he said. "They're in lock-up. There's a set fine, they can communicate with friends and family and legal representation, nobody died." He ducked his head, stretching out his palm, and switched to dabbing liquid skinplast over it. It stung, a little. The doctor who had done the internal stitches for his tendons had said he needed to keep the skinplast fresh. "The point is making sure nobody dies."

"And people aren't dying now — not like that." Janine tapped her chin gently. "It's… what did the news call it? Low intensity conflict?"

Edane nodded. "That's one of the terms." It got labelled low intensity conflict when people set up mortars to kill civilians — though none of the splintering factions grabbing at power, or the remains of the Azeri army, had done any of that yet. It was all blockades and prisoners of war and convoy ambushes, very little targeting civilians.

"So," she said. "When do you think you're coming home?"

Edane flexed his palm, waiting for the skinplast to finish drying.

"Sweetie?"

He ducked his head. "I'm not ready to come home."

"When will you be?"

"When I've found what I'm looking for, I guess." He perked his ears, trying to listen for the distant rumble of gunfire.

On the phone, Janine shifted her chin from palm to palm, head tilted. "And what are you looking for, Edane?"

There wasn't any gunfire, no matter how high he lifted his ears.

He crumpled in on himself, shoulders sagging forward, spine bending under his weight until his fingertips brushed the floor between his boots. His hand hurt. His ankle was better, but still tender. The constant ache in his body over the first few days of operations had faded to a dull heat by the time he went to bed.

For a little while, in bits and pieces, it had all felt good. But now…

"Some place I fit in," he told her, at last.

21. Reasonable Cause

::/ Baku, Azerbaijan.
::/ May, 2106.
::/ Eversen Estian.

"I'd like a second medical opinion," Eversen muttered.

"No, Mister Estian, what you want is to find a doctor who'll agree with you. And you'll find one if you look extensively enough." The teleoperation rig's manipulators twiddled the air, as the doctor in their office fiddled with a stylus. "You were shot in the leg. It was healing nicely, then you put pressure on it and it stopped healing nicely. It's healing nicely again." The manipulators clicked on the empty air, as the doctor turned the stylus around. "Give it another four days."

"How many hours a day can I spend on my feet?" He gestured restlessly. "The nurse said it was okay for me to get myself in and out of the bathroom, showered and all."

"That's fine, if you bathe sitting down — I wouldn't suggest standing in a shower. But you shouldn't be exerting yourself, putting any kind of load on it. And if you do, you risk more bleeding problems. Every time you flex the damaged muscle tissues, they're liable to tear. You understand?"

Eversen grit his teeth. This was why people didn't listen to doctors. Why they said 'screw it' and soldiered on anyway. Because it was easier to grind yourself to mush on the march with a bum knee than responsibly admit you were weak and needed to recover.

"I understand," he muttered.

"Now. Let me see you get in the chair." The manipulator waggled at it.

He braced himself on his arms, yanking the wheelchair up to the bed with a protesting squeal of its motors, and he levered himself into it, grimacing briefly as he pushed his wounded thigh down and into place, doing his best to keep it limp and unmoving as ordered.

"Are you in pain? Pain is one of the most distressing symptoms and the most easily treated, I can give you a dispensary script right now. Don't be stupid about this."

Eversen turned his snarl onto the doctor's screen. "Pain is your friend, sir. It lets you know you're *a*-live, as the drill instructors yelled at me."

"Pain is unnecessary."

"Ultimately, so is being alive, but I'm not a philosophy major, sir."

"You don't need to call me sir," the doctor replied, calmly.

Eversen shook his head, wheeling the chair around instead of just telling it where he wanted to go. "You're giving me orders, that makes you a sir, sir."

A chuckle. "My colleague across the hall, here, tells me your brothers say that to her, too. Call her sir. Why is that?"

"The drill instructors taught me that pain was my friend, sir, but not that there was more than just men in the world. You can imagine my surprise when I was later informed it didn't just stop with just *two* genders."

Outright laughter, and that, at least, made Eversen feel good. The good kind of laughter, anyway. It was like knowing how to smile at humans while exposing teeth and *still* making it friendly — the good kind of laughter meant people liked him.

It was good keeping things simple. People either liked Eversen, or they didn't.

Wheeling out of the underground parking lot that was still seeing use as an operating base, Eversen left behind the people who liked him, and went off to go and talk with off-site intelligence about the people who disliked him enough to kill his brother and put a hole through his thigh.

"As you can see, the social net is limited," the hired Intel officer said. She'd introduced herself as Lindiwe. Lindiwe threw a three dimensional network onto Eversen's screen — each axis on the network a set of linked points tagged with names and photographs — and then switched between various points of view, the lines thickening or changing color as she swept between options. "Microblogging links, instant messaging we picked up, sales and commerce, e-mail, voice calls… we have only two significant threads of background history that match all the attackers. They're former members of, or descended from members of, the Azeri armed forces circa twenty-sixty."

"So there's a link with the former regime?" Eversen asked, laid out on top of a cot. Maybe, he hoped, being good about resting would mean he got to stop resting.

"It's a tempting conclusion, but running a meta-analysis of thirty random Azeri citizens of the same gender and age demographic gave twenty-three similar linkages — it turns out that the former Aliyev regime resorted to widespread forced conscription before collapsing. For a majority sampling, a large proportion of a random group, their social links look typical. However, something this specific — that *all* of the attackers fit the army background profile — is atypical enough to be statistically significant, which led me to investigate the firearms used in the attack more closely."

"And?"

"All of them are from armed forces stocks which were either marked down as destroyed or sold on when the army reorganized in the eighties, post-war. As near as I can figure out, 'destroyed or sold on' seems to be a polite cover-up for the possibility that these weapons were in the hands of the exiled soldiers who splintered out of Azerbaijan's armed forces during the war and went rogue as Eurasian warlords. Specifically, this implicates four highly placed officers who fled Azerbaijan during Nesimi's coup. Two are currently active in Northern Persia — Generals Gayibov and Valiyev — but they can be disregarded, as both are settled in with autonomous states in the area. One was killed during the Tajik revolution, a Colonel Magsudov, and his armed forces shattered. I don't see his forces giving up their materiel to support the efforts of others right now.

"The fourth is the most likely candidate — General Abbasov, last seen in Uzbekistan four years ago. Abbasov was known as the liberator of Baku, having briefly retaken the capitol he held it for a period of three months during the Twenty-Sixty-Four in-fighting. Rumor indicates he was spirited away by supporters before Nesimi's coup. He's one of the few remaining hardcore Aliyev loyalists from the old regime's military cabinet — Nesimi executed the ones he could get his hands on."

Eversen picked up the spare smart-paper he'd set aside as a secondary display for the pad, glancing over the dossier on Abbasov and comparing it to the ambushers' social network. "What level of intelligence resource qualifies as 'rumor', Lindiwe?"

"Discussions on microblogging services at the time. That was the most popular speculation as to Abbasov's fate, seemingly based on 'friend of a friend' sourcing, but it fits with later sightings and the kind of people he associated with. It's probable he and his men are behind ransom kidnappings in the Karakalpakstan area."

"Karakalpakstan?"

"Western half of Uzbekistan. It's been its own country since Twenty-Seventy-Four. I'd never heard of it either. Just over the Caspian Sea from Azerbaijan and inland, behind Kazakhstan." She highlighted it on the pad.

"Don't suppose that provides a motivation for the ambush, does it?"

"Not clearly. We just don't have the information, but if you want, I can speculate."

"Affirmative. Do it."

"The only possibility that makes sense to me is that there's concern about the Transitionary Authority favoring some local factions at the exclusion of others. Panah Karimov leads what amounts to the most democracy-friendly militant faction in-country. If you and your brothers had armed his forces as an interim police force, as had been planned, this would have given him and his people a number of opportunities to stake a claim to leading the political discourse, even without abusing power."

That sounded probable. After the ambush Eversen had been forced to halt Ereli's plan — and it had been a *good* plan — to arm Karimov's people with non-lethals and use them for policing. As it was, they were bleeding money paying for additional European peacekeeping contractors from Ryder-Pryce. Thankfully, Ryder-Pryce were handling the streets well. But it didn't stop constant calls for them to be replaced by an Azeri police force — even though the only trained Azeri officers available were complicit in the brutal oppression of its own people, not a month past.

"I suspect it was hoped the Transitionary Authority would have enacted reprisals in the wake of the ambush — vendetta has a particular place in local political discourse — but even without doing so, removing Karimov from the field of play has changed the political landscape considerably, giving others the opportunity to make their own power-grabs unhindered.

"But, I must emphasize, this is speculation. It could just as easily have been disaffected elements of the militant protest groups, there have been a few minor attacks on patrols and your brothers. Regardless of the true motive behind the ambush, the best place to look for answers is with Abbasov and his men. The arms used during the attack are the only concrete link, and if they're not directly responsible for arming the ambushers, it's possible they know who were. Unfortunately, questioning them might be difficult. They're living off-grid, and it's hard to tell one gang of Eurasian warlords' bandits from another by satellite imaging.

"That's all I've got for you right now."

Lindiwe had a *lot* for him. The documentation she'd sent was more than he could reasonably read through himself. The summary he was getting now was the real thing he was paying for — signing off maybe a little more of the discretionary funds than he should have in getting the briefing prepared for him.

He wanted revenge. *Vendetta.* Sure. But the ambush was a military attack, with goals that had to make sense on either a tactical or strategic level. That's how he had to respond.

Eversen tapped the dossiers off. "Thanks, Lindiwe. Are you available if I have another job for you?"

"Certainly."

"Please draw up a list of suitable questions for an interrogation."

A pause. Uncertainly, she asked, "You have one of Abbasov's men?"

Eversen switched over to the tactical network. "Not yet, but I'm already looking for an excuse to go and grab one."

"You might want to check Andercom West's subsidiary listings, in that case. I saw a kidnapping insurance policy backed by the D&D Array's human resources team get pinged for a rescue and recovery in Karakalpakstan."

Eversen squinted. "The D&D Array? You mean those domes off-coast from San Iadras that keep the ocean clean?"

"The Defense and Decontamination Array does a little more than that, and it's the entire MACP coastline, but yes. It seems one of their employees has a spouse or family member missing. Would you like to know more?"

::/ BAUTINO, KAZAKHSTAN.
::/ EVERSEN ESTIAN.

THE ASSAULT BEGAN when Mark-Antony-Oversight One shot the closest two guards, seconds after they and the hostages made their move, bolting away from the hospital storage shacks. The guards had been lifting their weapons, potentially threatening the hostages, which meant they had to die.

With Mark Antony clearing the way, destroying any guards who could potentially execute the hostages, the job became both easier and a little more difficult. Mark Antony's infiltration team could bunker down in the center of the hospital — the only substantial building in the antique ruin of what had once been a mining town of some kind — and the drones could rise over the horizon with no fear that the hostages were in direct danger. The tricky part was that now half the guards in the compound were running towards the hostages, shooting.

What that translated to, in practice, was a dynamic response by Mark Antony, shooting down every living thing outside of the hospital. A much more achievable goal than fighting through the town of Bautino with every last hostage in tow.

"Could you reconfirm the headcount, please?" Eversen asked the chopper pilot, through the internal intercom.

"Thirty in and thirty out. Facial recognition confirms twenty-seven of the missing parties and three matches on the three clones." The pilot, huddled in the cockpit nook of the passenger cabin, his head swathed in high resolution imagers giving him the outside view, briefly lifted a thumbs up. "Hostages secure, just need to clear the town."

Thank God for the earbuds. Eversen could feel the pulsing of the vehicle's engine in his bones, the mesh fabric safety barriers across the open passenger bay's exits let every jolt of noise in, wind roaring as the chopper's companion drones flicked up and overhead with a scream of jets — which had to have been loud as artillery fire to get through the buds.

The helicopter tilted forward, and the g-force of sudden acceleration pushed Eversen down against his bench. In the shadowy space, he and seven more of his brothers waited, their camouflage gear displaying warped and distorted patterns of the metal plates beneath their feet. All indistinguishable from one another — the same gear, the same cut down rifles. Eidlitz was one of Eversen and Ereli's housemates, back home, though. He understood why this mission was important, why they were doing what they were doing. Exermont, Stelborn — to them it was just another mission. But through the narrow slit of their goggles they all had the same driven, intense gaze. The same emotionally detached glare.

The one Eversen wore. Or thought he might. A lot went on in his heart that never reached his face.

There wasn't any point in giving last minute instructions, even though Eversen burned to give them. Say some inspiring bullshit, give the fireteam that 'Yeehaw and Huzzah' pep talk out of the movies, but it was pointless. Morale wasn't in smiles and bravado and an impulse to yell swear words and pithy one-liners — morale was a measure of willingness to perform as required. The willingness was there. Cultural conditioning by years of action movies had fouled up his thinking on the matter, this was how it was supposed to be. Quiet and determined was his natural state of being.

Calm.

And when the helicopter rattled, gunfire pouring off its side-mounted gunpods, thundering down to the dust?

Calm.

Rushing out of the helicopter, teeth grit together because of the pain in his leg but trusting to the integrity of the splint Eversen had forced a doctor to print for him, moving in a swaggering run led by his good knee?

Calm.

Cold smoothness in every motion, hacking his hand down towards a target and watching two of his team move while Mark Antony's brethren spread out around the hospital, watching for targets. A sweet chill in his gut as the second and third helicopters gently eased down to earth on the nearby seabed, where the Caspian Sea had dried away, more brothers disembarking. The fourth backup chopper circled overhead, a black, armored star fixed in the sky.

Not waiting for the choppers, Eversen ran. Breaking into the barracks behind Erath and killing the first of General Abbasov's men to lift a firearm in his direction. The second of them Eversen chased out of the steel-shack barracks and into the dust around Bautino. Blood thundered in him — yet remained somehow silent in his ears — as the man turned, lifting a pistol from his waist. Eversen shot him in the shoulder with a double-tap, and the target's arm split where the bone broke, the limb flailing back down against his chest like an empty shirt-sleeve, his body collapsing to the earth.

Gunfire everywhere. Drones buzzing overhead, smoking vehicles, twisted masses of steel he could no longer recognize. The area was secure, and the pulsing in his ears faded until he was gasping down clean breaths of air, a strange kind of lucidity taking him as the hostages, twenty-seven humans and three black-furred clones, were brought out and led towards the helicopters, escorted along by his brothers.

The moments-long firefight was still fresh for Eversen, still real, but it existed in a dream-like state, an emotionally foggy trance despite the razor clarity in his head of what he'd seen, what he'd done.

The fog, if that's what it had been, lifted. And Eversen moved to join his brothers gathering the enemy survivors and prisoners outside Abbasov's interrogation room.

"Here's the deal," Eversen said, slowly, the vest-translator purring it out again in Azeri. "If you tell me what I want to know, I will pay you five hundred thousand Manat and give you safe passage to Baku, or a plane ticket and a ten year residency visa in the MACP, depending on your preference. A whole new life, think about it."

The whites of the man's eyes shuddered, his eyelids trembling as he frowned up at Eversen, lips stiffly locked together, listening to the translator in desperate silence.

Motes of dust hung in the air between he and Eversen, caught in the slashes of light penetrating the improvised steel walls of the cell. He hadn't been chained up to the rings welded into the walls — Eversen didn't work the way Abbasov's interrogators did.

He said something. "*And?*" the translator buzzed. "*Where is the threat?*"

"If you lie to me," Eversen replied, voice low, "I will kill you."

"*You can't do that. It's murder. You're mercenaries. You have laws to uphold to maintain your registrations. I'm not afraid.*"

"I'm not being paid to do this as a military combatant — this is a hostage recovery job. Do you know what that means?"

Abbasov's man didn't answer, glaring up, lip clamped tight between his teeth.

"It means," Eversen explained patiently, "that I'm operating as a private security consultant. I can kill whoever I want, for whatever reason I want, and the only thing that can stop me is if a lawyer sues me or the kidnapping insurance company I'm consulting for. That's how it works in the MACP. Do you have a lawyer registered with the Tri-Corporate Constitutional Bar Association? Norec-Naroi Insurance has some of the best."

The man listened to the translator, eyes glazing over with fear.

"No?" Eversen asked. "No lawyers? Then you better not lie to me."

The man's head fell forward, shoulders hunched, shivering — not just with blood loss and pain. Fear could do that to a man, too. "*And if I don't talk? You'll kill me also?"*

"No. If you don't talk I hand you over to the Kazakh police service and they charge you for kidnapping." Eversen smiled thinly — no teeth. "All I care about is making sure you don't fucking lie to me. Now. Do you want the money, or not?"

Four officers, four currency transfers after cross-referencing everything they said with Lindiwe, and one dead man later, they had their answers.

"Was that interrogation, bribery, torture, or execution?" Elwood, one of the subcontractors from Mark Antony, asked, while looking back at the lone corpse outside the interrogation chamber, and the neat rows of seated men in the square beside it.

No women — not one. Eversen didn't understand that. He'd never heard of an all-male military force, even the Liberation Fund had members of the older female production run integrated into it. Why would anyone bother with that kind of gender segregation? It'd cut available manpower too much.

Eversen shrugged, walking back towards the chopper. "I don't really care which it is."

"And?" Elwood asked. "Was it worth it?"

He turned around, shrugged again. "I don't fucking know. Apparently one of the former regime's kids — the Aliyev bunch — paid off Abbasov for weapons. And Abbasov sold them to the Aliyevs for *peanuts*. Like he was doing 'em a favor."

"So? You know who organized the ambush. Why don't you sound happy about that?"

"These Aliyevs are also bankrolling the fucking Citizen's Democracy Party."

Elwood paced after him, blinking in astonishment. "The party everybody thinks is going to run the next government? Malik Najafov? *That* CDP?"

"Yeah." Eversen pushed his earbuds back in, ducking his head against the chopper's rotor-wash as he moved to mount up. "Turns out that Malik is the kid of one of the Aliyev daughters. And it looks like Abbasov's trying to fucking get him elected."

22. Packing Up

::/ Baku, Azerbaijan
::/ May, 2106.
::/ Edane Estian.

Edane sat on his assigned bunk — the bed in the hotel room he'd been given — and packed his possessions into a new duffle. A spare shirt. A set of underwear. An unopened deodorant sprayer he'd picked up to use after the flight landed back home — he couldn't read the label, but it had flowery pictures and those were the kinds of smells Janine liked, and it'd be better than unwashed dog after a round-the-world flight.

He checked the interior of the shopping bag he'd gotten from the street vendor.

He didn't own anything else, other than his wallet and passport.

He'd wanted a rug. He'd missed out on getting one in Tajikistan, and the few market vendors who'd been willing to talk to him back then had all said rugs made fine gifts, but Baku didn't seem to have rugs.

Rubble, knock-off designer clothing, jewelry, novelty tea-sets and dusty old pre-war Chinese overproduced mass manufactured landfill — kid's toys and ornaments? Baku had plenty of all that. Not so much by way of rugs. He'd asked the desk manager, a man named Jabbar who'd been kept on mainly to open the doors for the handymen who shuffled in and out during the day to repair the hotel's battle-damage and get the water running on the upper floors again, but Jabbar didn't have any answers about where Edane could go to find keepsakes for his mothers.

His armor, his uniform, his equipment, his LAMW, that was all rented or being sold on. He couldn't take it back with him. He'd thrown away his MilSim scope after it'd been HERFed, and hadn't even saved any expended shell-casings from the fighting.

All of his personal possessions had been bought for less than ten New Dollars in the marketplace that morning. He'd almost have been better off waiting for the night markets at home, but he needed something to wear on the flight back.

He geared up, just with his pistol shoved into its oversized holster over his thigh, and headed out. Registered on the tactical network, but with no objectives to follow.

"*Going out on patrol, yes?*" Jabbar asked, looking up from his pad with a briefly-flashed smile.

Edane briefly consulted the phrase-guide he'd loaded into his goggles, and nodded, replying carefully — "*Just taking a walk.*"

"*Ah, you are learning Azeri? Going to stay on?*"

Edane shook his head slightly. "*It's good to, ah—*" He gaze-flicked through the loaded phrases. Settled on, "*It's good to try something new.*" He'd have been lost, without the goggles subtitling Jabbar live.

Thorne had maintained that learning the local language was part of integrating with the local population, back in Tajikistan. That to make any progress they had to connect with the people they were fighting for.

Edane didn't feel connected to the people of Azerbaijan. Just like how he didn't feel connected to the displaced Colombians he knew back home, the local peoples swept aside by the economic powerhouse of the MACP. They called it imperialism and capitalism-colonialism, but really, it was just that he had his own life to lead. Other things mattered to him.

The streets were safe, now — for a given level of safe. On the tactical network there were frequent calls for drone strikes, but that was outside of Baku proper. Complaints about looting weren't uncommon, nor were assaults — which Edane had taken a while to figure out was meant in legal terms, someone giving someone else a black eye, instead of in the context of armed forces attacking. But the police weren't attacking their own civilians now — most of them were either under arrest or discharged and left unemployed while Ryder-Pryce's trainers worked on getting a whole new PMC-led, locally-recruited paramilitary civil defense unit trained to the standards of European Union peacekeeping policy guidelines.

The job was done, the old regime had been shattered, but the new job of getting Azerbaijan rebuilt into a nation had barely begun. And Edane didn't care about that.

The shattered glass was still being swept off the streets in some places, local men and women watching him warily as he walked by, alone. They were Azeris and refugees who were no longer confined to ghettoes outside of the city, and Edane didn't think they wanted him there.

Why would anyone want him? He was just another capitalist-imperialist intervening in their lives, he hadn't fought because he liked them, or had some connection to the country. The only reason for him to be there was to do what they couldn't — fight back against a better armed and ruthlessly violent government. That had been done, and now there wasn't anything he could do that they couldn't.

Edane wandered through shattered alleyways, retracing his steps. He knew this street, but it was cleaner now. Rubble had been raked out of the road, smoke long ago blown away by the wind. He could make out the gaping wounds in the buildings' roofs to either side, where mortar rounds had slammed down, automated systems triangulating the sound and hunting him in the mad seconds after the thunder of a LAMW shot rocked through the city.

He stepped into a still empty apartment building, the brickwork shattered by machine gun rounds. Red caution tape blocked all the doors, but he simply ducked under it, looking up at the exposed steel frame where the floors had collapsed, at the open sky over the rubble of the fallen ceilings, and searched through the dusty corridors for a way up into the attics where he'd taken the shot.

Where he'd killed a soldier simply to terrify all his friends. To punish him for being part of the regime's military, for having received orders to take civilians hostage. Where Edane had done with a LAMW shell what had been done to him with a mortar round.

The torn away arm wasn't there anymore — Edane remembered seeing it slapping down on top of one of the armored vehicles, and the square was empty now, but through his uniform's lenses he could barely see the fuzzy brown mark covering the plaza stones, where the soldier had bled and died.

Edane pushed aside a shattered beam with his boot, amidst the fallen roof tiles, and bent down to pick up the glinting brass of a LAMW casing. It was dusty, dented in the center from when the roof had caved in on the attic, but it was one of his shells. How many shots had he taken? One, two? Edane thought it was only one.

It had been a long time ago, now.

Was there still a murky black-brown stain on the stones of the Tous marketplace, in Dushanbe? Or had Tajikistan forgotten all about him?

Tajikistan had been somewhere he'd fit in, for a time. While the people had hated him there, he'd done his best to defend them from the belligerents bullying them around. Now Azerbaijan was the same way, except Edane had pushed Azerbaijan's bully down by being a bigger, stronger bully.

Edane turned the cold metal around and around on the tip of his finger, staring at the shell casing thoughtfully. It was almost big enough to drink soda out of, if he wanted to. He didn't want to do that, though.

He wanted to go home.

23. Lifting Corners

::/ San Iadras, Middle American Corporate Preserve.
::/ May, 2106.
::/ Edane Estian.

Marianna flicked two extended fingers forward, her fist held at an angle, then chopped them up in a rising sweep. Two quick jerks of her hand. *Person of interest — J — Location?*

Edane slouched back into their foxhole, the match timer ticking down in the corner of his vision, the air sweet and wet through the cooling mesh in his mask. A glance towards the spy-eye spiked into the dirt over the top, to get its feed in his goggles, and he gaze-flicked through its interface until the spy-eye turned. The field was clear. Behind them, past the big orange mesh border fence, the field's rest area… There. Standing with a pad in one hand, and a soda in the other. He lifted his hand. *Person of interest — J — off-field — bearing one-three-five.*

Marianna looked up at the spy-eye, no doubt using her goggles to pull a feed from it too. She hauled her facemask down off her muzzle, and checked her wristwatch display, thumbing it over to a set of timers and countdowns. "She been here the whole match?"

"Think so." Another gaze-flick to get the spy-eye's focal lens pointed back downrange.

"You got off the plane, you got your ass here — she drive down with you?"

"No. Phoned her, though. Saw her for five minutes pre-match."

"And she's been standing around waiting for you for *eight fucking hours?*"

Edane shrugged, hugging his MilSim LAMW to his chest. The

weight was comforting, even if he'd had to readjust to its balance. "She said she wanted to meet up after the game."

"The fuck happened in Azerbaijan, kid?" Marianna cleared her goggles, blinking at him. "Hell. The *fuck* happened in the five minutes you saw her for? What'd they teach you about treating a woman over there?"

"We talked. In the five minutes." He perked his ears quizzically. "Is that a joke? I think it might have been but I don't know if I should laugh."

Marianna clamped her hand over the bridge of her muzzle, shaking her head. "Well at least I know they didn't issue you a sense of humor in that clusterfuck. They sent you back in one *piece*, even if you came back stupider."

"Ma'am, yes ma'am."

"Don't make me hurt you."

He grinned. Marianna made a snorting noise — could've been laughter. Was close enough, anyway.

Last game of the season. He hadn't really thought about it until he'd gotten onto the flight back and spotted Eissen by his dog tags.

Eissen hadn't wanted to talk about what he'd been up to, since splitting up with Edane. Said only that after thinking about it, he couldn't blame Edane for the whole thing about killing soldiers just to scare them. Admitted that maybe the need to punish them had seemed rational in the moment.

Edane got the impression that a lot of things that had seemed rational in the moment turned out to be downright ugly, later, for the both of them. But Eissen wasn't talking about his ugly feelings, just said he'd be glad to go back to MilSim. But he wasn't on the field — apparently he needed time to put his head back together. And there hadn't been much time in the headlong dash from the airport to the playing field.

Marianna, bless her, still had all of their gear in one of the trunks in the van. Waiting for them. Edane had untangled his stuff from Eissen's armor and equipment, setting it in place neatly to wait until Eissen felt ready to return.

The season hadn't gone as well as operations in Azerbaijan had. The team were hanging onto tenth place, barely enough to go pro with Hallman's sponsorship, but it didn't look like they'd be able to rank higher than that. Kacey, their old friend and EMWAR specialist, had been covering for Edane, while Eissen's cover was a skinny dude named Dahl. They were good players but trying to integrate good players into a team mid-season was a tough ask on anybody.

All the same, Edane's presence wouldn't pull their performance up or down all that much in just one match, even if he was out of sync now. But it felt good to be shooting again, and not at people.

"Okay," Marianna said. "Empty these out and leave the field." She hauled the last two spare magazines of LAMW shells off her webbing and flung them at him, one after the other.

He caught them both — one in his left hand, one in his right. No trembles, no fumbles. But Edane was worried anyway. "I do something wrong?"

"What? *No*," Marianna groaned. "Goddamn knucklehead. You seriously want to waste your time on-field when your girl's been waiting there the whole goddamn day?"

"No, but I think she understands why I'm out here."

"Enlighten me," Marianna said, unfolding a tactical pad while sagging back against the foxhole's torn earth side.

"This is as close to a place I belong as any." Edane started confirming the tagged targets she passed him, gesturing through them on his goggles and uniform's cameras.

She revealed teeth in a shark-tooth grin, thin, amused... not so vicious. "Find what you were looking for out there, did you?"

"Found out it wasn't in Azerbaijan," he said. "Wasn't in fighting."

"Sounds like you found it." Her grin eased down to a smile. "Just because they made you to be a killer, just because you *are* a killer, that doesn't mean that being a killer's all you want out of life, now is it?"

Edane touched the breast-pocket he'd put the LAMW shell casing into, from the roof in Baku. He dipped his nose to look at the bulge it made in his tactical webbing. "Doesn't mean it's not what I want, either."

"No," she agreed. "It doesn't. But it means it's not the whole story for you. Every time you walk off into the jungle on your own little *la guerra*, you'll discover whole new reasons to come back to civilization. And that ain't cowardice, or being unable to perform, it's—"

"—Living," Edane said. "Because they made me to do something, and I need to do it, but it isn't living. Killing makes me happy, I'm wired for it to make me happy, but if I let that be the only reason I'm happy, I don't walk back from *la guerra*, do I?"

Marianna shook her head. "You don't. You even want it to be the only reason you're happy? The only thing that *can* make you happy?"

"No."

"Welcome back from *la guerra*, Edane." She slapped his shoulder. "Now kill these targets like a good puppy and then get the *fuck* off my playing field before I beat your skull in. Go eat something with —" *Person of interest — J* "— at the snack bar. Clear?"

"Sir, yes sir."

"Good puppy."

The LAMW's recoil, kicking through three magazines of guided shells in rapid succession, felt almost as warm on his shoulder as Janine did just a few minutes later.

"It's amazing how fast and slow it goes, when I'm out here, really *watching*, instead of just keeping an eye on you at home." Janine poked at her paper cup of snack bar coffee distrustfully with the little wooden stirrer. "It's almost all waiting, and then something happens, and everything's fast, then it's all waiting again… almost peaceful. Is that weird?" She looked up at Edane, hesitant. "Calling MilSim peaceful?"

Edane leaned his head side to side thoughtfully. "Think I see what you mean. Most people think it's going to be like an action movie, constant firefights, but some of the best matches we've had have hardly any shooting."

"Not that it's not *fighting*, just…" Janine waved her hand, as if she could pluck the right words out of the air. To Edane, it seemed like she almost always could.

This time, he got to give her the words, though. "It's movement and position. Detection and evasion. Fighting for strategic advantage over tactical advantage."

"Hmn." She scrunched up the bridge of her snout, all the way down to her nose. "What's the difference between them?"

"It's not an easy line to draw, but strategy is decision-making towards a goal, tactics is executing those decisions." He folded his hands together on the picnic table-top. "Goal: Change the regime. Strategy: Capture the president. Tactic: Bottle him up in a building he can't escape from."

"Mmm." She watched him, eyes dancing across his face. "It was weird, getting those little e-mails from you, especially that first week."

Edane glanced down at his webbing's breast-pocket, as if he could see the shell casing inside. "Yeah," he said. "It was nice, though. Being able to stay in touch a little."

"It was."

Janine turned her head, watching the other teams filing in from the field. The players hopped off golf carts that turned around and went back out to pick up others. She stared at the gate into the play area, for a while.

"Think you'll go back?" she asked, voice small.

Edane glanced down at his right wrist. Brushed the fur back and forth, thoughtfully. "Maybe," he said. "Probably." He bowed his head. "But only to visit. I don't think I want to live that life full-time."

"Just might need to go and see if you can find a blue sky in the middle of all that, huh?"

He nodded. "It's a good way to say it."

"Moving back in?" she asked.

"If, uh. If you want me to." He thought back. "If... if you've had your moments feeling beautiful."

She smiled. A complex curve of her lips. Not happy, not pretending to be, either. Bittersweet, like she'd bitten into one of those awful-tasting lemon candy liqueur things she liked. "Might need a few more," she said. "But I'd prefer it if we could find a way to make that work. I still get to come back home to you, after, and we're all happy."

He ducked his head, a sort of nod, ears lifted. "We can give it a try."

"We can," she agreed, and her smile's sinful enjoyment of the sour turned soft as she reached for his hand. His right hand.

It was scarred, now. New scars. His scars.

Edane and Janine stayed for the announcement of the spring season's final standings, but what was unusual was that everyone else did, too.

Players, friends and family were waiting around the judging tents, to the left of the two off-field controller office tents. The off-field players were filing out, slinging their cold coffee in wide sprays out over the grass between the tents before vanishing back inside for refills, while team leaders shuffled in and out.

When Marianna returned from her session with the desk jockeys, her expression was grim, but it didn't have anything to do with the after-match post-mortem. Salzach was the target of her aggression, purely because he was the first one she reached, kneeing him along the picnic bench and into Dahl with an angry grunt before slumping down.

"Trouble?" Erlnicht asked, mildly.

Dahl and Kacey were to either side of Erlnicht, Kacey having stuck around to watch the match even though she'd stepped aside for Edane to rejoin the team. Across from them, Svarstad sat with his LSW's recoil engine's innards in oily pieces on a paper picnic plate. Eberstetten, Ellis, then Edane and Janine. The whole team, bar Eissen. A crowded table, but the others were worse — strangers sitting and standing on them to get a look at the still empty podium outside the judging tent.

Marianna shook her head, lips drawn in over her teeth. "Nothing confirmed, yet."

"But?" Edane asked. "What's going on?"

She glared at him squintily, then turned to the rest of the table. "Did none of you tell Edane?"

Ellis, wisely, got up and out arm's reach — even if Marianna didn't have her helmet with her. "I figured he knew."

"Well?" Edane asked, leaning back.

"Kennis-Purcelle Combat Games tabled a league policy addendum, signed off by their sponsored teams *and* three out of last year's top five." Ellis spread his hands, circling away from the growling Marianna. "They're calling it gene-doping, and guess whose performance they used in their charts to prove it?"

Marianna's growling grew as she rose, slouching forward over the table.

"Fuck," Edane murmured.

"Yeah. Dobson's warming up the crowd to it," Ellis said, flicking his head towards the judging tents. Dobson was the team captain of the KPC-Rush. Edane knew him. Everybody knew him.

Edane craned his head around, trying to see. Dobson, in his neon blue and green cap was standing out front, like *he* was one of the judges addressing the crowd...

"Shit," Edane murmured. "Janine, I gotta..." He hesitated, untangling his legs from the picnic bench, while she blinked up at him. "Is, uh Is this one of those things where I kiss your cheek before I run off? Like in movies?"

"Maybe?" She ventured, glancing off at Dobson in confusion.

He kissed Janine's cheek. "This right?"

She hunched up, smiling, embarrassed, looking around at the team. "Uhm. Maybe."

Dahl laughed, shaking his head.

"Where do you think you're going, knucklehead?" Marianna asked, though didn't protest when Edane pushed through the crowd.

He ducked around a genemod two inches shorter than him, the woman glaring icy daggers up at him, but only — he hoped — because he was pushing rudely by.

"Sorry!" He tried. "Gotta go talk to Dobson."

The offended player, one of the Chevaliers, Edane thought, lifted an eyebrow in surprise.

Getting through the crowd was easy, doing it without bruising anybody... That was another thing.

"See, it's not about discrimination. It's about this being a *sport*. It's not that they're doing anything intentionally to cheat," Dobson said, "they're just victims of circumstance, but we can't have a fair playing field with them on it. That's all there is to it. Our hands are tied, really."

"S'cuse me," Edane said, grabbing one of the players up front by the shoulder and shoving them aside. This one… this one Edane didn't care about offending, because he'd been nodding and smiling to Dobson's line of chatter.

Dobson blinked up at Edane from under the brim of his cap, eyes wide. "Problem?" He wore a self-satisfied smirk, as if Edane's mere height proved his point for him.

Edane shouldered up past the man to his left, a half foot shorter than him, and stood in the front row of players, clasping his hands in front of himself, gazing down on Dobson. "Sorry, I was just *real* interested in hearing what you had to say, Dobson. I'm Edane? Fireteam Eight-Eight-Zero, unofficially the Hallman Hairtrigger Hounds? I'm sorry, I ain't heard much about this — just got back from *Azerbaijan* today."

The players around him looked at him again, and differently, when he said that. He couldn't help but smile, a dark little feeling of satisfaction in his gut. Teams with actual military experience had a mystique in MilSim, and Dobson, good as he and his crew were, had never been on the wrong side of a schoolyard scuffle, let alone a rapid assault team.

Dobson flicked his lower lip under his foreteeth, made a sucking sound, and nodded. "Yeah. We were just discussing the situation, with the tabled addendum? I guess you heard about that."

"Yeah," Edane replied. "You were saying how me and my brothers are victims of circumstances?"

"Exactly. It's not like any of you intended to get yourselves an unfair advantage, now was it?"

"Sir, no sir," Edane said, smiling back down at him. "We all just got mugged by a gang of genetic engineers with a bodybuilding fetish. Their fault, right?"

People laughed. Not many, but enough. An unfamiliar, blissful sound of spasming breath.

Dobson, though. Dobson wasn't laughing. "That's right," he said, teeth grit. "Not your fault at all."

Edane spread his hands. "Wanna arm wrestle?"

"What?" Dobson stepped back.

"You heard me. Wanna arm wrestle? That's your point, isn't it? The one you're trying to make to everybody?" Edane gestured around in a sweep, stepping out of the front of the crowd. Just like he'd seen Thorne do a dozen times.

"No," Dobson said. "I think everyone here already knows you guys are pretty strong."

Edane laughed, his best fake laugh, his best lying smile, and nodded, as friendly as he never was. "Yeah? You sure? I think you could take me on. You sure you don't want to?"

Dobson stepped back, hands up, placating as Edane advanced on him. "We don't need an incident here, Edane…"

"*Incident?*" Edane laughed properly, this time. That *was* funny. "So you don't want to arm wrestle me because I'm bigger than you? That make you scared, Dobson?"

Crowds loved seeing blood. Oh, it didn't matter if it was a pack of old ladies trying to get to mosque or the MACP's MilSim players, they all wanted to see it. They all fell silent, staring expectantly.

But Dobson wasn't the kind of man to admit he was scared. He just glared up, and smoothly said, "I think you're making my point for me, Edane."

Edane nodded enthusiastically. "Okay. Kacey! Get out here."

She leapt down off the picnic table where she'd been standing, where the rest of the team was standing, staring at him over the crowd's heads. Grinning, Kacey waded through the crowd, people stepping back for her, blinking at her. In a moment she popped out the crowd's front ranks and came out to stand in front of Edane, his hands on her shoulders — her five feet nothing to his six and a half, Kacey shorter than even Janine.

Edane grinned. Shark-toothed, but *friendly*. "Wanna arm-wrestle my friend Kacey instead, Dobson? She was covering my spot on the team while I was gone. Don't worry, no gengineers mugged her, so you don't have to be scared of her, right?"

Dobson's upper lip stiffened, mouth flat lining. "That isn't the same."

But nobody heard him. Because when Kacey lifted up her slender, almost elfin arm, offering it out to Dobson, the crowd erupted into blazing laughter. One or two people even had their phones out for pictures. Nobody had much liked the ruling, it seemed, but none of them had been willing to speak up. And now the ice was broken, just about everyone was talking about it — just not listening to Dobson.

By the time the judges came out and announced that Edane and his brothers, along with Marianna and her sisters, were banned from play in the next season, there were already four petitions circling the crowd to overturn the ruling. A boycott against play that people had been talking about for weeks gathered so many pledges in the next half hour that it looked like the league might have to call off the next season, because they wouldn't have enough players.

"Wow. What was that all about?" Janine asked, after all the noise died down and he found her again at the picnic table, small in his arms — though bigger than Kacey.

Edane shrugged, and smiled. "Just lifting a corner, is all."

24. Game Theory

::/ BAKU, AZERBAIJAN.
::/ MAY, 2106.
::/ EVERSEN ESTIAN.

EVERSEN SIGNED OFF from the tactical network for the first time since arriving in-country. He'd seen some brothers do it — medical leave, a day's break, dead — but he hadn't. His location and status had been logged and recorded constantly, and now it wasn't.

He looked down at the folded sheaf of smart paper in his hand, flicking the edge to tap through the documents he'd offloaded from the network. The transcripts of confessions from the Bautino warlord's men. A dossier on the warlord himself, Abbasov, and his links with the Aliyev family and its heirs. Details on the amount of money the Neo-Aliyevs were pouring into the Citizen's Democracy Party now that the Nesimi regime had fallen, decades of old oil money and out of country investments coming home to roost. Malik Najafov's mother's birth certificate, naming her as Yasaman Aliyeva — the Azeri language specifying that women feminized their last names with an 'a' on the end.

The report also detailed the voter's pledges that'd been sent in to the Transitionary Authority's parliamentary electoral committee, registering the CDP and Malik Najafov as one of their candidates. There had been groundswell of support over the first week of campaigning, the slick election campaign run out of a London advertising company's office.

The pre-election polls predicted that Malik would get fifty to sixty percent of the vote to form a government, and the old oligarch's family web were pouring more and more money into the CDP's audited accounts. God alone knew how much the Neo-Aliyevs were passing the CDP under the table.

General Abbasov was the stick, ready to come home at a moment's notice now that Nesimi was gone. Abbasov came with guns, firearms, even biological weapons of mass destruction scavenged and bred from the Eurasian war's biowar fallout. The CDP already had the carrot of Malik's easy smile. Eversen understood how that game worked.

"Malik *Bey* will see you now," one of his suited cousins said, stepping from the restored glassy front of Malik's building. "Please, follow me."

Eversen tucked the smart-paper into his uniform jacket — camouflage off and hanging loosely around his chest, leaving him feeling naked without his armor.

They didn't go in through the front. He was led through a side-door into the parking area, where the cars took themselves to get off the streets. There weren't even any stairs for people, they had to walk down the ramps to the basement passenger pickup area where old red carpet was lain over the driving surface, just outside the elevator lobbies.

The limousine waiting there looked like an antique, but it obviously wasn't one. The faux-driver's compartment, separate from the front, hidden behind the dark windshield, actually contained a self-dispensing bar installation. Racks of drinks and glasses and spindly arms awaiting instruction. The rest of the long stretch cabin was lined in something that looked like suede, and the old-style doors were entirely faux, their hinges and half the side of the car lifting up on a gull-wing to reveal the interior.

Malik sat spider-like on the rose-petal red upholstery of the back seat, bottle of high-end Russian vodka and a plate of caviar and wafer-thin bread in a niche to his right, a map of the country's political support on a district-by-district basis displayed to his left.

He smiled, all bone white teeth, and gestured to the bench seat opposite. "Please, sit down."

Deactivated camouflage didn't quite look right in the limousine, sitting across from Malik's suit, even to Eversen, but he didn't say anything. Just sat down, and the limousine closed around them, leaving them alone but for Najafov's cousin waiting outside.

"So tell me," Malik said. "How are you? Well, I trust? Out of that wheelchair — it must be most enjoyable to walk along our streets, now that they're quiet and peaceful."

"Thank you. But I'd appreciate it if we could skip the overblown formalities." Eversen squirmed, unable to get his back comfortable against the plush seat.

"Still unwilling to engage with our national culture, *Mister* Eversen? A pity. You must learn to take your time — life can hardly be enjoyed, otherwise. But, certainly. How much will this cost me?"

"First, I have to ask you something." Eversen tried to settle back, couldn't get his back comfortably arranged. Eventually he gave up, and just leaned forward, tail bent to the side.

"Of course." Malik gestured airily.

"Two somethings, really. You're sure you and him are the only ones who know I'm here?" He nodded at the cousin, standing outside and watching the elevators. "This would look bad, if anyone knew."

"I know something of discretion." Malik leaned forward, steepling his fingers. "We would hardly want our association known, before the election. It would not look good, having your support, but afterward I will, of course, be able to rebuild my nation's armed forces as I choose."

"Of course." Eversen blinked across at him. "I and my brothers were treated well in Tajikistan, we simply didn't have enough governmental support."

"The revolution was a terrible thing. But your loyalty to the *legitimate* government was well noted, even if some chose to view it uncharitably."

Eversen pricked up his ears. "Yes," he agreed. He'd been young. He'd been stupid. He'd listened to orders. They all had, in Tajikistan. And it could have gone so much worse if the previous Tajik government had exploited that, instead of been too afraid to lean on their private military contractors.

Malik sat back, and dug a shard of wafery bread into his caviar.

"You had a second question?"

"Your involvement with the Aliyev regime's military. General Abbasov, Colonel Magsudov." He tilted his head. "They were planning to overthrow Nesimi and reinstall your grandfather, during the Eurasian War? Now they back you?"

Malik's eyebrows lifted. "And where did you hear that?"

"Magsudov died in Tajikistan," Eversen replied.

"You knew him?"

Eversen didn't answer that with anything more than a shrug.

Malik laughed. "How it all comes full circle. Yes. They back me, now."

Breathing slowly, very carefully and shallowly, Eversen leaned forward. "You intend to start a new regime?"

"I take after my great, great grandfather Heydar, don't you think?" Malik turned his head slightly, grinning again, as if posing for a photo-op. "Don't worry, Eversen *Bey*. There is still plenty of oil under the Caspian, if we start fracking deeply enough. You and your brothers will be well paid."

The air in his mouth was hot. Uncomfortably hot. Eversen took down a breath and blew out another. "Were you aware that General Hafiz Abbasov is seeking to develop a stockpile of reclaimed Eurasian-War era biological weapons of mass destruction?"

"Yes, of course. Part of the plan — make sure Russia and Armenia stay well back, keep the barbarians ruining Persia at bay with the threat of a bigger hammer. And it would certainly be good for… support at home? Hm?"

Eversen barely believed what he was hearing. He limited himself to a slow blink. "Use them to pacify your own population?"

"There would be no need. The threat of it will be enough." Malik smiled tightly.

Eversen had studied a little bit about authoritarian regimes. Social studies class. One of the few interesting things that they'd covered.

"So you understand the precepts of warfare of mass destruction?" Eversen stared at him. "The strategy behind it?"

Malik gestured airily, crunching another dose of caviar. "Enlighten me."

"The strategy was developed before nuclear weapons had been put into production," Eversen said, as if reciting it for history class, back in high school. "It was understood that a weapon of total annihilation held a unique place within military strategy. Strategic theory states that the first nation to develop one should immediately deploy the weapon against any nation attempting to develop another, to prevent them from doing so."

Malik waved his hand, watching Eversen with interest, while stuffing his face.

"The mere threat of suffering an attack by weapons of mass destruction justified launching an attack on a defenseless nation, purely because of a potential future threat. This was never done, leading the two superpowers of the era into the policy of Mutually Assured Destruction — in which two or more belligerents have, but do not deploy, their weapons. The defense is based around a mutual threat, if nation A attacks nation B, nation B attacks nation A. There is no way to attack your enemy without suffering equal, or greater loss."

"Then why were such weapons deployed in the Eurasian war?" Malik asked, eyebrow lifted. "There were nuclear bombs in China…"

Eversen shrugged. "The Eurasian War wasn't about nuclear weapons. It was about biological weapons. The MACP sold biowarfare agents so they could be deployed before the states of South-Eastern Asia could develop comparable bioengineering techniques themselves or begin to vaccinate their populations. It's a tricky subject, but you understand what I'm saying about what happens before Mutually Assured Destruction?"

"Yes." The future dictator of Azerbaijan nodded emphatically, grasping at his vodka. "Stamp out the enemy before they can even become your enemy. *Yes*."

"Good." Eversen nodded. "Then I guess it's okay, if you understand."

"Hm?"

Eversen leaned forward, and pulled the fucking captured Azeri EMWAR kit's panel antenna from where it just wouldn't sit right against his lower back.

"What is that?"

Eversen didn't answer, palming open the limousine's gull-wing door. Then Malik stared in horror as Eversen pulled a silenced side-arm from the holster that'd been under the antenna and shot Malik's cousin, with a thump no louder than a hammer hitting stone.

Malik sprawled, thumbing at a panic-button on his wrist-watch, legs scrabbling uselessly to get away — as if that'd do any good while sitting down.

"You see, Mister Najafov. In the near future you could potentially become this country's next authoritarian dictator. Presently, I occupy that role and you are defenseless."

The panic button blazed red. No matter how often Najafov hit it, it couldn't get a signal past the EMWAR kit's false all-clear being sent to his bodyguards upstairs.

"You can close your eyes, if you want, Mister Najafov."

Malik screamed instead, begging for help, begging for mercy, crying, offering money, drugs, women… anything to cling to life.

It was the first time Eversen ever felt *bad*, killing someone.

TRYING TO RUN a murder investigation in what was still effectively a warzone was… difficult. Granted, when the investigation had shown up on the tactical network, rather than leaving it for the European contractors Eversen grabbed it himself. So he could only blame himself for taking on a difficult job.

He spent plenty of time, weeks, even, following the guidelines and specified procedures, taking statements, grabbing surveillance footage from the area… but he didn't turn anything useful up. That dog who'd been walking around the area could have been almost anybody, especially given that a military grade EMWAR kit had spoofed and jammed surveillance camera and security signals in the area during the time surrounding the murder. The dog wasn't even a suspect, plenty of dogs had been walking around that day. Just because Eversen knew exactly who was guilty of the murder, that didn't necessarily mean he could find supporting evidence to prove it.

Heck, with all surveillance coverage blocked, it was plausible that nobody at all had gone down into the garage. You'd need some kind of expert to tell any different, and Eversen simply didn't have the skills. The police, and their forensic departments, had been dissolved.

Even if Malik Najafov's murder had been the news of the day, the fact of his death was far more interesting than the little details like who'd done it, or why. Popular theories for the killer's identity or backers included some of the pre-war Aliyev regime's supporters playing out an internal power struggle, the Armenians — Azerbaijan's historic enemy, members of opposing political parties, loyalists to the Nesimi regime, the Armenians, and even foreigners intervening in Azeri affairs. (Probably the Armenians.)

It was funny, in a sick way, but Eversen couldn't come to terms with it, even after removing the investigation from the tactical network and marking it as unsolved.

Malik hadn't been a threat. Not the kind Eversen understood. In all probability Malik's fists would crack like eggs if he'd tried hitting anything, and he'd probably never even held a gun.

As a kid, on the range, they'd had firing drills in which they were instructed to shoot only the armed targets projected in front of them, not the unarmed ones. In other drills, they had to kill both armed and unarmed targets — some firing drills only included unarmed targets. Sensitizing him into killing civilians, probably. But there was a world of difference between a static image in AugR or projected across a targeting board, and a man begging for his life.

Eversen should've cuffed Malik and hauled him in front of a court. Unfortunately it wasn't illegal to be a scumbag with plans. Wasn't illegal, so far as Eversen knew, to have rich people trying to put you into power.

Maybe if he'd dug more, maybe if he'd gotten Andercom's hired intelligence services to find more data, maybe if he'd recorded the conversation with Malik before shooting him, maybe this, maybe that... Maybe he wouldn't have had to shoot a man so terrified of dying he couldn't even *try* and fight back.

Eversen sipped his beer.

The beer theoretically belonged to one of the North American contractors, but the six-pack was part of the general foreign groceries delivery for Operations Post Delta. Nobody's name was on it, so the beer was his now.

Eversen'd tried running for office. Or looked into it, anyway. He couldn't — not an Azeri citizen. But he got to talking with some of the protest activists — the ones who'd bubbled up, pushed for the crowdfunding, then got shot by Nesimi for it. They liked what he had to say about the Transitionary Authority's system of organization through crowdfunding and collaborative networks.

One of them, a charismatic type, a guy named Subhi, had really bought into the idea. Pushed his friend Nahida to stand as a candidate, but she turned him down — said a woman would never get the vote. She talked him into doing it instead.

Eversen gave over all the operations procedure documentation he could, explaining the inner workings of the Transitionary Authority's decision-making processes, the way crowdfunded messages from the citizenry had directly influenced policy, the internal bidding procedures, the stop gaps and internal auditing procedures to avoid profiteering. Subhi and his friends had boiled it all down into a manifesto and gotten the required five hundred signatures.

Unfortunately, sitting in the dark, watching the news, doing his best to get drunk on too-little alcohol the way he and Ereli had, once or twice in the past, Eversen didn't think Subhi and his friends would even get five hundred votes.

The newsfeed was an ad-hoc indie media collective, patterned after some European group. Lots of young men and women liveblogging on the streets, while more of them stayed home and clipped it all together into five or ten minute sequences to watch over coffee, or two minute headline compilations you could watch or listen to while stuck in an elevator. Neat, bite sized, everywhere.

They were running live coverage at the election's voting stations. They opened at midnight. Malik's face loomed large from a graffitied billboard, the letters were unfamiliar but according to the subtitles the graffiti read, roughly, 'We will never forget your sacrifice — five *Manat*.'

Turned out, going through Malik's personal banking records,

that he'd thrown five Manat into the crowdfund for the liberation two hours after Nesimi was captured. Then, during all his campaign rallies, he'd spent a lot of time showing off his digital crowdfunder's token off on his phone.

The people were not, in retrospect, impressed by that.

Probably not legal to dump those kinds of files to the net in a public media folder, Eversen thought. After all, as an investigator he was supposed to have privileged access and responsibility for Malik's data, or some shit.

He didn't care, just then. Instead he watched the first rush of people surging into the voting stations to the sound of cheering he could hear, faintly, through his window as midnight hit.

Numbers popped up on the feed, racking higher and higher as the exit polls came in. It was a little like that first night, sitting on Stolnik's couch back home, in San Iadras. Ereli just to his side while they munched on Chinese food, staring at the crowdfunding total climbing up, and up and up.

Subhi had nine votes, on the exit polls. Pretty good, out of the first five hundred responses. Got a few more... the CDP's replacement candidate, who hadn't had the political standing to just smile and wave away the journalists like Malik could when they asked about where his campaign money came from, got his fair share. So did the lady campaigning on an environmental platform, the refugee guy from India who was a naturalized citizen, the ex-army guy who'd done most of his campaigning from a hospital bed while getting fitted for prosthetics...

The little bar chart wasn't flat, exactly, but after all the little tiny parties, like Subhi's, got filtered out, it left a near even split between a dozen contenders for the presidency.

By the time Eversen had emptied out the six-pack and flung the cans into a corner of his private room, losing the thread of everything and just staring at flashing lights on the screen, they were down to eight candidates.

With Malik dead, nobody had the upper hand anymore.

The politicians were out in the night, shaking hands, talking to people in the voting queues, trying to explain their views. Even Subhi had a spot, grinning madly for the camera as he explained that democracy by the dollar had already proven it could depose immoral rulers.

Well. Maybe it couldn't. After all, Malik had been wealthy, and so was the Citizen's Democracy Party. But they didn't have all the votes, just fifteen percent of the vote compared to the Indian refugee guy's fourteen point eight. Then the both of them took a tumble around dawn, when the ex-army guy tottered out of the hospital on a mechanical prosthetic leg to greet cheering nationalists.

Eversen got himself a cup of water and a pair of knock-out pills for forcing soldiers asleep after they'd been running on amphetamines and other stimulant drugs for too long, and used them to toast the morning's light. Between the pills and the beer, the rapidly starting debate on how a coalition government might be formed was just a little *too* complicated for him.

It was reassuring, though. After all. If six people had to share the presidential throne after Eversen was done with it, hopefully they'd keep each other in check.

He wished them the best of luck and bedded down into dreamless sleep.

I
Leaving

::/ San Iadras, Middle American Corporate Preserve.
::/ January, 2104.
::/ Edane Estian.

His plane wasn't there yet, but Edane didn't have anywhere else to go.

The passenger waiting area in the airport was all white tiles and glass and potted plants with small white squares of smart-paper hanging from them, explaining what brand they were and how they helped filter the air and detect contaminants. The air conditioning was on too hard, a blast of cold air being sucked through the Balcony Café's open doors and out into the pre-dawn heat, even though the Balcony Café wouldn't be open for another four hours.

The planes huddled under the terminal's crosswalks. Some big, some small, all of them dark and unlit. No life around them except for a couple of workers watching as trolley-trains loaded the planes up with commercial cargo. Edane tracked the motions with his nose, while on a skywalk service crews and flight engineers boarded a plane with a black and gold tail logo, so if anyone on the flight wanted a drink or the plane's software had to be updated or something there'd be a person to do it.

It'd be sunrise, soon.

Grandpa Jeff was dead.

Grandpa Jeff had left Edane money, but no instructions, and

Edane was trying at college, he'd really tried, but it was all so depressing. It was high-school all over again, people trying to teach him how to be anything but who he was, trying to teach him that meaningless things had meaning. That owning one kind of car instead of a different kind of car made a real difference over using the public transit trams and busses or getting a discount long-term use account with a cab company. As if every other person in college was born with the desire for a family, a job, an expensive pair of sunglasses.

He didn't understand, and he didn't want to understand. The PMC K-level certification had been a one week course, and it all *meant* something. What laws to follow, what a combatant was defined as, what kinds of orders were legal and what kinds weren't, what was good and *what was bad*. It wasn't just a movie he had to live beside, watching every day, full of people, human people who didn't look like him, being fulfilled by things he could never understand but things he'd be judged for all the same. Pretending that good was white fluffy clouds and bad was black spiky plastic. The licensing course was *real* and it had diagrams and standard operating procedures and coded citation references.

Even Grandpa Jeff would've understood that the PMC K-level certification was important. More important than college.

He would've listened. He would've been sore about it, but he would've listened, at least.

Cathy and Beth hadn't listened. They'd told Edane he was throwing his life away, that he was giving in to preconceived notions about what he was, that he was limiting all his options.

That he was making them unhappy.

Edane didn't want to make his mothers unhappy, but he didn't want to be unhappy either.

He pulled the suitcase he'd taken from the apartment's closet out from under his seat again, set it on his lap and looked inside.

His passport was still there. His registration documents and employment contract from the Tajik Republic's Private Military Contractor's Liaison Office were still there, safe-burnt into a few sheets of smart-paper. His ID was still there, the plastic sealed bag containing a wad of *Somoni* bills to spend in Tajikistan was still there, his pad was still there, and so was the black stretchy hairband one of his mothers had accidently forgotten to take out of the suitcase after unpacking last vacation, almost invisible against the lining.

Everything still there, even if he had to rearrange it all because the case was so empty that his things rattled around inside. A smaller case would have been better, except the flight ticket to Tajikistan had specified the dimensions of carry-on luggage very clearly and he didn't have enough to fill a suitcase that big.

Edane could have packed more clothes, but then when he came back the clothes might have to be delayed in quarantine.

If he came back. He didn't know whether or not he'd want to.

He hadn't been a soldier before. Not properly. He'd been in the barracks before the Emancipation, but that didn't count, he'd never actually fought anybody. And Grandpa Jeff had always been very firm, saying that war was a bad thing, but that didn't mean Edane was bad.

Edane had been made to be a soldier, and he wasn't one. Because it was bad to be a soldier. It was good to be an office admin, or a lawyer, or a business manager.

Edane wasn't any of those things, and he wasn't a soldier, either. He wasn't anything. He didn't know what he was, except that nobody wanted him to be it.

He carefully took the hairband out of the suitcase and looked at it. It could have been Cathy's, it could have been Beth's. It smelled a little bit like honeysuckle underneath the corridor closet's mustiness, but Cathy and Beth went through phases of using different smells for their shampoo, and he couldn't remember which of them had been using that kind of shampoo during the last vacation they took.

He just remembered the both of them slipping bands like the one in his palm over their wrists, holding back their hair and tugging the band over and around their hair into neat ponytails so they could run after him on the beach in Portobelo without getting their hair messed up by the wind.

Edane slipped the hairband over his wrist, with the same flex of the fingers his mothers had used. It sat black on his reddish fur.

The more he rolled it back and forth the closer it got to his skin, vanishing under the hairs. At last he couldn't even see it, just feel it around his wrist.

It pinched, a little, as he waited for his plane to arrive. The sensation faded, until the only way he knew it was there was if he checked, scratching at his wrist.

Being a soldier was important. It was the only important thing. Nobody else understood that, they all thought there were other things, but Edane knew different. Edane knew he'd been White-Six, and that once he'd had a place in the world, carrying the… the LAMW. The Light Anti-Materiel-Weapon. It'd been a long time, but he hadn't forgotten the weight of it, even if he had a little trouble remembering the words.

He'd been White-Six. Part of White Pack, Fireteam One. Partnered with White-Five. Back then he'd known what he was for, and what he was supposed to be, and nobody had ever told him that he wasn't who he thought he was.

Nervously, Edane picked at the hairband around his right wrist, scratching into his fur just to feel the soft flex of it under his clawish fingernail.

He was going to Tajikistan. He was going to be a soldier. He wasn't a child anymore, he was a man. An adult. He just had to wait a little longer, for his plane to get there, and then everything would be better. He'd find out who he was.

Edane waited, though he wasn't sure for what.

He scratched at his wrist, again, just to check for the hairband.

Edane kept waiting.

Sunrise was coming.

25. Stone Sparrow

::/ Baku, Azerbaijan.
::/ June, 2106.
::/ Alice Stein.

"Savage debate continues, with allegations of ulterior motives being slung back and forth on the floor of Azerbaijan's Transitionary Authority parliament. Sessions are currently being held on the front forecourt of the newly renamed *Kurban Said* building, also being called the poet's parliament building, while reconstruction continues as part of Azerbaijan's effort to reclaim its historic cultural heritage while mapping out a path towards its future."

The reporter ducked, a gust of wind blowing in off the Caspian tearing at her hair, but she didn't stop smiling manically at the camera, clutching at her earpiece. "With charges of corruption against both the Citizen's Democracy Party and the Baku Worker's Party, Vikram Khan's own refugee-backed United People's Front has been forced to submit to the same audit procedures — the Transitionary Authority's parliament coming under heavy pressure from the public for transparency in its attempt to form a coalition government in the wake of the failure to find a clear leader in the election. Public political interest has never been this high — as you can see behind me the wind hasn't been enough to scare off interested citizens who have plenty to say!"

She stepped to the side, gesturing — and there it was, the new parliament. Crowds surrounded the fenced off parliament steps, defense and public UAVs sharing the airspace overhead while clone Estian brothers and European PMC staff watched impassively. The crowds waved massive banners at their temporary government, lower parliament members walking around the fence's border, reaching out between the clear armor-glass slats to shake hands with the public between debate sessions.

It wasn't all an idyll. Large warning signs about search procedures and red tape marked out the surveillance area and protection cordon, but other than invasive back-scatter radar scans for weaponry by UAVs, anti-ordnance laser installations, and particulate detection masts surrounding the surveillance area's red tape, it was a public space.

"Wow, that's... a very busy looking place," the voice back in the studio said.

"It certainly is," the reporter replied. "Anyone can come and watch — or even yell at their elected officials. Four petitions for ministers to stand down have already been circulated, and two of them have stood down as a result. The people of Azerbaijan have tasted self-rule, and they seem set on keeping it."

"Nice to have some good news from the region for a change. Now then, coming up after the hour, we'll have special guests from Andercom West in studio to talk with members of the United Nations Committee on Eurasian Stability about just what this people-powered crowdfunded revolution might mean for civic rights in the region..."

26. Wasted land

::/ Ulytau, Central Asian Depopulated Zone
::/ July, 2106.
::/ Eversen Estian.

Eversen had no fucking idea why they were called rompers, but the bug-looking RVs ate up the terrain almost as easily as the jeeps and armored vehicles. What set the things apart, though, was that they had all this great anti-contamination gear the researchers working on biowar fallout could use to get in and out during dust storms and rain while everyone else in the convoy was stuck inside their vehicles.

Except for Eversen, but Eversen was immune to the fallout, so far as the researchers could figure. Except from the caustics. The facemask wrapped around Eversen's muzzle still let gritty little particles of the shit into his mouth, foaming on his tongue and burning like some kind of rancid disinfectant until he had to lift the mask to spit it all out, and at the moment he was officially classed a level three biohazard to the rest of the convoy.

He loved it. Even the spitting blood part — burnt mucous membranes were a small price to pay in exchange for fighting through the howling wind, gun in hand while nature and fallout tried and failed to murder him.

One of the unmanned cargo jeeps had overturned in the windstorm — a rock or something the driving system hadn't seen. Its cargo was scattered everywhere.

"I can't find the seedlings!" Subhi yelled, wrapped up in biohazard gear like the researchers scurrying back and forth.

"Get out've the wind!" Eversen grabbed the strap on the back of Subhi's biohazard suit — a hauling strap, just like on body armor for dragging downed teammates around — and shoved him into the lee side of one of the rompers. "The fuck are we gonna do if *you* get sick, huh?"

"The seedlings were my responsibility!" Subhi clutched his head through the biohazard suit's soft helmet. "I put money in for them!"

"So did *I*. Now stay out of the wind!"

"Okay, okay!"

Eversen stomped off into the roiling clouds. Siegen — or possibly Sieden — was running through the dust, a tire-jack in either hand. The jeep was still so laden with cargo that two brothers couldn't get the thing flipped over by themselves.

Hopefully the roll hadn't fucked the jeep up. They still had a long way to go to get to their unclaimed acres.

In the depths of the quarantined zones, there were places that the biowar contamination was so bad even the nomads didn't go there. Several governments still tried to claim the land, of course, but none of them could do shit with it — some areas were still buzzing with *nuclear* fallout.

But Subhi, and a bunch of his friends in the Crowdfunded Democracy Movement — now disbanded — had wanted to give democracy by the dollar a try. A real try. And they'd crowdfunded enough money to set up a commune, but there was nowhere to put the damn thing. So they'd voted it over in a mixture between a debate and a gambling session, Eversen even chipping in a few cents here and there to support the arguments he liked the looks of.

Having made their decision to go into the wastes, the group applied for and received grant funding from an MACP charitable fund to buy twenty tons of gengineered anti-contamination seedlings. The plants were designed to suck up old biowarfare agents and the chemical caustics and isolate the shit deep in their root structures. Philanthropic crowdfunding had gotten them the jeeps. Eversen and the rest had submitted a proposal for security provision on a part-volunteer basis, because there were still warlord nutbags and criminal gangs and all sorts of violence out here, when the dust itself wasn't trying to kill people.

Eversen spotted a steri-sealed plastic bag in the dust, a black hydroponics block sprouting a dozen fragile green stems visible inside, and hauled it up in one hand. He paused to sling his rifle over his back and chased down another bag rolling along in the howling wind.

Was the commune gonna work? Were the seedlings going to clear out the contaminants? Could the endless late night discussions and microfunding sessions to figure out how to put the commune's public works projects into place actually lead to a stable settlement?

Eversen had no fucking clue. But getting the seedlings back onto the jeep made a difference, and so did protecting the convoy, and he didn't have to question a goddamn thing about it.

It was a purpose that would've made Ereli happy, Eversen thought. He knew he was.

27. Real Blue

::/ SAN IADRAS, MIDDLE AMERICAN CORPORATE PRESERVE.
::/ JULY, 2106.
::/ EDANE ESTIAN.

A FOOTBALL SPIRALED overhead and into the shrubbery. Not a proper round one — a *Norteamericano* football. Ellis laughed, chasing after it. He bailed into the foliage and trudged back out grinning ear to ear.

"Don't you fucking track mud onto the picnic blankets, knucklehead! I will shove this thing so far down your throat that every time you wag you'll flip burgers!" Marianna yelled, shaking a metallic spatula threateningly from the barbecue.

"Are you *sure* the steak's not—"

She efficiently swatted it across Svarstad's ear. "*Back off*, knucklehead. I'm cooking, not you. Go sit down."

"Sir, yes sir." With exaggerated meekness and defeat, Svarstad trudged back to the picnic blankets and flopped down by the music player, thumbing its volume down.

Eberstetten started laughing at him, so did Louie, looking up from his pad and grinning. It was nice to see the kid around, today.

Hell, today was just *nice*. Marianna had decided to throw a barbecue at the park, celebrate the fact that the new MilSim league guidelines were in. The doping policy got rewritten to clarify its policy on genetic doping as allowing all declared genetweaks, genemods, and other gengineering related alterations that were certified as both legal and having existed for a minimum of five years prior to registration as a professional player. More recent alterations and those undeclared or acquired during the course of play would, as they always had, be reviewed on a case by case basis.

It had been a lot longer than five years since anyone'd tweaked Edane's genes.

It didn't stop there. There were new ranking modifiers, and a handicapping system, and a balancing clause that could theoretically force match organizers to keep high performing pro-level fireteams — like the newly pro Hallman Hairtrigger Hounds, or just Triple-H, and MA-Company sponsored by Mark Antony LLC — off the same faction, like they'd been asking for in the first place.

Janine came back from the barbecue, bearing a paper plate with two steaming, charred cans of meat on it. "*Seriously?*" she asked, squinting at them.

"Seriously. I still can't believe you've never even tried real meat before." Edane opened the lid on the cooler, took the plate from Janine, and dumped the cans into the left-over ice.

"Uh, Sweetie…" She smiled awkwardly. "I'm pretty sure this isn't real meat."

"Sure it is. Knitted on a spool right out of the vat, then compacted into cubes with preservatives and *everything*." He grinned at her until she laughed — he was getting good at that, lately.

When the cans had cooled enough to touch, he went and sat with her on one of the benches, showed her how to use the key to peel open the metal, and snap it off after to use as a little eating utensil.

Janine tasted it, pulled a face at him — but a cute face — and this time *he* laughed.

After they'd finished eating they went and lay on a couple of sun loungers, since he'd gotten her to try one of his things — meat — she was going to get him to try one of her things — sunbathing.

Before long, though, she lifted her sunglasses and glanced over at him. "Something wrong?" Janine asked, softly.

He shook his head.

"You're supposed to settle back and relax, Sweetie. Shut your eyes."

"Do I have to?"

"Relax, or shut your eyes?" she laughed, dropping the sunglasses back over her face.

Edane squirmed uncomfortably back. "Shut my eyes."

"Something wrong, Sweetie?"

"No, just…" Edane pointed up, at the sky.

Janine tensed, sitting up and glancing at him, the sky… him.

"Sky's blue today," he explained, carefully. "Real blue."

She took off her sunglasses, and lifted her head, staring up at the blue sky above.

"Huh. So it is." Janine smiled down at him. "Very blue."

Edane smiled back at her.

Blue.

Acknowledgments

I ORIGINALLY SELF-PUBLISHED this book in 2016, even though I'm not a particularly skilled self-publisher. I knew there would be some errors lurking around the manuscript I couldn't spot, even with the kind read-throughs of friends, and I didn't feel equal to the task of handling print typography by myself. I was proud of it, but I knew it didn't have the polish it deserved.

Now, in 2020, the support I've received through Patreon has made it possible for me to get just a little bit of professional help, including copy-edits, typography, and a brand new cover.

Patrons, thank you so much. Being able to launch a new edition of Dog Country with that extra polish and a matching print edition is an amazing gift you've all given me.

Thanks must also go to my friends, too, and my family, and very importantly, to my readers and other fans – you make what I do worth doing..

About the Author

MALCOLM F. CROSS, otherwise known by his internet handle 'foozzzball', lives in London and enjoys the personal space and privacy that the city is known for. When not misdirecting tourists to nonexistent landmarks and standing on the wrong side of escalators, Malcolm enjoys writing, catching up on his to-be-read book pile, and photographing graffiti and abandoned objects.

While Malcolm has yet to do any crowdfunding, he's sure it's perfectly safe, and is sure there are unlikely to be other consequences. Edane, Ereli, and Eversen disagree, particularly Ereli. More of their brethren can be found in Malcolm's short story collection 'War Dog & Marginalized Populations'.

He can be found online at http://www.sinisbeautiful.com, and found on twitter at @foozzzball.

Printed in Great Britain
by Amazon